TELEPATH

FRACTURED

GORDON G. BOWMAN

Published by Bowman Books.

www.bowmanbooks.ca

ISBN 978-0-9936057-6-5 (paperback - perfect bound)
ISBN 978-0-9936057-5-8 (hardcover - jacketed case laminate)
ISBN 978-0-9936057-8-9 (hardcover - case laminate)
ISBN 978-0-9936057-7-2 (EPUB)

For my daughters, Breana and Belinda.

1

CONFUSION

The alley was sideways. How long she'd been lying there, she couldn't say, but she slowly got to her feet and steadied herself against a brick wall. Everything hurt. Definitely some broken ribs, she thought, wincing. Her knuckles were bleeding and swollen, and her hoodie and jeans were dirty and scuffed. Gingerly, she touched the back of her head and her fingers came back covered in blood. She had clearly been in a fight.

She took stock of her surroundings. It was nighttime and a steady stream of people were walking past the entrance to the alley, hooting and hollering. Behind her, four bodies lay on the ground. She thought back, trying to remember where exactly she was and what had happened.

Uh-oh.

She bent over and abruptly vomited. Then, wiping her mouth on her sleeve, she staggered out to the sidewalk. Looking around, she realized that she knew where she was. She turned and saw a young woman staring at her expectantly.

"I'm sorry, what?" she said.

"I said, are you okay?" the young woman asked. Her friends gathered around. "Oh wow, you're bleeding."

"There's a bunch of people lying in the alley!" someone yelled.

A paramedic shone a light in her eyes. Where had he come from? She was sitting on the curb, shaking and wrapped in a blanket. Police officers were here, too, and ambulances. Her sense of time was wrong.

Concussion.

"I know," she said.

"What's that?" the paramedic asked.

"I said, I know. I have a concussion."

"That's right, you definitely do. My name's Riley, what's yours?" The paramedic's voice was slightly monotone but kind and gentle. She stared at him blankly.

"I don't know." She should be worried about that.

"That's okay. Do you have any ID on you, maybe? Or a phone?"

She checked her pockets. "No."

"Okay, let's try something else," Riley said. "Do you know where you are right now?"

She nodded. "I don't know how I got here, but this is the Market. Ottawa. And judging by all the red-and-white shirts and yelling, it's Canada Day."

"Heh. That's right. I'm going to ask you a few more questions now. Do you know when your birthday is?"

She shook her head, slowly because it hurt. "You don't understand. I literally don't remember anything about myself. Not my name, not my birthday, not my address. The last thing I remember is . . . nothing. It's all blank." She pulled her blanket tighter. "That's not good, is it?"

"Don't worry, it's not uncommon. You were hit pretty hard in the head, so it might take some time for everything to come back to you."

She could tell he was lying, though. Memory loss to her degree was apparently not common at all.

Neurological damage, maybe.

"You really think I have neurological damage?"

"What?" He seemed startled. "No, you just have a concussion, that's all. Nothing to worry about. But I'll tell you what, we're going to take you to the hospital now, and the doctors will check you out and make sure you're okay, all right?"

She stood and he helped her to the ambulance.

"Are they okay?" she asked, pointing to the four people on stretchers getting loaded into their own ambulances.

"They're still unconscious, but we think they'll be all right," the paramedic said. "Do you know them?"

She shrugged.

"Well, maybe they know you, and when they wake up, they can help us call your parents, okay?"

Her parents? That thought hadn't even occurred to her. "How old do I look to you?" she asked.

"I think . . . you look around fourteen or fifteen to me. Does that sound about right?"

She didn't answer. One of the injured men opened an eye—it darted around for a second and then closed again before she could be sure it had really happened. Weird.

She got into her own ambulance and lay down on the stretcher as the paramedic closed the rear doors.

∎ ∎ ∎

She was resting in a dim hospital room with two other sleeping kids. When had she come here? A nurse told her to try to sleep and she would come by to wake her up periodically due to her concussion. She was half-asleep when she heard whispering. She sat up. The kids were still sleeping. Had she been dreaming? The clock on the nightstand read 5:37 a.m. The whispering didn't seem to come from any one direction, but rather from inside her own head. Maybe she was still dreaming. Though she listened intently, she couldn't make out the words. Then a man strode into the room and stopped, seemingly surprised to find her awake. He had a neatly trimmed beard and wore a long coat.

"Hello there," he said. "I hope I didn't wake you. I'm Detective Nazari. You can call me Fasil. How are you feeling?"

"Fine," she lied. He had an accent. Arabic, she thought, but he'd learned his English in the UK. She wondered how she knew that.

"Good to hear," he said. "I spoke with the doctors and I have wonderful news for you." He flipped through the pages of his clipboard. "The blow you took to the back of your head definitely resulted in a concussion, but the cranial CT scan didn't reveal anything overly concerning. Other than some scrapes and bruises and a few broken ribs, you seem to be fine. I see they've bandaged your head up nicely and your ribs will heal on their own, so I expect you'll be right as rain in no time."

"That's good," she said, cautiously. "But . . . it's pretty early, and shouldn't a doctor be telling me this?"

The detective waved a hand dismissively as he drew up a chair, wincing almost imperceptibly. "It's all right." He crossed his legs. "I told the doctors I needed to have a chat with you first. About the incident earlier tonight. I'm the lead investigator, you see. It was quite the excitement, all those police and ambulances and reporters. Can you tell me what happened?"

"Like I told the paramedic and the doctors," she said, "I don't remember anything before stumbling out of the alley."

"Right," he said, riffling through his papers again. "Of course. It says that right here in your charts." He smiled disarmingly. "It says here that you don't remember . . . anything, really. So, not who attacked you, not the identities of the other four individuals, not your name . . . absolutely nothing at all." He looked up at her with sad eyes. "That must be scary, yeah? Not having any idea who you are or where you belong in the world? Unable to tell friend from foe? I can hardly imagine how alone and vulnerable you must feel."

She couldn't shake the feeling he was mocking her. Maybe he just had a terrible bedside manner? She switched topics. "Did the other people in the alley wake up yet? Do any of them know me?"

The detective shook his head. "Well now, that's a funny story. You see, they appear to be missing."

When he didn't continue, she asked, "What do you mean, missing?"

"Right. What I mean is, they never arrived at the hospital. It's all very mysterious," he said, waggling his fingers above his head like a ghost. "Of the five ambulances headed to the hospital, only yours arrived. Strange, yeah?"

What was going on here? How could that possibly happen? And why was he being so cavalier? She remembered how one of the men on the stretchers had opened his eye and looked around—had he been feigning unconsciousness so they could make an escape?

"I know you must be disappointed," he said. "I bet you were hoping they were your friends and they'd waltz on in here and tell you your name and take you home to Mum and Dad, yeah? Or maybe you were afraid they were the ones who gave you all those bumps and bruises—and now they're out there free, maybe plotting to do it again, only you'd never see them coming because you don't remember what they look like."

She met the man's gaze. Something was very off about him. She tried to push down her growing sense of unease.

"Detective? I forgot to ask to see your badge when you came in. Would you mind?"

"You know what else is strange?" he continued, ignoring her. "Having no memory of who you are, even though you've suffered no apparent brain injuries."

"Are you accusing me of lying?"

"Oh heavens, no, not at all. In fact, I can't think of a single reason you would possibly carry on such a charade, especially when it's just you and me here."

A shiver ran up her spine. "What do you mean? Do we … know each other, Detective?"

He smiled. "I'd like to pose a hypothetical scenario to you. Suppose someone was given everything she could desire as a child. Let's call her … oh, I don't know … *Zoe*. Let's say Zoe was given every advantage in life to allow her to get ahead in the world. Groomed for greatness, you might say. Yet she was utterly unappreciative. Always looking down her nose at her elders, as though she thought them inferior. And then suppose this ungrateful brat *betrayed* everyone she knew." He looked left and right conspiratorially. "And ran." He sat back in his chair.

Very carefully, she slid off the bed on the side opposite Fasil. He remained sitting as she looked out the window at the dark and the rain. It looked like they were three floors up, and there was no ledge to jump down. She was trapped.

"You're not a police detective," she said. She thought back to the alley and those four people on the ground. Had any of them been wearing a long jacket like his? "Who are you? Are you saying my name is Zoe?"

"Suppose you were ordered to bring this ingrate in," he continued, "by any means necessary. Those exact words."

She opened the cupboard and pulled out her clothes. If he was so confident that he intended to keep talking, then she was going to take advantage of that. She put her jeans on overtop her hospital gown.

"Now, suppose you found her. And she was every bit the arrogant child you remembered. And then . . . things happened. Didn't go according to plan. And the next thing you know, you're sitting across from her in a hospital room and she's looking at you with wide, innocent eyes, claiming she doesn't even know you. That she's a different person now. What would you do?"

Fighting her growing panic, she finished pulling her hoodie on over her shirt and slipped into her shoes. "That depends," she said, stalling as long as she could. Assuming she could escape somehow, keeping him talking meant she might learn something valuable. "Is she really as bad as you say? Or is she just a frightened kid who was trying to get away from a bad situation?"

Fasil snorted. "No, she's full of herself, this one. She deserves everything she'll get." He stroked his chin. "I wonder if not remembering why she deserves it will make her suffer more or less," he mused. "I think it might actually be worse, yeah? Because without memory . . . well, she's like an innocent victim, isn't she?" He nodded to himself. "I like that."

She judged the distance to the door. If she was quick, she could maybe make it past him before he got out of his chair. Or maybe she should scream for the hospital staff. "I honestly don't know who you are or who I am. Just tell me already."

He sat quietly, judging her through narrowed eyes. "It could be," he said, finally, "that you honestly don't remember. That you have . . ." He examined her charts. "Psychogenic amnesia, it says here. But it could be that you're pretending because you hope I won't kill a helpless, clueless, little girl."

She took a deep breath to steady her nerves. Her heart pounded and her hands trembled. Adrenaline. "I assume you must be one of the people from the alley. I woke up before you, remember? If I remembered anything, I could have run."

Fasil's eyes widened and moved back and forth as he thought it through. "You know what? That's a really solid argument you have there." He was silent a moment more as he stared into space. "Yeah." He nodded. "You would have run right there and then." He slapped his knees. "Right, then. You'll have to forgive my little ruse, but I'm clearly not a police detective. I thought you might be trying to pull one over on us, but you've convinced me. I believe you."

He met her gaze. *But I'm still going to kill you, Zoe.*

She staggered back. His lips hadn't moved—he had spoken directly in her mind. She screamed for help. She screamed as loud as she could for as long as she could and then waited for the hospital staff to come.

Fasil laughed. "Yeah, no one's coming, Zoe," he said, standing. "It's just you and me."

She bolted for the door and made it past him before he even tried to move. She ran through the doorway and turned left, only to skid to a stop. In front of her, three figures in long jackets blocked her path. She turned and ran the other way as Fasil stepped into the hall, but it was a dead end. She turned to face them.

"Well, you, me, and my companions," Fasil said. "Oh, and my good friend Fred, here," he said, indicating the uniformed police officer, staring blankly from his chair. "He was apparently keeping watch on your room in case the baddies who beat you up last night came back. Be a good lad and go back to sleep now, all right, Fred?" The police officer nodded and closed his eyes.

"You always thought you were better than us, didn't you?" Fasil continued. "As though it were your birthright to look down on us." He leaned in. "I'm not *supposed* to kill you, you know. Not strictly speaking, anyway. Our orders were to bring you in 'by any means necessary,' though, so I think that means I'm *allowed* to kill you if it's the only way, yeah? I wasn't going to before. I was going to capture you and bring you in to face your punishment. But after the alley?" He shook his head. "No, you're going to kneel and beg for your life. And then I'm going to take it from you."

Zoe could see the nurses at the other end of the hallway going about their business, as though nothing out of the ordinary was happening. She took a deep breath and forced herself to exude confidence. "I'm not going to beg you for anything."

He laughed. "No? Let's start with the first bit, then." He turned back to smirk at his companions before rounding upon her.

Kneel.

She staggered, clutching the doorframe. The power and compulsion of his voice in her mind almost overwhelmed her. It took all her strength to stay standing.

Kneel!

Her legs buckled, but she recovered. She was shaking, half from fear, half from the effort it took to refuse his command, but she stood her ground.

This didn't please him. The other three—a large, Slavic-looking man with a bushy beard, a young man with a blond bun, and an East Asian woman with short purple hair—exchanged glances and stepped forward to form a line with Fasil. He didn't look pleased by this, either.

KNEEL, their four voices said as one.

Her breath left her as her knees slammed to the floor. She couldn't withstand their combined will. If she could just get them out of her mind! How were they doing this?

Fasil stepped forward, grinning. "That's better," he said. "Now that we've got the kneeling part down, let's start with the begging part, yeah?"

Zoe was only vaguely paying attention to him, instead concentrating inward, into her own mind, where she could feel the presence of the four intruders. She needed to stall them, to give herself time to figure out how to get them out of her mind.

"I don't even understand who you all are," she said. "At least explain that before you kill me." She could *see* them inside her skull, like four points of light pressing on her synapses. Having no idea what to do, she visualized an explosion in her head to try to get them out, but there was no effect. She imagined her fingers prying the lights loose, but they were entrenched.

"*We* are your betters. *We* are skilled professionals who earned our places through hard work and dedication to our craft. *You* are a snot-nosed child who never had to earn anything and yet still somehow thinks she's better than everyone else."

Examining one point of light more closely, she saw that it had a . . .

string of some sort attached. "For someone so sure of himself, you sure seem to care an awful lot about what a teenage girl thinks of you," she said.

One of his companions snickered, and Fasil glowered. He took a deep breath. "I don't care what you think of me."

The strings were tethers. She could see them now, even when she closed her eyes. Four glowing tendrils leading from her head to each of the four figures facing her. "Pretty sure you do. Your friends even think so. Why else would you be going on and on about it?"

Fasil came closer, the others following in step. "Enough. Beg for your life. Convince me to spare you."

Zoe tugged gently on the strings. How was she even doing that? Regardless, they had a lot of tension in them. If she couldn't move the lights out of her mind, maybe she could cut their strings. She visualized cutting them with a sharp knife. Nothing happened. "I'm starting to think that there's something to this inferiority complex of yours," she said, goading him. "Four 'skilled professionals' couldn't handle one teenage girl alone in an alley? Imagine if it was just you against me. No wonder you're so insecure." Make him angry. Angry people make mistakes.

He sneered. "We were careless. It won't happen again, I assure you."

"You know what I think?" she said, trying to buy more time. Her mind raced. If they all had these mental powers, yet she'd been able to survive their attack before, then maybe she had the same powers. If they could speak directly into her mind, then maybe she could speak directly into theirs.

I think you're scared of me, she thought.

Fasil's eyes bulged out of his sockets. "Scared of you? God, amnesia hasn't dulled your arrogance. I am scared of no one. Certainly not a little girl, would-be prodigy or no!"

Prodigy. Well, that was encouraging. Tenderly, so that they wouldn't notice, she tried to follow the glowing tendril connecting her to Fasil, to move her consciousness along it. If she could get inside *his* mind. . . . But something stopped her. A shield of some sort, like frosted glass that she couldn't quite see through. That's what she needed, a mind-shield just like his.

"I think that if you could have killed me, or captured me, you would have," she said, not feeling nearly as brave as she was pretending to be. "But the four of you failed. And now you're scared of me. That's why you're keeping your distance." She tried to will a shield around herself, but nothing happened. It *felt* like something was trying to form, but the tendrils already attached to her mind prevented it.

Fasil was positively apoplectic now. Good. He took the final two steps toward her, his hands clenched into fists. "*You* will be silent!" Spittle flew from his mouth. "You will be silent and contrite and beg me for forgiveness and to spare your life!"

"Fasil, enough," said the woman behind him. "Finish this."

"You know what I think, Fasil?" Zoe smiled up at him.

"I don't care what you think!" he roared, pushing his boot into her chest and sending her sprawling.

The sudden jerk caused the four tendrils to stretch and grow thin. In that instant, using every bit of willpower she could muster, her mental shield surged into place like a solid metal door slamming down from above. It was euphoric. Suddenly, she felt powerful, like she had just donned armour. The four taut tendrils snapped back, dropping their stunned owners to their knees.

"I think you made another mistake," she said, getting to her feet and kicking Fasil hard in the nose. She leapt over him, dove between the legs of the large man, who was already rising, and sprinted down the dim hall toward the exit sign. The next moment, though, some unseen force picked her up and threw her through the air. She landed in a one-armed roll and came up running again. What just happened? And how had she rolled like that?

"Help!" she screamed as she ran past the nurses' station, but the night-duty nurse paid her no notice, seemingly oblivious.

Zoe darted down the first hallway and heard something whiz past her ear. Legs pumping, she took hallways at random, running past night staff who looked up in alarm but just as quickly turned away in disinterest. Why was no one helping her? How was Fasil doing this?

She overturned a supply cart and glanced back to see the lithe young man extend his hand just before the cart slid out of his path. Had he done that with his mind? Like the force that had flung her through the air?

There was no time to figure it out. She tore past the elevator—no time to wait—and slammed her shoulder into the stairwell door instead. She took the steps two at a time, her footsteps echoing off the concrete walls. Some instinct caused her to stop and duck as her pursuer leapt down the entire first flight of stairs. He landed in front of her and spun around but she was already past him and starting down the second flight of steps. He leapt again.

This time she was ready. She sidestepped and crouched, grabbed the underside of his jacket, and pushed off in the same direction as his flight. Her unexpected momentum added to his own sent his head colliding into the concrete wall with a loud crack. He didn't get up. Footsteps and shouts were right behind her, so she launched herself down the remaining flights of stairs as fast as she could.

Reaching the empty lobby, she sprinted for the glass doors of the hospital's main entrance. Ten feet away, she again felt herself lifted and then hurled into the door, cracking its glass. She collapsed in a heap, dazed.

The three remaining pursuers drew to a stop. The woman, dressed in a white, ankle-length coat, spoke. "I will make you pay for what you did to Anders back there." She reached into her coat and pulled out a sword. A very long, very sharp sword.

So, *that* was why they were all wearing long jackets in summer.

"No!" shouted Fasil. "She's mine! Tsuji!" But not only did Tsuji ignore him, the burly man drew his sword too. A heavy, two-handed broadsword. "Ivan!" Fasil swore and began drawing his own sword just as Tsuji raised her blade over her shoulder and lunged forward.

Time seemed to slow. Lying crumpled on the ground, Zoe couldn't possibly get out of the way. She *needed* a weapon or she was dead. So, with no other choice and nothing to lose, she reached out her hand and *willed* Fasil's sword to fly into her own.

It obeyed.

With no time to be shocked, she blocked the descending arc of Tsuji's sword as she rolled to her right and then slashed at her attacker's ankles. Caught off-balance and in no position to parry, Tsuji jumped and twisted, narrowly avoiding losing her legs but landing heavily on her shoulder.

Zoe's next attacker took his time, studying her while Tsuji got to her feet, rubbing her shoulder. Behind them, Fasil looked lost without his sword.

As her two attackers advanced warily, Zoe twirled her blade to test its weight and balance. It was a *katana*, she knew without knowing how. A Japanese sword, slightly curved, single-edged, and perfectly balanced. It felt natural in her hands, somehow. She might not consciously remember how to use it, but she felt certain that she could. She had multiple opponents, though, who were taller, heavier, and stronger than her. She needed a way to even the odds. Some way to use her smaller size to her advantage.

Her opponents tried to surround her, but she retreated through the lobby with her blade held low so she could keep all three in front of her. The bearded man, who Fasil had called Ivan, held his heavy broadsword with ease. She could never hope to block that. It looked like it could shatter her arm, if not her blade.

There was no more time to think as Ivan launched an overhead swing that left a crater in the tile floor where she had stood a second ago. Tsuji came at her from the left with a slash to her midsection. Zoe stepped forward to meet the attack. She blocked and countered in one fluid motion as she stepped to the side and swung at Tsuji's flank. The woman twisted, so the blade only sliced her long coat. Zoe knew she had just exposed her back to Fasil, and he must surely be moving in to take advantage of the opening, even without a weapon. This was her chance. Swordfights don't last long, she knew, especially when three-on-one. In the back of her mind, she wondered how she felt so certain of combat strategy. Regardless, even if she had been training her whole life, she was under no illusions she could win this fight. She needed another option. A hostage would do nicely.

She waited another moment until she was sure Fasil was just about to grab her from behind and then quickly pivoted her hips to face him. Stepping forward and to the left, she faked an upward strike and stepped behind him. She grabbed his hair to pull his head back, knocking him off-balance as she pressed her blade to his throat.

"Drop them," Zoe said.

Her two opponents hesitated, the man looking somewhat impressed, the woman looking very annoyed.

"Drop your blades or he dies," she repeated.

Tsuji and Ivan glanced at each other, and she heard whispering in her head, as though overhearing a conversation that she wasn't quite close enough to make out. Then, the man nodded and they turned and advanced on her again.

Uh-oh. "Fasil," she said, slowly retreating to the exit. "Tell them."

"Do what she says!" he yelled. "Drop your weapons!"

But Fasil was apparently not quite the respected leader he believed he was. Her attackers raised their swords into position and continued to advance.

Fasil, they're going to let me kill you, she said in his mind. *They don't care if you live or die.*

Then surrender, he said. *I promise I won't let them hurt you!*

That's not happening. She kept backing up. *It looks like we're both going to die here.* Was she bluffing about killing him? She wasn't sure, but she wasn't ready to give up. Her back was to the exit. She could still run.

Wait! he said. *I . . . I'll help you escape!*

Excellent. I've been thrown through the air twice by some force. Can you do that to them now?

Yes . . . but they'll kill me for it, Fasil said. *I'll need my sword back.*

She thought about it. *Fine. I'll give you your sword after you attack them. Do we have a deal?*

A moment of hesitation. *We do.*

Then do it, NOW, she said, as Tsuji and Ivan took their final step and began their killing strokes.

Suddenly, her attackers went flying back through the air and she went flying back through the exit while Fasil clung to the frame. Recoil, she thought, as she struggled to her feet. Physics still applied to these powers, it seemed. She tossed the sword to Fasil and ran without looking back. Steel clanged against steel behind her as she fled into the darkness and the rain.

2

THE ALLEY

Fleeing the hospital, she formulated a plan. So far, she knew her name was Zoe and she had escaped from some sort of organization of people with swords and crazy mental powers. She needed more information, and the morning newspaper would be the best place to start. She had some change in her pocket, so, pulling her hood over her head to obscure her face and bandages, she entered a gas station convenience store and bought a copy of the *Ottawa Citizen*—and there was her story right on the front page: Teen Attacked in ByWard Market.

She moved to the rear of the store, where she would be less visible from the street, and read the story. Apparently, the four unidentified adults found unconscious in the alley had all suffered injuries. Ambulances took everyone to the hospital and, like Fasil said, only her ambulance arrived. When the others failed to show up, the dispatch clerk got on the radio and found all the paramedics at a donut shop. When asked what they thought they were doing, they all seemed to suddenly remember what they were *supposed* to be doing—driving their injured patients to the hospital. They ran out to the ambulances but found them empty. None of the paramedics were able to offer any explanation for their bizarre actions.

So, it appeared that her attackers were not only capable of controlling minds but also erasing memories. They couldn't have been responsible for her memory loss, though, because Fasil had thought she was faking it. So, either someone else like them was involved or her amnesia really was from the blow she'd taken to the back of her head.

It was in her best interest to stay out of sight, maybe even get out of Ottawa entirely. But she had no intention of running aimlessly forever, which meant she couldn't leave the city just yet. She needed a plan, which required information, and the only place to start was at the scene of the crime, where maybe she could find some clues.

Tossing the paper in the garbage on her way out, Zoe froze at the sight of her reflection in the glass door. She reached up to gently touch the bruised face of a girl of maybe fourteen or so. Athletic build, shoulder-length ginger hair, light-blue eyes.

A complete stranger.

It was pouring rain, she was tired, hungry, and her ribs and head ached, but adrenaline kept her going. Noting that she apparently knew the layout of Ottawa, she headed northwest on foot, trying to stay off the main roads. After more than an hour, she finally made it back to the ByWard Market, just as the fruit and vegetable sellers were setting up their outdoor stands.

It didn't take long to find the alley from the newspaper article. She watched it from a distance, crouched behind a car parked across the street, scanning for any sign of movement. This was dangerous. The alley was probably the first place her pursuers would look. She examined the street in either direction, and seeing nothing suspicious, she ran across the street and into the alley.

She moved slowly, her senses heightened, expecting someone to jump out of hiding at any moment. She had no idea what she was looking for. Anything out of the ordinary, she supposed. Something that might jar her memory, might explain what she had been doing here. But she saw only garbage bins and folded cardboard boxes. This was foolish. She'd probably just entered the alley last night on impulse while being chased, in which case there was nothing here to—

"Zoe," said a voice from the shadows.

She froze. A few seconds later, she remembered to breathe.

"Zoe," it said again. "You shouldn't be here."

"How do you know me?" she asked.

The speaker stepped into the dingy light. It was a boy, around the same age as her and a little taller. His tussled blond hair partially obscured a bruised face, and his T-shirt and jeans were dirty and slightly torn. He stared at her for several seconds before answering.

"You . . . you don't know me? They must have hit you on the head really hard, Zoe. I'm Ethan. We're friends." He leaned forward, peering closely. "This is *weird*. How can you not remember me?"

She shrugged. "Okay, Ethan. What's my last name?"

He cocked his head. "You're just . . . Zoe."

"I have to have a last name," she said. "Who are my parents?"

"You don't have any parents," he said. "None of us do."

She let that sink in. She hadn't had much time to think, but she'd been hoping she had parents out there somewhere, looking for her. "Who's 'us'?"

"That'll take some explaining." His eyes widened suddenly. "We need to get out of here. They could be here any minute."

"Who?" But she already knew.

"Who do you think? They were in the Market less than an hour ago, looking for you. They even checked here. They did this," he said, indicating his bruised face. "They're questioning all of us. That's why I'm here—looking for you. I figured you must've left the hospital." He grabbed her wrist and pushed past her. "Come on, we have to go."

She pulled free. "Wait a minute. Who are 'all of us'?"

"I'll explain it all later. Let's go."

"Not yet. I have questions! Like, why are they after me? What did I do?"

He stared at her. "Everyone says you left, Zoe," he said. "Nobody leaves."

"Left where? What do you mean, nobody leaves?"

Ethan shook his head. "I'll explain everything but not here, all right? We have to go. They could be here any minute."

"You said they already checked here."

"They'll check *again*."

She didn't trust this boy yet, though. She needed to know more before going off with him somewhere. "Are you . . . like me? Can you do . . . things? Things that other people can't?"

Ethan smiled. "Things? You mean like this?" He held out his hand and the lid of a nearby garbage can flew into it.

Zoe nodded. "And there are more like us here in Ottawa?"

"Here and Toronto and other places. Can we go now?"

She stood firm. "Why are you here, in this particular alley? Were you following me?"

He scowled. "No, I came here because you told me to."

She processed this. "What exactly did I tell you and when?"

She could tell that he really was worried about the danger and that she was testing his patience, but she wanted answers. Eventually, he sighed and looked up as he searched his memory. "You said that if anything bad ever happened to you, or if you ever disappeared, that I should look for you here." Seeing her skepticism, he said, "Hey look, I'm not making this up. They're your words, not mine. I thought it was a really weird thing to say too, until last night when the ambulance took you away from this very spot."

She regarded him carefully, trying to read his face, trying to look into his mind to decide if he was telling the truth. What she was supposed to have said was so specific. She didn't get the sense he was lying, though that didn't necessarily mean he wasn't.

All right, let's say he was telling the truth. Why would she have said that? It couldn't be a coincidence that she'd told him to wait in this particular alley, where she was later attacked and found unconscious. What did it mean? She began pacing while Ethan watched in exasperation.

Maybe she had *known* she was going to be attacked and had chosen this alley ahead of time as the place where she would make her last stand. But why tell Ethan to meet her here instead of somewhere else? The only reason she was here was because she had lost her memory and this was the logical spot to look for clues to her identity. So . . . what if she had somehow known she might lose her memory—which would mean it wasn't necessarily from getting hit on the head—and figured that her memory-less self would come back here later searching for clues? If so, then maybe she would have purposefully left actual clues here ahead of time.

She stopped pacing. "All right, I believe you. And I agree, we need to get out of here in a hurry. But first I need your help. I need to find something."

"What?" Ethan asked, as she began inspecting the alley again.

"A clue. You might be the first clue, but if I planned this whole thing, then I would have left more clues here than just you. After all, what if you didn't show up? Or if we missed each other?" She shook her head. "It wouldn't make sense for you to be the only clue. I'd have left something else here. Like a . . . note or something. Something to help me remember who I am."

Ethan looked at her. "How could you have known that you'd lose your memory, Zoe?"

She opened her mouth, then closed it. How to explain something she couldn't really explain to herself? "I don't know, it's just a hunch. I have to assume that I'm still *me*, that I still think the way I used to. Just help me search, okay? Then we can get out of here."

They searched the alley together, feeling more tense and more exposed with each passing minute, yet they found nothing but garbage. Finally, she stopped. She needed to be smarter about this. Where would she have hidden it, where it couldn't blow away and nobody else would find it? What was special about her that would allow her to find it but no one else?

She went back to pacing. Well, apparently, she could move things with her mind, but that wouldn't be much help against brick walls and dirty pavement. She was fairly good with a sword. Again, not much use here. She had seemed pretty agile, even acrobatic, during her escape from the hospital. She was— Wait, could that be it? She looked up, scanning the walls. And then she saw it.

A small cloth bag was barely visible on the second-storey ledge of a boarded-up window. Ethan followed her gaze.

"You put that up there?" He raised his hand and the bag moved a little, but it was stuck, fastened to a hook or something screwed into the boards.

Zoe looked from one wall to the next, judging distances. She walked away ten feet, then, before she could change her mind, turned and ran full speed at the wall. She jumped up at the last moment and pushed off the bricks as hard as she could with her left foot toward the opposite building, then pushed off *that* wall with her right foot back to the first wall. Finally, with one last leap, she grabbed the window ledge with her fingertips and held on for dear life while her feet scrabbled to gain any sort of purchase. Releasing one hand, she seized the bag, untying it from the hook, then let go and dropped to the ground. Landing on two feet, she rolled to absorb the impact and came up kneeling.

Ethan seemed unimpressed. She studied the brown cloth bag in her hands, feeling its weight. Opening it, she pulled out a round silver pendant hanging from a long silver chain. It looked old, she thought, and featured an intricate carving of a tree with tiny green gems for leaves. It was two and a half inches in diameter and a full inch thick. Creatures were carved along the edge—a dragon, a bird, a stag, and a squirrel. Turning it over, she saw the pendant was actually a brooch, but with a metal loop over the pin to slide the chain through. The ornate craftmanship continued onto the back but not all the way. A one-inch plain silver circle lay in the centre with runes of some sort etched into it.

Ethan's crouched down opposite her. "Nice," he said. "Where did you get that?"

"I have no idea," she said. "No memory, remember?" It clearly had tiny hinges and she could see an almost invisible seam where the two halves met, but there was no latch to grab hold of. Try as she might, she simply couldn't open it.

"Here, let me try," Ethan said, holding out his hand.

She looked at his palm.

"It's okay, Zoe. I'm not going to steal it. We're friends." He smiled.

Still, she hesitated. He *seemed* like he really did know her, and she could sure use a friend. And she had to admit that his smile seemed genuine and sincere. Besides, she had to trust somebody sometime, right? She placed the brooch in his hand and shoved the empty bag into her pocket.

Ethan held the brooch up close to his face, examining it from all angles. "Look here. Look at this," he said, pointing at something. She leaned forward to see and suddenly found herself flat on her back with Ethan clutching her face and staring intently into her eyes.

Forget, said his voice in her mind. *Forget about the pendant. You never found it. You never found anything.*

No! How could he do this to her? He'd said he was her friend! How could she have been so stupid? Feelings of hurt and betrayal gave way to fury as she struggled to throw him from her mind.

Forget about the pendant. It never happened. You came into this alley and never found anything. Forget about the pendant . . .

He was too strong. She had been completely unprepared and now he was deep inside her mind, reaching for her memories of the past few minutes.

No! I don't want to forget! I don't want to forget anything else! She fought him as hard as she could, but she could feel him winning, feel her memories slipping away, feel—

Zoe stood in the alley, frustrated that she hadn't found anything. It didn't make any sense.

"There's nothing here, Zoe," Ethan said, looking back down the alley. "We've looked everywhere. If something were here, we would have found it by now. So, let's go before they show up."

He had a point. They were pushing their luck. If her pursuers were close by, every second she spent here was a risk. But she had been so sure she would have left herself some kind of message. Something that would help to bring her memories back. She began to pace back and forth as she thought.

"Zoe, let's go!"

"Not yet!" she snapped. Maybe she wasn't going about this the right way. Maybe she should try to think as though she were about to lose her memory right now and needed to hide something terribly important here. Where would she put it? There had to be no chance of anyone else finding it except for her. How would she do that?

Suddenly it came to her. She looked up and scanned the walls. There. That window ledge was a good fifteen feet high. She could hide something small there and tack it to the boards covering the window so that it wouldn't blow away. Nobody would notice it from the ground, let alone be able to get to it. Could *she* get to it, though?

"We have to leave *now*."

"Then leave," she said, absently, gauging the distance between the walls and visualizing the necessary acrobatics. She could do it. Not pausing to reconsider, she backed up a bit and then ran at the wall, running up it as far as she could before pushing off and leaping from one wall to the other until she could grab the ledge with her fingertips. While scrabbling with her feet to take some of her weight for just a few seconds, she felt along the ledge for a hidden package. There was nothing there. She dropped to the ground and rolled, coming up in a crouch.

Ethan looked amused. "Are you satisfied now? Can we go?"

Zoe didn't answer, though. Something was wrong. She had the strangest feeling that this had all happened before. Could she be remembering something at last? She could swear she had hung from that ledge before.

"Hello? Earth to Zoe. We are *leaving*. Before the bad guys get here, remember?" He started for the street.

She had felt along the ledge . . . grabbed something. Pulled it out, dropped to the ground . . . come up holding . . .

She reached into her pocket and felt the thing she had known would be there.

"Ethan, wait up," she said, getting to her feet and starting after him. "You forgot something."

"What?" he asked, not looking back.

"This." She pulled the small cloth bag from her pocket and dangled it in the air.

Ethan stopped. Slowly turned around. Neither said a word. Then, he made his move. She felt him rushing to enter her mind, only to bounce off her shield so hard that he staggered and steadied himself against the brick wall.

"You shouldn't have been able to remember," he said.

"So, you did this to me? You're the reason I can't remember who I am?"

He looked hurt. "No, I would never do that to you."

"You just did a minute ago!"

"I'm sorry. That was just erasing one little thing, a few minutes' worth, and it was for your own good. I had no choice. I would never erase your whole life, Zoe. I told you, we're friends."

"Whatever." She stepped closer. "You can tell me all about our friendship later. Right now, you can give me back whatever was in this bag. It belongs to me."

Ethan shook his head. "I can't do that. You should've left it alone, Zoe. You don't want what was in that bag. I don't know why you put it there in the first place, but it was a dumb idea!"

"Why?" she said, still approaching. "Why don't I want it? Why was it a dumb idea?" She needed to know. He had to tell her, no matter what.

But Ethan didn't answer, perhaps sensing he'd already said too much. "I was looking out for you, Zoe. I was trying to protect you."

Doubtful. "From whom?"

Ethan refused to answer.

"You're one of them," she said. "You're not trying to protect me from them, you are one of them."

"I'm your friend, Zoe."

"Yeah, you keep saying that. Now give me back whatever was in this bag."

He backed away. "No."

She clenched her teeth. "I mean it."

Ethan continued his slow retreat. "I can't, Zoe. I'm sorry, but you'll have to trust me."

"Trust you?" She couldn't believe it. "Are you seriously still trying to pretend that you're my friend?"

"I'm *not* pretending. I *am* your friend. I know it must not seem like it right now but—" His face contorted, as if in pain. "I would do . . . anything to keep you safe. Please forgive me."

"You're mental!" she shouted. "Don't walk away from me! You're going to give back whatever it is you took from me!"

Ethan didn't stop. "I'm sorry, Zoe, but I'm not going to do that."

This was ridiculous. She couldn't just let him walk away from her. But what was she going to do? Hit him, while he was standing there passively with his arms outstretched and palms open?

"I'm leaving now, Zoe. Plans have changed. Don't follow me. Go the other away. The others are coming any second. I can feel them approaching. You need to get moving." He turned and started walking away.

"No! Stop! STOP!" she yelled at his back. Ethan kept walking. *STOP!*

He stopped, compelled by her will.

Come here. She pushed the thought into his head with all her might. He turned and walked toward her, like a jerky marionette, his whole body trembling, clearly fighting her mental compulsion. She didn't know how she was doing this, but she was controlling him the way the others had controlled her last night. It felt repulsive, but she had no choice.

Ethan stood before her now, his face contorted with anger and genuine betrayal.

No time to process that now. *Give it to me.* Ethan reached into his pocket and pulled out a pendant hanging from a silver chain. He deposited it into her hand. "You're making a mistake," he grunted.

Zoe put the chain around her neck and the pendant under her shirt, trembling as much as Ethan. *Now, tell me everything. Who I am. Who you are. Who they are. Everything.*

Ethan scrunched his eyes shut and began shaking more violently. "Don't. Don't make me do this."

Tears ran down her cheeks. She felt vile, as if their roles had suddenly reversed and *she* had become the villain. She *had* to know these things, though.

Tell me.

Ethan hesitated a moment more, then opened his mouth to speak.

Two familiar figures in long coats stepped into the alley behind him.

Tsuji and Ivan.

Her connection to Ethan severed abruptly.

Ethan looked over his shoulder and saw them approaching. He turned back to Zoe.

Run.

What the—? He was protecting her now? What was going on here?

"Run!" he yelled. "Get to downtown Toronto! Others like us can help you!"

She turned and ran. Looking back, she saw the two pursuers run into some sort of invisible wall as they tried to pass Ethan. She reached the other end of the alley and paused, hearing a loud click behind her. Turning, she saw Ethan suddenly holding a long metal staff and refusing to budge. He looked back at her and their eyes locked.

Get out of here! They don't dare kill me. Just go!

For the second time in only a few hours, she fled.

3

IN HIDING

Unfortunately, Zoe's options were limited. She was a teenager with no friends, no family, and no money—not to mention in hiding from sword-wielding telepaths. She couldn't go to the police because they'd think she was crazy. For lack of any other plan, she headed down Elgin Street toward the bus station. Ethan had said to get to Toronto, where others like her could help. But could she really trust him? He'd stolen from her and wiped her memory. And yet, despite all that, he had *looked* anguished about it and asked for forgiveness. And he *felt* like a friend, which was a weird feeling to have for a stranger who'd attacked her. What was she to make of him?

A police station stood at the end of Elgin Street. She stopped. Shouldn't she at least try to ask the police for help? She marched in and asked to speak to a detective.

She told the detective everything that had happened from the moment she woke up in the alley to the moment she fled her pursuers for the second time in that alley. She talked all about being forced to kneel, about the tendrils connecting their minds, about how she'd learned to shield herself. She described how they'd tossed her through the air with their minds, and the swordfight in the hospital lobby. She talked about

Ethan, who'd almost succeeded in erasing her memory.

She suspected it was the stupidest thing she had ever done. What did she think would happen? The only good thing to come of it was the realization that she could read minds, even if not very well. In hindsight, that must have been what had happened with the paramedic—and maybe the whispering at the hospital had been her overhearing the telepathic conversations of her assailants.

Regardless, she didn't need to read the detective's mind to know she thought Zoe was crazy. But she did manage to pick up what the detective thought was in store for her. Plenty of psychological assessments and therapy, that's what.

She decided to prove she was telling the truth. But when she tried to move the soda can in front of her with her mind, it didn't budge. She had managed to make that sword fly into her hand instinctively under the pressure of knowing she had only a second left to live. But in the calm setting of the police station, she simply didn't know how to repeat such a feat and no amount of concentration helped.

So, she told the detective to think of something and she would read her mind. But while she could get general impressions from the detective's mind, she couldn't get enough actual detail to convince her these weren't just the delusions of a disturbed child. Zoe wasn't sure which frustrated her more—being thought of as crazy or being thought of as a child. Zoe knew she wasn't an adult yet, but she felt every bit as smart and capable as the detective.

So, while waiting dejectedly for someone from the Children's Aid Society to arrive, she asked to use the restroom, removed her head bandages and the hospital gown from under her clothes, and that was the last the police saw of her. She slipped out unnoticed and made her way to the bus station a few blocks away. After nearly getting caught in the Market and unable to rely on the police, she needed some distance so she could take a breath and figure out what was going on.

The departures board showed a bus was leaving for Toronto at nine thirty—in five minutes. Perfect. Now, she just had to figure out how to get aboard without a ticket. She wandered over to the glass wall facing the parked buses and found the one to Toronto. A dozen people waited in line, and a man checked their tickets in front of the glass doors to the bus platform. Out on the platform, the driver helped to load suitcases into the luggage hold. Easy enough. Zoe exited the building, walked around to the bus platform, waited until the driver was busy helping someone with their luggage, and then got confidently onto the bus. There was a chance they would check tickets again onboard—especially if they ran short on seats—but she would deal with that if it happened.

During the ride, she examined her hard-won necklace. It was clearly a brooch hanging from a chain. The brooch was so thick, though, that it had to be hollow, which meant there might be something inside. She held it to her ear and shook it but didn't hear any rattling. The one-inch circle of plain silver in the centre of the brooch's back seemed suspicious. Could it be a little door of some sort? She tried pushing and sliding and twisting it, to no avail. If it could be opened, she couldn't figure it out. She could maybe smash it open with a hammer, but no way did she want to break it. It had clearly been important to her former self, and she couldn't help thinking it could be the key to her identity. Plus, if it wasn't important, Ethan wouldn't have tried to steal it.

Five hours later, exhausted and half-starved, she arrived at the bus terminal in Toronto where Ethan had said there were others like her. This assumed he was telling the truth, of course. She was on high alert as she disembarked, half-expecting to find either a bunch of people in long jackets waiting for her or a bunch of police officers. She exited the station and found herself on Bay Street in busy downtown Toronto on a rainy afternoon.

She had spent most of the bus ride thinking about what she would do when she arrived. It was hard to come up with a plan, though, when there was so much she didn't know—not just about her pursuers but also about herself. She needed a secluded space to explore her mental abilities, but more than that, her first course of action had to be to obtain more information. Upon arriving, though, she realized that the first course of action actually had to be lunch, which meant either begging or stealing or finding a homeless shelter that might give her a free meal. She decided on the latter.

Immediately, she realized that unlike Ottawa, she did not recognize downtown Toronto at all. She asked some street kids sheltering from the rain and learned there was a youth shelter only a few blocks away. Sure enough, they gave her some food with few questions asked and told her to come back later for a proper dinner and a bed if she needed somewhere to spend the night. Zoe thanked them and asked for directions to the nearest library.

On her way there, she passed by an antique shop and had an idea. A bell rang as she entered the cozy little store. It was cluttered with all sorts of wonderfully old things, including a glass case full of jewellery. She doubted that whoever worked here would be an expert, but they'd certainly know more about her brooch than she did.

The elderly man behind the counter had disheveled white hair and wore a cardigan with elbow patches. "Hello, young lady," he said. "Is there something I can help you with?"

Zoe dangled her brooch. "I was wondering if you could tell me anything about this." She placed it in his outstretched hand.

"Oh my," he said, turning it over and examining it closely. "Well now, this is an interesting piece. How did you come by it?"

"I've had it for almost as long as I can remember," Zoe answered truthfully. "Is it old?"

"Hmm." The old man held a jewellery loupe to his eye for magnification. "That is an excellent question. Do you know anything about its history?"

Zoe shook her head. "I'm afraid not," she said. "And I have no parents to ask. I was hoping you might be able to tell me something."

"I'm sorry to hear that," the man said, kindly. "Here's what I can tell you right away. This is what is known as a box brooch. Like regular brooches, they were used to fasten your cloak or shawl, but these were thicker and hollow with a hole in the back so that you could place small objects inside. These are old Viking runes on the back, also known as Futhark, although whether it's Elder Futhark or Younger Futhark, I'm not sure. Hold on, I have a phonetic chart for Viking runes buried around here somewhere if you'd like to know what it says."

Zoe waited while he found the chart and began deciphering.

"It says . . . lif. Oh, well, that makes sense. Lif means 'life' in Old Norse, and this tree on the front," he said, turning it over, "is no doubt supposed to be the Tree of Life, also known as 'Yggdrasil.' Look, here's the dragon, the eagle, and the four stags that all lived in Yggdrasil—plus the squirrel who would run through the tree to deliver messages. This is beautiful craftsmanship." He squinted at it again, looking for something.

"You'll see the Tree of Life on a lot of modern Viking jewellery these days, but this definitely isn't modern. A modern piece can be identified by its hallmark, a little letter marking that offers insight into who created the piece or what time period it's from. This has none, though. I would say that this could actually be an authentic Viking box brooch. These little green gems are just glass, I think, which was common for Viking jewellery. And the clasp on the back is of the type you'd find back then. If you really wanted to date it, to verify its authenticity, I suspect you would have to get an expert to do a spectrographic analysis on the metal itself."

He beckoned her to look where he was pointing. "This box brooch is most peculiar, though. As you can see, there's no hole in the back. It looks like there used to be a hole, mind you, but it's been filled in . . . and there doesn't seem to be any way of opening it. I can't imagine why anyone would do that except to create some sort of time capsule, maybe, to ensure that whatever is inside remains undisturbed forever." He held it to his ear and shook it gently, as Zoe had earlier. "I don't feel anything rattling around in there, though."

"As for what this piece might be worth," the old man continued, "I wouldn't know how to price it. Antique jewellery from the Viking Age or, say, from the Roman Age can be worth thousands of dollars if it's in excellent condition, which this is, but it wouldn't be worth a fortune unless it had valuable gemstones, which this does not. However, this item is definitely unique in that an unopenable box brooch is unheard of, so that would increase its mystery and thus its value. There must be a story behind this piece and if we knew the story, that could increase its value by, well, any amount. Are you looking to sell it?"

"No!" Zoe blurted, quickly holding out her open hand. The old man hesitated, then placed the brooch back in her palm. "It's all I have," she said. "I can't sell it no matter what it's worth. I just wanted to know more about it, that's all. Thank you so much for your help."

The proprietor nodded. "I understand. Should you change your mind for any reason, I would be willing to purchase it from you. Again, I don't really know what it's worth, but I could do some research and pay a fair price or, if it's too much for me, put you in contact with a potential buyer. Honestly, if that piece is authentic, then I would say it could be in a museum."

She tucked the brooch back under her shirt and out of sight. "Thank you again, sir. For all your help. I really appreciate it."

■ ■ ■

The Toronto Reference Library was *huge*—and architecturally stunning. From the main atrium, four levels of beautifully curved white balconies looked down on Zoe, and people sat and studied in little circular glass rooms. She couldn't believe how many books there were about so many subjects. She could also use the computers to access the Internet.

She started by looking up psychogenic amnesia, a term her doctor had apparently written in her chart, and learned that identity loss is not commonly associated with head injuries but rather with some sort of psychological trauma. So maybe her amnesia wasn't caused by the blow to her head but rather someone had wiped her memory the same way Ethan had, except on a much larger scale.

She then moved on to searching for any evidence that there were other people out there like her and Ethan and her pursuers. She read lots of literature on parapsychology but quickly realized it was a dead-end. While some people believed in telepathy and telekinesis, there was zero scientific evidence to show these things were real. *She* knew it was real, though, so she searched for news articles—from anywhere in the world—about unexplained phenomena or even homicides in which the murder weapon may have been a sword, since that seemed to be her pursuers' weapon of choice. In the end, she found nothing. Their kind, she concluded, must either be brand new to the world or very careful to keep their abilities hidden.

When the library closed, she made her way back to the youth shelter for a meal. She avoided small talk with the other kids and they gave her space. In the morning, she was back at the library as soon as the doors opened. She continued to scour the web, but got nowhere. What would she do if she found nothing and her memories never returned and she never found these other people Ethan had referred to?

She was trying to block out the loud conversation at the neighbouring table when she suddenly realized they were speaking Mandarin—and she understood what they were saying! She quickly tested herself and was astonished to learn that she could *speak* it, too. That must surely be a clue. Maybe she had spent time in China? She wondered if she knew any other languages. After a few hours of research, she determined that she, in fact, spoke at least fourteen. She listened to some languages with headphones and spoke them quietly to herself. Some she felt fluent in, while others she knew just the bare basics of, but still, this flabbergasted her. Had she lived in many different countries and absorbed the languages, or was she some sort of language savant? She was briefly excited, hoping to find some mention of herself on the Internet but was unable to find any mention of a savant even remotely resembling her age and physical description.

Her morning research a bust, Zoe decided it was time to begin exploring her special talents. Moving to a quiet corner of the library's top floor and hiding behind a large book propped up on the table, she began to experiment.

She placed her pencil on the table, stared at it, and silently willed it to roll away. Nothing happened. She willed it to roll toward her. Still nothing. Rolling up her sleeves, she gritted her teeth, tensed all her muscles, and stared at it with such vigour that she thought her eyes would pop out of their sockets. For ten minutes, she tried, concentrating with all her might until she was actually sweating.

Finally, she stopped, utterly exhausted. That sword had flown a good eight feet through the air. How could she not make a little pencil move even a millimeter? Had she imagined the whole thing? *Was* she crazy?

Annoyed and frustrated, she folded her arms and leaned back in her chair, pouting. She flicked her hand angrily at the pencil—and watched it fly into the book, knocking it over with a loud thud.

Zoe stared in astonishment, then let out a squeal and quickly covered her mouth, checking that nobody was watching. Propping the book back up, she slouched down out of sight again and focused her attention on the pencil. The hand was the trick. It must be. Raising her hand, she gestured forward as she willed the pencil to roll away. Nothing. She pulled her hand back and willed the pencil to roll toward her. Nothing. She flicked her hand at it like before. Still nothing. This was ridiculous! She'd done it before without even trying, so why couldn't she do it now? Maybe not really trying was the key?

She leaned back in her chair like before and flicked her hand at the pencil nonchalantly, pretending like she didn't really care if it moved or not, but if it did, great. Nothing happened.

Furious, she lurched forward and focused all of her rage on the thing. *Stupid pencil!* she yelled in her mind as she willed it to rise.

The pencil shot upward and embedded itself deep in the ceiling. She gaped up at it. She'd done it! Then she looked down to see a middle-aged man standing in front of her, looking very displeased.

"*What* do you think you are doing?"

Startled, Zoe froze. How had he managed to sneak up on her like that? Had she just been too distracted? Something about the way he carried himself exuded authority and confidence. Instinctively, she knew that this man knew how to handle himself in a fight, although she couldn't point to anything in particular that explained *how* she knew this.

"I repeat," said the man, "exactly what do you think you are doing?" His gaze was hard, his voice cold.

Zoe opened her mouth, but nothing came out. Her mind raced. Who was this man? His reaction to seeing her fling a pencil into the ceiling with her mind was not one of shock but anger. Which could only mean one thing. He was one of *them*.

She looked around for an escape, but she was trapped. Why had she chosen to sit in a corner? There was only one choice. Looking up, she met the man's gaze.

Stand aside. Let me go, she said in his mind with as much power as she could muster.

His eyes widened in surprise. *You dare?* He threw her out of his head with such ferocity that the room spun. "What is your name?" Zoe saw several people look their way in concern, only to glaze over and turn back to their books. This was not good. She tried something else. Gathering her thoughts, she thrust out her hand and willed the man to fly away from her.

The man just stared incredulously. She tried to stand and kick him, but found herself unable to move, as if caught in a gigantic, invisible hand. He towered over her now, looking quite menacing. "You are in a great deal of trouble, young lady," he said in a very quiet voice. "And you test my patience. Your name. Now."

"I just want to go," Zoe said. "I didn't do anything."

"Other than attempting to compel a teacher and then attacking him, you mean? Other than performing feats of telekinesis in plain view of Typicals? Imagine my surprise while strolling downtown when I sensed a tremendous amount of unfocused psychokinetic power emanating from the fifth floor of the Toronto Reference Library. I felt it from *three* blocks away. What were you trying to do, lift the entire building off its foundation?"

"I was just trying to move the pencil," Zoe said, pointing helplessly up at the ceiling, while processing everything he had just said. He was like her and unsurprised to find someone else with abilities like his—and he was a *teacher*. Maybe he taught children with abilities? "Where do you teach?" she asked, trying to sound calm.

The man appeared taken aback, as if the answer should have been obvious. He was silent a moment, studying her. "I do not recognize you as one of my students. Did you recently arrive from Ottawa, by chance?"

A chill went up her spine. He knew who she was. But he didn't recognize her, so he probably wasn't from wherever she was from. Maybe he was the one of the people Ethan had said could help her.

"I will take your silence to mean yes." The man pulled up a chair and sat down in front of her, still blocking her exit. "I am going to release you now," he said. "I ask that you do not try to attack me again. I promise you that I intend you no harm. Agreed?"

Zoe hesitated, then nodded. What else could she do? The invisible hand let go.

"Now," the man said, crossing his legs. "Let us start over. My name is

Professor Chao. What is your name, and how is it that you are proficient enough in your Abilities to attempt compulsion on me yet you are not a student at my school?"

Zoe took a deep breath. "My name is Zoe. At least that's what I've been told. I don't actually remember anything before two nights ago." There, that was done. If he was allied with her pursuers, he'd know who she was for sure now. She hardly dared breathe.

"Interesting," was all he said. "Interesting. Who told you your name was Zoe?"

"A man named Fasil," she said, "and a boy named Ethan. The man said his name was Detective Fasil Nazari, except he wasn't actually a detective. He and three others apparently attacked me two nights ago in Ottawa and then tried to kill me in the hospital the next morning."

Chao showed no expression but for a very long time sat still. Then, he said, "I think you should tell me everything, Zoe. Start from the beginning."

■ ■ ■

And she did. She told the professor her whole story. Stumbling out of the alley. Escaping the hospital. Encountering Ethan. She paused a moment before telling him about the brooch. It was not just a clue to her identity, it was her only connection to her old life. She didn't want him to take it from her. But if this man was going to help her, then she would have to earn his trust, which meant being truthful about everything. He listened attentively for almost half an hour, stroking his chin and interjecting occasionally with a question or a request for clarification. When she finished, the professor sat quietly once again, deep in thought, almost oblivious to her presence.

Finally, he seemed to remember she was still there. "I want to help you, Zoe," he said. "I assure you that I have no association with those who attacked you, nor do any of my colleagues. I only became aware of their existence very recently. Whoever they are, they are *not* acting in accordance with the laws of our kind. Indeed, I find the very existence of these people—and what they said to you—to be extremely troubling. When we heard the bizarre story out of Ottawa yesterday of how four ambulances inexplicably lost their patients, we sent our people to investigate right away. However, you had already fled the hospital. None of the staff nor the police officer stationed outside your room remembered you leaving, and the security footage had been erased. It was obvious that our kind were involved."

He stood up. "Henceforth, you are under my protection. I will take you to a secure location where we can determine the best course of action. Come with me." But after a dozen paces, he noticed that Zoe wasn't following. Furrowing his brow, he beckoned. Zoe remained sitting, forcing the professor to return.

"Is there some reason you are still sitting here?" he asked, crossing his arms in annoyance.

"Yes, professor," Zoe said. "I mean no disrespect. I appreciate your offer very much—you have no idea how much I need help—but I have been fooled before by someone claiming to be my friend. How do I know you're not doing the same thing? I need more information before I can go with you."

The professor's expression changed from annoyance to respect. He nodded. "You have good sense. It is wise of you to be cautious." He thought for a moment. "I will answer all your questions to the best of my ability, but this is too quiet a location to discuss such delicate matters," he said, looking around the library. "Might I suggest we conduct our conversation in a loud, crowded location in which you will feel safe?" He looked at his wristwatch. "It is lunchtime. There is a restaurant nearby that I am fond of. My wife is running an errand in this neighbourhood. I will ask her to join us. Is that acceptable to you?"

Zoe nodded. The professor tapped his cellphone and held it to his ear.

"I know it is short notice but can you meet me for lunch? I have a young person here who you need to meet." A pause. "Actually, no, I think it would be best if Lin stayed home. I will explain everything there. The Green Kitchen?" Another pause. "Excellent. See you soon."

He put his phone away and handed Zoe his umbrella. "Here, take this. My raincoat will keep me dry enough."

Zoe paused a moment before getting to her feet and taking the umbrella. This might be a mistake, but she was not being foolish, she told herself. This "professor" seemed too good to be true, but she needed to take a chance. She desperately needed the sort of information he could provide. She was hopeful, but not stupid. She would stay on her guard.

4

REVELATIONS

She sat facing the solid wall of windows at the front of the restaurant. She felt safer being able to see who was walking by outside and, more importantly, who was walking in. The professor said he would wait for his wife to arrive before eating but encouraged her to start right away. He drank green tea and watched her every movement with interest.

"Interesting," he said.

She raised her eyebrow, unable to talk with her mouth full of food.

"I would like to try a little experiment, if you are willing. Close your eyes."

She swallowed. "Why?"

"Indulge me. It could help us learn about your childhood."

Zoe squinted, suspicious, but did as he asked.

"How many patrons are here?"

"Eleven plus us," Zoe replied with certainty.

"And where are they?"

"Four are sitting at the two tables by the windows, two at the table to my left, two at the table to my right, two at the table behind me, plus a man sitting alone at the bar."

"How many staff?"

"Two waiters—a woman and a man—plus the woman behind the bar who's in charge, and three men in the kitchen, I think."

"Where are the waiters now?"

"The woman is serving the table by the windows to the left of the door. The man just entered the kitchen."

"What is the owner wearing?"

"A green dress with white flowers."

"Who do you think is the most dangerous person here?"

"You."

He chuckled. "Other than me."

"The man at the bar," she said. "He isn't big, but he's quiet and sure of himself, and his movements are very controlled. Martial arts training, I think."

"What am I doing right now?"

"You are holding your cup of tea, looking at me."

"Open your eyes."

Zoe blinked her eyes open. "What was all that about?"

"Were you surprised you could do that?" the professor asked.

"No. Why would I be surprised at being able to describe what's going on around me?"

"It is called situational awareness. It is a skill taught to covert operatives, military, and law enforcement. It has been taught to you as well. When you are trained to notice everything and everyone around you at all times, as I have been, you notice when other people are doing the same, even when they are doing so subtly."

"So, most people can't do that? That has to be a clue, right? What school teaches that to kids?"

"No school that I am aware of near here. Schools that train children in espionage have existed in other parts of the world, though, and some still exist today."

"So you think I could be from one of those schools? Do they have people like us there?"

"I certainly hope not," he replied, his brow furrowed. "I am sorry to have interrupted your meal." He gestured toward her plate. "Please do continue."

After she finished wolfing down two plates of food, the professor smiled, rested his elbows on the table, his fingertips touching, and said, "So, tell me what you want to know."

"What are we?" Zoe blurted. She had so many questions, but this was the most obvious place to begin.

"Humans, of course," the professor said. "But different from most. We refer to ourselves most often as 'Telepaths' these days, but we have had other names throughout history, usually variants of the word 'Watchers' in different languages. We watch, we record, we sometimes guide in subtle ways, but we try not to interfere. Our kind have existed since the beginning of recorded history."

"How many of us are there?"

"At least ten thousand for certain. Fewer than one in three million people are born a Telepath. These days, around fifty of us are born into the world each year. It used to be far fewer back before the world's population skyrocketed. Our special Abilities tend to become apparent sometime during our early teens."

Zoe frowned. "Only fifty? Then how can there be so many of us? Most people live to be less than a hundred, so there should be fewer than five thousand of us."

"Once we reach adulthood, we age very slowly."

"How old can we live to be?"

Professor Chao shrugged. "It varies. Some age more slowly than others. We can actually die of old age after a thousand years or so, but most of us don't make it that far."

"You mean death by unnatural causes usually comes first?"

He nodded. "Usually, yes. We generally heal quickly, as you must have noticed with your own recent injuries. I can barely tell that you were in a fight a few days ago. That innate ability to heal may be what accounts for our longevity. We also have the ability to deliberately repair damaged tissue in ourselves and in others, but if you lose too much blood—or your head—death comes as easily to us as it does to Typicals."

"Typicals," Zoe said. That's what you call normal people? Non-Telepaths?

Professor Chao nodded. Something still wasn't right, though.

"Why are there so few Telepaths in the world? Abilities like ours should have given us an evolutionary advantage over Typicals. If we've always existed, then wouldn't natural selection have eventually made everyone Telepaths?"

Professor Chao nodded. "A very astute question, and one easily answered. Our Abilities are not hereditary. Even when both parents are Telepaths, there does not seem to be any greater chance of their offspring being Telepaths than that of two Typical parents."

Zoe thought about this. According to Ethan, they didn't have parents, but obviously they must have had biological parents somewhere, alive or dead. Somehow, she had always assumed they were like her, but if there was less than a one in three million chance of either of them being Telepaths, then they were almost certainly Typicals. "Is Lin your daughter? Is she a Typical?"

"Yes, Lin is my daughter. She *does* have our Abilities, though, but that is because she is adopted. My wife discovered her in an orphanage years ago, when her Abilities would normally not be detectable. It was a fluke that they found each other, one that we took as a sign, and so we adopted her. She will be attending the Academy in the fall."

"The Academy," said Zoe. "That's the school where you teach?"

"It is," he said. "It is officially called the Alexandria International Academy for the Gifted, named after the famous Library of Alexandria, of course, but people just refer to it as the Academy. It is currently located just east of Toronto. To the outside world of Typicals, it is an exclusive boarding school with admittance by invitation only. However, as I am sure you have deduced, those invitations are given solely to those children possessing our Abilities."

"But if they're born to Typical parents, how do you find them?" Zoe asked.

"With great difficulty," Chao said. "We have recruiters all over the world who search for children showing signs of telepathic powers of any kind. Often, we can sense their latent Abilities during the preteen years, in which case they are watched closely until their Abilities begin to manifest. It is imperative that we find them as quickly as possible to ensure they do not accidentally harm themselves or others. And to avoid unwanted exposure."

"You mean to keep our existence a secret from the rest of the world?" Professor Chao nodded.

"But why? Why keep it a secret at all?"

The professor sighed deeply, as though this were an age-old question. "Mainly, for our own protection, Zoe."

"*Our* protection? But . . . I don't understand. Our powers make us so much more powerful than Typicals. What do we have to fear from them? Shouldn't they be scared of us?"

"Exactly," said Professor Chao. "'Shouldn't they be scared of us?'" He paused to pour himself more tea. "Do you know what people do to things they fear, Zoe?"

Zoe shook her head.

"They destroy them." He sipped his tea. "There are almost eight *billion* Typicals in the world. Eight billion of them versus ten thousand of us. For all our strength, do you really think we could withstand an all-out war against them?"

"But Typicals aren't evil," Zoe protested. "How do we know they would try to hurt us?"

"No, they are not evil. No more so than us, at least. But they *would* fear us, Zoe. Four hundred years ago, in Europe, suspected witches were burned at the stake. In Salem, Massachusetts, they were hanged. To this day, in some countries, suspected witches are still persecuted. And then there are just those who are different. The persecution of minorities is as old as human society and is alive and well today. Imagine how people would react to our existence becoming known. We are not just different, we are powerful. We can read their private thoughts. Some of us can actually will a person's heart to stop beating. And many of us can use compulsion to make them obey our will even without their knowledge. Do you really think Typicals would allow us to live freely among them?"

Zoe considered this. "I don't know . . . I guess not. But how has such a huge secret been kept for so long? Hasn't anyone ever wanted to tell the world?"

"Yes," the professor said, slowly, "but they have all eventually complied with our laws. Anyone attempting to purposefully let the world know of our existence is dealt with severely, Zoe. Now that you know this, I expect to never see you attempting to levitate pencils in plain view of Typicals again. Understood?"

Zoe swallowed, then nodded. "Understood, sir. But there are exceptions, aren't there? I mean, if someone attacked you, for instance, you could use your powers to defend yourself, right?"

Chao nodded. "Yes, there are exceptions, such as the example you just provided. However, you must always use your Abilities in public as a very last resort. And afterward, you must clean up the mess."

"The mess?"

"It is not something that we are particularly proud of, Zoe, but it is imperative that Typicals remain ignorant of our existence. That means that whenever a Typical witnesses something they should not have seen, their memory of that event must be erased. *Carefully*, without injuring them or arousing their suspicions in any way. In recent times, covering up our messes has become exceedingly difficult due to the proliferation of video surveillance cameras as well as the fact that almost everyone walks around these days with cameras on their smartphones. Learning the skills to deal with these challenges takes a great deal of training. It is something you will learn, in time, at the Academy."

Zoe sat up straight. "What? Me? At the Academy?"

"Of course," Professor Chao said, matter-of-factly. "All of us attend the Academy as children, for a period of at least four years. Grades nine to twelve, plus an optional fifth year. If a child's Abilities manifest before grade nine, they must attend the Academy immediately. There are not many such children, though, so they are all together in one class. There is no choice in the matter. As I said, Telepaths must be trained to avoid hurting themselves and others."

"And you're absolutely positive I'm not a student at the Academy already?" Zoe asked. "Maybe I just wasn't in your class."

The professor shook his head. "Every student attends my class. I would remember you."

"So, I can just . . . go there? Just like that? Who would pay for me?" Zoe said, hardly daring to hope this was true.

"We take care of our own. Our kind have amassed a great deal of collective wealth over the centuries. The Academy is quite—" He stopped suddenly as Zoe tensed. No movement in his body suggested anything was out of the ordinary, but his eyes were sharp, and he was clearly aware of what Zoe was looking at.

"Quite self-sufficient," he said, finishing his thought. "I want you to stay calm, Zoe, and not show that anything is amiss. Do you recognize the people walking in?"

Zoe observed three familiar people entering the restaurant—two men and one woman, all dressed in long jackets.

"I knew it," she spat, shoving herself roughly away from the table and standing with her fists clenched. "I knew I shouldn't have trusted you. You brought them here." How could this have happened again? Was there no one she could trust? Was everyone in the world out to get her?

But the professor didn't react. He merely shook his head and said, "No. I did not."

Zoe held firm. "So, it's just a coincidence then, that they find me in another city as soon as I meet you?"

"Perhaps it is a coincidence, perhaps not. I do think we need to scan the brooch you are wearing beneath your shirt for a tracking device at our earliest opportunity, though." Zoe reflexively clutched her brooch. Why hadn't she thought of that? "Regardless," the professor continued, "it was not I who brought them here, I promise you."

The three long-coats had spotted them and fanned out. Tsuji, Ivan, and Anders, who appeared to have recovered from his head injury. She watched them approach from three sides.

"Don't be afraid," said the professor, still calmly drinking his tea. "I have sworn to protect you, remember? When the fighting starts, I want you to raise your shields, if you know how, and get out of the way. Let me deal with them."

"There are three of them," Zoe said, still unconvinced of his innocence. "And they have swords under their coats." She looked around the restaurant. "And we're in an entire room full of Typicals here."

"Yes, I know," he said. "But I am not without some small amount of skill in these matters."

No sooner had he said this than all the patrons in the restaurant suddenly stopped talking, laid their heads on the tables, and went to sleep. The waiters curled up on the floor. The abrupt silence was punctuated by the sound of the lock turning in the front door by . . . nobody.

Her three pursuers, who had now surrounded their table in the centre of the restaurant, exchanged glances.

"A neat trick, old man," Tsuji said. "We would have dealt with them more harshly, ourselves, but no matter. We've come for the girl. She belongs to us." Tsuji opened her coat to reveal her sword. Her companions did likewise.

Professor Chao still did not look at them, nor did he stand. Instead, he continued to drink his tea as though completely untroubled by their presence. "No," he said. "She belongs to no one. You will neither harm her nor take her. Also, I am afraid that I cannot allow any of you to leave this restaurant on your own. I recognize none of you and I am, as you accurately stated, quite old. You have not attended my school and therefore you should not exist. I must insist that you tell me everything about yourselves, where you trained, and who trained you."

Zoe saw the three assailants glance at each other again, suddenly wary. Anders stepped forward and drew his sword—a katana, like Tsuji's.

"Who are you to speak to us in this manner?" he said, puffing out his chest. "We will skewer you where you sit!"

"No," Professor Chao said, unperturbed. "Unless I have seriously misread your skills, by the subtleties you reveal through your stances, that will not happen. I promise you, however, that I will try my best not to kill you."

Zoe had to admit she was impressed by the professor's composure—assuming this wasn't staged for her benefit, that was—but she still didn't see how he could defeat all three of them, while also protecting her.

"Enough talk!" shouted Tsuji. She and the large man drew their swords.

What happened next was difficult for Zoe to describe, even after careful reflection. One moment, the three of them were attacking the professor. The next moment, he was standing beside Anders with his hand on the hilt of Anders's sword, and then Anders was spinning around and flipping over onto his back. Holding the man's sword, the professor brought his foot down on Anders's head. The other two launched another attack, but somehow lost their balance and became entangled with each other as the professor stepped between them, hitting each in the temple—Tsuji with his left elbow and the large man with the hilt of the sword. In the span of three seconds, before Zoe could even move from her chair, the fight was already over, with all three assailants lying unconscious on the floor.

Zoe stared at her new hero. "What subject do you teach, professor?"

He smiled. "Combat," he said. "Though many other professors could have handled these three amateurs." He began rummaging through their pockets.

"What are you doing?" Zoe asked, crouching down beside him.

"Looking for identification. Any information to tell us who these people are and where they come from."

"Can't you just…see into their minds now that they're unconscious?"

"Yes, and I intend to do just that in a moment. But it is a lengthy process, so we shall begin with the physical evidence." He frowned. "Except, there does not appear to be any. None are carrying personal items of any kind." He picked up one of the katanas and examined it closely. "Except for these."

"What can they tell you?" Zoe asked.

"A great deal about their maker. Whoever made this blade was very talented, but they are unknown to me. I have never seen their work before, which is very unusual."

"How so?"

"There are only a handful of sword makers in the world capable of creating a blade of this quality. A trained eye can quickly determine which maker made a particular sword, but none of them made this one. That means a new talent has emerged who is creating exceptional swords for an unknown group of Telepaths who have somehow kept their existence a secret from us until now. This is very disturbing."

The professor looked around. "We do not have much time. Nobody outside seems to have noticed the commotion in here, but someone could knock on the door at any moment and discover everyone unconscious. We need to get our prisoners out quickly. We are going to need some help. Let us see if my wife is almost here." He pulled out his phone and was about to dial a number when he suddenly stopped.

A man stood in the entrance. Zoe hadn't seen or heard him enter and neither, she thought, had the professor. He stood over six feet tall and was clearly very muscular beneath the long black jacket he wore with the hood pulled over his head. Piercing blue eyes stared out from above a cloth mask. A heavy, double-edged longsword rested easily in his hand. A chill ran up Zoe's spine. Everything about this man screamed danger.

The professor seemed to think so too. *Zoe*, said his voice in her head. *Get out. Go through the kitchen and out the back door. Call my wife.* He tossed her his phone. *She is the most recent number in the call history. Explain to her what is happening here. She will know what to do.*

Zoe picked up Tsuji's katana. *No*, she said. *I'm going to help you.*

The man in black walked toward them.

No time to argue, yelled the professor in her head. *DO IT!*

She felt herself being thrust toward the kitchen doors. Rolling, she came up to her feet and spun around to see the two men engaged in combat, their swords flying faster than she could discern.

It wasn't just swords, though. Both the professor and this man in black had mastered more than the physical martial arts—they were using their telekinetic Abilities in ways she had never contemplated. She could see, with her mind's eye, flashes of light as each used mental tricks to try to pull the other off-balance. Plates and chairs and other objects flew from all directions as they whirled around each other. It was impossible to follow, and she felt certain she was only seeing a fraction of the fight, as so many of the feints and parries, attacks and counterattacks were nonphysical in nature. She was also certain that Professor Chao had just met his match.

Zoe knew she should do what the professor had told her to do and run. But she also knew that calling that phone number would not bring help here soon enough. If she tried to enter the fight, she would most likely be cut down in an instant, but she couldn't just abandon the professor. There had to be something she could do.

She couldn't be certain, but the professor looked to be on the defensive more than the offensive, and he looked to be tiring more than his opponent. While the professor's movements looked crisp and smooth like a martial arts master, his opponent's looked vicious and unpredictable like a battle-hardened warrior. She didn't think Professor Chao had much time left. She had to help him. But how?

Then it hit her. This secret group of Telepaths had not only kept their existence a secret from others of their kind, they had also followed protocol and kept themselves hidden from the world of Typicals, too. Making her decision, Zoe sprinted to the front of the restaurant.

The man in black saw her instantly. Any hope she had that he might want to capture her instead of kill her was instantly dispelled when he disengaged from the professor and launched himself at her, his longsword arcing towards her midsection. She jumped into the air, twisting her body around to block his strike with her own sword. The force of his swing spun her in the opposite direction. She landed on her feet facing the wrong way and had to do a back flip and a twist to right herself. She landed, expecting a killing blow at any moment. Without looking back, she dove to the left and came up in a roll, to find that the professor had put himself between her and the man in black. He was barely surviving the onslaught, which seemed to have doubled in intensity.

Zoe wasted no more time. She reached out and pulled the fire alarm, the objective of her hasty plan, then grabbed the nearest chair and flung it through the window.

"Come on!" she yelled, jumping through the broken pane without looking back. She landed on the glass-ridden sidewalk, sword still in hand, in the midst of dozens of shocked pedestrians. Some gaped while others screamed. Then, the professor dove through the open window alongside her. He rolled to his feet and quickly scanned the crowd as the man in black stood inside the restaurant, regarding them coldly. A second later, the bystanders' eyes glazed over, and everyone walked away as if nothing was amiss. One woman who had pulled out her phone, no doubt to record the event, put it away with a shrug.

"Run!" Professor Chao yelled as he grabbed her wrist. They tore down the sidewalk, bloodied and still clutching their swords. Quite a spectacle, no doubt, for the many onlookers. Yet each one they passed, Zoe saw, seemed to lose interest immediately, just like the hospital staff had that night when she fled down the halls.

5

THE MEETING

When it became clear that the man in black was not pursuing them, Professor Chao took Zoe's sword and hid both blades within his long coat. Zoe tried to ask him if he was all right, but he shushed her and held out his hand.

"My phone, please."

Zoe pulled it out of her pocket and gave it to him. He dialed a number and held it to his ear while continuing to walk briskly.

"Turn back," he said in Mandarin. "Do *not* go near the restaurant. Stay as far away from there as you can." A pause. "Excellent. I am glad you were running late. Meet me at the safe house. I am on my way. I just had an encounter with rogues." Another pause. "We are both fine. See you soon. Make sure you are not followed."

He hung up and dialed another number.

"This is Chao," he said, in English this time. "There has been an incident. We need a cleanup crew at the Green Kitchen restaurant near Yonge and Bloor. A lot of bystanders saw me and a young lady jump out of a broken window with swords in hand. I cleaned it up as best I could, but I had only seconds before we had to flee. Inside are four rogue Telepaths. Three were unconscious when I left, the other is dressed in black and is *extremely* dangerous. I doubt he is still there, but just in case, bring as many agents as you can gather. If he is there, though, do *not* engage—call me and wait for my arrival."

He paused to listen.

"Yes, please make the appropriate calls to gather everyone there. Before I return, though, I need a bug sweep for my companion. Send a van for us. We are walking south on Yonge Street, south of Bloor." He put his phone away and quickened their pace.

"Professor," Zoe said, cautiously, "you're giving orders to people . . . I thought you said you're a teacher." She left her question hanging and readied herself to bolt if needed.

The professor didn't slow his gait, though. "I did not lie," he said. "I am indeed the professor of combat at the Academy and have been for very many years. But I am also a member of the Council and in charge of security operations."

Minutes later, a dark van pulled up alongside them. The side door opened and Professor Chao motioned for Zoe to jump in. She took a deep breath and did as instructed. The professor followed her and closed the door as the van resumed driving.

"Sir," said a man in the back, who was holding a device. "This is the companion you spoke of?" He began moving the device around Zoe.

"Yes," said the professor. "This is just a precaution, but there is reason to suspect she has a tracker on her. It could be anywhere in her clothes—or even inside her—but I am especially suspicious of her brooch. Zoe, could you hold it out, please?"

Zoe fished it out from under her shirt and held it out, but kept it hanging around her neck. The man shook his head.

"I'm not detecting anything, sir. No radio signals are being emitted from her or the brooch. Let me check for metal, though, in case it's broadcasting sporadically to avoid detection." He held up a different device and moved it around her. It made noise only when it neared the brooch. "Nothing metal in her clothes or under her skin. Just the brooch, sir. Since it's metal, I don't think anything inside it could manage to broadcast very well. If you're concerned, though, we could take it for examination and see what's inside. There's no way to scan it, but I'm sure we could open it by force."

Zoe's heart skipped a beat as she hurriedly put her brooch back under her shirt, but Professor Chao shook his head. "No, that will not be necessary. Thank you, William. You can let us out here. We will continue on foot. If we are being followed, it will be easier for me to notice them on foot than from within this vehicle." He pulled out the two swords from his jacket and handed them to the man. "I need a forensics analysis on these. Anything out of the ordinary, anything to help track down where they came from."

"Yes, sir," the man said, taking the weapons as the van slowed to a stop. The professor and Zoe exited and the van sped away.

"This way," Professor Chao said. They walked in silence for about fifteen minutes, turning down streets seemingly at random. If anyone was following them, Zoe couldn't tell. Suddenly, the professor stopped and looked around, then bent down with his fingers entwined.

"Over the fence," he said. Zoe raised her eyebrows but stepped into his hand and allowed herself to be tossed up and over the six-foot-high fence, twisting in the air and landing in a crouch. She was in the heavily treed backyard of an old house. A second later, the professor landed beside her and together they descended a small flight of concrete steps into the house's dark basement.

Professor Chao locked the door behind them. Then, he turned to Zoe. "Now that we have some privacy, let us reflect on what just transpired. I explicitly told you to leave the restaurant. What did you think you were doing?"

Zoe was stunned. She didn't know how she had expected him to react—with gratitude maybe? Definitely not this. Her eyes narrowed as her own anger rose to meet his.

"I thought I was saving your life, Professor."

"*I* did not require saving. *You* did. Now, I have to explain to the minister why I was seen by dozens of Typicals jumping through a smashed window with a bloodied sword and running down the street with a child!"

"Your sword wasn't bloodied, sir. *His* was," she said, pointing at the rip in his shirt beneath which a bloody gash was clearly visible. "I don't doubt that you are among the finest fighters in the world, professor. I can hardly believe what I just saw. But you were *not* winning that fight and you know it. I don't run away while others die for me."

Professor Chao's nostrils flared and his body tensed. He started to say something, then stopped. Then started again and stopped. Finally, he closed his eyes and breathed deeply. After regaining some semblance of composure, he opened his eyes.

"I am unaccustomed to losing fights. Nor am I accustomed to having children point that out to me. I admit my opponent was indeed extremely skilled—more skilled, perhaps, than anyone I have ever encountered. And I *do* appreciate your effort to assist me, Zoe. Thank you. You handled yourself very well. But I can take care of myself. In the future, I want you to trust that I know what I am doing and do as I instruct. Understood?"

Zoe was silent for a moment, then reluctantly looked down and said, "Yes, sir."

The professor nodded, seeming to accept the matter as settled. "Now, we have a serious situation here that must be resolved." He climbed a wooden flight of stairs. "Am I correct in assuming that our first three assailants were the same ones who attacked you before?"

"Yes, sir," Zoe said, following him up the steps.

"But you have never seen the man in black before, correct?"

"Correct, sir."

"A lucky thing. Had you encountered him alone or in the company of anyone other than myself or a handful of others I know, you would not have escaped."

At the landing, he opened a door and together they entered the foyer of a small, old home with high ceilings. Two sheathed samurai swords, one long and one short, rested in a stand on a small table against one wall.

"Is this your house, sir?" Zoe asked.

"No. It is a safe house."

"A what?"

"A place we've set up in the event we are ever discovered by the Typicals and forced to flee. Our current situation, while quite a bit different, is equally dangerous. I have requested that others of our kind in this city meet us here."

The professor spun around as a man descended the stairway from the second level. He stepped in front of Zoe, then relaxed as the figure came into view. "Gabriel. You got here quickly."

The man swaggering down the stairs looked to be in his late twenties. He wore plain jeans and a black T-shirt under a black button-down with the sleeves rolled up. He hadn't shaved in possibly a week. Hazel eyes looked out from behind a mop of unruly hair.

The man grinned. "I was close by when I got the call, Professor," he said. He spoke with a British accent. A West Country accent, to be precise. Wait, how did she *know* that? He nodded toward the upstairs. "Just checked the second level. All clear. Lin is fine." He turned his gaze upon Zoe and paused. "And who's this? One of us, I presume?"

"Yes and no," said the professor. "Gabriel, this is Zoe. Zoe, this is Gabriel. Gabriel is one of my former students."

"Not a very good one, though," he said, extending his hand. Zoe shook it. "All that punching and kicking, rolling and flipping, grunting and groaning." He wrinkled his nose. "Not my cup of tea. Couldn't even manage the meditating, really."

"You managed more than most, Gabriel, despite your best efforts not to." Professor Chao peered through the front door's peephole. "Your problem, as I told you many times, was that you were simply too lazy to achieve your potential."

Gabriel shrugged and grinned at Zoe. "I don't deny it. Although I do prefer the term 'leisurely.'" He cleared his throat. "So, Professor, the phone call was a tad brief with the details. I can't help but wonder why we're here. Has the world of Typicals discovered us after all this time? Are their tanks closing in on us as we speak?"

Professor Chao turned away from the peephole and frowned. "I have warned you before, Gabriel, not to underestimate the Typicals. But no, they have not discovered us. Although, if my fears are well founded, our current predicament could be much worse."

The sound of a key turning in the lock kept him from elaborating. The front door opened and an elegant woman entered. She looked to be about Professor Chao's age, with long dark hair, high cheekbones, and a regal, no-nonsense air. Her mouth was set in a grim line. She shut and locked the door behind her, then turned and hugged the professor. "You're hurt," she said, stepping back to examine him. "Let me see."

"It's nothing," he said, wincing as she pulled up his shirt and felt his wound with her fingers. "Just a scratch. It will be fine, don't worry."

"It will be fine once I tend to it. Now, sit down like a good husband and let me work." She led him to the dining room table and sat him in a chair. He did not seem pleased, but he didn't complain either. Gabriel looked amused.

"Zoe, this is my wife, Professor Mei Yeoh," Professor Chao said. "She teaches healing at the Academy."

"Hello," Zoe said. "Nice to meet you, Professor Yeoh."

The professor's wife looked up briefly, then nodded. "And you as well," she said. Placing her hand over the wound, she closed her eyes and took on a look of deep concentration. Zoe could see, with her mind's eye, a golden glow emanating from her hand.

"What's going on?" said a girl entering the room. She was several inches shorter than Zoe, East Asian features, slight of build, with long black hair tied back in a ponytail. "Are you okay, Dad?"

"It's nothing," the professor said. "Zoe, this is my daughter, Lin. Lin, this is Zoe."

"Hello," Lin said, shaking Zoe's hand enthusiastically. "Are you one of my parents' students? Do you live here in Toronto or are you just visiting?"

"I just arrived yesterday, actually," Zoe replied. "But I think I'll be starting at the Academy in the fall."

"Cool! You'll be a first-year like me! Come on, I'll show you the rest of the safe house." And before Zoe knew what was happening, she was being led by the hand up the stairs.

■ ■ ■

"So, you really don't remember *anything*?" Lin gaped at her. They were sitting on the floor in her bedroom. "Not your parents, your home, your friends . . . nothing?"

Zoe shook her head. "Nothing before two nights ago." It hadn't taken long for Lin to grow suspicious of Zoe's noncommittal answers to all of her questions, and so within minutes, Zoe had found herself once again telling her whole story, only this time including her most recent encounter at the restaurant.

"And you really had a swordfight in the Green Kitchen?" Her eyes bulged.

Zoe nodded. "Your dad did all the fighting, really. I just tried not to get hit as I ran past."

But Lin stared at her in admiration anyway. "Still, nothing like that has ever happened to me, and I eat at that restaurant with Mom and Dad all the time."

"Your dad's an amazing fighter. I've never seen anything like it. At least, not that I remember, which isn't saying much. But still, I can't imagine many people being better than him."

Lin nodded, obviously proud. "Yeah, I think he's probably the best in the world. When I was little, Mom used to take me to the Academy with her sometimes and I'd sit and watch his classes. Sometimes he'd take on his entire senior class single-handed and he always won. I hope I can be that good someday."

"Has he taught you?" Zoe asked.

"Yup. Since I was little. We have a training room in our basement. Not here, but at home. I practice every day. I can't wait until I get to practice with other kids, though, when I go to the Academy." She suddenly got excited. "Hey, we can practice together! You can fight, right? What kinds of martial arts do you know?"

Zoe shrugged. "I don't know. I know I can roll and do flips. And I can use a sword. But I have no idea what else I know."

"Let's find out!" Lin jumped up.

Zoe stood too, feeling a little nervous. "How?"

"Let's start with something simple. This is called *chi sao*, or 'sticky hands.' It's a training method you do with a partner in Wing Chun. It's meant to develop your sensitivity to your opponent's openings and attacks. Dad says I'm getting pretty good at it. Here, put your hands like this." Lin took Zoe's hands and placed them in the air in front of her chest, palms flat and vertical, facing each other. "Good. Now, I put my hands like this." She put her hands in the same position and placed them between Zoe's hands, just barely touching.

"The idea is that I'm going to move my hands left and right until suddenly I attack with a punch that's either high, medium, or low. Your job is to keep your hands touching mine and block my attacks. It's supposed to give you a feel for sensing your opponent's movements and responding instinctively. Ready?"

Zoe nodded.

"I'll start slow." Lin moved her hands to the right and to the left, rocking her whole body back and forth, back and forth. Zoe did as instructed and kept her hands in contact with Lin's, rocking her own body slightly left and right. "That's it, good," Lin said. "Now, I'm going to attack. But don't worry, I'll pull my punch. I won't actually hit you if you don't block."

Suddenly, Zoe felt Lin's body movements change slightly, and the next thing she knew, she had twisted her torso and blocked a punch aimed at her chest and, in the same single motion, countered with her own punch square to Lin's chest.

"Ow!" Lin took a step back and rubbed where Zoe had hit her.

"I'm sorry!" Zoe cried. "I didn't mean to! Are you okay?" She felt awful. Her first friend, and she had just punched her.

"It's okay, I'm fine. Just pull your punch next time, all right?" She smiled. "We just proved something, though. You've *definitely* done this exercise before. That was classic Wing Chun you did there. Did you notice how you blocked my punch and countered all in one movement? Most other martial arts do that in two movements—a block, then a strike. Plus, you punched with your fist vertical, not horizontal." She nodded. "Definitely Wing Chun. Want to try it again?"

"I don't know," Zoe said. She really didn't want to risk hurting Lin again. As a fighter, so much of what she did was instinctive. She just did it without thinking. What if she really hurt her?

Lin seemed to read her thoughts. She looked her in the eyes and held her hands. "Hey. It'll be okay, Zoe. We're just practicing here. Besides, I can take care of myself." She raised Zoe's hands into position again. "Ready?"

And their practice continued. Lin's attacks came at random, and Zoe somehow always managed to sense when they were coming and how to block and counter. After a few minutes, Lin said, "Now, close your eyes."

"What?" She wasn't serious, was she?

"I'm serious. Close your eyes. Don't worry, I'll pull my punches."

Zoe closed her eyes.

"Now, with your eyes closed you'll have no choice but to rely on your other senses. You need to feel me attacking you, not see me. Here we go."

And suddenly Zoe was countering as easily as before. It was an amazing sensation—more so, she thought, because it felt so natural, as if she had been doing it all her life.

"You see? You're great at this," Lin said. "Now, let's try something slightly different. This time, when you counter, we're not going to stop and start over again. Instead, we're going to keep going. Ready?"

They began again, and after a few seconds, Zoe sensed Lin's attack and countered, only this time she needn't have pulled her punch because Lin countered too. Zoe felt herself reacting, and before she knew what was happening, they were trading rapid punches as fast as they could, each one trying to trap and outmaneuver the other. Suddenly, Lin's foot moved inside hers and Zoe was again reacting with her own footwork, the two of them spinning around each other crazily, trading blow after blow, each trying to get past the other's defences.

Zoe didn't know how she was doing half of this stuff—*any* of this stuff, really—but she still wasn't sure who she was more amazed by, herself or Lin. Lin hadn't been kidding. She really could take care of herself. She could see in Lin's face that Lin too was shocked that her partner was keeping up with her. So, Zoe decided to see what they were both capable of and stepped it up a notch.

Faster and faster they went, their hands, feet, knees, and elbows becoming blurs, neither of them really thinking any longer, neither pulling their punches anymore, both in their "zone."

"Ahem."

They both stopped at once and looked guiltily at the doorway, where Professor Chao stood watching.

"Hi Daddy," Lin said, quickly. "Zoe knows Wing Chun."

"I can see that," he said. Zoe didn't think he looked angry, but he did look . . . concerned? And deep in thought. "Everyone has arrived. Please come downstairs." He turned and left. Zoe and Lin stared at each other in disbelief. They were both sweaty and out of breath.

"I didn't know I could do that," Lin said.

"I didn't know I could do any of that," Zoe said.

Beaming, they went downstairs arm in arm, each having discovered a kindred spirit and a new friend.

■ ■ ■

Zoe's smile faded when she got downstairs and saw how many people had arrived. All talk abruptly stopped as everyone turned to look at her. No one looked pleased.

"Is this the one, then?" said a woman with a thick Parisian accent. She was a beautiful young blonde, dressed in a long, expensive-looking white coat, and scowling. "This girl in filthy clothes is the one who has caused all this trouble? The girl you want us to leave our homes for? Leave our *lives* for?"

The room broke out in murmuring, some people nodding in assent, others frowning in disapproval.

"This is Zoe, of whom I spoke," Professor Chao said above the noise. "But your accusations are highly unfair, Genevieve. She is still a child, as you can plainly see, and in need of our help. She no more caused this situation than you did."

"That is doubtful," she said, rounding on the professor. "*I* have not been fighting other Telepaths in public spaces. We don't know anything about this girl. Except that she is not one of us. Which means she is one of them. Whoever *they* are."

"Whoever *they* are," the professor said, calmly, "they are trying to kill her, so wherever she is from, she is *not* one of them. At least not any longer."

"We do not know they are trying to kill her. It could all be a ruse to get their own agent close to us." She narrowed her eyes at Zoe. "I find this amnesia of hers far too convenient."

"That will be enough, Genevieve," Professor Chao said. His mild tone had disappeared. "It is not for you to decide whether Zoe is speaking the truth, nor is it up to you to decide whether she will be attending the Academy. That is for the headmaster to decide. And unless you have completely missed the point of everything I have said, Zoe did not cause our current danger. Indeed, this girl may have saved all of us, by forcing our enemies to expose themselves earlier than intended. Therefore, I must ask that you kindly refrain from directing your anger at her. If you have nothing constructive to say, then be silent."

Zoe wished she were anywhere else in the world but here. This woman scared her, but she was glad the professor had defended her.

"Do not speak to me like I am still your student, *Ling*. Do you know who I am in the real world? I buy and sell more in a single day than you will earn in your entire lifetime."

"Your status in the world of finance is of no interest to me, Genevieve. Should war befall us, you know the role I will play. I also currently sit on the Council, and I speak on their behalf now. I have told you of the danger we face, and I have given my recommendations. You may disregard those recommendations as you please, but I will not permit you to put any of us in danger."

"*Permit?*" The woman was seething. "I will do exactly as I please! I will not run and cower in fear from half-trained pups as you do, Chao! I—"

"Enough, Genevieve!" snapped an older woman, also impeccably dressed. "I did not come here to listen to your immature prattle." She turned to Professor Chao, leaving Genevieve sputtering. "Ling, you would not have summoned us here if you did not think the danger very grave, of that I am certain. But are you not overreacting? As you yourself have said, we know nothing about these rogues. For all we know, there could be only a handful of them, whereas we number almost ten thousand. Why should we fear them?"

Professor Chao chose his next words carefully. "Because they exist at all, Sunita. It would be bad enough if a handful of us went rogue. We have dealt with that sort of thing many times over the centuries. But I did not recognize any of those who attacked us in the restaurant. Every one of us has attended the Academy and I have taught there for a very long time. The first three seemed to be as young as they looked—one even referred to me as an old man—so I would remember them if I had taught them. Also, Zoe here should just be coming into her Abilities, yet she has obviously already been trained. I do not think these Telepaths have ever been among us. They have somehow managed to keep themselves hidden their entire lives. And as an organized group. Three weeks ago, I became suspicious that I was being watched. Typicals with whom I regularly interact had been questioned regarding my movements and then had their memories of this questioning erased. It is only by luck that I became aware of it. That is why I moved my family here to this safe house, out of caution."

He took a deep breath. "The man I fought today was formidable and his style unorthodox." The professor paused, as if remembering something.

"Was he stronger than you?" an elderly man asked. Zoe wondered how old he must be to actually look elderly. How old were any of them for that matter? Centuries?

"Perhaps," Chao said, glancing at Zoe.

"But that's impossible," said another man, who looked to be in his early twenties. "Where could he have learned to fight like that? Who could have taught him?"

"Indeed," the professor said. "That is exactly what troubles me so, Stuart. He could have learned his hand-to-hand martial arts from Typicals, most assuredly. But his telepathic combat techniques were both highly untraditional and highly refined—except sometimes it seemed like he was trying something new, something he had just learned and not yet perfected. Despite his prowess, I think he may actually be the student, not the master."

He turned back to the woman named Sunita. "So, we have a highly skilled master recruiting children before we can find them and training them in combat. And since the oldest of the three individuals I incapacitated looked to be in his mid-thirties, this Master has been doing this for at least two decades without our knowledge. Ask yourself why he or she might be doing this if they do not wish us harm. They have had a long time to learn all about us. Where we live. Where we work. For all we know, some of them may even be among us now. If they intend us harm, how will we stop them? We surely outnumber them, but we are scattered across the globe. They could kill us one by one, in our homes."

"They'll not kill me without a fight," growled a burly Scotsman in the back of the room.

"I do not doubt you would get your licks in, Jamie," Professor Chao said, smiling. "But I was not exaggerating when I spoke of the man in black's skills. I barely held my own against him. If a group of such men attacked any of us unsuspecting in our homes, I can guarantee the outcome."

He turned to address them all again. "The fact is that the world has changed for us today. Our danger is no longer just that of being discovered by Typicals, but of being killed by highly skilled enemy Telepaths. Time will tell what their true intentions are, but they have already shown today that they are willing and able to kill us. Therefore, I highly recommend that you all take this danger seriously. We all have lives to live, I know. Nobody wants to leave their homes, their jobs, their friends, their family.

But we will all be safer if we do so. We have people trained in espionage, and they can help you to disappear and relocate elsewhere in the world if you choose. I advise you to avail yourselves of their services."

"That is not to say that I advise you all to run in fear," he added, looking at Genevieve again. "There will come a time to fight. But it must be on our terms. We must be the hunters, not the hunted."

"And if we choose to stay and take our chances?" asked the Scotsman.

"Then be vigilant. Be smart. Stay together as much as possible. Keep your sword within reach at all times."

"And what of the children?" asked Sunita.

"I will be asking the headmaster to start school early this year. Immediately, in fact. I will escort Zoe and Lin there later tonight, regardless of the headmaster's decision, since Zoe is the most obvious target. There is no safer place for the children than the Academy. We can protect them there."

"So, not only have you revealed all of us to this girl, a possible spy, as well as revealing our safe house, but you also intend to bring her to the Academy," Genevieve said.

"I'm not a spy!" Zoe shouted, surprising herself.

"And how would you know?" the woman sneered. "You don't remember anything about your past. Is that not so?"

"If I were a spy, they wouldn't be trying to kill me," Zoe said.

"Again, we do not know that is the case."

"I will vouch for her character," Chao said, stepping beside Zoe. "A great deal can be learned about a person's character when in combat. I have had the opportunity to observe her in such a situation, and I trust she is telling the truth. Once she is safe within the walls of the Academy, we will help her to recover her lost memories and that will end any debate on this matter. Those memories, incidentally, will quite likely prove to be of great benefit to us all."

"We shall see," Genevieve said, determined to have the last word.

"I have nothing else to say," Professor Chao said to everyone. "For those wishing to take my advice and disappear, Gabriel can assist you in making contact with our agents." Gabriel nodded. "For those choosing to remain, be careful. This safe house may no longer be safe—I am taking no chances. Never come here again. You will be informed when a new meeting place is ready. Good luck to you all."

6

THE ACADEMY

"So, we're going to the Academy now, Dad?" Lin asked from the back seat of the car. "I mean, we're actually on our way there *right* now?"

"That is correct," Professor Chao answered. He was driving. Lin's mom, Professor Yeoh, sat next to him with her eyes closed, perhaps sleeping. She had seemed tired since healing Professor Chao's wound. Zoe wished she could see it, to see how healed it really was. Had it left a scar?

"This is so cool! I thought we wouldn't be going for months. I can't believe it's happening already!" Lin seemed positively bubbly, even though they were only going early because their lives were in danger.

"So, how far away is the Academy?" asked Zoe.

"Less than an hour away, with no traffic," Professor Chao said.

"I figured it would be hidden somewhere far off," Zoe said. "Tucked away in the Himalayas or something. Why is it here?"

"It is an international school, Zoe," Professor Yeoh said, without opening her eyes. "Toronto is a very cosmopolitan city, so it's as good a location as any. It *has* been hidden away someplace more obscure in past centuries. But these days, with military spy satellites in orbit, a school in a remote location is actually more likely to attract unwanted attention than a school close to a major urban centre."

"So, how long has the Academy been here?"

"Nine years now. Before then, it was in Brussels. Before that, it was in Shanghai. It moves every few decades to give other countries the opportunity to host it, but mostly because we do not want it to stay in any one place long enough to attract too much attention."

"But doesn't that attract attention in itself?" Zoe asked. "I mean, most schools stay put, right?"

Professor Yeoh shrugged. "The Academy is officially an international school that relocates to a different country every so often. This campus was built in the mid-1800s as a private school for girls. It *is* unusual for a school to move around, but it would hardly make anyone suspect it's actually a school for Telepaths."

"I can't believe I'm going to a school for Telepaths," Lin repeated.

Zoe smiled. She couldn't believe it either.

■ ■ ■

The Academy, as it turned out, wasn't just a school—it was a compound. A fortress clearly designed to keep people out, as well as to prevent spying. A ten-foot-high stone wall stretched down the road on both sides of the gate, and the driveway immediately took a sharp turn, lined by tall hedges.

Professor Chao stopped at the gate and rolled down the window as a uniformed guard—one of a half dozen—bent down to peer inside the car.

"Evening, Professor Chao. Professor Yeoh. The headmaster said you'd be coming."

"Good evening, Sam," said Professor Yeoh, leaning across her husband. "How have your first few weeks of summer been?"

"Can't complain, ma'am. Though it sounds like summer vacation's been cut short. I've been told to expect a lot of arrivals in the coming days." He cocked his head. "Haven't been told why, though."

"Come by our quarters later, Sam," said Professor Chao. "We will have a drink and fill you in."

Sam smiled at this. "Thank you, sir, I'd like that very much." He looked into the back seat. "Is that Lin I see back there? She can't be old enough to start at the Academy already, can she?"

"I am too old enough!" Lin yelled at him, grinning uncontrollably.

Sam whistled. "Time flies, it does." He turned to Zoe. "And this young miss must be . . ." He looked down at his clipboard.

"Zoe," Professor Chao finished for him. "I trust the headmaster informed you she was coming as well?"

Sam nodded. "He did, sir. He also requested that you bring her to see him immediately upon your arrival." He cocked his head again. "He didn't say why, though."

This time the professor was silent, and Sam took the hint.

"Well, welcome back, professors." He nodded to Zoe and Lin. "And welcome to the Academy, girls. Most likely to be some of the most memorable years of your lives." He straightened and motioned to another guard to open the gates.

Professor Chao drove in and turned right at the hedges, then left at another set of hedges. Zoe's jaw dropped. The school grounds were *huge*. And beautiful. Acres of finely cut grass, tall trees, walking paths, a little stream, a little lake, a forest. . . . It was incredible.

"How big is this place?" Zoe asked nobody in particular, her mouth agape as she watched two Border Collies run across the lawn toward the woods.

"Fifty acres," Professor Yeoh answered. "Beautiful, isn't it? They really did a lovely job with it."

Zoe nodded. She couldn't believe she was actually going to *live* here.

As they drove down the lane, they passed a barn with sheep, goats, pigs, cows, and a few horses out wandering. "What?" Zoe exclaimed in delight.

Professor Chao smiled. "You like our animals? We run an animal sanctuary here. A recent graduate started it last year, and we think it has been a tremendous success already. The students love the animals and, more importantly, it teaches them that we Telepaths are the stewards of this world, not its rulers. With our Abilities comes the very real danger of feeling superior to Typicals and treating them as lesser beings. Such an attitude cannot be allowed to flourish. By learning empathy and compassion for animals, the hope is that students will also learn empathy and compassion for people."

A goat yelled at Zoe as they passed, and she burst into laughter. They rounded the barn and turned right past some more hedges and suddenly the school itself came into view. Zoe gasped. They'd never mentioned it was a castle! It was clearly designed in the spirit of Gothic or Elizabethan architecture—she wondered what kind of education she'd had that she would know this—with its limestone and stone walls, tall towers, and crenelated roofline. A large lawn with tall trees spread in front of the school, and a cobblestone walkway and stone steps led to enormous, arched double doors.

The curved driveway deposited them at the entrance, and they got out of the car.

"Umm, I just thought of something," Zoe said, suddenly embarrassed. "I don't have any clothes other than what I'm wearing . . . and I don't have any money either . . ."

Professor Yeoh put a gentle hand on Zoe's shoulder and said, "Don't worry. Everyone at the Academy wears the same school uniform, which the Academy provides along with everything else you'll need, including a laptop for your studies. And we will buy you clothes to wear outside of the Academy in the future. You'll be just like everyone else." She smiled.

Zoe suddenly and quite unexpectedly felt a tear roll down her cheek and a sob escaped her lips, which she quickly pushed down. She didn't know what had prompted this sudden outburst. It was a very nice act of kindness to be sure, offering to buy her clothes. Yet, she hadn't cried when Professor Chao saved her life earlier, so why was she feeling so emotional now? All she knew was that she felt safe. And she felt like someone cared about her. And although her memories were lost to her, she felt strangely sure that this was the first time in her life that she had ever felt this way.

Professor Yeoh was startled but rubbed her shoulder comfortingly. "There, there," she said. "It will be all right, Zoe. Don't worry. We're here for you. Everything will be all right, I promise."

The large front foyer featured gleaming wooden floors and an arched cathedral ceiling from which hung an ornate chandelier. A suit of armour stood in the corner to her left. Solid oak doors with frosted windows led to rooms on the left and right. At the end of the foyer, through an archway bearing the inscription Dispensatores De Terrae, was an enormous staircase that split and reversed halfway up.

Zoe had thought the school would be mostly deserted, but the place buzzed with activity as the hastily gathered cleaning staff readied the school for its early start. In the centre of it all was a short, stout woman with grey hair shouting orders and waving her arms like an orchestra conductor. When she saw them enter, she rounded on Professor Chao, crying, "You!" She stormed across the hall and stopped inches away from the professor, who looked both surprised and amused. She glared at him with her fists planted on her hips. "I hear *you* are to blame for all of this?"

"Lin, Zoe," Professor Chao said, "meet Amelia Zehringer, head housemaid of the Academy. There is virtually nothing that goes on here that she does not know about first, and she has the uncanny ability to know what mischief a student will cause before the student ever dreams it up. At least, that is how it seemed to me during my student years, long ago."

"Flattery will get you nowhere, Ling. And don't change the subject."

She raised her chin even higher. "Is it your doing that my staff and I have had to cut our holidays short? That we are killing ourselves to prepare the school to open in just one day? You realize this would normally take us weeks?"

Professor Chao nodded. "I did indeed request that the Academy be opened early, Amelia, yes. The reasons for my request, however, were quite beyond my control."

"Is that so?" she said, not backing down. "That is not what I heard, Ling. I heard you got into a fight, just like you always did as a schoolboy. Only this time, you chose the wrong person to fight with, and now we're all paying the price, scurrying to safety in fear of what this man might do to us now. Is that an accurate description?"

Professor Chao furrowed his brow. "No. That is not an accurate description. It is considerably more complex than that. And—"

"And that man was trying to kill me!" Zoe blurted. "Professor Chao saved my life!"

Amelia studied her for several seconds. Zoe had the feeling that those eyes were very perceptive, taking in every detail and arriving at conclusions she couldn't imagine. Amelia looked back to the professor. "Is this true? He was trying to kill the girl?"

Again, Professor Chao nodded.

Her demeanour changed abruptly. "*Sehr gut*, Ling," she said, approvingly. "Well done. Anyone who would harm a child is my enemy. There is no further need to explain the 'complexities' of the situation. We will just have to have the school ready in one day. That is all there is to it."

"We can help," Lin said, apparently speaking for both herself and Zoe. "Just tell us what to do."

Amelia raised her eyebrows. "I see you have both done an excellent job of raising this child. Sehr gut. I could use some extra workers."

"It will have to wait until the morning, I'm afraid," Professor Yeoh said. "It's late and these girls need their sleep."

Amelia nodded. "Very well, tomorrow morning then. I shall have a list of chores for you both." She walked off and resumed shouting orders at her staff.

"I'll show Lin to the girls' dormitory," Professor Yeoh said to her husband. "Can you bring Zoe there after your meeting with the headmaster?"

"Of course," Professor Chao said. "Zoe, come with me."

■ ■ ■

The castle was a maze. After several staircases and multiple turns down identical-looking hallways, Zoe felt a little lost.

"Professor," Zoe said, "is everyone here a Telepath? Even Sam and Amelia?"

"Yes," the professor answered. "Absolutely everyone. A Typical would quickly notice this is not a regular school, and that is simply too dangerous to allow. Some may think that our Abilities are wasted on such tasks as cleaning and cooking and gardening, but being a part of the Academy in any way is considered a great honour."

"But what about all the parents? Don't they know what their children are?"

Professor Chao sighed. "You have hit upon a controversial policy. We have tried keeping the nature of the children a secret from their parents, but it never really worked. Most children had shown no signs of being particularly gifted academically and deserving of admittance, plus some parents had already witnessed their child's nascent Abilities. Also, there were always some students who could not resist the urge to reveal their Abilities to their parents during visits home, which then required a lot of cleanup. These days, we are honest with the parents, but we do compel them to keep our existence secret. It is like a subliminal suggestion so as to be as minimally invasive as possible. It is not ideal, but we have never found a better solution."

"We are here," he said, as they arrived at a large oak door. They entered a waiting room where a serious-looking woman was typing. She looked up at them.

"Professor Chao, please go right on in. The headmaster is expecting you and your guest." She nodded toward Zoe.

"Thank you, Abby," Professor Chao said, without breaking stride. He knocked on another oak door, this one more ornate, and walked in with Zoe trailing behind.

The office was massive and littered with an eclectic array of antiques spanning centuries. The walls were adorned with paintings with no unifying theme. At the far end, an old man sat at a gigantic wooden desk cluttered with books and papers. He was clean-shaven with long, scraggly grey hair and large glasses. He wore an ill-fitting suit that looked like it had gone out of fashion many decades ago. The headmaster, presumably. He sat with his hands interlocked on the desk in front of him, watching them. He was not alone. Six others, three men and three women, stood silently in front of his desk. All eyes were on Zoe and Professor Chao.

As they approached the desk, Zoe heard Chao's voice in her head.

Be careful. Let me do the talking.

Zoe's heart skipped a beat. Be careful? What did *that* mean? If she'd thought she was nervous before, she was doubly so now.

"Good evening, Headmaster," Professor Chao said. "I do hope I am not interrupting. I had expected a private meeting. To what do I owe the pleasure of our minister and fellow Council members' attendance?"

"Good evening, Ling. Your colleagues," the headmaster said, gesturing to the still-silent men and women, "have just been sharing their grave concerns regarding your actions today, and the dangerous situation they feel you have put us in."

"Indeed," Chao said. "Surely, though, that is a matter between them and me, Headmaster. Why are they troubling you?"

"I asked them the same question. It would seem their primary concern is regarding your young guest here—specifically, my granting your request to bring her here." The old man looked around the room, smiling. "Have I got that right, everyone?"

"You had no right to bring her here!" a large man shouted, stepping forward. He was meticulously groomed and wore an expensive-looking suit.

"I had every right," Chao replied, calmly. "And more, I had permission from this school's headmaster. How, exactly, is this any of your concern?"

"I notice you didn't ask *what* our concern is," a tall, stately woman said. She was almost regal in her demeanour. "Because you know it already."

"I can guess," Chao said, facing her. "But please tell me anyway, Minister. I dislike guessing."

"She's a spy."

"You have been talking to your protégé, Genevieve, I see."

"Yes," the woman said. "She called me moments after your impromptu gathering today. A meeting you saw fit to bring this spy to, thus putting every attendee in danger."

"I see. And upon hearing Genevieve's concerns, you promptly organized an investigation to determine Zoe's origin and have, in mere hours, found proof that she is a spy? Truly, your reputation does not do you justice."

The woman sneered. "I have all the proof I require."

"Which is to say you have none."

"Headmaster!" she said, rounding on him—the only person sitting. "This is intolerable! I demand this child be given into our custody immediately for interrogation!"

Zoe could hardly believe what she was hearing. "No! Headmaster, you can't let them take me!" She began backing away, instinctively assessing which Council members were likely to be the most dangerous, which objects nearby might make good weapons, and what her best escape route would be. Professor Chao put a soothing hand on her shoulder and held her in place.

"Headmaster," Professor Chao said. "You can't seriously—"

But the old man put a hand up for silence. Still smiling, he looked at the minister. "Gabrielle, I agree with you. This is indeed intolerable. I have shown an extreme lack of judgment in this matter." He nodded to himself. "And now I must rectify things."

He stood and Zoe felt her heart sink into her stomach. This couldn't be happening. Not after everything she'd been through. Not after everything she'd been promised. Professor Chao squeezed her shoulder. The minister, she saw, was smug.

"Minister," the headmaster said, looking her in the eye. "Get out."

Stunned silence filled the room as the minister's smile faded and her face began to turn purple. Her eyes narrowed. "This is the biggest mistake you have made in your overly long life, *Headmaster*. You do *not* want me as your enemy."

The headmaster sighed and shook his head. "Ah, Gabrielle. We have been adversaries for so very many years now. We just never said it out loud. How could we be otherwise? Our philosophies on life are so radically different." He gestured toward Zoe. "For instance, I believe that people are innocent until proven guilty, and deserve every opportunity to defend themselves against accusations of wrongdoing. You, on the other hand, don't care whether people are guilty *or* innocent—you will label them whichever way best suits your own interests, which usually revolve around your lust for wealth and power." The old man's eyes narrowed. "You seriously thought I would turn one of my students over to your custody just because you wished it?"

The minister clenched her teeth. "This isn't over."

"I have no doubt. But you are not taking the girl. Now, get out of my office." He waved his hand dismissively. "And take your lackeys with you."

The minister stormed out, her bewildered entourage hurrying to keep up, leaving Zoe and the professor alone with the headmaster.

Professor Chao whistled. "Well, that was unexpected. I had not figured on our beloved minister arriving until tomorrow morning at the earliest. You handled that very well."

"You think so?" the headmaster said. "I do hope you're correct. She's right about one thing—I *don't* want her as my enemy. She's a powerful woman with powerful friends." He shrugged. "But some things can't be avoided."

He turned to Zoe. "And she was right about something else, too. Our newest arrival here could indeed be a spy."

"Headmaster!" Professor Chao said. "You cannot believe—"

"Calm yourself, Ling. You know it's possible, whether you wish it to be otherwise or not."

"I'm not a spy, sir!" Zoe said. "I swear!"

The headmaster studied her a moment. "Zoe, I believe you are most likely telling the truth. And I believe even more firmly that *you* believe you are telling the truth. Nevertheless, there is certainly a chance that you are a spy."

"But, sir, I don't remember *anything*! Even if they did send me to be a spy, I've forgotten all about it, so how can I still *be* one? And why would they have tried to kill me? I wouldn't even *be* here if Professor Chao hadn't stumbled across me at the library."

"Zoe," the headmaster said, folding his hands. "I realize it must be terribly difficult for you to look at this objectively, but still, you must try." He held up one finger. "First, I have only your word that you have amnesia at all." He held up another finger. "Second, their attempts to kill you may have been staged for our benefit." He held up a third finger. "Third—and this is the most important point, my dear—it is entirely possible that you are a spy, or *worse*, without even knowing it."

Zoe felt stunned. What did he mean? How was that possible? "You mean," she said thinking out loud, "that the rogues might have planted me here, intending to capture me later and learn what I know about the Academy? But that doesn't make sense. They could capture any student—or teacher, for that matter—and learn the same information."

"You are correct. That wouldn't make sense, but it is not what I meant. Professor Chao tells me he has given you an overview regarding the nature of our kind and what we are capable of. But there are many details you don't know and won't be taught for years to come. Some things are not taught until the post-graduate years, in fact. And this is one of them."

He leaned forward. "It is possible to erase a person's memory and to compel a person into doing your will. But it is also possible for an extremely skilled practitioner of mental manipulation to do more subtle and . . . insidious things. Such as programming an individual to perform a specific task, perhaps in response to a specific trigger, without them ever being aware of it. Or even worse, suppressing an entire *identity* until it emerges again in response to a trigger."

Zoe felt like her life—her entire existence—had just been pulled out from under her. She stared vacantly at the headmaster. Her legs felt weak, and she dropped into one of the chairs in front of his desk. The headmaster said nothing. Professor Chao looked at her helplessly.

"That's not . . . that's not fair," she said, finally, in a voice so weak she could barely even hear it. "Not only do I not know who I used to be, but you're saying that who I am *now* might not be real? That I might actually be a horrible person—a spy or an assassin—and I have no way of even knowing?"

The headmaster was silent, then nodded. "Yes."

Her lower lip quivered. Tears came unbidden again. "No!" she cried. "I may not remember anything, but I at least thought that my personality, my . . . my moral compass . . . was my own. And now you're telling me it might not be? That someone might snap their fingers one day and I'll suddenly become someone else, with an entirely different personality?" She could hear the panic in her own voice.

"Zoe," Professor Chao began, reaching for her.

"No!" she said, violently throwing off his hand. "No, I don't believe what you're saying! It isn't true! I *know* who I am, I *know*!"

The headmaster had risen to his feet. "Zoe, calm yourself."

"Calm?" she shrieked at him. A part of her brain could tell she was losing control, but it was as though she was watching another person. "You tell me that everything about me might be a lie and expect me to stay calm?" She rounded on the professor. "If this is what you think, then why did you promise to protect me?" She looked back to the headmaster. "Why did you bring me here?"

Zoe felt invisible tendrils wrap themselves around her, pinning her arms in place. "Zoe," the headmaster said, sternly, "I insist that you calm down this instant. I do not want to have to hurt you."

So, this was it then. It was a trap after all.

"No!" She felt for the tendrils with her mind and saw them, golden and glowing, flowing from the headmaster to herself. Acting on instinct, she yanked hard on them, so hard that the headmaster flew across the desk and right past her. As he did, she writhed and twirled and somehow untangled herself from the tendrils. Without stopping to ponder how she had done it, she bolted for the door, but the headmaster was on his feet and had moved to block her path. He erected a psychic force field, like a transparent wall between her and him. Seeing no other exit, she threw herself directly at him with all her strength, creating her own force field ahead of her. She focused it into a precise point—a wedge that she drove through his wall—creating an opening that she was able to dive through. Rolling, she came up nose-to-nose with the old man—and hesitated. What was she supposed to do now? Hit him? How had this meeting spun so far out of control so quickly?

Then she felt a hand on the back of her head. "Sleep," said Professor

Chao.

She crumpled into the professor's arms and felt him lay her gently on the floor.

"My god, Chao," she heard the muffled voice of the headmaster say, as though from very far away. "What have you brought into my school?"

"A child, sir," Professor Chao said in the distance. "A very frightened child."

"Frightened? Did you see what she just did? What kind of child can do that?"

"A particularly gifted one. With respect, Headmaster, could you have handled that any more poorly? What did you think would happen, telling her what you did? And then forcibly restraining her?"

"With all due respect to *you*, Ling, I acted exactly as I intended. I needed to see how she would react."

"And?"

"And it is as I feared. She has been highly trained and conditioned. I can't imagine how, given her age, but she is dangerous to those around her."

"You are reaching, sir. I will grant you that she has clearly been training her entire life, and her Abilities must have manifested unusually early, but we do not know she is dangerous. You have only proven that she is scared, which is to be expected considering what she has been through. You have had to deal with problem students before—students who would not have stopped themselves from hitting you."

"I've never had a problem student who could drill through my shield."

"We do not lock up students for being strong, Headmaster. If she has been conditioned to have dangerous instincts, then all the more reason to retrain her. As for the possibility that she is an unwitting sleeper agent, the same could be said for *anyone*—including either one of us."

"So, you're comfortable with her being friends with your daughter, are you? She's—"

"Wait . . . I think she is still awake."

"Impossible."

"Sleep," she heard the professor say again, as she felt his hand touch her forehead. The sounds of the two men arguing above her faded into the distance.

. . .

Zoe awoke to the sounds of birds singing. She opened her eyes and squinted. She was in bed in what must have been the room she shared with Lin in the girls' dormitory. The beige curtains were pulled open and sunlight streamed in through the open window beside Lin's bed. She could hear lawn mowers outside. She sat up and discovered Lin sitting cross-legged on the end of her bed, gaping at her.

"You're crazy," Lin said. "You *attacked* the headmaster? Are you mental?"

Zoe swung her legs out of the bed. "Good morning," she grumbled. Everything was so bright. All the furniture in the room—two captain's beds, two desks, and two dressers—were white. The walls were light green and white. The floor was a light-coloured hardwood and shiny.

"Zoe, do you know how serious this is?"

Zoe yawned and rubbed the back of her neck. "How'd I get here?"

"Dad carried you in about half an hour after I got here. I heard him tell Mom that you got really upset about something and attacked the headmaster and that he had to make you sleep."

Zoe winced, remembering it all. How could she have been so stupid? How could she have let herself panic like that?

"Mom came in a few minutes after Dad left and did her healing thing on your head, but I don't think anything was wrong. She said you'd probably sleep 'til morning."

Zoe looked at her feet. She felt sick to her stomach.

"Zoe, why'd you do it?"

She looked up. She didn't want to tell Lin. She knew there was a good chance she would lose her new friend over this, but she couldn't very well be Lin's friend and *not* tell her. She took a deep breath. "He told me that I might be a spy or an assassin and not even know it. That I might have some deep programming or whatever that would make me do something bad when the time was right."

Lin looked genuinely distressed. "Jeez."

"That wasn't the worst part. He said I might not even be me. That I might actually be somebody else—somebody not nice, maybe—and that everything I think I am could all be a lie and just . . . change one day when the real me wakes up."

Lin didn't speak for about five seconds. Then, she said, "And you believed that? What a load of crap!"

"Huh?" That certainly wasn't the reaction Zoe had expected.

"Look." Lin sat forward. "*If* you have some sort of hidden programming inside your brain—and I've never heard of such a thing—Mom or one of the other professors will be able to find it and get rid of it. As for being someone other than who you think you are—which I find pretty hard to believe—what makes you think *that* person is any more real than *you*?"

Zoe blinked. She didn't know what to say to this. Lin continued, "Think about it, Zoe. No matter who you might have been before, *you're* the one in control of your brain and your body now. You just have to make sure that you *stay* in control. Assuming there's someone else inside you at all, which sounds ridiculous to me."

Zoe smiled. Lin was smarter than she had given her credit for. She reached out and took her friend's hand. "Thanks, Lin. Wish you were there to talk some sense into me last night." She sighed. "I guess now I just have to wait and see if I'm expelled or not. I imagine I'll know soon."

Lin squeezed her hand. "Don't worry. Mom and Dad like you. I'm sure they'll convince the headmaster that it was all a misunderstanding and all you'll get is a week of detention or something."

...

It turned out, in fact, to be four weeks of detention. Zoe hadn't waited to see if she would be expelled or not. After talking to Lin, she decided to take matters into her own hands and went directly to the headmaster's office to apologize, plead her case, and beg his forgiveness. He wasn't been particularly pleased to see her, especially first thing in the morning, he said, nor was he very forgiving. But he did hear her out, accepting her apology, and in the end said he would not expel her from the Academy. He made a point, however, of clarifying that nobody *ever* gets expelled from the Academy, for the same reason that all Telepaths *must* attend the Academy—namely, that untrained Telepaths are a danger to themselves and others and risk exposing their kind to the world. Instead, he said, problem students are made to "wish" they could be expelled.

So, her punishment was four weeks of detention after classes each day in *his* office. In the headmaster's office. With him. Zoe shivered every time she thought about it. In addition, she was to see a Professor Sharapova, the school's psychologist, on a regular basis. That scared her even more, but part of her welcomed the opportunity, too. Maybe this psychologist could help her unlock her hidden memories and lay to rest everyone's concerns about her being some sort of secret agent.

The headmaster had also instructed Professor Yeoh to give Zoe a full physical exam as soon as possible, to ensure she was in good health and to perhaps provide further clues as to where she was from.

Zoe told all this to Lin over breakfast in the Great Hall. The room was filled with round wooden tables that would seat eight each. It had twelve-foot ceilings and an entire wall of windows, and it felt weird with just the two of them there. But the kitchen staff told them that half of the students would arrive by dinner and the other half by the following evening. Those must be the ones from overseas, Zoe guessed. She wondered how everyone would feel about having their summer vacation cut so short. She hoped they wouldn't be upset with her. Lin promised that nobody could possibly blame her, but Zoe didn't share her optimism.

"Come on," Lin said, standing up with her tray. "Let's go explore."

"Not so fast," said the head housemaid, Miss Zehringer, walking briskly toward them with her finger pointed. "Here is your list of chores." She placed a piece of paper in Lin's hand and a mop in Zoe's and continued past them without breaking stride. "If you put your backs into it," she called back to them, "you should be done before noon!"

The girls looked at the paper. It read simply, *Clean Great Hall. That means EVERYTHING*. They looked at each other and then at the vast expanse of the room.

"We're going to need a bigger mop," Lin said.

7

CONFRONTATIONS

Cleaning the Great Hall took a full five hours, after which they collapsed in a sweaty mess before wolfing down lunch and quickly ducking out before Miss Zehringer decided to give them more to do.

They didn't get far, though, before Professor Yeoh came to escort Zoe to the infirmary for her physical exam.

"Aww, Mom," Lin protested. "We were just about to go exploring."

"This will only take a few hours," Professor Yeoh said. "But if you think you will be bored without Zoe, I can ask Miss Zehringer to find another task for you."

"Nope, I'm good!" Lin said, already running away and waving back. "See you soon, Zoe!"

Zoe frowned, feeling abandoned as she followed Professor Yeoh. The infirmary seemed to be quite a full-fledged medical facility with all sorts of machines—not at all what Zoe had expected to find in a school.

"We try to keep a low profile, as you know," Professor Yeoh explained. "So the more we can handle here, the less likely we are to need the services of hospitals and doctors in the world of Typicals."

She measured Zoe's blood pressure and listened to her heart and lungs with a stethoscope, looked in her ears and throat, and drew several vials of blood to test for all sorts of ailments and nutritional deficiencies, she said. The main test, though, was a full-body MRI.

"This is a very expensive machine," Professor Yeoh said, "but worth every penny. Magnetic Resonance Imaging is noninvasive, no radiation like X-rays, and will give us thousands of highly detailed images of your body and brain. If there is anything wrong with you, we will see it. This will take a full ninety minutes, though, and it will be loud, so wear these." She handed Zoe earplugs. "Do you have claustrophobia?"

Zoe shook her head. "I don't think so."

"Good. In you go, then."

Professor Yeoh hadn't been kidding when she said it was loud, and lying still inside a machine for ninety minutes was not fun in the slightest. When it was all over and she slid out of the machine, Professor Yeoh looked somber.

"What's wrong?" Zoe asked, expecting the worst for some reason. "Is it my brain?"

The professor shook her head. "No, I don't see anything wrong with your brain at all. But . . . the rest of you. Come sit," she said, patting the chair next to her, "and we'll go over these images together."

Zoe immediately saw what had made the professor so concerned. Bone fractures. Hundreds of them.

"You seem to have broken almost every bone in your body, Zoe. Many of them multiple times. They are all nicely healed, and definitely with the aid of a skilled Telepath. But injuries like these . . . and the sheer number of them. . . . Our students tend to suffer more injuries than those of Typical children because we train them in combat, and our games are rougher than those of Typicals as well, but those injuries are nothing compared to this. I'm afraid that you have clearly been abused. I can't imagine what you must have gone through." She touched Zoe's arm. "I'm so sorry."

"It's okay," Zoe said, staring at the images. "I don't remember any of it."

. . .

The campus took them all afternoon to explore. Aside from the castle, there was a wooded area and a little lake with a pile of stones that were perfect for skipping on the water. There was also the sanctuary, run by the warmest, kindest young woman Zoe had ever met. Her name was Elizabeth, and she took such good care of the animals. Zoe spotted the white goat from the day before and instantly fell in love. His name was Vincent. Vincent van Goat. Lin befriended a piglet name Napoleon. Zoe suddenly had a thought.

"Elizabeth, can we communicate with animals telepathically?"

Elizabeth nodded, smiling. "To an extent, yes. They don't have language like we do, but they understand ideas and they have all the same emotions we do. Happiness, excitement, love." A look of sadness came over her. "Also fear, anxiety, sorrow. These are all rescues who experienced absolute horrors. Just like us, that sort of trauma scars them for life. Poor things." She kissed the goat's head. "You're safe now, Vincent."

"Wow, so you literally speak to them and they understand you."

"All the time," Elizabeth said. "I send them words and images. It's useful for getting them back in the barn at night, although my two munchkins help with that, too," she said, pointing to the two Border Collies rolling around in the dirt. "The more time you spend with the animals, the easier it is to communicate. You can't help but realize that they're just like us, with just as much right to exist and live peacefully." She shrugged. "They're my friends. I hope to one day teach an actual course in communicating with animals. Telepaths have rules against using compulsion on Typicals but for too long have felt it is perfectly fine to use compulsion on animals. I'm trying to change that mindset. For now, I just want to help students to feel compassion and respect for all living creatures. Too many of us leave the Academy too full of ourselves."

Zoe decided she never wanted to leave this place. "Goodbye, Vincent," she said, rubbing his nose. "I'll visit every day."

There was one other building to see. It was clearly an old church that had been deconsecrated and now served as Professor Chao's dojo. Lin said she'd visited it several times. It was an immense wooden room with a high triangular ceiling and horizontal beams. Rays of sunlight came through stained glass windows. But these windows were not religious in nature, depicting instead what seemed to be a history of martial arts. Monks in kung fu fighting poses, farmers wielding tools as weapons, and samurai in battle. Mats covered much of the floor, while other portions were hardwood. Hundreds of weapons of all shapes and sizes hung on the walls. Some of the swords were wooden for practice while others were metal and very sharp.

Zoe walked slowly along the walls, staring at the weapons with a strange feeling of déjà vu. They all looked so familiar. She couldn't remember ever using them, but she was fairly certain that she knew how to.

Shuddering, she turned to see Lin executing a half dozen backflips down the mats, landing on her feet with an exuberant smile.

"Nice," Zoe said, impressed. "I didn't know you were into gymnastics too."

"I'm not. But Wushu was the first martial art I ever learned." Seeing Zoe's blank look, she elaborated. "Wushu is a form of kung fu, just like Wing Chun is. It's effective but also more . . . artistic, more stylish and acrobatic. You see it a lot in movies. Dad told me it's a good martial art to start kids out on because it teaches you a lot of techniques before you're ready to actually fight anyone. When I got older, he started teaching me Wing Chun, which is more about being super effective in real-life combat, without any of the flashy stuff."

Zoe nodded. She couldn't remember actually watching any martial arts movies—or *any* movies, really. "I wonder if I know any Wushu."

"Students are not allowed in the Combat Room without my permission," said an authoritative voice from above. They both looked up to see Professor Chao falling from a rafter high above. Zoe let out a tiny shriek as he hit the mat, rolled once, and came up standing in front of them. They could *do* that?

"But that doesn't apply to me, does it, Dad?" Lin said, unperturbed. "I mean, I'm your daughter."

Lin's father walked over, looking quite annoyed. "You thought you would receive special privileges, daughter dearest? I am sorry to disappoint you, but you must adhere to the rules even *more* than the other students *because* you are my daughter."

He held up his hand to pre-empt Lin's protest. "Trust me, Lin, I am doing you a favour. You do not want your classmates accusing you of receiving preferential treatment. I will not hear another word on the matter. Now, get out of my classroom or you will both be serving detention with me this evening."

"Yes, sir," they said in unison as they scrambled for the exit. The last thing Zoe wanted was more detention.

"Zoe," Professor Chao said a second later. "A moment, if you please. Lin, you can wait outside. Zoe will join you momentarily."

Lin looked helplessly at Zoe before closing the door behind her, leaving an ominous silence in the vast room. Zoe waited for the professor to speak, afraid to make eye contact. She knew what must be coming.

"Our meeting with the headmaster did not go as anticipated. Would you care to explain what happened, Zoe?"

Zoe fidgeted uncomfortably and looked at her shoes. "I don't know what to say, sir. I didn't like what he said about me not being who I say I am . . . who I *think* I am. I got . . . scared. And then he grabbed me, with his mind, and wouldn't let me go and . . . I thought this was all a trap. All of it—him and you. I panicked." She looked up briefly, then down again.

"I'm sorry, sir."

Professor Chao considered her. "Zoe," he said, finally, "the headmaster did *not* say you are not who you say, or think, you are—merely that it is a possibility. I would have broached the subject more gently, but nevertheless it is something you must be aware of and must learn to deal with. I can assure you that some of the students will have heard similar theories and the rumours will no doubt spread quickly."

Seeing her horror, the professor put a hand on her shoulder. "It is not fair, I know, but it is the situation you must now navigate. Do not let the other students provoke you into becoming the person some will accuse you of being. This goes for the faculty as well. Not every professor is happy you are here."

Zoe was amazed that he was speaking so openly to her. He looked her in the eye. "You must remain confident in who you are, Zoe. No matter what your past turns out to be—and we will discover the truth of it in time, I promise. You are who you *choose* to be. There is no greater advice I can give you than this. No one can force us to be something that we do not wish to be. Our actions, our choices, are always our own to make, even when it may seem they are not. There is always a choice. Do you understand?"

"Yes, sir," Zoe said, uncertain what else to say.

"Go then. Lin is waiting for you and I wish to return to my meditation."

Zoe made for the exit, then turned to ask one more question, only to find the professor was gone. Looking up, she found him sitting cross-legged on a rafter. How the—? Shaking her head, she said, "Professor? Do *you* believe in me?"

He opened his eyes and turned to face her. Again, he was silent as he considered his response. Zoe liked that. Here was a man who took the time to say what he meant and thus would always mean what he said.

"I consider myself to be a good judge of character, Zoe. I see great qualities in you, and even greater potential. I think it is highly likely that you will have a difficult path ahead of you and will face many difficult choices in your life. But I do believe that ultimately, you will make the *right* choices."

Zoe felt a lump in her throat, managed a quiet, "Thank you," and went to meet her friend outside.

■ ■ ■

By dinnertime, the castle was in a state of chaos. Not only were students arriving months ahead of schedule to a school that was still being readied by a skeleton staff, but parents who would normally just drop off their children with a hug and a kiss goodbye were instead milling about in the main lobby looking for anyone who could explain exactly what was going on and why they had been forced to bring their children in early.

As they ate dinner in the Great Hall, Zoe and Lin watched the students returning from all over the world greet each other after just a few weeks apart.

The first-years were easy to spot. They were the ones looking scared and confused, but they all managed to find each other with relative ease.

It turned out that Zoe had been wrong. Rather than bitter about losing their vacations, the students seemed excited by the sense of emergency. The "Rogues" were all anyone could talk about—that and the girl with no memory who the Rogues were chasing and who might actually be a spy or sleeper agent or assassin. Everyone was looking around, trying to figure out which student she was. Zoe felt like hiding under the table.

Lin leaned forward. "Don't let it bother you. Once they get to know you, everything will be fine. Look on the bright side—you're a celebrity. Everyone wants to be famous, right?"

Zoe grimaced. "Why would anyone want to be famous? Everyone

watching you, talking about you . . ." She shuddered. "Not for me, thanks. Besides, this seems more like *infamous*, to me."

"Nah, it'll be fun. You'll see."

Zoe opened her mouth to refute this when something caught her attention. A small, terribly frightened first-year was being teased by a group of four much bigger first-year boys. Zoe sized them up quickly. Clearly, they had all recognized in each other a common need to feel important by picking on someone weaker. The leader of their pack was the tallest, with intentionally messy brown hair and expensive-looking clothes. He had probably started it but now leaned against a wall, smirking.

The small boy looked like he barely understood what they were saying—most of which mocked his short stature. He kept saying, "*Lo siento*" and "*No entiendo*," and Zoe guessed he was probably from South America. He understood the intent behind their remarks well enough, though, and tried to smile and shrug it off and quietly get away, but the boys kept blocking his escape.

Lin followed Zoe's gaze and furrowed her eyebrows. "Oh, that's not right. Why don't they leave the poor kid alone?"

"It's not in their nature," Zoe said. "They're predators. Like a group of lions attacking their prey."

"More like a bunch of hyenas," Lin said. "Look at them, laughing at him like that."

But Zoe was already up and walking, her body moving of its own accord. Lin hurried around the table to follow.

"What's the matter, you little Pygmy?" one of them was saying. "Don't they speak English in the jungle?"

"Geography certainly isn't your strongest subject," Zoe said. She looked at the small boy. "*De dónde eres?*" she asked.

"Peru," he said, obviously relieved that she had moved the boys' focus away from him. She turned back to the boy who'd made the Pygmy comment.

"You see? Wrong continent. I guess you can't expect racist bullies to be smart, though, can you?"

All the boys stared at her, as shocked as if she had just slapped them. All talking ceased as people elbowed each other and pointed at the brewing confrontation. Zoe could sense Lin standing slightly behind her to the left, which was comforting. Not that she wanted this to end up in a fistfight.

The bullies looked to their leader for instructions. When none were forthcoming, the one she had just insulted lifted his chin and said, cockily, "Well, he looks like a Pygmy to me."

"Then you don't just *look* stupid," Zoe said and waited for that to sink in.

"Who the bloody 'ell are you?" said a boy with a distinctive Cockney accent. He was the biggest and meanest looking of the bunch.

"Zoe," she said, simply.

"Well, mind your business, *Zoe*," he said, puffing up his chest, "before we decide to mind it for you."

Zoe ignored him and instead looked directly at their leader, still leaning casually against the wall. "Tell your boys to leave him alone."

The boy raised one eyebrow. "Fancy him as your new boyfriend, do you?" he said in a lilting Irish accent. The other boys snickered. He sauntered toward her, hands in his pockets. "And what if we don't leave him alone, yeah? What then?"

"Then you'll regret it." Oh, what was she doing? Didn't she have enough enemies already? But there was no turning back now.

"Is that a fact?" He stepped right in front of her. "And how's that? You going to beat me up then?"

Zoe shrugged. "Yes."

He looked at his mates and laughed. "Oho! She's a lively one, isn't she?" He turned back to her. "I don't usually hit girls. But if they want to act like boys, well, that's a different story."

Zoe sighed and closed her eyes. She really didn't need this. She was in enough trouble with the headmaster already. Who knew what would happen if she got caught fighting? She opened her eyes and forced herself to smile. Beckoning him to lean closer, she whispered in his ear so only he could hear.

"Do you really want to get beat up by a girl in front of everyone on the first day of school? Just say something witty to save face and we'll both walk away. Otherwise, I'll end all your hopes of being the leader of your little pack right here and now."

She leaned back and watched his smirk fade, to be replaced by a venomous glare. She could almost see the wheels turning in his head as he tried to decide whether she was bluffing or not. After several seconds, he was sneering again.

"All right, Zoe," he said aloud so everyone could hear. "We'll leave your little boyfriend alone for now." He pointed at her. "But you owe me, understand? You owe Liam Murphy." He started to walk away, gesturing for his gang to follow.

"That's not good enough, *Liam*," Zoe called to his back. She'd offered to let him save face, but not at her expense. That was going too far. And who referred to themselves in the third person anyway? "You'll leave him alone from now on. And I don't owe you anything." Ouch. Had she gone too far? Forced his hand?

But he just laughed and continued to walk away. "No, you owe me," he said over his shoulder. "Whether you like it or not. And I'll collect, you can be sure of that."

As he and his gang walked off, Zoe looked for the first time at the crowd that had gathered. Many were looking at her with open admiration. One girl, though, who seemed to have her own gang of followers, had her eyes narrowed in blatant suspicion. She stood with her arms crossed, looking very haughty.

"It's you, isn't it?" she said in a voice dripping with accusation. "You're the reason we're all here early. You're one of those Rogues. The one they say *claims* to have amnesia but could really be their spy."

Oh no. That hadn't taken long. She knew that how she handled the next few moments could affect her next four or five years here at the Academy. She opened her mouth to speak but Lin beat her to it.

"Zoe is my friend," she said, stepping between Zoe and her accuser. "My *best* friend. I guarantee she's no spy. She fought the Rogues. Twice. The second time alongside my dad, Professor Chao. She could have run—he told her to—but she stayed and helped. She may have saved his life. If she was one of the Rogues, she wouldn't have done that." Lin drew herself up defiantly. "I don't care where she's from—I'd trust her with my life any day."

The entire Great Hall had gone silent during Lin's speech, broken only by whispers of, "It's her!" or, "She's the one!" Most gawked at Zoe as though she were walking on water. Her accuser, however, was not giving up so easily.

"How nice for you," she said to Lin in what must have been the most condescending tone she could muster. "But you are horribly naïve." She spoke to the crowd now. "Helping your daddy doesn't mean anything. If the Rogues wanted to send a spy here to gain our trust, they could have staged everything, made it look as though they were trying to kill her and that she was trying to help us. Are we really supposed to believe that a kid no older than us could fight a group of fully grown Telepaths and survive? As if. They must have let her escape, because she's still one of them."

Lin looked as though she wanted to counter but couldn't quite figure out how, so Zoe stepped forward to fight her own battle. She had a feeling she'd be doing this a lot.

"I survived the first time with a lot of luck. I survived the second time only because of Professor Chao. I owe him my life." She didn't bother to address her accuser—that would be playing right into the girl's hand, making it look as though she were important enough to demand and receive an explanation. Instead, she raised her voice to address all the gathered students. "I have no memory before a few days ago. And as far as I can tell, the Rogues *were* trying to either capture me or kill me. And as far as I am aware, I am *not* a spy. But—" she paused, "there's no way for me to ever *prove* any of this to you."

This prompted a lot of murmuring, and Accusatory Girl looked smug. Zoe held up her hand. "I can tell you this, though. If I were one of the Rogues and I wanted to send a spy here, I'd send someone a lot *more* useful and a lot *less* conspicuous than me. I'd wait until summer vacation and then capture a teacher, who has access to information none of us are privy to and work some mind control mojo on them to create a sleeper agent." This raised a lot of eyebrows. "Or I'd do the same thing to a senior who everyone already knows and trusts." This caused a lot of sideways glances. "Or I'd just send a first-year who nobody knows or suspects."

Now Zoe looked directly at her accuser. "Or maybe I'd be really smart and send two students—a decoy who everyone would suspect, and the real spy, who would throw as much suspicion on to the decoy as possible, so that nobody would ever think to suspect her." This caused everyone to look at Accusatory Girl, who now appeared thoroughly displeased at this turn in the conversation.

"I can't prove I'm not a spy for the Rogues," Zoe finished. "But neither can anyone else. If there's a spy here, it could be anyone." Now she looked genuinely contrite. "I'm sorry your summer vacations got cut short, everyone. Really, I am. But it wasn't my fault." She turned and walked back to her table, picked up her dinner tray and strode out of the hall without a backward glance.

. . .

"That was totally awesome!" Lin said, giddily, as they walked to their dorm room. "I mean, first you face down that Liam dude and his pack and *then* you face down that mean girl, give a speech to the entire hall, and totally turn the tables on her! Talk about first impressions—everyone's going to be talking about what you did in there! Where did all that stuff come from anyway?"

Zoe smiled contentedly to herself. She had done rather well. "You mean the bit about how anyone could be a spy, not just me?" She shrugged. "I don't know, it just sort of occurred to me. It makes sense though, doesn't it?"

"Sure, it makes total sense. And I'll bet you just convinced half the school of it, too. It was brilliant."

Zoe stopped abruptly. "Uh-oh," she said. "I almost forgot. I'm supposed to be in detention with the headmaster in . . ." She spied a clock on the wall. "Two minutes!"

Lin winced sympathetically. "Better get going then. Don't worry, it'll be fine. You'll see."

■ ■ ■

It wasn't fine. It was . . . weird.

Zoe knocked at the headmaster's office one minute late.

"Come in," said a voice and she entered. The headmaster (what was his actual name anyway?) was writing at his desk way at the other end of his cluttered office. "Have a seat, please," he said without looking up. Zoe scanned the room for a seat as far away from him as possible, but the only chairs were the two directly facing his desk. Sighing inwardly, she made the journey across the long office, dutifully sat down with hands folded in her lap, and waited quietly.

She waited for fifteen minutes. Had he forgotten about her somehow? Was this part of the punishment? Was he playing mind games? She spent the time examining his wonderful assortment of antiques. It wasn't an eclectic collection, like she had first thought. It was a collection of inventions that had changed the world. From where she was sitting, she could see an old phone, a phonograph, a box camera, an old crystal radio, and an old computer with the words Altair 8800 on it.

Finally, the headmaster put down his pen and looked up. "Do you have any idea, Miss . . ." He scowled. "Do you have a last name?"

Zoe shook her head. "Not that I know of, sir."

"Well, that will never do. When a teacher is angry with a student, the teacher typically addresses that student in a formal manner using his or her surname. Miss or Mr. whatever. If they're always calling you 'Zoe,' how will you know when they're angry with you?" He picked up his pen again and jotted down a note, mumbling something about first priority. Then, he looked up again. "Right, then. As I was saying, Miss . . . Miss Zoe. Do you have any idea how much trouble you have caused me?"

Oh no, she wasn't about to fall into that trap. "If you are referring to the commotion out in the lobby today and the general displeasure of the parents—and the Council—then yes, sir, I have a very good idea." She paused. "None at all."

He blinked. "Excuse me?"

"None at all, sir," she repeated. "With the exception of our unfortunate misunderstanding last night, I bear no responsibility for any of the trouble you are currently experiencing."

"Is that so?" he said, very quiet and controlled.

Zoe nodded. "Yes, sir." She tried to keep her own voice steady. "I never asked to come here. And even if I had, it was your decision to allow it. Just as it was your decision to not allow the Council to take me away. You have been very kind to me, sir, and I am in your debt. But my presence here was your decision, not mine."

"Do you not *wish* to be here?"

"Sir, I wish to be here more than anything else in the world! But I refuse to feel guilty about it."

The headmaster said nothing for a while, and they sat in silence, staring at each other. Zoe tried to keep her gaze calm and nonconfrontational. She was in enough trouble already. But she had to stand up for herself, didn't she? Finally, the headmaster spoke.

"Good for you." Was that a smile she saw at the corner of his mouth? Impossible. "You are correct. None of this is your fault and it was wrong of me to imply otherwise." He removed his glasses and rubbed the bridge of his nose. "Nevertheless, your presence here *has* caused me a great deal of trouble. Every parent—*every* parent—has made a point to inform me of their displeasure and their grave concerns about you." He put his glasses back on. "So, tell me, *should* they be concerned?"

"No, sir," Zoe said. Why was he asking this? What other answer would she give?

"But you attacked me yesterday."

"No, sir. As I explained to you this morning, I thought you were attacking *me*. I was just trying to escape."

"You didn't like it when I forcibly restrained you."

"Of course not, sir. Nobody would."

"You reacted instinctively, to defend yourself."

"Yes, sir."

"Like you reacted in the hospital when you were attacked."

"Yes, sir."

"You fought off four trained, adult Telepaths. You did things you didn't know you were capable of that night, didn't you?"

"Yes, sir."

"And yesterday when you penetrated my shield—*my* shield, which I would appreciate you keeping between us, thank you—I'll wager you had no idea that was even possible. You just . . . reacted. Instinctively."

Zoe paused this time but still had nothing to add. "That's correct, sir."

The headmaster leaned forward. "And *that* is exactly what concerns me, Zoe," he said, pointing at her. "You must have been training in physical combat for many years now. And telepathic combat too, it would seem, even though your Abilities shouldn't have surfaced until fairly recently. Yet we have no idea what you've been taught. How do we know that you won't get into a fight with another student and react instinctively—in a *lethal* manner?"

"I won't, sir. I would never do that."

"How do you know that?"

"I don't like hurting people, sir. I only fight to defend myself."

"Killing your opponent is the best way to defend yourself, wouldn't you agree? He can't hurt you if he's dead."

"No, sir." Zoe shook her head emphatically. "That's only when you're in a fight to the death, which I would never expect to happen here. I'll avoid fights as much as possible, and if I'm forced to defend myself, I'll try my best not to hurt anyone."

"But how can I be sure of that, Zoe?" Why was he pressing her so hard? "I believe that you believe what you are saying. But it is the nature of martial arts training to replace our natural instincts with new ones, so that instead of flinching when we are suddenly attacked, we meet the attack head-on using techniques that our training has given us. So, how can we be sure that your instincts are not to use lethal force?"

"It doesn't matter what my instincts are, sir," Zoe said, raising her voice with finality. "My instincts don't rule me. I can control my actions."

"And how can you be certain of that?"

Zoe paused. Looked away. Took a deep breath and looked back. "Because I didn't kill you last night when I had the chance—and the instinct—to do so. Sir."

Once again, they sat in silence, this truth hanging in the air between them.

"Well, thank you for that," he said, finally.

8

THE FACULTY

The next day was much calmer. Zoe was determined to stay beneath everyone's radar and avoid any more confrontations. Lin seemed a little disappointed, as the rest of the students were arriving today, and she wanted to meet as many of them as possible. Zoe admired that about Lin—she was an extrovert, able to talk with complete strangers and learn all their secrets within minutes. They discovered, though, that many of the first-years could barely speak English. This made sense, since most of the students had only recently discovered their emerging telepathic talents and had no idea that they would soon be attending an English-speaking school. Once word got out that Zoe was a polyglot, she became quite popular as the first-years' official translator.

Later, she and Lin went exploring again. They hung out by the lake for a while, skipping stones, before visiting their friends at the animal sanctuary.

By detention time, Zoe was pretty tired and was almost looking forward to just sitting for an hour. The headmaster, however, had other plans.

"You are late, young lady," he said the instant she entered his office.

Zoe looked at the wall clock. She was right on time.

"By twenty seconds," he continued.

She peered at the second hand on the clock. It was true. "I'm sorry, sir. From now on, I'll arrive several minutes early."

"Certainly not," he said, putting away his pen. "Do you think I have nothing better to do than entertain you?"

Zoe didn't answer that.

"From now on, you will arrive at the exact time I requested," he finished, standing up and walking around his desk. "Now then. Classes start tomorrow. What do you hope to learn this year?"

"As much as possible, sir. I want to learn everything there is to know about using our Abilities. I want to be able to control them completely."

"Why?" he asked.

"Pardon me?"

"Why, Zoe?"

"Because . . . I need to." When he didn't reply, she continued, "I need to be . . . powerful, and controlled, for when the Rogues come for me."

"You think they will come for you here?" he said.

"Yes," Zoe said, simply.

"Does that scare you?"

"Of course."

The headmaster looked sympathetic. "That's nothing to be ashamed of. You've been through a lot. You're perfectly safe here, Zoe. Trust me."

Zoe winced.

"What?" the headmaster said.

"Sir . . . with all due respect, please don't tell me to trust you right after a lie." She met his eyes. "We both know I'm not perfectly safe here. The Telepaths who attacked me could try to sneak in—or worse, the man in black. Don't get me wrong, I appreciate that you're trying to comfort me, but I'm not a child. I mean, I *am* a child, but I'm not stupid."

The headmaster raised his eyebrows, then slowly walked back behind his desk and sat down again.

"Rest assured, young lady, I will not try comfort you again."

Zoe spent the remainder of her detention writing *I will not accuse the headmaster of lying* on his chalkboard and wondering when she would learn to keep her mouth shut.

* * *

By five o'clock, most of the students had arrived. Zoe was impressed that so many kids could get to Toronto so quickly considering how far some had to travel. Everyone assembled in the auditorium for the welcome ceremony.

The headmaster strode onstage and took his place at the podium. "Welcome everyone, to another year at the Academy. I do apologize for the early start and for the haste with which you have all been gathered here. I will explain in a moment, but first I would like to address our new cohort of first-years. For those of you who do not yet speak English, we have retained the services of translators for this welcome assembly. I trust your earpieces are functioning properly. Have no fear that you will all be receiving English language classes to get you up to speed as quickly as possible.

"My name is Richard Harrington," he began. So that was his name, Zoe thought. "I have the honour and privilege of being the headmaster of this school, and that is how you should all address me. 'Headmaster.' Nothing else." Nodding, he continued. "You have all recently become aware that you are different from your friends and family. Some of you were approached by one of us before you were aware of your special Abilities, others shortly afterward. Whoever found you has no doubt already explained to you everything that I am about to say, but repetition never hurts.

"Discovering that you have Abilities that most people do not can be both exciting and frightening. Some of you may not wish to be here and may resent that you were forced to leave your friends and family behind. To those of you, I do sympathize, but there simply is no other choice in the matter. Without proper training, you would be a danger to everyone around you. Also, the world is simply not ready to learn of our existence. Someday, perhaps, but not now. It is vital that you never reveal your Abilities or the existence of our kind to the world of Typicals—i.e., non-Telepaths. Any accidental exposure must be reported immediately so that we can control it. Any deliberate exposure is an offence for which you *will* be imprisoned—even if you are a child. There are simply no exceptions. This is why cellphones are prohibited at the Academy. The risk that someone might accidentally post something to social media that exposes us is too great. You *will* all have a laptop and access to the Internet, but be warned that all Internet activity is monitored. We have no desire in intrude on anyone's privacy, but we cannot risk discovery.

"Speaking of privacy, one of the Abilities that you will soon discover, if you have not already, is the ability to read minds—to know what others are thinking. This is considered to be a fundamental violation of an individual's privacy, unless that individual has granted express permission. This applies not only to your classmates but also to Typicals. The only exception is if there is reasonable suspicion that a Typical has learned of our existence. Anyone breaking this rule shall be dealt with harshly.

"Another Ability that you will develop in later years is compulsion—forcing your will upon someone to make them obey. The punishment for any student doing this is *extremely* severe." He paused to let his words sink in.

"Now that I have hopefully scared you all sufficiently, I will tell you the bright side. This will be, without a doubt, the most exciting year of your lives thus far. You have a very rare gift, and you will soon learn that you are capable of feats you never dreamed of. These gifts are not to be taken lightly. When you first entered this school, you saw the words 'Dispensatores De Terrae.' This is our school's motto, Latin for 'Stewards of the Earth.' That is our role. We do not use our gifts to assert superiority over Typicals but rather to help them and all other creatures of this world. In this spirit, we do not assert superiority over each other, either. We continually strive to make this school as safe and welcoming to students of all backgrounds as possible. No matter your race, ethnicity, religion, disability, gender, or sexual orientation, you are welcome here, and absolutely no forms of discrimination will be tolerated.

"Now, on to the important business of the day. Why did our school year begin early?" He paused. "In short, we have just discovered that we are not alone. Other Telepaths exist of whom we were not aware, and their intentions toward us may very well be hostile." There was a great deal of murmuring in the audience. "They recently attacked a young Telepath, who we believe was defecting from them, and she suffered memory loss as a result. We believe that she was fleeing them when the attack occurred. When they found her again, our own Professor Chao was luckily there to help. She is now with us and we welcome her wholeheartedly into our Academy. Until we know more about these unknown Telepaths, we have decided to err on the side of caution and so gathered all of you here where we can properly protect you.

"That is all I have to say on this matter for now. Now, let me introduce you to your professors and then we can all eat!"

■ ■ ■

The following day, classes began. The student timetables were posted in the halls when they awoke. Zoe was excited as she read her list of subjects, but Lin seemed disappointed.

"What's wrong? Don't you like these? There's telekinesis, healing, ESP, combat . . ."

Lin shrugged. "Yeah, but we've also got English, math, history, geography. . . . What's with all that? I thought this was supposed to be a school for Telepaths, not Typicals."

"Well, we don't want to be dumber than Typical kids when it comes to . . . typical stuff, right?"

Lin shrugged again. "I guess. I just thought I was done with that stuff, that's all." She swung her backpack over her shoulder. "Come on, let's go get breakfast."

Their first class was Telekinesis 101, taught by Professor Martinov, a Russian man with a greying goatee and a mass of hair that stuck out in all directions. He swept into the classroom like a madman, black cape billowing behind him, gesturing frantically at textbooks that flew from their shelves to lie open on the desk before each shocked student.

"Good morning!" he shouted. "My name is Professor Martinov. And this," he said as he took his place behind the front desk, "is my class. Ha!"

The silence that ensued was total but only lasted a few seconds before he rushed on.

"Before we begin, let me address the burning question—the one every new crop of first-years asks: Why am I wearing a cape? It is *not* a cape; it is a *cloak*. A highly functional garment that was in fashion when I first began teaching and I am waiting for it to come back into style. Now, who here can already move objects with their mind? Hmm? Who? Who? Who?"

No hands went up. Lin elbowed Zoe in the ribs. "Put your hand up," she whispered.

"No one? What about you?" he asked a blond boy in the front row. "What is your name?"

"Anton, sir," the boy said.

"Ah, I detect a Russian accent!" Professor Martinov said, excitedly. "You must have moved something by now. We Russians have always excelled at telekinesis! No? Are you sure? Ah well, you will soon, I've no doubt." He addressed the entire class again. "Anyone else? Hmm?"

Lin stomped on Zoe's foot. "Ow!" Zoe yelled.

The professor whirled on her. "Yes! You have? Excellent. What is your name?"

Zoe glared at Lin. "Just you wait," she whispered, as Lin smiled innocently. "Zoe," she said, loudly.

"Zoe? Zoe. So, Zoe, what have you managed to move?"

"A pencil, sir."

"A pencil? Excellent. To the front of the class please, Zoe."

Zoe reluctantly got up, shooting a last dirty look at Lin, and stood next to the professor in front of the entire class.

"Here," he said, holding up a pencil. "Stop it from falling."

He dropped the pencil and Zoe watched it fall to the floor. Zoe heard giggles. "Don't worry. Don't worry. You weren't ready." Professor Martinov picked up the pencil and held it up again. "Here, on the count of three. One. Two. Three." He dropped it again. Zoe concentrated and willed the pencil to float, then watched it hit the floor a split-second later. More giggles.

"Don't be embarrassed. Don't be embarrassed," Martinov said, bending down again to pick up the pencil. "Maybe you weren't ready again."

"Or maybe she's a big liar," said a familiar voice. Zoe felt anger flare as she turned to face Accusatory Girl, whose name she had since learned was Helen Hawkesbury. Helen shrieked in surprise as her textbook suddenly jumped up and snapped shut on her nose.

"Good! Good!" Martinov shouted amid the class's laughter. "Excellent, Zoe. That book weighed much more than a pencil, plus you had to not only lift it but close it as well. That is a tremendous achievement." He pointed a finger at Zoe. "But unfortunately, you have no idea how you just did that, do you?" He waited for an answer and Zoe reluctantly shook her head. The professor nodded. "I thought as much. You reacted out of anger, without thinking. Sit down, please."

Zoe sat, feeling both pleased with herself and chastised at the same time. The professor told the class, "Anger can be both a friend and a foe. Just as it can increase our physical strength temporarily, so too can it increase our mental strength temporarily." He held up a finger. "But at a cost, especially during your formative years when you are just beginning to learn to use your emerging Abilities. Many students turn to anger to achieve a level of strength that would otherwise be beyond them. It is only natural, especially in combat. But I *strongly* caution you against this, because by doing so, you will become dependent upon that anger for even the simplest of tasks.

"I have known students who possessed the potential to be among the greatest of us in terms of raw power, yet who amounted to nothing because they could not tap into that power while calm. Remember this: Nobody can be angry all the time. And nobody *should* be angry all the time—that is a terrible way to live your life. Do not fall into that trap. Now, who else here would like to demonstrate their telekinetic prowess? Anyone?" He looked around the room and then chose someone at random. "You," he said pointing to the Peruvian boy Zoe had defended earlier. "What is your name?"

The boy looked around and then hesitantly pointed to himself and said, "Pacha."

"And can you move objects with your mind yet, Pacha?" he asked, levitating the pencil and bringing it to rest on his desk. Seeing that Pacha didn't understand, he pointed to him and then the pencil. Pacha nodded, put his hand out in front of him, and suddenly the entire desk was levitating six feet off the ground. Everyone's jaw dropped, and then the classroom erupted in hoots and hollers. Pacha was a powerhouse! Professor Martinov grinned from ear to ear. He motioned for Pacha to put the desk back down and then motioned for quiet. He stood stunned and blinking, before finally saying, "Wow! You will all want *him* on your team at our end-of-year tug-of-war competition." He returned to his desk and opened the textbook.

"Now, we shall begin with your first lesson. In order to move objects, you must understand about forces. Who here has heard of Sir Isaac Newton?"

· · ·

English class was pretty much the same as at any Typical school. They would be studying Shakespeare's *The Merchant of Venice*, which Zoe already knew, even though she had no recollection of reading it, so she was glad when ESP class came along.

Unfortunately, ESP was taught by a woman who, Zoe would later learn, had been voted Most Annoyingly Patronizing by the students ten years in a row.

"Hello, class," the professor said with a smile and a tone perfectly suited for five-year-olds. "My name is Professor Tilly. Welcome to ESP 101. Can any of you tell me what ESP stands for? Hmm?"

She waited patiently until a boy in the back row said, "Extrasensory perception, Professor."

"Oh dear," Professor Tilly said, concern on her face. "I didn't see a hand being raised."

After another long pause, a girl finally raised her hand and waited until the professor granted her permission to speak. "Extrasensory perception," she repeated.

"*Very* good!" Professor Tilly said, smiling and clapping joyously. Zoe had the distinct impression this woman was not all there upstairs. "And can someone here tell me what any of those complicated words mean?" Zoe's mouth fell open. Was this woman for real? She couldn't endure another minute of this, let alone an entire semester. She had read about parapsychology at the Toronto Reference Library, so she blurted, "Extrasensory perception means perceiving information by means other than our five senses. It includes clairvoyance, telepathy, and precognition."

"Oh dear," the professor said again. "I didn't see someone raise her hand."

Zoe buried her face in her desk. Lin raised her hand and made a small "ahem" until Professor Tilly granted her permission to speak.

"What she said," Lin said, jerking her thumb at Zoe.

■ ■ ■

After the horror that had been ESP class, Zoe was thrilled to be able to work off some of her angst and frustration in their next class, Combat 101, taught by Professor Chao. She sat on the mat in a line with the rest of the class, in classic *seiza* position—on her knees with her feet tucked underneath her. She was dressed in her white martial arts uniform. As always, she and Lin sat next to each other.

Professor Chao sat in seiza position in the middle of the mat, eyes closed, with his back to the students as he had been since class started. Perhaps waiting for them all to sit still and be quiet? If so, it had worked. No one had spoken for several minutes now. Finally, he extended his hands, leaned forward, and touched his forehead to the mat, bowing to the two photographs on the wall—one of a stoic, elderly, balding Japanese man with a long white beard, the other of a smiling, clean-shaven, middle-aged Chinese man. Lin and a few others followed suit and Zoe and the other students quickly followed their example. Then, the professor turned to face them and bowed again. The students bowed in return. Professor Chao smiled.

"The men you see in the photos behind me are legendary masters. On the left is Morihei Ueshiba, founder of the Japanese martial art of Aikido. He is more commonly referred to as O'Sensei. On the right is Grandmaster Ip Man, who forever changed the history of the Chinese martial art of Wing Chun. What I will teach you throughout your years here at the Academy is a fighting system that I designed over a very long period to suit our specific purposes. Much like Krav Maga, the fighting system developed by Hungarian–Israeli martial artist Imi Lichtenfeld, it borrows from other martial arts, such as Aikido and Wing Chun, but also Muay Thai, Jiu Jitsu, and others. Unlike Krav Maga, which was designed to inflict as much damage to your opponent as necessary and get away safely, my system is designed to subdue your opponent while inflicting minimal damage. It is for that reason that Aikido is at the core of the fighting system I have designed, and Aikido is all you shall study during your first year of training."

"Why spare your opponent?" Liam asked. "They'll just attack you again. Krav Maga sounds more my style." Liam's cohort murmured their agreement.

Professor Chao shook his head. "We are not soldiers. We fight only as a last resort to protect ourselves."

"Sir?" Zoe said, raising her hand. The professor looked her way. "Sir, you said it suits our specific purposes. What purposes are those?"

Professor Chao held up one finger. "To stay alive." He added a second finger. "To stay hidden, in a world where we are outnumbered almost a million to one." He raised his third finger. "To do no harm. With our Abilities, it would be very easy to consider ourselves above Typicals, but that is not our way. We are the caretakers of this world. We guide when necessary, but we try to minimize our interference."

"Wouldn't our mental Abilities be more suitable for dealing with Typicals, Professor?" Zoe said.

"Usually, that is the case," he said. "But it is sometimes necessary to use more conventional means."

"But why, sir?" Zoe said. "I should think—"

Professor Chao held up his hand. "All in good time, Zoe. Leave something for me to teach in future lessons."

"Can we use sword?" asked another student, in broken English.

"Yes," the professor said. There were murmurs of, "Cool!" and, "Awesome!" among the students. "Some Aikido instructors choose to teach Kenjutsu—the art of the sword—only to senior students. I, however, introduce the sword right from the start. Much of Aikido has its origin in Kenjutsu, and many of the empty-hand techniques have their complementary form with the sword. Thus, learning swordsmanship early on can improve your empty-hand technique by forcing you to do it properly with sword in hand."

"Sir," Zoe began. "What about other weap—"

"If you will kindly allow me to teach the class now? Thank you. As I was saying, I will be teaching you very different styles of martial arts. In the beginning, though, it is better to focus on just one. We will start with Aikido this semester. Who among you has had any training in martial arts?" Professor Chao asked, looking up and down the row of students.

Two hands went up, including Lin's. Zoe kept hers firmly in her lap.

"Put your hand up," Lin whispered once again. Zoe shook her head.

"Your name is?" the professor asked a small, wiry boy near the end.

"Panom," he said, in a mouse-like voice.

"And what style have you trained in, Panom?"

"Muay Thai, sir."

"A most effective martial art," Professor Chao said. "I will teach some aspects of it in later years."

"Come on, put your hand up, Zoe," Lin urged, trying to raise Zoe's resistant arm herself.

Professor Chao's gaze fell on Lin. "And my daughter, Lin, has studied under me for a number of years now, of course. Anyone else?"

All eyes turned to Zoe, who resolutely kept her arm down and her eyes on the mat. After a moment's silence, Professor Chao said, "Well, then, let us begin our first lesson." He extended his hand. "Zoe, you can be my first volunteer."

Zoe groaned inwardly as she got to her feet. Was this punishment for not raising her hand? She just wanted to keep a low profile, so everyone would forget that she had these freakish fighting skills. This wasn't fair.

She walked to the centre of the mats and faced her teacher. Silently, he extended his left hand, and motioned for her to grab his wrist with her right. She obliged and he slowly twisted clockwise, his left hand kept close to his body, his right foot sweeping out in a semicircle until he stood beside her and she was leaning slightly forward, off-balance.

He stood facing her again and this time extended his right hand. She grabbed his wrist and he made the same motion as last time but mirrored.

"Pay attention to my feet," he said to the class. "This sweeping motion is called *tenkan*. It is a highly effective method of getting out of the way of your opponent's attack while at the same time controlling it. You might think that at this point I have not really done much to counter her attack. I am, after all, standing beside her now. I haven't punched or kicked her. But compare my stance to hers. Notice how I am well grounded, while she is twisted up. Now, keep in mind that we are doing this technique slowly. Were you really intent on attacking me, Zoe, and your attack was at speed, what would you do?"

Zoe thought. She didn't know what to say. This wasn't at all what she had expected. This wasn't a fight. It was like some sort of slow-motion ballet. After an extended silence, during which she realized that he would wait until she answered, she said, "I guess . . . if this were all happening really fast, and I was determined to attack you . . . I would swing around toward you to hit you . . . like this." As she swung her left foot out in front and twisted to the right to slowly punch him with her left hand, he gently bent her right wrist and she found herself on the mat unable to escape.

"Notice how I barely had to do anything here. No punches, no kicks. Just the slightest motion and I was able to use her own energy against her, to redirect her attack into a submissive hold." He released her wrist and Zoe stood up again.

"Aikido is sometimes referred to as the gentleman's martial art, because it bears no ill will towards another, even your opponent. It allows you to incapacitate your enemy without hurting them." His eyes narrowed. "However, do not be fooled into thinking Aikido is a weak martial art. With proper training, it can be as effective and deadly as you need it to be."

"Here in the dojo, though, we are 'nice' to each other. Everyone must check their ego at the door. Our purpose here is to learn. Aikido does not have sparring practice as many other martial arts do, although once you become more advanced it does have *randori*, in which you must defend yourself against multiple attackers who can attack any way they choose. Even then, however, the purpose is to practice—not to hurt, not to win. We practice techniques with each other slowly at first, then with greater speed as your technique improves. And by technique, I mean not only your ability to perform a technique but also your ability to withstand it being performed on you. You will learn how to roll so that you can be thrown across the room without harm. You will learn how to breakfall so that your partner can flip you and slam you into the mat with great force without injuring you. Anyone who deliberately injures their partner will answer to me personally. This is not something you want to happen."

He faced Zoe again. "Now, back to tenkan. Like Kenjutsu, proper footwork is the key to Aikido. Footwork allows you to elude your opponent, to position yourself perfectly for a strike or takedown or to redirect your opponent's motion as you wish. Aikido is second to none in this regard. By always keeping positioning in mind, Aikido allows you to handle multiple attackers better than any other martial art, in my opinion. You can play your opponents against each other, tangle them up.

"Tenkan is the first footwork you will learn. Here is another common example of its use. Zoe, punch me. Midsection, at speed. As hard and fast as you can."

Zoe hesitated. "Don't worry," he said. "You can do this. Your body remembers how." She took a deep breath and punched her teacher as hard as she could with her right hand. And it was *fast*. As before, though, his right foot swept out in an arc as he pivoted on his left while placing his left hand on her right wrist. His right hand gently twisted and bent her hand and she found herself flipping through the air. Instinctively, she splayed her legs out straight and slammed her left hand down hard as she hit the mat.

"The technique I have done is called *kotegaeshi*—wrist-turning throw. And Zoe has just demonstrated how to do a proper breakfall so as not to get hurt. We will learn this later this semester after you have first learned front rolls."

He released Zoe and waited for her to stand again. He bowed to her and she did the same. He gestured for her to return to her spot in line.

"Spread out, please. Every other person, take a step forward." He turned his back to the class. "Stand as I stand. Left foot in front and facing forward. Right foot behind and perpendicular. Not too close, not too far apart. You must be stable but also able to move quickly. Now, we will practise tenkan. Do as I do."

. . .

Zoe loved combat class. It didn't take long to realize that she had learned Aikido before. She had to relearn all the names of the techniques, and when she had to perform them slowly, she discovered that her form was quite good. She couldn't explain the reasons why she did what she did, though, so she wasn't able to teach the other students like Lin could. But as the weeks went on, she progressed quickly, and Professor Chao told her and Lin that they could move up to a more advanced class soon. Right now, they were all in the beginners' class with the rest of their cohort, but martial arts classes were unlike others at the Academy, he said. It was useful to have senior, intermediate, and junior students all in the same class so the more experienced students could help teach. "You never truly understand a subject until you have to teach it," he said. Soon, once the beginners were at a slightly higher level, he would mix Zoe and Lin into the other classes. Zoe could hardly wait.

The normal courses like math and geography were, in a strange way, the most enjoyable for Zoe. Lin thought she was crazy, but they made Zoe feel like a normal kid for once. History was her favourite. She knew a lot of history without remembering where and when she'd learned it, but the history taught here was, Professor Grant said, unlike anything you'd find in Typical textbooks. It seemed that Telepaths had been keeping records for a very long time and had played a significant role in shaping world events. Also, the Telepaths were not always one big happy family working together benevolently for the good of all. There had been a period of many centuries during which they were split and warring. The Telepaths were the generals and the Typicals their unwitting pawns. It made Zoe wonder, though, how much of a role their kind played in the events of the modern world. But when she asked Professor Grant, a man who looked *old* despite being a Telepath, he just waved the question away, saying they would learn all that in a few years.

...

Zoe wanted to spend as much time as she could in the school's library. She had heard rumours from other students concerning how the pyramids were "really" built and she couldn't wait to find out for herself—but class and detention kept her very busy. Plus, every teacher, it seemed, was intrigued by her for one reason or another, and kept scheduling one-on-one meetings with her to figure out this mystery girl for themselves. It was all very annoying.

So, after the first week, Zoe began to turn the one-on-one sessions to her advantage and began asking questions of her own. Subtly at first, then with increased probing, learning as much as she could about their kind's history, about the Academy, about their ethics, and about the curriculum for upcoming years. In the end, they each became nervous that they were perhaps revealing too many of their secrets to a first-year, and to one who *could* turn out to be a spy after all, and they finally left her alone.

She did learn some interesting information, though—something the headmaster had touched on in his welcome speech. Compulsion—forcing a person to do something you want—wasn't taught until the senior years, and a heavy part of the course involved ethics. Compulsion could not only injure the individual, especially if they resisted, but it was also considered to be a method of last resort, as it represented a fundamental violation of a person's rights.

Zoe settled into a pattern, of sorts. She and Lin hung out a lot, and because Lin was so well liked, Zoe was accepted by the rest of the students too—if grudgingly. She managed to stay clear of further confrontations with Liam Murphy and Helen Hawkesbury, and even her daily detentions became routine. All in all, she felt happy and the weeks passed by.

Still, she wasn't as sociable as Lin and needed time to herself sometimes. So, in addition to visiting Vincent and her other animal friends at the Sanctuary, she spent a few hours of each day alone in the library, just reading. She enjoyed her classes, but they were not advancing quickly enough for her, so she tried to learn everything about her Abilities that she could from books. This was easier said than done, however. It was one thing to learn math from a book, quite another to learn telepathic techniques. Knowing the theory simply wasn't enough. Improvement required practice.

So, Zoe and Lin began practising in the woods. Lin had managed to move some light stones with her mind but still could not manage to read Zoe's thoughts or create a shield to keep Zoe from reading hers. Zoe was not faring much better. She could move heavier rocks than Lin, but it always took so much concentration and her control was shaky. Eventually she would become frustrated and angry, and suddenly the rock would fly away like it had been flung from a slingshot. This always impressed Lin, but it left Zoe feeling like a failure. She knew she was strong, but she couldn't get past her mental block. Anger seemed to be the only way to tap into that strength.

She was getting better at reading thoughts, though. Lin said she had no secrets and so didn't mind Zoe rummaging around in her mind. Zoe was extremely careful and gentle—she didn't want to risk hurting Lin in any way. This was a technique, however, that was even harder to learn from books than telekinesis. The human mind was so complex! Once you let your consciousness slide into another's mind, it was like being in a whole new world, and was a bit scary. Sometimes she felt like if she weren't careful, she could get lost. When Lin thought of specific things, Zoe could see the images bubbling into her awareness. It almost felt like *she* was thinking the thoughts and not Lin. And when Lin thought of something sad, like the time her dog died, Zoe could feel the sadness welling up inside herself, too.

This was the easy part, though, Zoe discovered. The really hard part was trying to access memories Lin was not actively thinking about. In fact, she still didn't have a clue how to do it. Now she understood how some Telepaths could spend their entire lives studying the human mind.

She wondered when her sessions with the school psychologist, Professor Sharapova, would begin. Whenever she asked the headmaster about it, he said her arrival at the Academy had been delayed but would not elaborate further. Zoe had at first dreaded the idea of allowing someone into her mind, but now she couldn't wait. The idea of therapy still frightened her, but not as much as living with so many unanswered questions. What scared her the most, though, was the thought that if she did have some sort of secret programming hidden deep inside her mind, then when it was activated, those closest to her would likely get hurt. And that meant Lin. She never voiced this worry to Lin, but silently vowed that she would never allow that to happen.

9

MEMORIES

On her last day of detention, the headmaster informed Zoe that Professor Sharapova, the school psychologist, had arrived and was expecting Zoe in her office immediately after detention. Zoe spent her last hour with the headmaster meditating quietly in her chair. She hadn't been taught how to properly meditate, unless it was by the Rogues, but she found that if she breathed slowly and purposefully and focused all of her awareness on her breathing, it settled her mind whenever she felt stressed or angry or worried. It helped her to feel in control of herself, which was a feeling she liked a great deal.

She found Professor Sharapova's office and knocked lightly. A quiet voice bid her enter. Taking a deep breath to steel herself, she entered. A beautiful woman with long blond hair and a warm but weary smile looked up from behind a tidy desk. "You must be Zoe," she said, getting up slowly and shaking Zoe's hand. "It's so good to finally meet you," she said. She spoke with a Russian accent, not too thick, just enough to sound pleasant to Zoe's ears. "Please make yourself comfortable."

"Hello, Professor," Zoe said, as she took a seat and looked around. It was a beautiful office, tastefully decorated with paintings, a large leafy plant in the corner, and a very comfortable-looking brown sofa.

"Please, call me Natasha." She waved her hand. "I don't teach anything. I am the school psychologist. You can call me 'Doctor,' if you prefer, but Natasha is fine." She sat opposite Zoe and crossed her legs. "I am sorry to be late in arriving. I am afraid I was very ill and could not travel." She smiled and raised her hands in front of her. "I am no longer contagious, though, not to worry."

"What did you catch?" Zoe asked.

"Typhoid fever, if you can believe it," she said, rolling her eyes. "Not something I wish to ever experience again. I highly recommend getting your proper immunizations before visiting Thailand, especially if straying from the major cities. I was visiting an old friend, but she recently moved from Bangkok to a rural area. It completely incapacitated me for over month. We Telepaths don't usually have to worry too much about diseases due to our natural healing ability, but we can still catch things sometimes. It was not a pleasant visit, I am afraid."

"I'm sorry to hear that," Zoe said, warming quickly to the woman. Something about her demeanour put Zoe very much at ease. "Is that where you went?" she said, pointing at a painting of what looked to be a fishing village in Thailand.

"It is! My friend actually painted it herself and gave it to me. She's very talented. Now, do you know why the headmaster asked me to see you, Zoe?"

"Yes," Zoe said. "He wants you to unblock my memories and make sure I have no hidden programming. He wants to learn all he can about the Rogues and ensure that I am not a danger to anyone here."

"And how do you feel about that?"

"Scared. Anxious. But eager. I want to know who I am."

"It is normal to be scared. I can hardly imagine what you must have gone through, and what you are still going through. You must be a very strong young woman, and that inner strength will serve you well during our sessions together. I will not lie to you, Zoe. This is not an easy process what we are about to undertake, you and I. Memory retrieval is very delicate, and if it does turn out to be a deliberate block and not just the result of a natural injury, it will be much more difficult. But I am confident that I can help you. Do you have any questions before we begin?"

"Lots," Zoe said. "You call yourself a psychologist. Do you use that term in the same way that Typicals do? Did you study in their schools?"

Dr. Sharapova smiled. "A good question. I always wanted to be a doctor of the mind and I wanted to learn what the Typicals had to offer first, so I went to medical school and then became a psychiatrist." She pointed to a degree from Harvard hanging on the wall. "After that, I became a clinical psychologist." She pointed to a degree from Oxford. "It's somewhat unheard of to be both but we are long-lived, so it was always part of my plan. Afterward, my studies began in earnest as I apprenticed under one of our own. Illnesses are either physical or mental in nature. The brain is a physical organ, but it's incredibly complex. We don't understand how most mental illnesses manifest themselves in the brain, so we treat them with psychotherapy or drugs or both. Our Abilities, though, give us a third, incredibly powerful tool—we can peer directly into a patient's mind. We can follow neural pathways to locate and repair damaged areas. We can rewire pathways formed due to trauma. We can fix the source of chemical imbalances. We can cure many mental illnesses that would otherwise be difficult to treat. There is a limit to what we can do, so psychotherapy is still useful, but even then, our ability to actually see a patient's memories greatly facilitates that."

"Why does a school need a psychologist? Is that normal?"

"For Typicals, no, although they do have guidance counsellors. But for our kind . . . Telepaths have unique stresses . . . and dangers. You've heard the saying that power corrupts? Well, it's true. And Telepaths are very powerful. It is my job to ensure that this does not happen to our students as their Abilities develop."

"I see," Zoe said. This seemed to be a theme here, the idea of making sure that the kids didn't feel superior to Typicals. She focused back on the present. "Is what we're going to do here dangerous in any way?"

Natasha shook her head. "Not really. This is fundamentally brain surgery, of course, and so should not be taken lightly and should never be attempted by anyone other than a highly trained Telepath. But I have been doing this for decades now and I am very good at it. You are in good hands with me." She smiled. "Any other questions?"

"How long will it take?"

"That all depends on the nature of your block. But if you would like to begin right now, I should be able to give you a better answer at the end of this session. Do you feel you are ready?"

"One last question. Are you going to tell the headmaster or anyone else what happens during our sessions? Tell them what you learn about me?"

"Ah," Natasha said. "Yes, we must discuss this for certain. In the world of Typicals, there exists the practice of client confidentiality, whereby the mental health professional protects the privacy of their patient by not revealing anything about their therapy to anyone. We abide by this same rule. The only real exceptions to the rule are when there is suspicion that a child is being abused or when a patient is a threat to themselves or to others. The headmaster wants to be assured that the students and staff here are safe, both from you and from these so-called Rogues that have been pursuing you. So, while I do not need to tell him everything that we learn together, I *do* need to tell him about anything relating specifically to his concerns. Are you all right with this arrangement?"

Zoe nodded.

"Then let us begin. Please, lie down on the couch. It may seem cliché, but I don't want you falling out of your chair should you experience any disorientation while I am inside your mind."

Zoe lay down. The couch was as comfy as it looked. Natasha pulled her chair over next to her.

"What I want you to do is just lie still, close your eyes, and relax as much as possible. You have the advantage of being very young, so your Abilities have only just started to manifest themselves. You may not even notice me inside your mind at all, which would be best. If you do notice me, however, you will have the instinct to push me out of your mind, and you must resist this instinct as it makes my job much harder. Do you understand?"

Zoe nodded.

"Good. Now, take a few moments to relax before we begin."

Zoe was scared. She had no idea what would come of this. Might it be possible that in just a few minutes, her entire life would come flooding back to her? She would know who she was and where she was from? She concentrated on her breathing and within a minute entered the meditative state she had been practicing. Soon she felt the doctor's hands on her head.

"I need you to drop your shield, Zoe. Can you do that for me?"

"My shield?"

"I cannot help you if you are shielded. I am actually surprised you *can* shield yourself at your age. But you must trust me and lower it so that I can get inside."

Zoe didn't remember raising her shield, but Natasha was right—there it was and as strong as ever. She willed it to drop and for a moment it seemed like it might not obey, as though someone else were controlling it. A moment later, though, she felt it dissipate.

"There we go, much better. Now, Zoe, I am going to gently enter your mind. Remember, if you notice me, don't fight me. I am here to help. Are you ready?"

She took a deep breath. "Yes," she said.

"Then let us begin."

Zoe spasmed and gripped the couch tightly with both hands.

You felt that, I assume.

Yes. It was a horribly invasive feeling to have another person in your mind. She couldn't actually remember what it had felt like when Ethan did it to her—she had only been aware that he had done so. She imagined it as a battle, in which she'd fought with all her strength. This was much more insidious. It was like being instructed to breathe water, against every instinct in your body. To intentionally drown and pretend it was normal.

I am sorry, I had hoped you would not notice my presence at all. I know it is a very strange sensation. But you controlled yourself and resisted the urge to throw me out. You are doing well. Try to relax now while I do some exploring.

Zoe forced her hands to relax their grip on the couch. She could feel the doctor probing, gently pushing here, slowly sliding there, still on the outskirts of her—what? Her consciousness? The sensations were all so strange and so new, she knew she wouldn't be able to properly describe them if asked later. This went on for several minutes before the doctor spoke again.

All right, Zoe, I'm going to need your help now. I want you to think, in as much detail as you can, of the moment you entered this room and saw me.

The memory came forth immediately, but Zoe could *feel* that she was not the only observer this time. She felt the fuzzy presence that she knew was Natasha move within her mind, closer to where the memory had originated.

Good. That was easy, wasn't it? Now, I want you to remember when you first met Professor Chao.

The Toronto Reference Library. She had just thrown a pencil into the ceiling and suddenly there he was beside her, looking so cross. *What do you think you are doing?* he had said.

She felt another sliding in her mind. Maybe the doctor was zeroing in on the location of her memories?

Dr. Sharapova chuckled. *You did that? You tried to use compulsion on Professor Chao? I can't imagine he liked that. Let's go back further now.*

They told me what happened to you in the alley, when Ethan entered your mind.

She was lying flat on her back, Ethan on top of her, clutching her face. *Forget. Forget about the pendant. You never found it. You never found anything.* Shock. Betrayal. Zoe grabbed him by the shoulders, tried to push him off.

It's me, Zoe! It's Natasha. This is just a memory. He can't hurt you.

Zoe forced herself to relax again and took her hands off the doctor.

That was nasty. He was reckless, using brute force to overpower you. No precision at all. He could have seriously hurt you. Luckily there wasn't too much damage. I should be able to . . . wait . . . there was damage. He made you forget . . . but you repaired part of the damage yourself moments later and then remembered. Partly, at least. Incredible. You should not have been able to do that.

You shouldn't have been able to remember, Ethan had said, eyes wide.

However, you didn't repair it entirely or retrieve the whole memory. Let me see what I can do. This will not hurt, Zoe, though it may feel a bit strange.

Zoe felt pressure. Focused and refined, though. *What are you doing, Doctor?*

I am rewiring the synapses that were damaged when that beastly boy blocked your memories of those few minutes in the alley. As messy as his handiwork was, I am astounded that he was able to do it at all. He didn't look any older than you, Zoe. I also have to fix your own repairs. As unprecedented as they were, they were still sloppy. No offence intended.

The feeling of pressure and manipulation continued for several more minutes. *Bear with me, Zoe. This is delicate. I've had to put my own block on the entire memory section to prevent you from remembering the events while I am doing the repairs, otherwise it would be like trying to repair a heart while it's still beating.*

What memories? Zoe asked. She didn't know what Natasha was talking about.

Exactly. You don't know what I'm talking about. You will in a moment, though.

She felt a snap. Jumping up the wall, grabbing the pouch. A silver pendant inside. Look here. Look at this. He was on top of her. *Forget. Forget about the pendant. You never found it. You never found anything.* Fighting him with all her strength. Too strong, though. Feeling him winning. Her memories slipping away . . . but not anymore. Now, it was fully intact. Clearer than before. In fact . . . there was more than before.

Listen to me closely, Zoe. It was Ethan's voice. *You're probably lying on a couch in an office while some doctor is trying to repair your memories. They're probably in your head right now, but don't worry, they can't hear this—I've placed this message within a memory bubble in another part of your mind, loosely linked via a random neural pathway from the synapses the doctor just repaired. That pathway is unnatural and will evaporate soon, leaving only this copy. The doctor will only see it if you deliberately access your memories of this moment later while they're in your mind. So, don't do that, okay? Here's what I have to say: Do NOT let them access your blocked memories from before the night you were attacked in the alley. Not under any circumstances. This is important, Zoe. I don't know why you lost your memories, but I have a theory—and if I'm right, your life is at stake. Who you are now might literally cease to exist. You cannot let them do it. A pause. I love you, Zoe. Be careful.*

Zoe? Are you all right? Does that feel better?

Holy crap! *What did you say, Doctor?* Holy crap!

I said, does that feel better? I have repaired the damaged area. It should be almost as good as new.

What was that all about? You might cease to exist? I love you? What was she supposed to do now?

It—it feels great. Thank you. I can remember it better now.

Excellent. Now, I want you to remember when you woke up in the hospital.

Again, the memories came unbidden. Hearing the whispers in her head. Jumping out of bed to discover where she was. Another shift in her mind. Each shift felt like a dull scalpel slowly twisting, sliding deeper. She needed time to think. What should she do? She wanted to remember, but he said she shouldn't. But why not? Why should she trust him when he'd erased her memory? But then he took on the Rogues so she could escape. Whose side was he on? He *loved* her?

Good. Now, go to a few moments later, when you first saw the Rogues.

Four figures in long coats were walking down the hall toward her. Okay, good, she was going forward, not backwards. That was okay. That was safe.

I see them, Zoe. Were they the ones who chased you into the alley that night?

Uh-oh.

I see it. I see the block. Hold on.

Pressure in her head again as the doctor worked her magic. Then, she was running through crowded streets. Young people were whooping and hollering. Fireworks were exploding behind her. Then—

Another one. Just a minute.

More pressure. Darting down the alley, pulling the cloth bag from her pocket, stuffing the brooch into it. One giant leap straight up, crouching on the window ledge while she fastened the pouch to the hook. Then jumping down and turning around to face—

More blocks, they are everywhere. I am afraid this does not look natural, Zoe. Although I think it was supposed to appear natural. Still, we are making good progress. What happened then? Try to remember what happened next.

She couldn't remember. Good, she needed time to think this through.

Got it.

Two figures advanced on her. Fasil and Ivan. "You little brat," Fasil said. "Why'd you run? You know what has to happen here."

Zoe looked back. Anders and Tsuji approached from the other end of the alley. She lowered her head in resignation, then looked up. "Just do it," she said. "I'm done running from you." They surrounded her.

"I'm so glad you feel that way," said Fasil, smiling. "Because we're done chasing you." He stepped forward to slap her but missed as she spun and dropped and swept his legs out from under him. Something—a boot maybe—hit her hard in the back of her head as she dove forward overtop of Fasil and punched the massive Ivan in the only place a man of that size was vulnerable. He dropped to his knees but so did she, already seeing stars. Someone grabbed her from behind and picked her up. She lunged to the left and ran up the wall with her feet, then pushed off, flipping backwards over Anders's head. He lost his grip and she hit him hard on either side of his neck with the blades of her hands. Her strikes were *hard*. She channelled all her power into them.

Then she took a blow to the backs of her knees and went down. Someone grabbed her by the hair and twisted her around. Tsuji. The woman punched her in the face. Again and again. Then Fasil kicked her in the ribs and sent her sprawling. They were all around her now, all of them kicking her. Every time she tried to get up, another boot would shove her down. She screamed in frustration, her anger boiling over. Finally, the kicking stopped.

Fasil panted above her. He sounded miles away. "So, the great prodigy isn't so strong after all, is she?"

She slowly got to her hands and knees. Blood streamed from her face into a dirty puddle beneath her. She clenched her fists, gritted her teeth. "I never said I was strong," she spat. She gathered all her strength, everything she had. Pulled it all in, like a coiled spring ready to explode. "Just stronger than you!"

She threw her hands up as she released psychokinetic force in all directions. It was like an explosion, slamming her surprised assailants into the brick walls of the narrow alley. They slid to the ground, unmoving. Zoe collapsed. She had nothing left in her. She couldn't move. She could barely breathe. She lay there for several minutes, hearing the cheers of the Canada Day partygoers in the streets, the boom of fireworks in the air. Then, the sound of someone's footsteps approaching. She couldn't turn her head but sensed him crouching over her, wordlessly examining the scene. "It's time," he whispered in her ear. Then, she sensed him stand. Heard a familiar metallic click. Felt something hard hit the back of her head.

Then nothing.

Zoe? Are you there? Come back to me. Zoe?

She opened her eyes. Dr. Sharapova looked down at her in concern. Zoe sat up and touched the back of her head where she had been hit. Nothing.

"What happened?"

"You reexperienced an intense, traumatic memory. When you remembered being hit that final time and then losing consciousness, you blacked out for real. You have been unconscious for several minutes."

Zoe felt groggy. "So . . . I remember that night in the alley now. But I don't remember anyone erasing my memories. Was it caused by that final blow to my head after all? Can you fix it?"

Natasha sat back and furrowed her brow. "I am not certain, Zoe. For a while, I suspected your memories were blocked intentionally, but they might not have been. As you saw, you were hit very hard in the head. That could have resulted in memory loss, but complete memory loss is very uncommon. It is still possible that whoever hit you blocked your memories after rendering you unconscious. A clever way to disguise his actions." She paused. "You do not remember anything before you were chased into that alley?"

Zoe shook her head.

"Strange," she mused, "that you can now remember the moments before your injury but still nothing before that."

"So, what now?" Zoe asked. "Where do we go from here?"

"That is definitely enough for one day. It is possible that your memories from before that night will begin to return to you now that some of your neural pathways have been repaired. That would be preferable to my manual intervention. I would like to give your brain some time to heal and see if your memories return on their own. Let's see each other again in a week. Would that be all right?

"Sure," Zoe said with mixed feelings. A week seemed so far away, and she wanted so much to retrieve her memories. Yet she needed to think about Ethan's message.

"Zoe, I will have to tell the headmaster about what we learned here. It is information about you and the Rogues. I hope you understand."

Zoe nodded. "I do. It's all right." She stood up. "Can I go now?"

"Of course." Natasha stood as well. "Unless you want to talk more about what we learned here today."

Zoe shook her head. "Maybe next time. I feel tired. I just want to nap."

"This was an excellent first session, Zoe. Wonderful, in fact. We retrieved some of your lost memories already. I feel confident that we will be able to retrieve them all in time."

She shook Zoe's hand. "See you a week from today. Same time. If you feel the need to talk about anything before that, though, my door is always open."

Zoe nodded, said goodbye, and shuffled off to her dorm. She slid into bed and closed her eyes.

10
DREAMS

"Very good, Zoe. Now, can you lift both blocks at the same time?"

Zoe scrunched up her face and concentrated as hard as she could. The other boys and girls in her kindergarten class sat cross-legged on the carpet around her, trying to make their wooden toy blocks rise. Their blocks hovered only a little bit in the air, and they were all wobbly. Zoe could make her block rise all the way to the ceiling if she wanted and it stayed really steady. But whenever she tried to move two blocks at the same time, they both got *really* wobbly and then one would start to fall and when she tried to make it stop then the other one would fall. She wanted Miss Jenkins to be proud of her, though, so she tried with all her might.

"Concentrate, Zoe. You can do it. The trick is not to focus on one block at a time but on both of them at the *same* time. It's like when people learn to play the piano. They have to play a different rhythm with each hand, and it can feel very confusing and difficult at first, but it gets easier the more you practice. If you practice very hard, then someday, years from now, you'll be able to manipulate many blocks all at once."

Zoe's blocks kept alternating, though. It was frustrating and she was starting to get angry that the blocks wouldn't do what she wanted. She didn't want to wait until she was a big kid. She wanted to do it *now*.

"Another trick is to remain calm, Zoe," Miss Jenkins said in a soothing voice. "I know it can be frustrating, but it takes a long time to learn to levitate two blocks at once. You are doing extremely well for a five-year-old, so don't worry."

"No, I can do it," Zoe insisted. "Really, I can."

Miss Jenkins smiled and patted her shoulder. "Patience, Zoe. Just do your best." She moved on to assist one of the other children.

Zoe kept trying. She knew she was supposed to stay calm, but it was so frustrating! Suddenly, something whacked her in the back of the head and both her blocks fell to the ground. She whirled around to see Ethan smiling innocently, his block hanging in the air behind her head. She saw red. Wrestling the block out of his mental grasp, she sent it flying at him and it whacked him on the forehead.

"Ow!" he yelped. Scrunching up his eyes, he sent another kid's block flying at her and then another and another. Zoe held up her arms to protect her face. The blocks kept hitting her and they *hurt*.

"Ethan!" Miss Jenkins yelled. "Stop that!"

Zoe lost it. With venomous rage, she opened her arms wide and lifted every block in the classroom. She sent them all whirling in a circle, gaining speed while children shrieked and Ethan watched slack-jawed, and then she hurled them at him, all at once, from every angle. She picked them up again and sent them flying again and again, a hurricane with a cowering, bloodied little boy in the centre.

"Zoe, stop it! Stop it!" Miss Jenkins was crouched in front of her shaking her shoulders. Zoe blinked, her fury suddenly gone. All of the blocks paused midair, hovered a moment, then dropped to the floor. Silence followed, broken only by Zoe's panting and Ethan's wails.

Miss Jenkins stared at Zoe. But she didn't look proud. She looked scared.

Standing in the corner, a man dressed all in black began to clap.

. . .

Zoe bolted upright. She was in bed in her dorm room, and it looked like a hurricane had just blown through. Lin's stuff was scattered everywhere. She remembered the blocks. Had she done this while she dreamed? She got to her feet and hurriedly began to tidy up. Some of the items were broken—she would have some explaining to do. That dream must have been a real memory. She was certain of it.

"What the—?"

Zoe froze, but it was only Lin standing in the doorway. She breathed a sigh of relief. "Help me? Please?"

Lin nodded and wordlessly joined her in the cleanup. When they finished, Lin said, "I came to find you for dinner. Hungry?"

Together they walked to the Great Hall. Zoe was quiet all throughout dinner, thinking about her dream and sorting through its implications. It had to be real. That boy looked just like a young Ethan. And there were more kids, a whole classroom full of them, just like her.

Not exactly like her, though. She remembered the look in her teacher's eyes. Little kids weren't supposed to be able to do what she had done. Those other kids couldn't, not at five years old anyway. Maybe adults couldn't either. Why was she so powerful? Maybe she was just an early bloomer. Maybe those other kids grew up to be just as strong. But more importantly: How were those children, who were so young, able to use their powers at *all*? And why were there so many of them? They were all the same age, so it might have been just a single class among many. There could be other classrooms with older kids or maybe even younger kids. Professor Chao had said that Academy scouts scoured the world for children with their Abilities. How could they have missed so many kids? Unless they just never bothered looking at children that young. Could there be children being born, for at least the past fifteen years or so, whose powers manifested earlier than in previous generations?

Finally, who had that clapping man been? She couldn't picture his face clearly, but he felt chillingly familiar. Was he clapping because she had displayed such strength and control? Or because she had exhibited such anger and violence? More questions than answers, but at least she had some answers now. A single memory of her childhood. She clung to it, like she never wanted to let go.

Lin, to her credit, ate in silence, clearly desperate to know what was up, but showing great restraint and respect. Zoe had already decided to tell her about everything, though. No matter what she learned of her past, she would share it with her friend, so when they both finished eating, Zoe said, "Let's go down to the lake and talk."

■ ■ ■

"So, Ethan *loves* you?" Lin said with wide eyes after Zoe had related everything about her therapy session and dream. "What the heck does that mean?"

Zoe shrugged and skipped another stone across the lake. "That he loves me, I guess."

"Yeah, but I thought he was your arch enemy or something. He stole your brooch, attacked you, and erased your memory, for crying out loud."

"He also fought off the Rogues so I could escape."

"You don't know that," Lin said. "You don't know what happened after you ran. It could have all been an act to gain your trust."

Zoe nodded. "I know."

"And telling you that he loves you? He could be trying to confuse you—to try to get you to believe that he has your best interest at heart when he says you shouldn't try to get your memories back."

"I don't know what to think about any of it, Lin. I don't know if he's my friend or my enemy, but I can't shake the feeling. . . . He just *feels* like he's my friend, despite everything he did. Anyway, right now, I'm more concerned about the dream. I think we should talk to your parents."

. . .

That night, they visited Lin's parents in their chambers. A familiar face was getting up to leave just as they entered.

"Gabriel!" Zoe exclaimed. "We met at the safe house."

"I'd not soon forget it," he said, smiling and shaking her hand. "You caused quite the kerfuffle, as I recall."

Zoe looked sheepish. "What are you doing here? Do you work at the Academy?"

He shook his head. "No, I just come and go from time to time. Keeping this one's dad aware of the goings on out in the world," he said, nodding to Lin. "And how are you, Lin? Busy keeping this troublemaker safe, I'll bet?"

Wait, troublemaker? She wasn't a troublemaker!

"You have no idea." Lin shook her head.

Wait, what? Zoe looked from Lin to Gabriel and back.

"Thank you for coming, Gabriel," Professor Chao said, shaking his hand warmly.

Professor Yeoh gave him a hug. "Be careful out there," she said.

"Always," Gabriel said. "We'll speak soon, Professors. Lin, Zoe, it was good seeing you both."

After Gabriel left, Professors Chao and Yeoh sat quietly throughout Zoe's tale, interrupting only occasionally with questions. They exchanged looks when Zoe told them about what she had done with the dozens of blocks. They mostly asked about Miss Jenkins and the man in black. What did they look like; how old did they appear; what clothes were they wearing; were they wearing jewellery; did they have any tattoos or birthmarks; did they have an accent?

"Do you know them?" Zoe asked, after she'd told them all she knew.

They both shook their heads. "I do not know a Miss Jenkins," Professor Chao said, "but it will not take long to search for her. If she is or was one of us, however, Jenkins may not be her real name."

"What does it all mean?" she pleaded, looking from one to the other. "An entire kindergarten full of Telepaths. How is that possible? Have children ever been able to use their powers at that age?"

"No," Professor Yeoh said. "Not ever. It simply does not happen."

"Do you think it was just a dream, then?" Zoe asked.

They exchanged looks once again, then said in unison, "No."

Zoe waited for more but neither elaborated.

"That's it?" Lin urged. "That's all you have to say? Mom, Dad, this is *huge*. We are all in serious danger here."

"I am aware of the implications, Lin," Professor Chao said.

"So am I," Zoe said, quietly. "If our Abilities were hereditary, then I could imagine a secret community of Telepaths forming without your knowledge, but since they're *not* hereditary, there are only a few scenarios I can think of to explain it. One is that someone has learned a way to find Telepaths before their powers manifest. They're finding a generation of Telepaths before you can. And knowing that these children are Telepaths, they're able to train them at a much earlier age."

Professor Yeoh nodded. "Yes, this is a possibility."

"But it's not likely, is it?" Zoe said. "It would mean that they have hundreds of scouts just like you, recruiting children right under your noses without anyone noticing."

The professors were silent. Zoe went on. "Another possibility is that humans are undergoing a sudden evolutionary change. There's a new breed of Telepaths, whose powers manifest at a much younger age, and the Rogues' scouts are finding them all while your scouts are missing them, presumably because they are not looking at children that young. That this could be going on for so many years, though, without anyone noticing, seems equally unlikely. Which leaves the third possibility—the only other one I can think of."

All eyes were on her. "These Telepaths—myself included—weren't found. We were *made*," she said. "Professors, do we know what makes a Telepath a Telepath? Do we know which genes are responsible for our Abilities?"

...

You really think you're genetically engineered? Lin whispered in her mind. They lay in their beds, talking using the mindlink Zoe had taught her. Lin had picked it up pretty quickly, though she still couldn't make a shield, so it wasn't a secure link. Still, it was better than talking out loud. Zoe shrugged in the dark.

It makes sense, doesn't it? You heard what your parents said. They've been researching this for decades now. Trying to figure out what makes us tick. Maybe someone succeeded.

And started creating an army of Telepaths?

Maybe worse. I'm not . . . normal, Lin. I have trouble using my Abilities unless I'm angry, but when I do use them, they're freakishly strong. And I've had them since I was a little kid—that's not normal, either. If there was an entire classroom of kids who all developed their Abilities as young as I did, then it stands to reason that they might all be as strong as I am. What if it's not one single gene but a bunch of them that give us our Abilities, and most Telepaths only have some of the genes? If you could create a baby with all of those genes, maybe you'd have a Super-Telepath whose Abilities develop far sooner than normal.

Or maybe it was just a dream, Zoe! You want it to be real because you desperately want your memories back.

Wouldn't you? Besides, your parents don't think it was a dream and neither do you. What I'm wondering is: Who's behind it? Typicals or Telepaths?

What do you mean? Lin said. *It can't be Typicals. Those were adult Telepaths chasing you.*

If you actually know which genes give Telepaths their Abilities, then you could do two different things. The first would be to create babies that have those Telepathic genes. The second would be to use gene therapy to give those genes to Typicals and hope they develop Telepathic Abilities.

No way. You're serious? How do you know this stuff?

Zoe shrugged again. *I read a lot. I'd expect Typicals-turned-Telepaths wouldn't be as strong as genetically engineered babies, though. Injecting Telepathic genes into someone, even on a regular basis, isn't the same as putting those genes into an embryo where the genes would get into every single cell.*

If you're right, Zoe, then it doesn't seem likely that either Typicals or augmented Typicals could hope to control an army of genetically engineered Super-Telepaths. You'd need a Telepath who was naturally super strong. Or maybe you could use gene therapy, like you said, but on a regular Telepath to give them whatever genes they were missing and turn them into a Super-Telepath.

Yeah, Zoe said. *I guess so.*

Or it's possible, Lin said, *that their leader is just a regular Telepath who is in for a big surprise one day when his creations decide they don't want to follow orders anymore.*

They were quiet for a while. Then, Lin said, *Zoe, there's another possibility. Maybe you're right about them creating genetically engineered Telepaths. But maybe they're not any more super than naturally born Telepaths. Maybe it's just you that's special.*

Why would I be special?

I don't know. But special people are just born sometimes. Geniuses like Einstein. Musicians like Mozart. Maybe you're just special like them.

Zoe thought about it. *I guess,* she said, yawning. *I sure hope they're no more powerful than the rest of us. Otherwise, we're all in trouble.*

11

BREAKTHROUGHS

Zoe had trouble paying attention in class in the days that followed. Every night, she hoped for similar dreams but nothing else had come so far. She was both excited about her next session with Dr. Sharapova and also increasingly worried. Ethan had warned her to not allow any doctor to retrieve her memories from before the night she was attacked in the alley. But how could she possibly go along with that? First, she had no reason to trust him. Second, she could hardly live the rest of her life without trying to discover her past. And third, she was unable to think of any scenario in which retrieving her memories would be bad for the Academy. She could, however, think of many reasons it could be bad for her personally—such as being exposed as an evil assassin on a secret mission. But if that was the case, she *wanted* to be found out before she could harm anyone.

If she was honest with herself, she didn't know what to think about Ethan. He had demonstrated that he wasn't to be trusted, and yet she *felt* like she could trust him. Was it because they'd been friends before and some part of her mind still felt that connection? Or was it just because he happened to be cute? Regardless, she wasn't going to blindly obey him just because he had a nice smile. What really troubled her, though, was what he had said about her ceasing to exist. It was one thing to want her memories back, or to keep the school safe—but to literally cease to exist? Could that even happen?

Her concerns came to a head during her next weekly therapy session. After initial pleasantries, Dr. Sharapova said, "I heard you had a dream. Can you tell me about it?"

Zoe nodded. She had assumed that Lin's parents would inform the headmaster or Dr. Sharapova directly about her dream. She recounted it in detail while the doctor listened and took notes.

"My goodness," she said, finally.

"You think it was real?" Zoe asked.

"Oh, almost certainly. Especially considering it came right after we restored some of your memories. I thought more memories might start to surface, and to have them return as dreams is not unheard of."

"But how do you explain children that young having their Abilities already?"

"That," Sharapova said, "is something I cannot explain. But hopefully as we return more of your memories, the answers will reveal themselves. This memory is good for us, because it now gives us a jumping-off point for this session, which is years before you lost your memory. This could be the key to restoring all of your memories. I'll get you to go back to this memory, and I will see if we can find any loosely connected memories that I can restore. Hopefully, we can start a cascade effect and you will remember everything." She smiled. "Are you ready to begin?"

Zoe balked. "Actually, Doctor, there's something I need to ask you first. Is there any chance that by returning my old memories, all of my new memories might disappear? That who I am now might, in effect, cease to exist?"

Dr. Sharapova seemed taken aback. She opened her mouth to speak, then stopped. Then started again and stopped, as if unsure how to respond. Finally, she said, "If your memory loss was natural, then there is no way that could happen. You would lose no memories by recovering your old ones. If your memory loss was not natural, your memories would probably have been blocked in the same way they would have naturally, via a blow to the head, which would mean that again, you would be in no danger of losing your new memories."

Zoe cut in. "The headmaster said that a skilled practitioner of mental manipulation could suppress an entire *identity* until it emerged again in response to a trigger. If that was done to me, would my current identity remain?"

Dr. Sharapova hesitated again. "It probably would. It would be entwined with your former identity, of course, but your new memories would most likely remain intact."

"You keep saying 'probably' and 'most likely,'" Zoe said. "Is there something you're not telling me? Is there any scenario in which I could essentially cease to exist?"

Dr. Sharapova seemed to struggle with herself as she formulated her reply. "I do not think this is at all likely, Zoe . . . but yes, the headmaster is correct in that it is *theoretically* possible. I have never heard of this being done, but if a mind were intentionally . . . fractured . . . segmented into two, so that old memories were moved to one section and made inaccessible, and new memories were stored in the other section, then . . . yes, when the old section became accessible again, it might be possible to render the new section inaccessible. But I can assure you, Zoe, this is highly unlikely. It would be extremely unethical to do something like this, so it's something that would never be taught to anyone. Someone would have to be incredibly skilled to pull something like this off."

"Could you do it?" Zoe said.

Dr. Sharapova stared at her helplessly. Finally, she said, "Maybe? I don't know. I would never dream of doing something so horrible. And there aren't many other Telepaths in the world who *could* do it. Unless we have a good reason to believe this has been done to you, Zoe, I honestly don't think it's something you need to worry about. Is there anything you're not telling me? Do you have some reason to suspect this is a danger?"

Now it was Zoe's turn to pause. Should she reveal what Ethan had told her? She had only told Lin so far, but if she told Sharapova, she would tell the headmaster, and who knew what would happen? But if there was a chance that she was a bad person here for nefarious purposes, shouldn't she tell them?

"There was a memory bubble," she said. "During our last session, you triggered a message from Ethan. He called it a memory bubble that would dissipate, leaving no trace. He said that he didn't know why I had amnesia, but that he had a theory, and he was worried that by allowing anyone to restore my memories, I might 'cease to exist.' Those were his exact words."

She stood up. "I'm sorry, Doctor. I can't do this. I want to remember my past, even if I won't like who I used to be, and I don't want to be a danger to anyone here—but if there's even a slight chance that Ethan is telling the truth and that he's right, that I might just . . . disappear . . . that terrifies me. That's the same as dying, as far as I'm concerned. I don't know if I can trust him, but I have to take his warning seriously. I'm sorry, but I just can't do this."

She left Dr. Sharapova sitting there, looking dumbfounded.

■ ■ ■

What would happen now? The headmaster would soon find out, and then what? She'd been permitted to attend the Academy on the condition that she undergo these therapy sessions to restore her memories. Would they let her stay now that she had refused?

While she awaited the consequences, there was school to deal with, and it was getting more complicated. Liam Murphy and Helen

Hawkesbury were dating and had been busy solidifying their leadership status among the first-years. They had been making life miserable for anyone who either didn't want to follow them or who just didn't fit in. Their Abilities were pretty strong already and they made sure everyone knew it. Using powers on fellow students was forbidden, and when one girl named Jessica made the mistake of informing the teachers, Helen quickly proved that she was perfectly capable of punishing Jessica without the use of any Abilities. Not only had the poor girl suddenly found herself ostracized, but Helen and her minions spread mean-spirited rumours about her. At first, Zoe was happy enough that Helen and Liam had chosen to leave her and Lin alone, though she doubted she would be able to sit by and watch while they bullied someone else in front of her. After awhile, though, she began to suspect that they'd realized this, too, and were purposefully doing their bullying when she wasn't around.

It was Liam who actually concerned Zoe the most. It wasn't because his powers were strong, or because he was big for his age, or because he seemed to be a pretty tough street fighter—as he'd been quick to demonstrate on more than a few unfortunate first-years. It was because he was vicious. Sadistic, even. He did things that others wouldn't even think of, let alone dare. Zoe began to regret letting him save face that first day. If she had instead humiliated him in front of everyone, maybe she could have prevented his reign of terror.

The last straw was when she heard what he did to Pacha. She had thought Pacha was safe after demonstrating himself to be the strongest telekinetic in their class. But he had woken up screaming during the night, convinced that thousands of spiders were crawling all over his body. He freaked out and had to be telepathically sedated and taken to the infirmary. Word around school was that Liam was responsible. When Zoe saw Liam and Helen and their gangs laughing over the incident at their breakfast table the next morning, she lost it. Her face turned red and she rose from her chair.

"Zoe, no!" Lin said. "Not like this!"

Part of her brain heard Lin and recognized she was right, that she needed to calm down and think of a way to punish Liam that wouldn't get her expelled. But she couldn't seem to stop herself. Pacha was . . . *good*. And innocent. He would never hurt anyone. The thought of him experiencing such terror because someone thought it would be funny made her furious. She wanted Liam to experience everything he had inflicted on Pacha so that he would know what it felt like. She wanted everyone to see him cry and beg her to make it stop. She was almost upon him when someone grabbed her hand. She looked back and saw that it was Pacha himself.

"No," he said, looking her in the eyes.

"Pacha . . ." she began, but he held up a hand and stepped in front of her to face Liam, who grinned.

"Hey there, Pacha," he sneered. "Heard you had a bad dream last night." Everyone at the table snickered.

Zoe's hands balled into fists, but Pacha calmly extended his arms out wide. Suddenly Liam's heavy wooden table rose to the ceiling. As Liam's eyes widened, another table rose to the ceiling. And another, and another, and another. His jaw dropped and he stared at Pacha in disbelief.

"Just because I choose not to fight," Pacha said, "doesn't mean I can't."

Slowly, the tables all drifted gently back to the ground. No one at Liam's table said a thing as Pacha turned and strode to the breakfast buffet as if nothing had just happened.

Zoe was astounded. First, she wasn't sure if she could have pulled off such a telekinetic feat no matter how angry she was. More importantly, though, without resorting to violence, Pacha had effectively put an end to Liam's bullying. When your victim demonstrates to everyone that the only reason he doesn't swat you like a bug is because he chooses not to, how can you continue to instill fear in others? Liam was finished, and so was Helen, because Pacha had just shown everyone what real strength and leadership looked like. Zoe stared after Pacha in admiration.

Then she saw the headmaster in the doorway, beckoning her. Oh no, that hadn't taken long. She followed him in silence to his office and sat while he closed the door.

"Professor Sharapova came to see me earlier," he said.

"Yes, sir. I figured she would."

"You should have told us about the memory bubble right away."

"I know, sir. I'm sorry. I got . . . scared."

"Hmm. Tell me what this boy said."

Zoe recounted his message, omitting nothing—except for three words. It just didn't seem right to tell everyone that he'd said he loved her.

"So, he didn't say that you are a spy or an assassin. He didn't say that your amnesia was deliberate. And he didn't say that you would actually cease to exist if you tried to restore your memories, only that he had a theory. A theory that Professor Sharapova says is highly unlikely. Does that sum it up?"

Zoe nodded. The headmaster sighed, closed his eyes, and rubbed his temple. "You have, once again, put me in a difficult position, Zoe."

"I'm sorry, sir. I don't mean to be difficult. I just . . ." She shrugged. "I just don't want to die."

The headmaster made a helpless gesture and sighed again. "Fine. I cannot, in good conscience, ask a student to put herself at risk. I will ask Professor Sharapova, however, to dedicate herself to researching the possibility of a mind being segmented and what to do should that turn out to be the case. Until we know more, we will put therapy sessions on hold. But let us know of any more memories or dreams or messages, agreed?"

"Yes, sir." Zoe nodded. "Agreed. And thank you, sir."

. . .

Pacha's display of calm telekinetic prowess inspired Zoe to focus. She knew her Abilities were strong. Scary strong. Yet it was becoming painfully obvious that she couldn't properly control them. She had to be angry to do anything but the simplest of tricks. She could *feel* the power there, waiting, but it refused to come out in anything more than a trickle. She did everything her teachers said. She tried all their calming, meditative techniques, but it always ended with her getting terribly frustrated and eventually she would fly into a rage—and then suddenly she was a powerhouse. Her teachers were, for the most part, patient. She was beginning to wonder, though, if she was ever going to get past this. Her professors all said that she might have a mental block as a result of many years of relying on anger to control her Abilities. She wondered if it was also possible, though, that her Abilities were being blocked in the same way as her memories.

It would be easy to just give up and give in to anger all the time, but Lin would literally get in her face and point her finger and order her to calm down and behave. And then Lin would threaten her with a punishment so comical that Zoe's anger would instantly evaporate as she burst into laughter, collected her composure, and tried once again to calmly perform the task at hand.

It was during Professor Martinov's telekinesis class that she had a breakthrough. She'd been up half the night reading through piles of library books about amnesia and dreams and compulsion and blocking memories. So, she found herself yawning and nodding off as she stared with droopy eyes at the hundred-gram stainless steel calibration weight on her desk. The other students' weights were all levitating, though wobbly, several centimeters above their desks. Her weight, though, had stubbornly been refusing to move for weeks, and she was too tired to put in any effort and to get mad at yet another failure. So, she was surprised when she slowly realized that the lead weight was hovering utterly motionless a foot above her desk. Upon realizing it, the weight instantly dropped to the desk with a loud thud.

She looked beside her where Lin had apparently been holding her breath, afraid to interrupt. "How long?" Zoe whispered.

"About ten seconds," Lin whispered back. "What happened? How'd you do it?"

"I wish I knew," Zoe mumbled, staring at the once again unmoving weight.

"Excellent control, Zoe," Professor Martinov said, coming up behind her. "It felt effortless, yes? Were you even aware you were doing it?"

Zoe shook her head. "No, Professor," she said, unable to stifle another yawn. "I don't know how I did it and now it won't move again."

"Aha! As I thought." He smiled, clearly pleased. "You were sleeping in my class, yes? Or almost sleeping."

"I'm sorry, Professor. I was up late last night. It won't happen again."

"Nonsense! Stay up late every night if this is the result. This was a breakthrough for you!"

Zoe blinked. "But I can't do it anymore," she said. "It's as still as ever."

"But you did it once, Zoe, and without getting angry. You did it using your subconscious mind. You have shown that you can remove your mental block not only by losing your temper but also via a state of deep relaxation. Now, all you must do is try to achieve a similar state of calm without actually being asleep."

He patted her on the head and moved on to another student. But try as she might, the weight would not move for her again that class.

■ ■ ■

Any hope she'd had that this minor breakthrough would lead to a major one withered and died over the next few days. She kept that stupid hundred-gram weight in her pocket at all times and tried to levitate it every chance she got. She tried everything to recreate the circumstances of her one-time success. She tried yawning. She tried dozing. She tried to pretend that she just didn't care about whether the weight moved or not. She tried reading late into the night again and trying in the morning. She tried not sleeping at all. Nothing worked.

"Maybe the problem is that you're still trying too hard," Lin said.

"If I try any less hard, I'll fall asleep!" Zoe retorted.

"Well then, that must be the problem. You're not trying quite hard enough."

"*What?* Which is it? Am I trying too hard or too little? It can't be both!"

"Exactly," Lin said.

"That doesn't even make sense!" Zoe sputtered.

Lin raised her hands in surrender. "Okay, okay. No need to get mad at me."

"I'm not mad!" Zoe yelled, throwing her hands up in the air.

Lin calmly waited a moment, then a moment longer. Then she said, "I think you're a *little* mad."

■ ■ ■

Zoe was in a particularly belligerent mood during that afternoon's combat class. Professor Chao was instructing them in the use of the *bokken*, the wooden sword, when Zoe suddenly interrupted without raising her hand.

"Professor?"

Professor Chao stopped mid-sentence and looked at her.

"Why are you teaching us this?"

He raised an eyebrow. "Perhaps you should be more specific, Zoe."

"The sword. Why are you teaching us to use swords? It's the twenty-first century. People don't use swords anymore. This is a waste of time."

If Professor Chao was irritated by her tone, he didn't show it.

"As I told you during our first class, all the empty-hand techniques in

Aikido have their basis in sword techniques. If you learn to use the sword, it becomes more obvious why the empty-hand techniques are the way—"

"No, Professor, that's not why you're teaching us the sword. Typicals who practice Aikido learn to use the bokken too, but they don't carry a sword around under their jacket and have swordfights in restaurants. So, what's the real reason?"

Now Professor Chao's brow furrowed. "Zoe . . ." he began.

"Typicals use guns! Not swords, guns! What's the *point* of all this? What good is your fancy swordsmanship going to do you if I pulled out a gun right now and shot you?"

Professor Chao's eyes narrowed dangerously. "Let's find out, shall we?" He walked slowly over to the wall and placed his hand on a locked metal cabinet that she had never seen opened before. She heard a click. Had he just unlocked it with his mind? It opened to reveal a single pistol. He took the pistol, popped a clip into it, and stood before Zoe. The rest of the class moved well away from them.

Zoe tensed. Had she gone too far? What was he doing?

He held out the gun, grip first. "Take it."

Zoe hesitated, then slowly reached out and took it.

"You are holding a Beretta 9mm semiautomatic handgun," he said, as he strode to a Kevlar wall panel and turned to face her, his bokken at his side. "I dislike guns, but I keep it locked in that safe for the sole purpose of this demonstration. I want you to point it at me."

Zoe's heart skipped a beat. "What?" she asked, dumbly.

"You wanted to know what good my sword would do against a gun, so now I am going to show you."

Zoe just stood still, too stunned to speak or move. What was he *doing*?

"Dad, no!" Lin cried. "Zoe, don't you dare!"

He raised his hand. "It's all right, Lin. Don't worry. Zoe, I want you to point the gun at me and then disengage the safety. It's on the left side.

Just push it down with your thumb."

The class was deathly quiet. Zoe could literally hear her heart pounding. The pistol trembled in her hand. "I don't want to, Professor. I'm sorry I was rude. It won't happen again."

Professor Chao nodded. "Apology accepted. Now, if you don't mind, please be so kind as to do as I asked."

Zoe stood still for what seemed an eternity, then slowly raised the Beretta. Her hand shook as she found the safety and disengaged it.

Professor Chao smiled. "Excellent. Now, shoot me, Zoe. It will be all right. I have given this demonstration to students many, many times. You will not hurt me, I promise."

Zoe licked her dry lips. "You promise?" she whispered.

"I promise."

Wincing, she slowly squeezed the trigger.

What happened next was difficult to say. One moment he was standing in front of her, the next she heard a loud noise and the gun jerked violently in her hand, and then he was standing slightly to the left, as if nothing at all had happened. A bullet lay on the floor where he had stood a moment earlier, blocked by the Kevlar wall panel.

"Excellent. Now, again."

Zoe swallowed and squeezed again.

Another loud bang and the professor stood slightly to the right this time, one step closer to Zoe, another bullet on the ground behind him.

"Again. This time, I want you to keep firing until you have no more bullets left."

Zoe took a deep breath and closed her eyes. Then, she opened them and started firing.

This time, she could see what happened. He didn't dodge quickly. He just calmly sidestepped the bullets as he slowly moved toward her. Each time she began pulling the trigger, he began his motion. It was as though he knew where the bullet would go, and he had all the time in the world to get out of its path. Finally, the gunshots turned to empty clicks and Professor Chao stood before her, his bokken against her neck. He held out his left hand, palm up, and she placed the pistol into it.

Professor Chao quietly removed the empty clip and returned the pistol to the metal gun cabinet—definitely locking it with his mind, Zoe observed—then sat in the middle of the mats and gestured for the class to do the same. Zoe sat. Nobody dared to speak. The whole thing felt surreal.

"I will tell you a story now," Professor Chao began. "When O'Sensei was a man of forty years, he and his companions were ambushed by mounted bandits while traveling through Mongolia. They were being fired upon. He was certain he was going to die, so he calmed his mind, and it was then that a strange thing happened—he began to see golden flashes of light streaking through the air just before each gun fired, and the bullets followed the path of those streaks. By avoiding the streaks of light, he was able to dodge the bullets and survive the attack.

"Word of Ueshiba's encounter in Mongolia spread over the years and eventually reached my ears. I had heard of Morihei Ueshiba's martial arts prowess before and been intrigued, as a lifelong practitioner of martial arts myself. When I heard the stories of how he dodged bullets and his assertion that bullets could not touch him, I was stunned. He clearly had to be a Telepath, so how could he have gone unnoticed all this time? I set out right away and soon presented myself at the doorstep to his dojo and asked to be his student.

"I immediately discerned that he was not, in fact, one of us. He was definitely a Typical. Yet he was anything but typical. For one, he clearly *could* sense the enemy's intent a split-second before they attacked. I had never before heard of this talent in a Typical. And he was truthful about his ability to dodge bullets. I witnessed this firsthand years later. A group of arms inspectors from the army came to the dojo to see a demonstration of this new martial art 'Aikido' that they had heard so much about. During conversation, O'Sensei casually mentioned that bullets could not touch him. These inspectors were all trained marksmen and they challenged him to prove his outlandish claim. On the arranged date, O'Sensei calmly walked out onto the shooting range and stood twenty-five metres away from six marksmen, who all leveled their pistols at him. I remember being extremely worried. I knew that I could dodge a bullet, but as much respect as I had for O'Sensei, he *was* still a Typical and there were *six* guns pointed at him."

Professor Chao paused. "What happened?" Lin asked.

"All six guns fired simultaneously, and we were enveloped in a cloud of smoke. Then, I saw one of the marksmen literally flying through the air and O'Sensei standing behind the men laughing."

Professor Chao chuckled. "I still remember the shock on everyone's faces. The marksmen had just witnessed something so utterly impossible that they refused to believe it and asked O'Sensei to do it again. He just shrugged and agreed, and again six guns fired and once again a man went flying through the air. They did not ask for a third demonstration.

"Later, though, a master hunter by the name of Sadajiro Sato came down from the mountains to challenge O'Sensei. This time, I was very worried, as this man was said to never miss. I watched nervously as O'Sensei sat in seiza at the far end of the dojo and Sato took aim. It was then that I saw a troubled look appear on O'Sensei's face, and I knew something was wrong. Just as Sato was about to pull the trigger, O'Sensei said, 'Wait! Your bullet will hit me. Your thoughts are clear and undistorted. You have no doubt that you will hit your target. I cannot avoid the gun of such a true master.'

"And so, Sato left the dojo and went back to his mountain, feeling quite pleased with himself. But I had only questions. I had witnessed O'Sensei's abilities firsthand, so I knew he could dodge bullets as well as I could. How was it that he could not see the golden streaks? Or if he did see them, why did he think he could not avoid them? Later, I was able to get O'Sensei alone and I questioned him. I remember his brow furrowed as he told me of his strange experience. He said it was not that he could see no golden streak but that he could see an infinite number of them. He knew with profound certainty that the bullet would hit him, no matter which way he moved.

"It was then I suspected that Sadajiro Sato was not what he seemed," Professor Chao continued. "He must have been a Telepath, who took advantage of O'Sensei's inability to shield his mind, so as to somehow interfere with his ability to see the streaks or make him hallucinate so as to see streaks everywhere. I had never heard of a Telepath named Sato before, so I went off in search of him. To my surprise, he turned out to be a Typical as well. I questioned him about what had happened with O'Sensei and about his excellent marksmanship in general, but all he would say was that he had always been able to somehow anticipate his prey's movement. From that description, I developed a theory as to what had happened.

"The golden streaks are a form of precognition, which you will learn to control in Professor Tilly's ESP class. Typicals do not usually possess precognitive abilities, but O'Sensei certainly did. Sadajiro Sato was known to be such a good shot with his rifle that he could hit the smallest target, no matter how quickly it moved, every single time. It is my belief that he possessed a precognitive ability of his own to see his prey's movement slightly before it happened. When two men with precognitive abilities faced each other, the result was that O'Sensei saw a golden streak and chose a direction to move so as to avoid it, which Sato saw and thus changed where he would fire, resulting in another golden streak that O'Sensei would avoid, resulting in a new direction of fire from Sato, and so on and so forth, like two mirrors facing each other, reflecting to infinity."

Professor Chao paused and looked around the class. "Nevertheless, the point of my demonstration today is that a gun is not a good weapon against a Telepath. Sato's precognitive ability to sense a person's movements is an ability never recorded in any Telepath. We can see the golden streak of a bullet because once it leaves the barrel of the gun, its trajectory is no longer under our control. I have tried many experiments over the years to bend the path of a bullet midflight, but a fired bullet is simply too fast to control. The best you can accomplish is to create a strong electromagnetic field in its path to cause it to bend, but that merely results in bent streaks of light, which are just as easy to avoid. The bow and arrow is almost the same story. It is slower than a bullet but still fast enough to be incredibly difficult to manipulate mid-flight, so the streaks of light will always give it away.

"The sword, though," he said, rising and picking up a bokken, "is another matter altogether. A sword is a weapon that you control right until the instant it strikes your enemy's flesh. Even if your enemy could see a golden arc telegraphing your strike and react to it, he would see that golden arc change as you then react to his reaction. On a metaphysical level, some believe this to be profound evidence that the future is not set but is rather controlled by our will. On a physical level, it means that two Telepaths dueling with swords are on equal footing, neither one able to predict the other.

"And that, Zoe," he said, leveling his gaze at her, "is why the sword is our weapon of choice and has been for thousands of years. Now, form a line, and let us continue with today's lesson."

"Professor?" Zoe said, unable to stop herself. "Does this mean you're training us to kill other Telepaths?"

Sorrow flickered across his face. "No. Never that. Our kind have always learned the ways of combat. In the past, our fighting styles have been much more brutal, as befitted the times, perhaps. I am old enough to have trained in these styles. But with Aikido, I am teaching you to defend yourselves against Typicals and Telepaths alike, inflicting only as much harm as needed, none if possible. Even a sword need not be lethal when striking with the blunt end. But make no mistake, where Telepaths are concerned, we have always been our own worst enemy."

· · ·

Zoe lay in bed that night reflecting on the day's events and turning her box brooch over and over in her hands. Professor Chao had given her an idea. He had opened his safe with his *mind*. She'd never been able to figure out how to open her brooch. There was simply no way to do so from the outside—but maybe there was a way to open it from the *inside*. It made total sense. If you're a Telepath, why have a combination lock that a Typical could open? A skilled-enough Telepath should be able to manipulate the tumblers from the inside, right? She focused on the brooch and tried to extend her consciousness to *feel* what was inside of it. She had never tried anything like this before and, at first, felt like she was stumbling in the dark. Gradually, though, she became aware of structures within the brooch. They were tumblers, she was sure of it! She started to apply pressure to one to make it move, when suddenly she stopped. What if it was rigged? What if any attempt to guess the combination resulted in the contents being destroyed somehow? It seemed far-fetched, but was it worth the risk? Since it would be impossible to guess the combination of any decent lock, she determined that no, it wasn't worth it. But without knowing the combination, what good was the brooch? She had clearly thought it was so important that she hid it in that alley for herself to find. Why would she do that unless—

And then it all clicked.

She knew what the brooch was for.

"Lin!" she cried, racing across the bedroom and shaking her friend awake. "Lin, wake up!"

Lin squinted. "What? What's going on?"

She dangled the brooch above her. "I think I know what the brooch is for."

"What?" Lin bolted upright and turned on her lamp, instantly awake. "For real?"

"For real."

"How'd you figure it out?"

"I made myself think like her. Like Zoe 1.0. If my amnesia is really due to getting conked on the head, then honestly, this could just be some worthless piece of sentimental jewellery that I didn't want to lose. But if my amnesia *wasn't* an accident, then I can only think of one purpose for this thing. If I were her, I'd want to know."

"Want to know what?" Lin asked, barely able to contain herself.

"Starting tomorrow, I'm going to teach you to make a really strong shield. We'll work on it every day. It's important. Now, listen carefully, because we can never, *ever* speak of this again, okay? Here's what I think the brooch is for—and if I'm right, here's what I need you to do when it's time."

■ ■ ■

The next morning, though, Zoe's excitement gave way to a somber mood. The other kids were still talking about Professor Chao's incredible bullet dodging demonstration, but all Zoe could think about was the future. Why were they learning to fight? What did adult Telepaths *do* in the real world? Whenever she asked teachers, she always got the same answer—anything they wanted, just like Typicals.

But we *aren't* Typicals, she wanted to scream. Years of training, learning to use our Abilities, learning to fight. Just so they wouldn't accidentally hurt anyone? So they wouldn't accidentally expose our kind to the world? To work in an office and never actually use anything they learned? Ridiculous! She refused to believe it. Plus, she knew that Professor Chao had people working for him out in the world. Gabriel, for instance, and that man in the van who'd scanned her for tracking devices. How many of them were there and what exactly did they do?

"What exactly are you suspicious of, Zoe?" Lin finally asked in exasperation one day between classes. "You think this is all a big conspiracy? That we're all being groomed to be soldiers and spies to control the world? I refuse to believe my parents are lying to me about this!"

"I never said they're lying," Zoe countered. "I just don't think they're telling us everything. Maybe we really are free to do whatever we want when we grow up. But we barely *age*, Lin. That must limit our options quite a bit. We can't become famous or people will notice. We can't even become well-known in our communities or people will notice."

"But you're making my point for me," Lin said. "We might be able to join the military, but we could never stay in it long enough to rise to a powerful position or people would notice that we're not aging. We can never become high-ranking politicians because everyone would be looking into our past, which we'd probably have to fabricate every few decades."

"Which means," said Zoe, "that if we want to make a difference in the world, we have to work in the shadows. Be in positions of influence but not of authority."

"So, what's wrong with that? You make it sound sinister to want to make a difference in the world."

"That depends. There's influence through ideas and then there's mind compulsion. My point is that we're powerful, Lin. And power corrupts people. Maybe we're not supposed to influence the minds of Typicals, but we can if we want to. And there are at least ten thousand of us in the world. Surely some of us do."

"It's against our laws, Zoe. We all know that."

"Even if it's good influence, for the betterment of the world? It's illegal to compel a warlord into thinking that slaughtering a whole village is wrong? Or to compel a dictator into relinquishing power? Or to compel world leaders into taking the climate crisis seriously?"

Lin had no answer.

"And who punishes Telepaths who break our laws? How do we even know when a Telepath is breaking them?"

They walked in silence the rest of the way. As they sat down in Professor Yeoh's healing class, Lin said, "What are you *really* afraid of, Zoe?"

Zoe bit her lip. That was the real question, wasn't it? If the world really worked as she suspected, was that so bad? The world was full of good Typicals and bad Typicals. It must be full of good Telepaths and bad Telepaths. Maybe they were free to choose their own path, but by necessity they would be steered in one particular direction that she didn't quite understand yet. But that didn't mean it was a bad direction. So, what was she really so worried about?

"I want us to be the good guys," she said, finally. "If the Rogues are the bad guys, then we have to be the good guys. Right?"

12

DISTRACTIONS

With no satisfactory answers to her questions, Zoe threw herself into her studies. The normal courses like math and English took no effort at all, so she focused on the others. Even though she still found herself blocked—a continual source of frustration—she was determined to at least learn the theory behind everything. That meant books. She devoured everything she could find. All the textbooks for first-years right through to fifth-years and then every advanced book she could find in the library.

Lin was ever the good friend and kept her company most of the time—after all, she was quite studious herself—but Zoe couldn't seem to shake her disquiet. No, it was more than that—it was a feeling of dread, of time running out. As though she had to learn as much as she could from this place before they decided to kick her out. Or before the Rogues came for her. Or before she "woke up" and her secret programming kicked in.

Unfortunately, she soon had to admit to what she already knew to be true: All the books in the world would not help her. When it came to Abilities, you could only learn by *doing*.

Fortunately, she soon found a new distraction, and one that perhaps both she and Lin could enjoy together. It was called Doom. And it was brutal. Brutally awesome. While the Academy had all of the Typical sports, Telepaths had invented their own game designed for their specific talents way back during the Babylonian Empire—or maybe even earlier, during the Akkadian Empire. The word Doom had morphed from its original name, *Kasādum*, which was Akkadian for "capture." This made sense, because the game was essentially capture the flag with two teams of five players. You won by stealing the opponent's flag from their end and placing it next to your own flag at your end. There were a few differences, though. First, the "flag" was actually a metal disc nine inches across, so you could throw it. Second, each player carried a wooden sword or staff and was allowed to hit others mercilessly with them. Third, players were allowed to use whatever Abilities they possessed in pretty much any manner they pleased, except compulsion.

A few rules had developed in recent times to make the sport more civilized. Players wore body armor and helmets, were no longer allowed to hit someone who was already unconscious, and were not allowed to intentionally kill anyone. Any number of teams could sign up for the season, as long as they had their final list of players within two weeks.

The season started with exhibition matches between last year's teams. From the very first moment of the very first match, Zoe and Lin were hooked. Forget basketball, this was like . . . telepathic super-samurai in a Roman gladiator pit all wrapped up in a screaming high school pep rally.

The boys playing this match had obviously been playing for years, perfecting their tactics. And there were a lot of tactics. You could hold someone back to defend your disc or you could go for broke and send everyone after the other team's disc. Once you got the disc, either by grabbing it physically or with your mind, you could run it back to your end or work it back by throwing it to your teammates—which got really cool because you could control its flight, either psychokinetically or ferrokinetically, because the disc was made of metal. You could also use it as a weapon and throw it at an opponent's head. And then, of course, there was the tried-and-true tactic of pummeling your opponents into submission.

This match was fairly mild, a third year boy told Lin. In fact, there always seemed to be quite a few boys hanging around Lin, though she never seemed to return their attentions. Each team, the boy said, was mainly trying out different strategies and giving their new potential players a chance to show what they were capable of. It ended with three of the ten players headed to the infirmary on stretchers. It was utterly awesome in every way.

"We have to do this!" she yelled in Lin's ear over all the clapping and cheering. "You and me, we have to form a team! Woo!" When she heard no reply, she eventually looked over to see Lin staring at her, slack-jawed.

"What? What'd I do?" she asked.

. . .

"Are you nuts?" Lin cried, as everyone headed back to their dorms before dinner. "You want us to get killed? Didn't you see those boys getting hauled off on stretchers?"

"They'll be fine," Zoe waved this off. "Your mom and her assistants will fix them up. Doom would never even be allowed if we couldn't heal each other."

"One of them lost his front teeth, Zoe!"

"I'm pretty sure he can grow them back. It'll just take six months or so." Zoe couldn't understand why Lin was carrying on like this.

"We're *girls*, Zoe. In case you haven't noticed, I'm kind of small. Some of those boys were probably over two hundred pounds! I wouldn't want to play Doom with them any more than I'd want to play tackle football with them!"

"There's no rule saying girls can't play," Zoe said, reasonably. "And being small can be a good thing. It means we're lighter on our feet. Faster, more agile."

"We're first-years, Zoe! Most of those boys have been taking combat classes for years, plus training specifically for Doom."

"But we're good at martial arts. You know we are. And this isn't football—you can have weapons. We could probably take those boys we saw today, no problem."

Lin just stood there, arms crossed. "You're insane."

■ ■ ■

All the other first-years thought so too, it seemed. Even the boys were too scared to play. "We can just play for fun," they said, "against each other. We don't have to play in the league." Lin nodded in vigorous agreement, but Zoe thought that was just stupid. What was the point of playing for fun against a bunch of babies? She'd only asked them anyway because each team needed five players. So, instead, she approached the captains of the teams that had already signed up but needed more players. The first was Tyrell Johnson, a senior, who was captain of the Crushers—last year's champions. He was six foot four and very athletic. His girlfriend draped herself annoyingly around his shoulder when Zoe approached him in the hall with Lin reluctantly in tow.

"Umm, no . . ." He smirked.

"You haven't even seen us play," Zoe said. "Just let us try out, you'll see what we can do."

"Yeah, umm, that's okay. I'm pretty happy with my new guys," Tyrell said. The girlfriend giggled.

"Fine," Zoe said, stiffly, marching away.

It was the same story with the other team captains, except they weren't quite so gracious.

"You're little girls," said Takeshi Yamamoto of the Flying Dragons, utterly confused and shaking his head.

Zoe was not pleased. "Boys are stupid," she kept muttering to herself. "Who needs them?"

"Let's just forget it, Zoe," Lin told her. "We'll try again when we're older."

"We're old enough *now*," Zoe growled.

"Well, nobody wants to play with us, so what do you want to do? Take them all on, just the two of us?"

"Of course not," Zoe said. "The rules say you need five people for a team. We'll just have to find three more girls."

"Wait, what?"

"Forget boys!" Zoe said. "We'll form an all-girls team. I have a plan." She stormed off with Lin following helplessly. First, they asked Professor Chao who the three best female martial artists were in the school. Then, they found Professor Martinov and asked him to identify the three best female telekinetics. Finally, they approached Professor Geller, who taught ferrokinesis—moving or bending metal by creating electromagnetic fields with your mind. She identified the three best female metal benders. They now had three lists of people, some of whom were on multiple lists, so in total there were six girls they could talk to: three from grade thirteen, two from grade twelve, and one from grade eleven.

They spent the rest of the day tracking down each girl and making their pitch. Or rather Zoe made the pitch. Lin still thought she was nuts. Three of them flat-out refused. The other three, though, were intrigued and agreed to meet in the dojo during open hours.

. . .

"Thanks for coming," Zoe said to the three girls standing awkwardly, unsure if they thought this was a good idea. "Every single team captain basically laughed us off when we asked to try out. That makes me really mad and I want to make them regret it."

The oldest girl, Makena, stood taller than any of them. She was probably the most kick-ass girl Zoe had ever seen.

"The same thing happened to me when I was a first-year," Makena said in her beautiful Kenyan accent. "And every year since then. I am as good a fighter as any boy. This is my last year here. I share your desire to humiliate them."

Priya, a diminutive third-year, raised her hand. "I'm here more out of curiosity. I'm not saying I'm joining yet. I'm small, I'm not terribly good at fighting, and I don't especially want to get hurt. What makes you think I'd be good at Doom?"

"That's easy," Zoe said. "I hear you're the best metal bender in the school."

"Thanks," Priya said. "But I don't see how that helps much against wooden weapons. I get that the disc itself is metal, but what am I going to do when five huge boys come at me with wooden swords?"

Zoe picked up a game disc and tossed it up a few times. "This is pretty heavy," she said. She tossed the metal disc to Priya, who easily stopped it in midair with her ferrokinesis. "I'll bet this would really hurt if a powerful metal bender threw it at someone's head, helmet or no helmet." Priya grinned. "Also," Zoe continued, "I'll bet you could grab the other team's disc from pretty far away, am I right?"

Priya nodded. "From further away than any of them, I'll bet."

"That sounds like an advantage to me," Zoe said.

"Is that why I'm here too?" the fifth girl asked. Paige was a fourth-year from Australia who had short blue hair. They were of average size but exuded confidence and attitude. "You want me to throw the disc around with my telekinesis?"

Zoe nodded. "Yes, but I'm also hoping you might be able to throw the boys around, too."

"What, like this, you mean?" Paige said, stepping forward and throwing their hands out in front of her. Zoe suddenly flew backwards.

She resisted the urge to counterattack and instead did a back flip and landed softly in a crouched position.

"All right!" She rose, beaming from ear to ear. "I think this is going to work. Who's up for our first practice?"

"Wait," Makena said. "I can fight, and we've seen what these two can do. Lin is Professor Chao's daughter, so I assume she can fight. But what about you? What can you do?"

Zoe took a deep breath. If she tried to demonstrate any kind of Ability without being angry or threatened or in imminent danger, she knew she would just embarrass herself.

"Everyone, grab their favourite weapon," she said. She walked to the wall and grabbed a bokken. Lin and Paige did likewise, and Makena grabbed a *bo*, a six-foot staff, and twirled it nonchalantly. Priya just held on to the metal disc. Zoe walked to the centre of the dojo and instructed everyone to form a circle around her.

"Okay," she said, steeling herself. "Attack me."

■ ■ ■

After two weeks of training, they had their first match—the last of the exhibition matches. The gymnasium was filled to capacity. Everyone wanted to see what the Valkyries—the first all-girls team in decades—could do. The drums pounded, and the crowd cheered as each player was announced. Zoe adjusted her gear and stretched her neck as she took stock of her opponents, the Untouchables. They were big and cocky and behaving as if this match was a joke.

Each team lined up beside their discs at either end of the gym. Zoe and Lin held their bokkens and Makena held her bo. Paige and Priya, however, were weaponless—a fact that prompted a lot of murmuring in the stands. When the whistle blew, the five boys all charged, leaving no one behind to protect their disc. The Valkyries were prepared for this.

They charged forward too, with Zoe in the middle, flanked by Makena and Lin. Paige and Priya held back for a bit and then Paige ran as fast as they could.

"Now!" Zoe shouted, as Paige leapt up high, giving themselves an impressive telekinetic boost. Zoe, Lin, and Makena together used their combined telekinesis to slingshot Paige even further up and over the boys, just before the boys came crashing into them. All three dropped to their knees and slashed at the nearest boys' legs, sending them sprawling.

The remaining Untouchables stopped and stared slack-jawed at the girl soaring over their heads. As they tried to run back to their disc, Paige descended close enough to grab the disc telekinetically. They flung it back toward the Valkyrie's side and then used their telekinesis to slow their descent. Frantic, the two boys tried to stop their disc either telekinetically or ferrokinetically, but were suddenly walloped on the back of the head by Lin and Makena.

Zoe stayed behind to take on the three remaining boys who were now getting back on their feet. She leapt up and kicked one of them in the head. Her kick pushed her toward the second boy, who she took out with a sword slash to the side of the neck as she spun in the air. As she landed, she rolled and came up with an upward slash to the chin of the third boy, knocking him unconscious. Meanwhile, Priya had advanced just enough to grab the disc ferrokinetically and guide it in toward her. Catching it, she placed it on their baseline beside their own disc.

The airhorn sounded. The clocked was stopped at 9.87 seconds—the fastest victory ever recorded in the history of Doom. The students in the stands went nuts. The Valkyries ran to hug each other in celebration as the Untouchables just stood there, stunned—all except the one who was still unconscious.

The girls waved to their new fans, who chanted, "Valkyries! Valkyries!"

"I *told* you an all-girls team was a good idea!" Lin shouted in Zoe's ear. "I don't know what you were so worried about!"

• • •

Days stretched into weeks and then months. As the leaves started changing colours, the students had settled into a routine. There were assignments and tests, plus daily combat classes, and also daily chores—which Zoe guessed differed from most private schools. Zoe and Lin volunteered to help at the Sanctuary as much as possible. Zoe didn't mind getting dirty, and she loved spending time with the animals. The more time she spent with them, the more she was able to communicate with them. What struck her the most was how the minds of animals were so uncomplicated and pure and full of love.

The Valkyries practised as much as possible, as they all felt they had something to prove. Some boys thought their first match was a fluke, but they were quickly silenced as the girls won their next three matches, too. The keys to their success were teamwork, playing to their strengths, and thinking outside the box to develop novel, unanticipated strategies. The other team captains nodded with grudging respect now whenever they passed in the halls.

In late November, the snow came, turning the Academy grounds into a winter wonderland. Professor Martinov took the class outside to practise telekinesis with snowballs. Everyone made a snowball and then, on the count of three, threw them at him—and watched in awe as all the snowballs entered into orbit around him, like a tornado, his hands slowly moving in circles around his head. How could he possibly focus on so many objects at once? She remembered the wooden blocks in her dream. How had she been able to do that as a small child? In answer to her unspoken question, he explained that the trick was to not even attempt to focus on the snowballs separately.

"The human mind," he said, "has a finite amount of focus. When you attempt to focus on more than one thing at a time, you actually have less focus on each of them. This is how a magician can steal everything in your pockets and even your wristwatch—by continually distracting you and splitting your attention. I could never focus on all of these snowballs individually, so I instead connect them all telekinetically to form a single object that I can spin around myself. It is as though they are all connected by flexible strings. I can then, if I wish, briefly focus on one snowball at a time . . . like this!"

Snowballs suddenly began flying at everyone's heads. Professor Martinov laughed uproariously as the students shrieked and ducked for cover. Then, they started throwing snowballs back at him, and the snowball fight began in earnest—everyone versus the professor. It was the best class ever, Zoe thought.

* * *

In mid-December came the unfortunate news that the students would not be allowed to return home for the holidays. The reason, the headmaster explained, was that they were no closer to locating the Rogues than they had been when school began. Until the Rogues were found and dealt with, the Academy couldn't take any chances with the students' safety. Everyone was disappointed, and there were lots of tears, as some students—the first-years especially—were terribly homesick. Zoe had no such concerns, of course, but it *was* a reminder that unlike everyone else, she had no parents to miss her—if Ethan was to be believed.

To make things worse, classes weren't even cancelled. Something about an idle mind being a dangerous thing. They did hold a big New Year's Eve dance in the gym, though. Lin volunteered to be on the decorating committee, so Zoe helped. But the dance itself was . . . awkward. Zoe liked to think of herself as pretty coordinated. She could learn new martial arts moves quicker than most. But when the music started and everyone got up on the dance floor, she had never felt clumsier. Luckily, nobody seemed to notice or, at least, care, so she just tried to mimic everyone else and jumped around a lot.

Slow dancing was a whole different story, though. When couples started forming on the dance floor, waddling left and right like penguins, she literally ran to the edge of the gym to hide. Why would anyone want to *do* that? Several boys and girls approached her but suddenly thought better of it and turned around when they saw her don't-even-think-about-it face. One particularly confident boy, though, literally tried to pull her out onto the dance floor and quickly found himself on his knees, begging for mercy in a painful wristlock.

"Zoe!" Lin admonished her. "Not cool!" Zoe let go of the boy, and Lin gave Zoe her sternest what-the-hell expression as he darted off. Zoe hung her head. Dances were stupid.

13

THE ARRIVAL

Zoe held the frog gently in her hands. It was cold and squishy and made her laugh.

"Can you feel its heart beating, Zoe?" asked Miss Gillespie. "Hmm? Can you sense it?"

Zoe tenderly examined the frog, probing its tiny mind and moving on to its organs. "I feel it," Zoe said. "It's fast. A lot faster than mine." She and her teacher sat on the carpet in the centre of a circle of cross-legged children. They all watched intently, eagerly awaiting their turn.

"Very good, Zoe. You're such a smart girl. Frogs' hearts beat faster than ours. But can you make it beat a little faster? Give it a try."

Zoe focused on the heart, imagining it beating faster, and was astonished when it obeyed. "I did it!" she shrieked in delight. "I made it beat faster!"

"That's wonderful, Zoe! You're so good at this. Now, make it beat faster still. You can do it."

Zoe loved Miss Gillespie's praise. She'd do anything to hear it. Concentrating, she increased its heart rate further. The frog began to struggle in her grasp.

"Faster, Zoe. Make it beat faster."

Zoe obeyed, increasing her will on the frog as it fought to escape. She could sense that its heart would not be able to take much more.

"Make it beat as fast as you can, Zoe. As fast as you possibly can."

Zoe paused. "It will die," she said.

"It's just a frog, Zoe," Miss Gillespie chided. "It's not alive like us. It doesn't feel anything."

But Zoe knew that wasn't true—she could feel the frog's panic. "It's afraid." Her lower lip started to quiver, and tears began to form.

"Stop crying," her teacher said, suddenly very stern. "So what if it's afraid? It's a frog. Just do it."

Zoe could hear the frog's frenzied heartbeat, could feel its fear. "I don't want to . . ."

"Zoe, I am getting very angry with you. I told you do something, and I expect you to do it. It's only a frog, for crying out loud! It's no better than a filthy Anunnaki. What if they were killing your friend Ethan? What if they captured him and were slicing him up slowly with their sharp swords and laughing? Would you be such a little baby then, not wanting to hurt the Anunnaki while Ethan lies screaming, all cut up? Of course not. You would kill them to protect your friend. Now, kill the damn frog!"

Zoe was sobbing now. "Please, Miss Gillespie, don't make me—"

"Now!"

This wasn't fair. She didn't *want* to hurt the frog. It didn't deserve this. It wasn't fair that Miss Gillespie was making her do this.

"Do it!"

"*No!*" Zoe shouted, rounding on her teacher and sending a surge of will straight into *her* heart instead. It was so sudden that Miss Gillespie didn't even have time to gasp. Her eyes went wide as she convulsed and collapsed onto the floor, twitching. The children screamed. Zoe picked up her frog and held it close as she went to sit in the corner. Another teacher poked her nose into the classroom to investigate, and yelled into the hall for help. Then she ran to the fallen teacher, rolled her onto her back, and began performing chest compressions.

"There, there," Zoe said to her frog, rocking back and forth as more people swarmed into the classroom. "It'll be okay. There, there."

. . .

Zoe sat up in bed and hugged her knees, rocking back and forth and feeling sick to her stomach. She remembered that day in the restaurant with Professor Chao. *Some of us can stop a person's heart just by thinking about it.* They had been teaching her to do just that. What kind of school would do that to children?

She looked over at Lin, sleeping soundly. Thus far, she had told Lin everything, but how could she share this? Lin would want to tell her parents, who would then tell the headmaster. She had promised to let him know of any future dreams, but how could she share this? He was so concerned that she might accidentally hurt someone on instinct, or that she might actually be an assassin. This was worse than anything he had ever imagined, no doubt. He would never allow her to stay if he knew. She couldn't ask Lin to keep this secret—it wouldn't be fair to her. No, she would just have to keep this to herself. For now, at least, while she figured out what to do.

Zoe rocked for another hour or so, thinking about the word her old teacher had used.

Anunnaki.

. . .

It was difficult to concentrate on anything the next day when all she wanted to do was head to the library. The headmaster had said at the welcome assembly that all Internet traffic was monitored. What would they think about her searching for the word "Annunaki"? It was impossible to say, without knowing what it meant. But if it triggered an alarm on the headmaster's computer, she would have to explain where she'd heard the word, which meant recounting her dream and admitting she could make people's hearts explode.

Deciding it was better to be safe than sorry, she searched the old-fashioned way: in the library, starting in the history section. This would take some time.

. . .

"Spill it."

Zoe looked up in surprise, which was odd because she usually had that situational awareness Professor Chao had pointed out to her. Not this time.

"Lin! You scared me."

Lin sat across the table, staring. "You've been here for more than five hours. And you missed dinner. And now we have to hurry before we miss curfew."

Zoe's jaw dropped. Five hours? She saw through the window that it was indeed getting dark. How was that possible? She could have sworn she hadn't been here for more than a single hour.

"I . . . I guess I lost track of time. Thanks for coming to find me. We'd better go." She began gathering the books scattered across the table, but Lin seized her wrist.

"You think I don't know something's going on? You were fine last night and then this morning you started acting all weird." She leaned forward. "You asked me if I was enjoying my bagel during breakfast. Who says that, Zoe?"

Zoe felt like a deer caught in the headlights. "I was just wondering . . ."

Lin jabbed at her. "You said sorry to Helen Hawkesbury when she intentionally bumped into you during math and knocked all your books to the ground. You!"

"It might have been my fault . . ."

"Your mind has been somewhere else all day, Zoe. Something obviously happened during the night. So, out with it."

"I . . ." Zoe struggled to think of something to say, then finally gave up. "I can't."

Lin looked genuinely hurt. "But we tell each other everything, Zoe," she said, softly.

Zoe shook her head. "Not this, Lin. I want to, believe me, but I can't."

Silence hung in the air. "You had another dream, didn't you?"

Zoe bit her lower lip.

"A dream where you did something bad?"

She looked away.

"Something really bad? Did you kill someone?"

"I . . . I'm not sure," Zoe admitted.

"Was it an accident? Or self-defence?"

"Not exactly . . . maybe . . . kind of both?"

"Zoe," Lin said, taking her hands in her own, "tell me what happened."

Zoe sighed, defeated. She repeated the entire dream as she remembered it, then pulled away and hugged herself as she waited for Lin's reaction.

"Oh, Zoe," Lin said. "I'm sorry you went through that. It wasn't your fault. She was a horrible woman who was trying to make you do a horrible thing. You did what you had to do to save your frog."

"Yeah, by killing her. I was so little, Lin! I remember the little kids sitting in a circle, and we didn't look more than seven years old."

"You don't know that you killed her. She might have been okay."

"But even if I didn't, I *tried* to! I lashed out in a moment of anger, just like I always do! I can stop a person's heart, Lin! Can you imagine what everyone here would do if they knew that? The headmaster was right, I'm a trained killer. It's the only—"

Zoe!

Zoe looked around, alarmed.

"What is it?" Lin asked.

Zoe! Help me!

"It's Ethan."

"What?"

How could she be hearing his voice? Didn't you have to be in close proximity for that? Ethan?

I'm coming in over the west wall. They're chasing me. There are too many of them. I need help, Zoe!

Zoe was up and running. "Get your dad!" she shouted to Lin. "West wall! Rogues are chasing Ethan!"

Not waiting for a response, she sprinted down the hall, down the main stairs into the lobby, and burst out the front doors toward the setting sun. The west wall was pretty far away, and it was long. What was she doing? What if this was a trap?

Where are you?

Then she saw the silhouette of a boy arcing gracefully over the ten-foot-high stone wall, landing in a roll and running toward her across the snow-covered grounds. He was followed by a man's silhouette. And another. And another. Soon she counted a dozen figures, leaping over the wall. All were identically dressed in dark black-and-green uniforms, like some sort of special forces. She heard what sounded like an air raid siren.

We can't take them on ourselves, Zoe. We're outnumbered.

She looked back at the castle but saw no one. She tried to do some rough calculations in her head. He would never be able to reach the castle before they caught him.

Help's coming, but not in time. We're going to have to fight.

Then she saw the first yellow streak. It went right through Ethan and passed by her on the left. She screamed, thinking he had just been shot. But a split-second later, Ethan casually moved aside, apparently unhurt, and Zoe heard a bullet whiz by to her left where the streak had been. And then it clicked.

The streaks! It was just like Professor Chao had described. The yellow streaks were the paths the bullets were *going* to take. She could dodge bullets!

But then the streaks erupted everywhere. The Rogues had formed a line, firing automatic weapons as they ran. Ethan did a crazy acrobatic maneuver to avoid the streaks and then, unable to dodge a maelstrom of bullets, turned and faced his pursuers. A metal staff had suddenly appeared in his hand. He held his other hand out, and Zoe saw the yellow streaks bending around his shield, which he had formed into a conical shape in front of him. Zoe kept running, staying directly behind him where there were no streaks. She was almost there.

Then the streaks stopped, and she saw the Rogues draw their swords in unison. They were close enough now that she could see they all wore masks and body armour, but not enough to hinder their movements. Those in the middle slowed, allowing those on the edges to move ahead, so that they formed an arc where every man would reach Ethan at the same time. Ethan glanced back, gauging her distance.

One, she said.

Two, he answered.

Three! He threw his staff up above him and launched himself at the legs of the man in front of him just as Zoe sailed overhead, catching the staff midair and bringing it down with all her might on the same man's sword, knocking it from his grasp and bowling him over. Rolling to her feet, she threw the staff back to Ethan, who grabbed it just in time to engage the closest assailant. She willed the fallen sword into her hand and, without pausing to think, threw herself into the fray, skewering a man who was attacking Ethan from behind.

God, she'd just killed someone.

One part of her mind watched events unfold, a passive observer, incredulous at what her body was doing. The other part had no time to think. She was operating on instinct now. This was like the randori she had practiced in the dojo, defending against multiple attackers. But instead of empty hands, these were deadly swords. Her movements fluid and graceful, she never paused, never waited for an attack but instead chose her targets one after another and brought the attack to them. Positioning was key. Only allow one person within reach at a time. Play them against each other, let them trip themselves up. Always keep moving. Don't go for the kill if it takes too long. Use her small size and speed to her advantage—slashing the legs is almost as good as the throat. Find their vulnerable spots between the armour. Use her Abilities as an extension of herself, as a shield to defend against their telepathic attacks and as a weapon to subtly turn their strikes and put them off-balance. Blend with the attacks. Harmonize. This was a dance.

And then they were the only two left standing. Ethan and Zoe locked eyes, panting and bloody. A dozen men lay on the bloodstained snow, many dead, a few still alive. How much time had passed? Twenty seconds maybe? Ethan smiled, then gasped, as he looked down to see an arrow protruding from his chest.

"Ethan!" There had been no warning, no yellow streak. How was this possible? She rushed to his side to cradle him as he slumped to his knees. This couldn't be happening, not now—not after having done the impossible. She created a shield around them and scanned the horizon. The archer stood in the distance, atop the west wall. The man in black. He nodded to her.

Then Professor Yeoh was kneeling beside her and examining Ethan.

Without hesitation, she snapped the arrow in half and ripped it out of his back before laying her glowing hands over the entrance and exit wounds. Zoe was dimly aware of people around them, shouting orders, surveying the carnage, staring at her. Some were teachers, others she didn't recognize. Lin was next to her, saying something about being sorry and ignoring people telling her to get back. Professor Chao stood at the front of the crowd, glaring up at the man atop the wall. Two trucks raced that way. She felt disembodied, like this was all happening to someone else.

The man in black made a fist, held it front of him, and twisted it violently. Five of the still-living assailants suddenly convulsed and lay still.

"No!" she heard the headmaster yell.

The man in black turned his back on them and stepped off the wall.

14

MYTHS

Zoe slowly realized she lay in the infirmary. She couldn't remember sleeping, but she didn't remember coming here, either. She examined herself and her surroundings. Someone had washed off the blood, although there was still some on her clothes. A man stood guard by the door, and at the far end of the room, two more guarded Ethan's bed, where he lay unconscious and wrapped in bandages. Someone was speaking to her.

"... safe now. You're coming out of shock. It's completely normal so don't worry. Do you know where you are?"

Dr. Sharapova.

Zoe nodded.

"Your injuries have been treated. You'll have a few scars, but nothing too bad. Your left side will be sore for a few days though, they said."

"How's Ethan?"

Dr. Sharapova looked at him. "He's alive, thanks to you, and thanks to Professor Yeoh. I heard her say that if she had arrived seconds later, he wouldn't have survived. I'm sure that her being one of the world's preeminent healers also had something to do with it." She turned back to Zoe. "How much do you remember?"

"It's a blur," she said. "Like it happened to someone else. I don't really remember the details of the fight. But I remember the start and the end. And the arrow, and the man in black, and then lots of people. Nothing really after that."

Natasha nodded. "That's completely normal. Most people feel numb or disconnected for a short time after a traumatic experience. The important thing to know is that you're safe now. You took control of the situation, and thanks to you, Ethan is alive. Now you can relax and let everyone take care of you. Everything will be okay."

"I killed people," she said, softly. There had been no time to think about it during the fight, but now it sunk in. "I actually killed people. Every one of them probably had loved ones, probably thought they were the good guys. They all started off as innocent children and now they're dead."

"Zoe," Natasha began before someone cleared his throat. Professor Chao stood in the doorway.

"May I have a moment alone with Zoe please, Natasha?"

"Of course, Ling." She patted Zoe's hand. "Zoe, I want you to feel free to come see me, okay? Not to restore any memories—just to talk about anything you want to discuss, okay?"

Zoe nodded. When she was gone, Professor Chao approached her bedside.

"It wasn't your fault," he said.

"Sir?"

He was quiet a moment. "I was twenty years old when I first killed a man. It was 1542. I had been trained at the Academy, so I knew how to fight, but I was a simple man of peace, so when my training was completed, I returned to the life I loved as a farmer. The Mongols had been raiding inland into China, plundering and stealing livestock. One day, they attacked my village and slaughtered every man, woman, and child. I fought them, and killed many of them, but their numbers were too great. They left me for dead, but I was able to heal myself just enough to stay alive.

"It changes you, Zoe. The act of taking a human life is something nobody can understand until they experience it. No matter how noble your cause, there is always the guilt, always the faces of the dead when you close your eyes. But it does dissipate over time—especially if you know you were in the right, that your cause was just. And you were. It was. Those men gave you no choice. You fought to save the life of another, as well as your own. You acted with honour and courage and skill far beyond your years, and I have never been more proud of one of my students."

"Thank you, sir," Zoe murmured.

"I encourage you to avail yourself of Professor Sharapova's services. I admit that I am old-school, having lived for many centuries before the advent of modern psychology. But if she thinks she can help, then I am certain she can. If you ever need to talk with someone who knows firsthand what you are going through, however, my door is always open to you."

"Thank you, sir," she said again. "I appreciate that."

"There will be a lot of questions in the morning, especially concerning that boy over there. He has been sedated, so he won't wake up for a while. Before that, we need to revisit everything you know about him. For right now, though, someone has been waiting anxiously to see you. Lin!"

Lin flew through the door and seconds later, wrapped her arms tight around Zoe. Professor Chao smiled. "One more thing. The dormitory, unfortunately, faces west. I am afraid that many of the students saw what transpired here tonight, and those who did not definitely saw the aftermath. I honestly do not know how they will react, but the headmaster will speak to everyone in the great hall tomorrow morning. Now, it is almost midnight and Professor Yeoh has said there is no reason you should not spend the night in the comfort of your own bed. Lin, I trust you can take her?"

Lin nodded and the two of them made their way to the dormitory, each leaning on the other, neither feeling the need to say anything.

...

Zoe hid under her bedcovers the next morning until the noise in the hallway died down and she was certain everyone had gone to breakfast. Everyone except for Lin, who said, "It's all clear. You can come out now."

Zoe poked her head out. "I'm starving."

"Go shower," Lin said. "We'll head down together after."

"You don't have to wait," Zoe said, as she grabbed her towel and started down the hall to the washroom.

"I know."

They arrived at the Great Hall with their food trays in hand just as the headmaster was concluding his speech. Zoe stopped, frightened. What had he told them? What must the students think of her now? Were they afraid of her? Would they call her a killer? Would they even be wrong?

"It'll be okay, you'll see," Lin said.

Taking a deep breath, she steeled herself and entered.

The headmaster stopped midsentence and all eyes turned to her.

The silence seemed to last an eternity. Then, the room erupted—in applause and cheers and whistles.

"And there she is now," the headmaster shouted over the noise, "Zoe, our hero from last night, who rushed headlong into danger without a thought for her own safety, to protect us all from those who would do us harm. Let's hear it for her!"

Zoe's jaw dropped, and Lin had to prod her to get moving. Students patted her on the back and yelled, "Good job!" and, "We love you, Zoe!" as she made her way to an empty seat. She sat, feeling stunned.

"Now, everyone, I've kept you all longer than usual, so please make your way to class and apologize to your teachers on my behalf. Everyone except for you, Zoe. You just relax and eat your well-earned breakfast. The rest of you, off you go!"

"Wait," Lin protested, her mouth full of cereal, "that's not fair, I just got here."

"Everyone out!" Amelia Zehringer yelled. "Off to class! That means you, too," she said, shooing away Lin, who hastily grabbed her toast to go.

■ ■ ■

When the room was empty of everyone but the two of them, the headmaster took the seat opposite her and folded his hands in front of him.

"I think that went quite well, wouldn't you agree?"

"What did you say to them, sir?"

"The truth, of course. That another student who grew up among these Rogues escaped and came here seeking sanctuary. That he was pursued by said Rogues onto the Academy grounds. That together, you and he successfully fought them off before help could arrive."

"That's it?"

"Well, I was more wordy, more colourful, and complimentary of your bravery and prowess, but yes, that's essentially it."

"You didn't mention that I killed people? And that the man in black killed the rest?"

"Heavens, no, why would I say any of that? Do you think I want to start a panic and have hundreds of frightened parents clamoring at our door? No, thank you. Besides," he paused, "I see no reason to give those particular details to people who might not be capable of understanding—and being sensitive to—the full ramifications of last night's ordeal. I think you have enough to deal with, don't you agree?"

Zoe let that sink in. "Thank you, sir," she said, finally. "Honestly, though, I'm not sure what to think. I'm relieved that people won't be calling me a killer, but I didn't expect them to call me a hero instead. I'm not comfortable with that. . . . In fact, I think that's even worse. Plus, they deserve to know the danger we're all in."

"Zoe, in my opinion and in the opinion of most faculty members, you *are* a hero." He held up his hand to stop her protests. "You are. And as for the danger, we are taking last night's incident very seriously, I can assure you. This is a security matter and all protocols are being followed. We are officially in a state of high alert. Extra guards have been posted on all the walls, and those Telepaths we think will be of particular assistance are being flown in from all over the world. The faculty are not to provide students with any further details. A meeting of the Council is scheduled for later this morning and it will take place *here*, at my insistence, because until we know the extent of the Rogue threat, I am keeping you and that boy here where you can be properly protected. Your presence is requested at this meeting."

"Now," he said, "if you are done with your breakfast, I need you to accompany me to a *pre*-Council meeting in my office where several people are waiting. I need to know who that boy is, what he is capable of, whether he is a friend or foe. Everything that you know, I need to know. It is in both our best interests that there be no surprise revelations during the Council meeting, understood?"

Zoe just nodded. The headmaster stood.

"Let's be off, then."

. . .

Professors Chao, Yeoh, and Sharapova were all waiting in the headmaster's office, along with a tall, muscular man who was introduced as Lee Martin, the Academy's Head of Security. He was obviously ex-military, but his body language also seemed very contrite and apologetic, Zoe thought, as if he had recently been reprimanded. The security breach had clearly revealed the Academy's defences to be inadequate.

A large monitor showed security camera footage from different angles with a running time in milliseconds in the bottom-right corner. In the videos, Zoe and Ethan could be seen running toward each other as men jumped over the west wall. Zoe stood in front of the monitor, staring transfixed at the event she only barely remembered.

"Back up to before the boy jumped over," the headmaster said to Lee. The video paused and reversed, then paused again as Ethan reverse-jumped over the wall.

"Exterior camera."

The view changed to show the forest beyond the west wall.

"Go back a minute and play."

The video jumped to show a still forest of trees and snow-covered ground. Then, a boy appeared in the distance, running as fast as he could toward the camera. A moment later, a dozen men followed in pursuit. Without looking back, the boy jumped up and over the ten-foot wall like it was nothing. The men poured over the wall seconds later.

"It was here that we first became aware of the breach, sir," Lee Martin said. "Unfortunately, our response time was simply not fast enough."

"Clearly," said the headmaster. "You have a plan to prevent this from happening again?"

"I do, sir. We own an extensive amount of the land outside our walls. I have already ordered the installation of security cameras and motion sensors throughout the woods as well as along the road in either direction. In addition, I—"

The headmaster put up a hand. "I don't need the details now, Lee. After this meeting will do."

The head of security nodded and glanced quickly at Zoe. "Yes, sir."

"Ling, I would like your opinion on what happens next."

In the video, Ethan stood still with one hand outstretched while a dozen soldiers fired automatic weapons at him. Without being able to "see" his shield in the video, nor the yellow streaks of bullets warping around it, it looked like the soldiers were firing blanks.

"Pause. Ling?"

"It's a remarkable display of strength, finesse, and confidence, especially in one so young. This is both raw strength and serious training. Zoe, did you know what was happening here? Zoe?"

Lost in her dim memories, trying to remember that this girl in the footage was actually her, Zoe startled. "Sorry, sir. Not at first, but when I saw the yellow streaks, I remembered what you taught us in class, and it clicked."

Professor Chao nodded. "Yes, I thought you must have seen the streaks judging by how you changed your path to align perfectly with his shield."

"I am most interested in what happened next," the headmaster said. "Play."

The video continued and suddenly Zoe jumped over Ethan as he threw his staff in the air for her. Once again, she brought it down on the nearest soldier.

"Pause. Zoe, how was this choreographed so well? How did you know to do this?"

Zoe thought back. "I'm not sure, sir. . . . We were communicating via mindlink from the time I was in the library and I heard his call for help. As I got close to him, we counted to three and then it just . . . happened. We both just somehow knew what the other would do."

"Like you had done this before."

Zoe shrugged.

"Continue, Lee."

Zoe watched the fight ensue. She remembered this part the least, and it felt surreal to watch herself moving so gracefully among the soldiers, their swords almost always missing their mark, hers always seeming to find their vulnerable spots. Was she actually that girl? How had she done that?

"Play it again," Professor Chao said. "Zoe, I would like you to tell us what you see."

This time Zoe watched Ethan. He was like her twin. The same poise, the same grace, the same calm expression. "He fights just like me," she said. He disarmed the first man almost immediately and swapped his staff for the man's sword, with which he dispatched his opponents as handily as she did hers. She noticed something else, too. "We're not just better than our opponents, we're coordinating with each other. Whenever it seems like one of us makes a mistake and accidentally exposes themself to an attack, the other is there to block it. Sometimes it almost looks like I deliberately exposed myself so as to invite an attack, leaving my attacker vulnerable to Ethan who just happens to be in the right spot. Other times it looks like Ethan did the same thing and I took out his attacker. It can't be a coincidence. Even if we were in constant telepathic communication, there would be no way to coordinate such tactics through words. It's as if we just intuitively know what the other is planning, as though we've been fighting together our whole lives. And then there's the way we employ telekinesis with such subtlety, gently pushing their swords just off the line of attack so that we don't have to block but can strike instead. It's incredible."

Professor Chao nodded. "I could not have said it better myself."

"What does this mean?" asked Lee Martin. "I've never seen anything like it." He pointed at the screen. "They're *children*, for god's sake. How can they possibly possess such skill at their age? Those soldiers were well-trained with a six-to-one advantage, and they were taken out effortlessly. Children cannot do that."

"Normal children, no," said the professor. "Children with regular lives, who go to school and play with their friends and spend time with their families—but children who have been trained ruthlessly every waking hour since they were old enough to walk? It's possible. I've seen what some nations have accomplished over the centuries in their efforts to create the perfect assassins or spies. I would say we can be certain that is the sort of childhood Zoe and Ethan have had."

"So, it's true then," Zoe said. "I'm a trained killer."

"You and me both," said Professor Chao. "What of it? I can kill more effectively than most people on the planet, but I only choose to do so when absolutely necessary, in self-defence or to save the lives of others. I have not seen you do any differently."

Zoe thought about that. He had said something similar to her once before, when they spoke about choosing the sort of person she wanted to be.

"And now we have two of them," said the headmaster, cheerfully. "Two lethal rogue assassins from a shadowy organization attending classes in my school. How wonderful." He smiled.

"Why did you go to him?" asked Professor Chao.

"Sir?"

"You said he called to you while you were in the library. You ran to his aid and took on those men without hesitation. Why?"

Zoe thought about it. "I don't know, sir. I just . . . knew I had to help him."

"Why? Why did you care if he was in trouble?"

"Well, I figured he was being chased by the same people who chased me . . ."

"So what? Why risk your life and take on a dozen armed men for this boy?"

"Because he's my—" Zoe stopped as Professor Chao scrutinized her.

"Your friend? Is that what you were going to say?"

Reluctantly, Zoe nodded.

"Do you actually remember him being your friend?"

"No, sir. It's just a feeling I have."

Professor Chao stroked his chin, deep in thought. "The only

interaction you have had with Ethan since your memory loss has been one in which he attacked you. Granted, he helped you escape afterward, but still, a feeling of friendship? I doubt that comes from nowhere."

Zoe wondered again if she should confess that he had professed his love for her in that memory bubble. Despite everything, though, it just didn't seem right. It was private. Telling Lin was one thing, but everyone?

Professor Chao turned to Dr. Sharapova. "What do you think? Can emotions survive amnesia?"

"Absolutely," she said, nodding. "It's been well-established. If she feels this boy is her friend, then I think that is most likely the case."

"We can use this!" the headmaster said, excitedly, and pointing at Zoe. "Zoe, you must gain this boy's trust when he wakes up. Find out everything you can about him, about yourself, about the men who were chasing him, about the man who shot him, about where they're from. Find out *everything*. And then report back to me."

Zoe blinked. "Sir? You're asking me to spy?"

"Yes."

"Even though you already think I might be a spy for them?"

"Yes."

"You want me to spy on someone I may very well have grown up with, someone who may be my friend?"

"Yes."

"But . . . but . . ." she sputtered, unable to articulate her protest.

"But nothing, Zoe," the headmaster said. "I have defended you from your enemies in the Council since your first day here. It has not been an easy task. I have had to call in nearly every favour owed to me from many, many people over a very long period of time. Now, I need you to return the favour. Events are accelerating and there is no more time to waste. We need answers and we need them now. Our enemy has attacked us and we still have no idea who they are or where they are located. Ethan will be interrogated at length when he wakes, and it could be that he will willingly give us every answer we require. But I need you to independently obtain all the answers you can from him, and if there is any discrepancy, I need to know. If his arrival is a ruse to gain our trust, I need to know. If we are in danger from him or these Rogues or even from you, I need to know. Do you have a problem with any of this?"

Zoe looked at the other professors, but neither offered any assistance. She shook her head. "No, sir. I'll do it."

"Thank you, Zoe. That will be all. You can go to class now."

■ ■ ■

Zoe was in no hurry to get to class and deal with her peers just yet, so she stopped by the infirmary to check on Ethan. She stood at his bedside, surprised that nobody stopped her. Maybe the headmaster had already ordered the staff to allow her access. How else could she be an effective spy? She didn't like the idea, but she had to admit that she was indebted to the headmaster and she had no idea whose side Ethan was on. This could all be a ruse.

He breathed easily now, clearly on the mend. She leaned in close.

Ethan.

He didn't react.

Ethan!

Still nothing. She put her hand on his forehead and closed her eyes, not really sure what she was doing. Dr. Sharapova could access her memories, so maybe she could access Ethan's. They *did* seem to have some kind of bond, so it couldn't hurt to try, right? For a long time, she saw nothing and felt foolish. But she kept at it. She tried to imagine her consciousness moving into him, her thoughts merging with his. And then it happened.

Images in her mind. Hazy, but they were his, not hers, she was sure of it. He was in a dojo and fighting someone in a dark-red martial arts uniform. A boy, maybe twelve years old. Other children, dressed in the same red uniforms, were fighting one-on-one all around them, too, and brutally. No one pulled their punches. He waded in past the boy's kick, grabbed him, threw him over his back into the mat, and then grabbed his arm and hyperextended it until the boy screamed. Ethan stood up and bowed to a man dressed in black at the front of the room, then looked to his right . . . and saw Zoe. She was fighting a boy much larger than her. She caught Ethan's gaze and smiled slightly before launching a vicious attack against her opponent, a series of punches and kicks that forced him back until finally she jumped up and landed her knees onto his shoulders, driving her elbow into the top of his head. The boy crumpled. She stood and bowed to the man in black, then stole a quick glance at Ethan, smiling ever so slightly again.

The scene changed. Now, he was fighting Zoe amid a circle of watching children. She looked older. They punched, kicked, wrestled, both sweating and breathing heavily, as though this had already been a lengthy fight. Suddenly, she landed her knees on his shoulders and drove her elbow down, but he was already twisting and turning and driving her down into the mat. Dazed, she seemed to have the wind knocked out of her. He straddled her and raised his fist . . . and hesitated. He looked down into her face.

"Finish!" a man yelled. Ethan looked up at the man in black, who scowled. He looked down at Zoe again, then shook his head and stood up. The man in black walked briskly toward him and then struck him over and over as he tried helplessly to defend himself. Ethan lay on the ground, and then Zoe was on the man's back, trying to drive her elbows down, but he threw her off. Livid, the man punched Ethan in the face, and everything went black.

Zoe removed her hand from Ethan's head and came back to herself with a shudder. She looked down on this boy who had refused to hurt her when ordered. She tenderly brushed a wisp of hair off his forehead, then turned and left the infirmary, trying to make sense of what she had just seen.

...

Everyone wanted to know about the boy in the infirmary who Zoe had rescued. Everyone wanted to know his name, if he was her friend, her boyfriend, her brother. They wanted to know if he was a prisoner or an ally. Was he was going to be a student? How had they been able to defeat so many grown men? Where had those men come from? Were they really trying to kill her? Did she kill any of them herself, or did the boy do it, or were they all killed by the man in black on the wall? It all made Zoe very uncomfortable. She stuck with her story of not knowing who the boy was, really, except that his name was Ethan and she had met him once on the streets of Ottawa. She maintained that the fight was all a blur and that she didn't really want to talk about it. Lin helped to keep the swarm of students at bay and fielded most of the questions.

In the halls between classes, some students seemed to give her a wide berth, some avoided her gaze, and others eyed her warily. Others, though, nodded in respect as they passed. Her fellow Valkyries offered their support and told her to take some time off from training. She had been looking forward to their next match but now she didn't know how to feel. The idea of beating up boys with a wooden sword didn't hold the same appeal now that she'd killed men in combat. She wondered if anything would ever feel the same again. Would she be able to forget what she had done and laugh again? Would her life be forever divided in two—the time before she'd killed and after? She went through the motions of class and school, but nothing the teachers said seemed to matter. Everything seemed so trivial now.

During her third class, she felt Ethan reach out to her.

Zoe? You there?

She bolted upright. *Ethan?*

Yeah, it's me. I'm awake, which is surprising considering the last thing I remember is an arrow sticking out of my chest. Ouch, I'm sore. Should I open my eyes and let them know I'm awake? I can tell there are two men standing near my bed, and another two at the door. How much trouble am I in?

I don't know, Zoe said, truthfully. *It depends on why you're here and how helpful you're willing to be. Everyone here has a lot of questions, and I have even more.*

I'll bet. He paused. *Thanks for coming for me, Zoe. I . . . didn't know if you would or not, considering our last encounter in the alley. I'm sorry about that. I was just trying to protect you.*

Protect me from what?

From yourself. You always were impulsive. I visited you in the hospital, by the way.

What? Zoe was shocked.

I made sure nobody there remembered. I'm sorry I wasn't still there when they came for you. I didn't know they would do that. I still don't know if they were ordered to or if they were acting on their own because you humiliated them.

Zoe didn't know what to say. *You know I don't remember you,* she finally blurted. *I don't know who you are at all.*

Oh. A pause. *I guess you heard the memory bubble I left for you?*

Zoe thought quickly. How much to reveal to this boy? She wanted to gain his trust to get him talking, so some truth would probably help to accomplish that. *Yes, I got your message. But I assumed you put it in my brain after you attacked me, so I wasn't about to trust it. I don't know you. I don't know whose side you're on.*

And you don't know whose side you're on, either. I can't imagine how hard this has been for you, Zoe. But that's why I'm here—to help you.

Help me how?

First things first. Do I dare open my eyes? I don't know if I can take four guards. I'm in pretty bad shape at the moment.

Zoe bit her lip and looked up at the clock on the wall. *I honestly don't know what's going to happen when they know you're awake. Just keep pretending to sleep, and I'll come when I get out of class. We'll figure it out from there.*

Okay. I can use a nap anyway . . . kinda tired.

Zoe felt him fade from her mind as he fell asleep. What a strange sensation.

So, Ethan's awake, Lin's voice said in her mind.

Startled, Zoe looked at Lin sitting calmly beside her, pretending to pay attention to the professor.

You heard that?

Of course not, Zoe. But I've been poking your leg for the past few minutes without any response so I could tell you were talking to someone. So, what's up? Did he profess his undying love for you again?

What? No! Zoe felt instantly flustered. Lin was almost, but not quite, successful at hiding her amusement.

He apologized for the alley, though, right?

Umm. Yes . . . how did you know that?

Because if he loves you, then he would apologize. And if he's playing you, he would apologize. Either way, he'd apologize. She paused. *You know you can't trust him yet, right? You have no idea why he's here.*

I know, Zoe said. *I know.*

∎ ∎ ∎

When the bell rang, Zoe headed straight to the infirmary. Though Lin had wanted to come, Zoe held firm. If Ethan had secrets to tell, he'd be more likely to share them in private.

She stood at the side of his bed. *Ethan? You awake?*

He opened his eyes. "Hey."

"Hey."

One of the guards nearby nodded to another at the door, who promptly disappeared, off to the headmaster's office, no doubt. "How are you feeling?"

"Sore," he said, touching his chest delicately. "But I'll take it. Someone here must be a talented healer."

Zoe nodded. "Professor Yeoh. I don't think anyone else could've pulled off that miracle."

"I'll have to thank her." He looked into her eyes. *It's so good to see you again, Zoe.* He reached timidly for her face, then quickly drew back.

"I'm sure you'll get your chance soon enough." *We might not have much time. I've no idea what's going to happen, but I don't think you're in any actual danger.* "Now that you're awake, I'm sure she'll be here soon to check on you." *I have so many questions, Ethan. Let's start with who am I. Did I defect or is this all some elaborate plan?*

"What happened to the men we fought? Are any of them still alive?" *I don't know, Zoe. They say you defected but . . . I just find it hard to believe. I never saw it coming.*

Zoe shook her head. "No, the man in black on the wall killed them all. Stopped their hearts. Didn't want any prisoners who could talk, I guess." *So, you think my amnesia could be a ruse?*

"I was afraid of that. Too bad. Now, they'll have nobody else to interrogate. Nobody to corroborate what I say." *I don't know, Zoe, but it's an awfully big coincidence that you'd lose your memory when it would be the perfect cover for coming here. That's why I left you the message. If your amnesia was intentional, then I didn't want you to accidentally get your memories back too soon.* "Do you think they'll torture me?"

"Torture? No, these people are good. Well, maybe not the Council, but here at the Academy they've given me sanctuary and treated me as one of them." *What do you mean "get my memories back too soon"? Why would that be a danger? And why did you try to steal my brooch?*

Don't place too much trust in these people. They're not what you think.
"I hope you're right. I'm feeling a little too weak for torture right now."
The brooch isn't yours. I wanted to put it back before he discovered it missing. If you really defected, then you were already in enough trouble. After I made you forget that I took it, I could see my blocks repairing themselves immediately. I never heard of such a thing—I was worried that might mean your memories would return way sooner than planned, if your defection was a ruse, so I left you the memory bubble to warn you.

These multiple conversations were getting too difficult to continue inconspicuously. "There's no way Professors Yeoh and Chao will let you be tortured. I just don't believe it." *You're saying I stole it? From who?*

"I guess we'll see. I imagine they have a lot of questions for me." *From the same man who put the arrow in my chest.*

"No more questions than I have." *Why would I do that? Who's the man in black?*

"What do you want to know?" *His name is Ragnar. Our master. He taught us to fight.*

"Why are you here, Ethan?"

He stared into her eyes. "For you, of course." *I had to be sure you were safe.*

Zoe trembled. She was also holding his hand—when had that happened? She quickly let go. Flustered, she was glad to see Professor Yeoh approaching.

"How is my patient?" Professor Yeoh asked, looking down on Ethan. *Zoe, is everything all right?* Now Professor Yeoh was speaking in her head, too.

Zoe swallowed. *Yes, ma'am.*

"Much better than expected, thank you," Ethan said. "You must be Professor Yeoh. Zoe says I have you to thank for saving my life." He smiled. Oh, he had a nice smile. "Thank you."

"You can thank me by not getting shot with any more arrows. You are very lucky to be alive, young man. Let me see how you are healing. Do you mind?"

Ethan shook his head and the professor laid her hands on his chest and closed her eyes.

"Your name is Ethan?"

"Yes, ma'am."

"Take a deep breath, Ethan." Ethan did so and winced. "How is the pain when you do that, on a scale of one to ten?"

Ethan thought. "Four?"

Professor Yeoh opened her eyes. "Four? It should hurt much more than that."

"Oh, it *hurts*, ma'am. Just in comparison . . . yeah, four."

She looked at him. "What was ten, if you don't mind my asking?"

"Torture resistance training, ma'am," he answered, matter-of-factly.

"*What*?" Zoe exclaimed.

Ethan looked startled. "What? What's wrong?"

"You've been tortured? When? Why? By whom?"

Ethan looked genuinely taken aback. "Of course. It's standard training. You've endured it, too. So we won't break if we're captured by the Anunnaki."

"What did you say?" both Zoe and Professor Yeoh blurted in unison.

"Wait," Professor Yeoh said, rounding on Zoe. "How do *you* know that word?"

"I . . . I heard it recently. In a dream. The night before Ethan arrived. I'm sorry I didn't tell anyone. I would have—I *should* have—but . . . it was really disturbing. Someone was trying to make me do something . . . bad . . . to a frog. I was scared. I just wanted to learn what 'Anunnaki' meant first. That's why I was in the library when Ethan arrived."

"You dreamt about Miss Gillespie's class?" Ethan said. "I *hated* her. Always wanting us to kill the bloody frogs. Make its heart explode! Remember when you made her—"

"What does it mean, Professor?" Zoe interrupted, quickly. "Who are the Anunnaki?"

Professor Yeoh looked troubled. "The ancient Sumerian gods," she said, quietly.

Zoe blinked. She certainly hadn't been expecting *that*. "I don't understand. What do Sumerian gods have to do with us?"

When the professor didn't answer, Ethan did it for her.

"It's them, Zoe," he said, slowly, indicating Professor Yeoh and the guards. "Everyone here. They're the Anunnaki."

15

THE COUNCIL

"You're telling me," Professor Yeoh said, slowly and deliberately, "that the Rogues, your people, refer to us as Anunnaki?"

"Well, we don't call ourselves Rogues, but yes. You are the Anunnaki. Why? Do you call yourselves something different?" Ethan seemed genuinely surprised by the possibility.

The professor didn't answer.

"Professor?" Zoe asked. "Is this . . . true?"

"It . . . may be," she said, finally. "It's a theory, at least. Most myths have some basis in fact. Telepaths could certainly have been seen as gods to ancient peoples. Some of our scholars have speculated that Telepaths could actually be the Anunnaki from Sumerian texts."

"And the so-called Watchers from biblical texts," Ethan said. Was that contempt in his voice? Professor Chao had mentioned Telepaths were often called Watchers.

"Then who are we, Ethan? Who are the Rogues?"

"We're the Igigi. The former slaves of the Anunnaki, who were persecuted and hunted after daring to rise up. That's why we've been hiding from them, Zoe. They've been trying to destroy us for millennia. They call us the *lesser* gods, but we're not lesser anymore."

Zoe was literally speechless.

"Ethan," Professor Yeoh said, carefully, "I understand that what you're saying is what you have been raised to believe, but we do not call ourselves Anunnaki nor do we think of ourselves as gods. To my knowledge, we have never been aware of any group of Telepaths called the Igigi and we have not been hunting them. I think you have been misled."

Ethan seemed to consider this. "I see," he said finally. "Well, professor, if what you are saying is what you have been raised to believe, then it would seem that either someone has been lying to me or someone has been lying to you."

"Professor," Zoe said, "the headmaster and maybe the Council will want to talk to Ethan now that he's awake. But he's still weak and in pain, and he must be starving. Do they really need to talk to him right away?" *What are you willing to reveal, Ethan?*

"Not right away, but I have no reason to deny their request for more than a few hours. I ordered a meal for Ethan on my way here. And after another healing session, he will be healthy enough for questioning."

I'll tell them whatever you want me to, Zoe. But I don't think we should tell them that you might be here on purpose.

"Since your food hasn't arrived yet, are you ready for another healing session?" Professor Yeoh asked.

"Yes, ma'am. Thank you, ma'am."

"As for you, Zoe, I expect you to inform the headmaster of your dream. No matter what it contained. You made a promise."

"Yes, ma'am."

They already know that I might be here on purpose, Ethan. They're not idiots. And you said that you don't actually know one way or the other. So just tell them everything. The headmaster has been good to me so far. And I trust Professor Chao. He sits on the Council. I don't think we can trust anyone else on the Council, but we can trust him.

...

Several hours later, after shamefacedly describing her dream to the headmaster and apologizing for not telling him earlier, Zoe and a weak but walking Ethan were escorted into a large, high-ceilinged room she had never seen before. They sat before a raised, semicircular table, surrounded by fourteen men and women in robes. The Council. She recognized some faces from her first meeting with the headmaster, who was sitting slightly to the side with Professor Chao. She pointed them out to Ethan so he would know who their friends were.

Don't worry, said Professor Chao's familiar voice in her head. *Everything will be all right. Just answer truthfully.*

A woman stood up. "The meeting of the Council is now in session," she said. The minister, Zoe remembered. The nameplate in front of her read Gabrielle Lafleur. "I would like to thank our two guests, Zoe and Ethan, for being with us today. Ethan especially, considering he is still recovering from his near-fatal injury. I think we all know why we are here. Before any questions, I must ask that our guests be shielded so as to prevent any mindlink communication between them. It's not that we don't trust you both, but these are very troubling circumstances and we need to ensure as much veracity as possible. If there are no objections?"

Zoe looked to Professor Chao, who raised an eyebrow but nodded. She felt a shield surround her. *Ethan?* There was no answer. She wondered who was actually creating the shield. She could see it around her with her mind's eye, but she couldn't see a tether connecting it to anyone. Was that because the shield itself prevented her from seeing anything outside of it?

"Shall we begin then?" The minister sat down. "Let's start with your full name, young man."

"Ethan, ma'am."

"No, your *full* name."

"I'm afraid I don't have a last name, ma'am. It's just . . . Ethan."

"Well now, this is getting off to a bad start already," said a man with a southern drawl. His nameplate read Horace Bailey. "You expect us to believe you don't have a last name?"

Ethan shrugged. "I have no expectations of any kind, sir. But if I have a last name, I've never known it."

"How *is* it that you don't have a last name, Ethan?" said the minister. "Who are your parents?"

"I have no parents, ma'am. None of the Igigi do."

A hush fell across the room. Zoe watched everyone carefully. Only Professor Chao and the headmaster appeared unperturbed. Either Professor Yeoh had tipped them off or the name Igigi meant nothing to them. It clearly meant something to the others, though—the blood seemed to have drained from their faces. They all looked at each other.

"Ahem," the minister cleared her throat, "let's come back to the matter of your parents later. What was that name you just said?"

"We are the Igigi, ma'am. And this is the Anunnaki Council."

A very uncomfortable silence ensued. Ethan waited calmly. Finally, the minister spoke again, "Young man, I'm not sure what you have been told but—"

"Please, Minister," Ethan interrupted her. "Let's not waste our time here with lies and denials. I admit that until now, I have only heard one side of the story. I grew up with the Igigi, hearing all about the crimes of the Anunnaki—crimes against us in particular and crimes against mankind in general. I admit, though, that I may have been lied to, or at least that there may be another side to the story, that things might be less black and white than I have been taught. Zoe says she trusts Professor Chao and the headmaster, and that I should cooperate fully. I am here for her sake, because I trust her instincts regardless of her memory loss. So, I will give you the benefit of the doubt. I am willing to tell you everything I know and to help you with what lies ahead. Believe me when I say that you need my help. Mine and Zoe's."

The Minister scowled, apparently not happy to be called a liar. "And why do we need your help? What lies ahead?"

"Your imminent destruction," Ethan said, simply. "Marduk, leader of the Igigi, intends to destroy you all."

The room erupted. Council members leapt from their chairs, shouting angrily. The minister pounded her gavel on the table, screaming for order above the cacophony. When the noise subsided, one Council member, a very large and pompous-looking man named Charles Baggarley, said, "Minister, this is outrageous! Nothing this boy says can be trusted! He should be locked up and in chains. And this girl with him. This nonsense has gone on long enough."

"Hear, hear!" someone else yelled. Zoe and Ethan exchanged glances. This wasn't going well. Zoe studied the Council members and the guards, trying to determine who was holding their shields in place. If this went bad, she needed to be able to act quickly.

The minister demanded silence. "Are you saying, Ethan, that the leader of this band of Rogues you hail from is named Marduk?"

"Yes, ma'am," Ethan replied.

"And are you aware of the historical meaning of this name?"

"Yes, ma'am. Marduk is the Sumerian god, originally of the Igigi, who was elevated to be the champion of the Anunnaki during the war of the gods. He defeated Tiamat for you, and later Kingu. When he defended the Igigi after they rebelled, you bided your time and eventually betrayed him. You killed most of the Igigi and have been hunting them ever since. You thought Marduk was dead, but he is not. He has been planning his revenge. And now he is almost ready to put his plan into action."

"Fairy tales!" someone shouted. The minister raised her hand again to stop any other outbursts.

"Do you expect us to believe," the minister said, "that your leader is *the* Marduk of myth and legend? That Marduk actually existed and has been alive and well for thousands of years?"

Ethan spread his arms. "Again, I don't really expect anything. I can only tell you that this is what the Igigi believe. I have never seen Lord Marduk myself and I cannot attest to his being the god of legend, but I have no doubt that he exists and that he is *powerful*. He is both revered and feared among the Igigi. Even his champion, Master Ragnar, who trains us in combat, serves him without question."

"You were right, Ling," said the headmaster, who had been sitting quietly until now. "The man you fought was the pupil, not the master."

Ethan looked at Professor Chao with newfound respect. "You fought Ragnar and lived? Impressive, sir. I don't think anyone else can claim that distinction." His expression changed to one of puzzlement. "Why are you not the one in charge here?"

"This is ridiculous," said Baggarley. "This boy is living in a fantasy world! What is the point of listening further to this nonsense? Next, he'll say that this Ragnar is *the* Ragnar Lodbrok of legend."

"I must say, sir," Ethan said to Baggarley, "you are not doing anything to counter the stories I've heard about this Council."

"And what have you heard?"

Oh no, thought Zoe. *This won't be good.* "Ethan . . ." she whispered.

"That you are buffoons. Effete snobs, decadents, and bureaucrats caught up in your own petty power struggles, using your positions of influence to further your own wealth and personal ambitions rather than to help the world."

"Ha!" the headmaster guffawed, slapping his thigh. "I like this boy," he said, pointing at Ethan while grinning at the Council members. "What an astute young man."

Baggarley sputtered and the minister glowered. "You are out of order, child!" she said. "And you do not seem to understand the gravity of your situation. The only reason you are not currently in a cell facing charges of treason is because we have thus far been persuaded otherwise." She stared at Professor Chao and the headmaster. "A decision I am beginning to reconsider."

"Oh no, Minister, your original decision was the correct one. I could hardly commit treason against your people when I have never been *one* of your people. And please," Ethan addressed the entire Council, "I ask you do not take offence at anything I've said or will say. I know I may seem impudent, but I simply have no experience with subtlety . . . or patience. I often find it difficult to deal with people of lesser intelligence."

Seeing the jaws drop, he hastily added, "Again, I mean no offence. Other than to you, perhaps, sir," he said to Baggarley, "But Zoe and I are almost certainly the most intelligent people in this room. It's not your fault. We were *genetically engineered* to be more intelligent, as well as stronger, faster, and more powerful in terms of our telepathic Abilities."

"You were *engineered*?" the minister repeated, softly.

"Yes, ma'am. That's why we don't have parents."

"For what purpose were you engineered?"

"To destroy the Anunnaki, of course," Ethan said. "And to, quote, 'establish a new world order, one in which the Igigi rule the world—not from the shadows but openly, guiding mankind with a firm but loving hand, to end its downward spiral into violence and self-destruction and bring about a new golden age.' That's the mantra we were fed, anyway. It's hard to brainwash highly intelligent people, though, even if you *can* indoctrinate them from birth. Still, I think most of the New Gods believe it. Certainly, the godlings do."

Stunned silence ensued.

"Bloody hell," someone muttered.

"Ethan," Professor Chao said, "what do you mean by 'New Gods' and 'godlings'?"

"Zoe and I, and the other children, are the New Gods, created to be more powerful than any living Anunnaki. We are the first generation—the first successful generation, anyway. There are thirteen subsequent generations who might be even more powerful than we are, and there are fifty children per generation. We have been trained since birth to be spies, soldiers, and assassins. The godlings are what we call the adults, the Typicals who were granted their telepathic Abilities via artificial means, like the ones who were after Zoe. They'll never be as strong as us or as strong as you, but they serve as excellent foot soldiers, especially since the first generation of New Gods are still children. I don't know their number, as most of them are scattered throughout the world. To be honest, Professor, I've always suspected the Igigi would wait to attack until a number of generations of New Gods reached adulthood. Now, I'm not so sure. The idea was always that you would never see us coming since you didn't even know we existed. The battle would be over as soon as it began. But Zoe's defection and your subsequent awareness of our existence may have caused Marduk to accelerate his plans. The fact that I am here, alive and with all my memories intact, will be an even bigger blow to him. I wouldn't be surprised if this prompts him to accelerate things even more." He turned to the minister. "I hope you appreciate the gravity of your situation, Minister."

"You're saying," the minister replied, "that you can turn Typicals into Telepaths and also create superior Telepaths? How?"

"Not me personally, ma'am. I don't know for certain how it's done. If I had to guess, however, I would say genetic engineering for us and gene therapy for the godlings. I've seen them regularly injecting something into their arms, anyway."

Chaos erupted again. Shouts of, "This is insane!" and, "Does anyone seriously believe this?" clamored for prominence as everyone tried to speak at once. Zoe studied the Council's faces. Some were genuinely afraid, she could see. Others, the loud ones especially, were not smart enough to be afraid yet. The headmaster and Professor Chao kept exchanging concerned glances. Were they talking via mindlink?

The minister pounded her gavel again. When she could be heard, she said, "Why did you defect? Why are you telling us this? And why should we trust anything you say?"

"I'm here for Zoe, ma'am. When she fled Ottawa, I lost her for a time. When I learned she was here, I fled the Igigi immediately and came to make sure she's safe and being treated well. I didn't think I would put in her in such immediate danger. As long as she continues to be treated well here, I will cooperate with you, tell you anything you want to know, even fight for you." His eyes narrowed. "However, should you ever attempt to harm her, or to separate us, please understand that our relationship will change drastically. You should trust me, ma'am, because Marduk is coming and you need all the help you can get. In addition to the information I can provide regarding the Igigi, I can also, no doubt, help Professor Chao to understand our combat techniques and strategies so that he can more effectively train you. Time is of the essence. There is no way to know when he will make his move."

"I see," was the minister's only response. "I see. You have given us a great deal to think about. I appreciate your candor. However, I don't take kindly to being threatened. It is very clear to me that both you and Zoe—now that we know you to be trained killers—cannot be allowed to remain at this school where you can harm other children and learn inside information, nor can you be allowed to remain together where you can conspire freely."

She looked to the other Council members. "I move that these two children be arrested immediately. All in favour?" She raised her hand.

"Minister!" the headmaster boomed, rising. "You have no right! This is my school and you will not remove these children!"

The minister ignored him. Other Council members raised their hands eagerly, shouting, "Aye!" and, "Hear, hear!" Six, plus the minister. Zoe committed their names and faces to memory—these were her enemies. She turned to Professor Chao, who met her gaze and shook his head almost imperceptibly.

"The motion is passed seven to six," the minister said, slamming her gavel down. She motioned to the guards. "Please handcuff these children and escort them to the front entrance. We will join you momentarily."

Zoe and Ethan nodded to each other and, in unison, stood to face the guards, relaxed but alert, their chairs between them and the approaching men. Suddenly, each man collapsed. The Council members cried out. The shield that had been erected around her was gone. *Ethan?*

I'm here.

"What's going on?" the minister yelled, her gaze darting frantically about the room. "Are we under attack?"

Amid the uproar, Professor Chao calmly rose and stood beside Zoe and Ethan. "Minister, I'm afraid I cannot allow this to continue."

Her eyes widened. "You did this? How dare you? You're finished, Chao! I will have you in chains for this!"

Professor Chao shook his head sadly. "No, Minister, you will not. I despise politics and have reluctantly participated in this corrupt Council for many years, for the sole reason of keeping an eye on all of you. Ethan's assessment of you was surprisingly accurate. I can only assume the Igigi have well-placed spies and are very well-informed indeed. It might surprise you to know that I have my own network of informants. For instance, I know that since we first became aware of Zoe's existence, you and some of the other Council members have been busy creating a secret, state-of-the-art laboratory, complete with holding cells. I know that you have been assembling a team of talented geneticists from around the world—both Telepaths *and* compelled Typicals—who have been told that they will be studying two individuals with extraordinary abilities."

"Of course I want to study her!" the minister shouted. "She's a threat to us all, and now this boy has provided us with proof of our suspicions! They are our enemy! We need to find out what makes them different, what makes them powerful, the extent of their capabilities. You and your bleeding-heart headmaster here would have them frolic happily with our children until they and their brethren destroy us."

"And you would jail children—who have never does us any harm and who have even offered to help us—and treat them like lab rats," Professor Chao said, coldly.

"They *are* lab rats! They're experiments created in a laboratory!" She pointed at Ethan. "He said so himself, or weren't you listening?"

"No one is responsible for the circumstances of their birth or their upbringing, Minister. And regardless, they are *children*."

"They are Igigi!" she spat.

Professor Chao's eyes narrowed. "A name you seem all too familiar with and contemptuous of, Minister. According to what we've heard here today, they hate us for crimes we have supposedly committed against them, for hunting them like animals. You would have us prove them right by perpetuating even greater crimes. You would have us cage their children and experiment on them. You would have us prove that we deserve all of their hatred and more."

"And what would *you* have us do, Chao?" she sneered. "Ask them to be our *friends*? You know nothing. I am far older than you, in case you have forgotten. The Igigi are known to me. They are beasts."

"Clearly you possess knowledge that needs to be shared with the rest of us, Minister. Nevertheless—"

"I do not answer to you," the minister interrupted. "*I* am responsible for our people, and I will tell you what I think you need to know when I think you need to know it."

"That is unacceptable, Minister." Professor Chao raised his voice. "I will not allow you to take these children. Furthermore, by withholding relevant information and conspiring to conduct illegal and unethical medical experiments on these children—thereby sabotaging any hope of a peaceful relationship between us and the Igigi—you have shown that you are no longer fit to lead this Council."

"And who is more fit, Chao? You?"

"Yes, Minister," he replied. "I hereby place you under arrest. You and everyone else who knew about your secret laboratory, who coincidentally are the same Council members who voted to arrest these children moments ago." He nodded to the headmaster, and suddenly the doors burst open and Lee Martin, the Academy's head of security, strode in alongside a dozen men armed with swords.

"Have you gone mad?" the minister shouted, standing so quickly her chair toppled. She pointed at Professor Chao. "Arrest this man!" she shouted, but the security team ignored her. She turned to the Council members. "He's a traitor, arrest him!" No one dared move, their faces ashen.

"Mr. Martin," the headmaster said, calmly, "please escort the honourable minister and her co-conspirators to their cells in the basement."

"Yes, sir," he said, stepping forward—before finding himself flying unceremoniously backwards. The headmaster's security men drew their swords, but Professor Chao's raised hand held them back. A silence hung in the air as the minister lowered her outstretched hand and then jumped lithely over the table, landing without a sound. Suddenly, Zoe realized the extent to which she had misread this woman. Gone was the pompous politician, replaced by a graceful warrior calmly preparing for battle. Zoe and Ethan cautiously spread out to surround her from either side as Lee Martin got back to his feet. The minister ignored them as she regarded Professor Chao.

"So, what is it to be, Ling?" she said, smiling coldly. "You would seek to usurp this Council without getting your hands dirty? You think I will go meekly to my cell because you say so? You have been in your little world of academia for too long. You forget who I am. You'll need more men than this to take me."

Professor Chao spread his arms out wide. "Minister, you do not want to do this."

"Don't I? I was killing people long, long before you came into this world, Ling. Who was it who taught you to fight when you were a snot-nosed whelp? You think that the pupil has become the master? *This* is how you repay me?"

"You have given me no choice."

"You had every choice!" she spat. "You have no idea what is going on. No idea the danger we face. You act out of ignorance and hubris and by doing so will get us all killed. No, I will not give up my seat."

She snapped her fingers and her six co-conspirators sprang to their feet and placed daggers to the throats of the five remaining Council members and the headmaster.

The minister smirked. "I ask you again, Ling. What is it to be?"

Zoe had never seen Professor Chao angry before. It was scary. A cold, controlled anger, like a coiled viper about to strike. He stepped forward. "You would take the lives of your fellow Council members just to cling to your power?" His voice was ice.

She spread her arms mockingly. "You have given me no choice. Drop your swords and your mental shields or your fellow Council members and the good headmaster will all bleed out here in this chamber."

Zoe looked at the professor as he considered this ultimatum. *Professor? Tell us what to do.*

Finally, he spoke. "No."

The minister snarled. "I'm not joking, Ling. Surrender or their blood will be on your hands."

Professor Chao nodded. "I believe you, Gabrielle. And I believe you are willing to die here. But they aren't," he said. motioning to the men and women nervously holding their daggers to their hostages' necks. He raised his voice. "I give all of you my word that if you drop your weapons and surrender, you will not be harmed. Any one of you who dares to spill a drop of blood, however, I swear will not leave this room alive. The choice is yours."

The minister's lips tightened with displeasure.

"Minister?" said a shaky voice behind her. She raised her hand.

"Hold fast!" she said. She regarded Professor Chao with skepticism. "You crave power so badly that you are willing to sacrifice their lives? I don't believe it. You may be talented with the sword, Chao, but you have always been soft. Weak. You don't have the stomach for this. Adrian!" she yelled to the man threatening the headmaster. "When I count to three, slit his throat."

She crossed her arms smugly. "One."

Professor Chao met the headmaster's gaze. "I am sorry, old friend." He turned to Zoe, who stood closest to the headmaster. "Zoe." He tossed her the sword that had belonged to the guard to his left. "If he hurts the headmaster, I want you to kill him without hesitation."

"Yes, sir," she said, her voice steady. She walked around the table to face Adrian and gave her blade a few twirls, just to reinforce the fact that she knew how to use it. The man looked from his knife to her sword and swallowed nervously.

"Two," the minister said, less smugly.

Zoe stepped forward and raised her sword with both hands. Her eyes narrowed. She didn't dare look at the headmaster. Instead, she stared into the eyes of the man she was about to kill. Time seemed to slow as she calculated her next move. She couldn't possibly stop Adrian from slicing the headmaster's throat, but her sword would find its mark a split-second afterward. Sweat trickled down Adrian's face. She stood firm. Calm. A killing machine.

"Three!"

Adrian dropped the knife and stepped back with his hands up. The headmaster quickly whirled and punched him in the face, knocking him out cold. He stretched out his hand, and Zoe tossed him her sword as he moved behind the next hostage-taker. He placed the point of the sword into the man's back and smiled.

"I'd drop that little knife, if I were you."

The knife clattered to the floor. The headmaster hit this man on the back of the head with his sword's hilt and the man crumpled. He moved on to the next conspirator.

"It's over, Gabrielle," Professor Chao said. "Your gambit has failed."

The minister seethed, her fists clenched. "I am the leader of this Council!"

"No. You have played your hand. After word gets out of what you have done here today, your career in politics will be over. You may think you are able to defeat me in single combat, but this is not a duel. You are outnumbered, and you are under arrest. Surrender peacefully. Your death will serve no purpose."

"You are killing us all! You do not have the knowledge to see our people through the dark times ahead!"

"All the more reason to surrender peacefully. If you truly care for our people, you can still help them. You can begin to redeem yourself by sharing whatever knowledge you have of the threat we face."

The minister fell silent, her mind clearly racing. Which way would she go? Would a fight to the death erupt?

"Please, Gabrielle," Professor Chao said, softly. "Don't let this be your legacy."

The minister closed her eyes, squeezed them tight, then her body relaxed, and she held her arms out, wrists together.

Professor Chao nodded and a security guard placed her hands behind her back and handcuffed her. The remaining daggers dropped to the ground and the former Council members were all taken into custody.

Zoe breathed a sigh of relief.

16

PREPARATIONS

It was decided the school would keep no secrets from the students. Zoe approved. If they were all in danger from the Igigi, then they deserved the opportunity to prepare. The headmaster called an assembly for all students and staff.

"Thank you all for coming," he began. "I know there are many rumours swirling and that you all have many questions. That is why we are here." He took a deep breath, perhaps trying to decide where to begin. "You are all, I think, familiar with the events of the past summer. Your vacations were cut short when we became aware of the existence of an unknown group of rogue Telepaths pursuing a young lady named Zoe, who you have all since come to know. It would seem that she was raised by these Rogues—through no fault of her own, of course—but because she suffers from amnesia, there was little she could tell us about them. Now, another student has defected from their ranks and joined us. A young man named Ethan. He has told us much, and we believe his information to be credible." The headmaster placed his hands on the podium.

"They call themselves the Igigi. And they call *us* the Anunnaki. You will find these names in ancient Sumerian myths. Their leader claims to be the Sumerian god known as Marduk. We believe he is actually of one us, just another Telepath who has gone rogue because he believes we should rule the world of Typicals. Unlike other rogues who have attempted to lure Telepaths to their cause, he has pursued a very different strategy." He paused. "He has somehow learned which genes are responsible for our Abilities and created his own cult of genetically engineered Telepaths."

The auditorium erupted and the headmaster had to wait for quiet. "He has done this in two ways, we are told. He has used a technique called gene therapy to inject telepathic genes into Typicals, thereby endowing them with our Abilities. Their Abilities are weaker than ours, but they still pose a threat. The other technique he has used is to create human embryos with the telepathic genes, as well as with advanced cognitive and physical abilities. This goes beyond anything today's science is capable of, so we can only assume that he has been secretly—and unethically—experimenting on humans for many years. Fourteen years ago, he successfully created fifty babies whose telepathic Abilities manifested at an early age. Our own Zoe, and her classmate Ethan, are from this first generation. He has, every year since then, created a new generation of fifty children, each one an attempted improvement over the last."

Silence reigned in the auditorium as everyone—students and teachers alike—hung on his every word. "We must remember these children are innocents. They did not ask to come into this world, and they are every bit as human as we are. What is more, they have been subjected to physical and emotional abuse throughout their entire lives, the likes of which I sincerely hope none of you will ever have to experience. They have been fed lies, told that we are their enemy, and have been trained as soldiers since they were old enough to walk. And yet, as a testament to the human spirit, two of them have now shown that they are still free thinkers and have come to warn us of the danger we now face. That danger is considerable. This cult of Igigi wishes to destroy us and then rule this planet. But thanks to Zoe and Ethan, we now know of their existence and can prepare.

"Now," he continued, "you may have heard rumours that Minster Gabrielle Lafleur has been arrested along with six members of the Council. These rumours are true. She and her co-conspirators illegally compelled Typicals—scientists—to work in a secret laboratory designed to imprison and experiment upon our two latest students. They are now in jail awaiting their trials. Until such time as we can hold elections, our acting Minister is our own Professor Chao, who detected and put a stop to Minister Lafleur's despicable scheme.

"There was much debate among the Council, with its new minister and six new members, regarding whether it would be safer to send our students back home to their parents and hide them around the world or to stay put, on high alert, with built-up security forces. In the end, we have decided that while it is one thing to hide from the world of Typicals, it is quite another to hide from other Telepaths. This is our home and we shall not run from it. We shall not be intimidated. We will protect each other—and should they dare to attack us here—we *will* be ready for them."

He paused as many in the audience applauded and cheered. "An hour ago, I told your professors everything that I have just told you. They agree that until this danger has passed, all of our lives will be different. We have a network of people scattered throughout the world who are working tirelessly to locate these Igigi. But should we be attacked first, we must be ready. While it is best to have a solid foundation in how to use your Abilities before learning advanced techniques, your training must, unfortunately, be accelerated. Starting immediately, all classes unrelated to the use of Abilities are officially suspended. Instead, our entire curriculum will focus on two things—physical combat and using your Abilities for battle. Also, grades nine to thirteen are being done away with altogether. The levels for each class will now be sorted by proficiency rather than by age, so that if a particular skill comes easily to you, you can progress at whatever pace you can manage. Your professors will work together tonight and in the coming days to draw up new course outlines and will provide you with details soon.

"In addition, all sports are now suspended with the exception of Doom, in which students are strongly encouraged to participate as a way to hone your skills.

"Now," he said, "I would like to leave you with this. Our kind has seen crises before, and we have always prevailed. We will do so again. You are all much stronger than you realize. Starting tomorrow, we will begin to teach you just how powerful you are. Dismissed."

• • •

Although the headmaster's speech left the student body stunned, it was nevertheless a tremendous success. Everyone was onboard with the new curriculum, and suddenly, everyone wanted to know everything about ancient Sumeria and how to defend against mind control, how to form a shield, how to best fight against larger opponents.

Ethan was a celebrity. He clearly had a roguish charm with the girls, who fawned over him to an embarrassing degree, Zoe thought. The boys seemed to hold him in awe, immediately treating him as their de facto leader despite the fact that he was only fourteen and thus a first-year. It was nice to know that she was officially fourteen years old, too, since she came from the same "batch" of babies as Ethan, but she was disappointed to learn that he had no idea when their birthdays were. Apparently, birthdays just weren't a thing among the Igigi.

The Crushers, who were currently in second place behind the Valkyries, asked Ethan to join their team as their "secret weapon" and he accepted. Zoe wondered what it would be like to face off against him if their teams had to play against each other again. Doom hadn't held much interest for her since the night of the Igigi attack, but she couldn't let her teammates down.

Ethan was true to his word and taught Professor Chao as much as he knew of the Igigi's fighting style. It turned out that they really did have formal Aikido and Wing Chun training, but only because that was what Professor Chao taught. Ragnar also taught them a fighting style that seemed to have no name but was very old and very brutal and clearly designed for killing multiple opponents as efficiently as possible. It was Ethan's theory that this was a Viking fighting style, since Ragnar had a Norse name and certainly *looked* like a Viking, with his blue eyes, blond hair, and Scandinavian tattoos. With the help of a sketch artist, he also provided drawings of Ragnar and other Igigi teachers and children.

Or Marduk could have taught Ragnar this ancient fighting style, Ethan conceded. In any event, Ragnar was someone who could incorporate the best of any fighting style into his own. Professor Chao was, of course, quick to learn this ancient martial art but was cognizant of the fact that he was only learning a portion of it from a teenager. Nevertheless, he had already modified his classes to teach the students how to defend against the unconventional, bone-breaking attacks and had Ethan doing likewise.

Ethan was particularly hard on the students, never hesitating to land full-contact blows—even though he said he was going easy compared to the training he and Zoe had endured. Professor Chao approved, if reluctantly, saying that he was sorry, but they just didn't have enough time and that they had to get used to full contact quickly.

Initially, Ethan was surprised that he had to teach Zoe the techniques, too. But just like Aikido, she couldn't remember ever having learned it, so she could only react to attacks. However, because her muscle memory remained, she was able to pick it back up quickly and was helping to teach the others before long.

Ethan also kept his promise to tell them all he knew of the Igigi. The most obvious information, of course, was their location. He knew the last location at which he'd been barracked—a warehouse in Toronto—as well as the location of a smaller base in Ottawa, but both were abandoned by the time Professor Chao's agents could raid them. It still seemed odd to Zoe to think of Professor Chao as acting minister, giving orders to a network of agents and officials all over the world. The man must have been busy. The main base, where Zoe and Ethan had spent their childhoods, was supposedly some underground bunker, but Ethan couldn't say where it was because its location was kept secret even from the children who lived there. He and Zoe had left it on a private plane from a private runway—the windows were blacked out and all of the passengers given sleeping pills. All he could say was that whenever they'd gone outside, it was always warm and the foliage looked tropical.

Ethan said he couldn't remember a time when he had no Abilities—that as far as he knew, he and Zoe had been able to use their Abilities even before the age of five. All of their training and academic education seemed to centre around two purposes: assassinating and spying. Ethan claimed that neither he nor Zoe had ever assassinated anyone, but over the summer they had taken part in their first spy mission. That was why they were in Ottawa, which housed embassies from all over the world. They had been enrolled in a private school where they were to get close to the children of a Russian diplomat.

The goal, he said, had been to befriend them and get invited to their home. Once inside, they planned to use mental compulsion on the father to gain entrance to the Russian Embassy. They never learned why, though, because the mission got called off after Zoe escaped. Ethan said he was questioned extensively afterward about why she had defected and if he'd helped her. Zoe suspected he was seriously downplaying the extent of this "questioning," but whenever she pressed him on it, he changed the subject.

■ ■ ■

They spent the cold winter months in training. They trained in combat. They trained in the practical use of Abilities in combat. And some of them trained for Doom—which was good practice for combat. The teachers pushed the students hard, and Zoe wondered how long they could withstand this pressure. March break had been cancelled, as expected, and they didn't even get any time off at all.

What was I like before? Zoe asked Ethan one cold morning in early April. It was technically spring but she couldn't tell, and they ran together along the snow-packed trail through the woods, ahead of the rest of their class. *Before I lost my memory?*

Ethan thought a moment. *Pretty much like you are now. But more . . .* He jumped up to a branch, swung around like a gymnast, and landed again. *Demure*, he said, smirking and darting ahead.

What?? Zoe leapt to the same branch, swung around it and off again, making sure she got a little bit more air than Ethan had.

Mm-hmm. And more . . . He dove headfirst over a log blocking the trail, rolled, and came up running again. *Girly. Yeah, more girly. Dainty, even. You were always busy doing your makeup, painting your nails . . .*

WHAT???? Zoe dove over the log, flipping midair rather than rolling.

Always flirting with me, too.

Zoe tackled him to the snowy ground. "Ethan, I know darn well you're lying!" she yelled, as she pinned his arm behind him. "Tell the truth!"

Ethan laughed uncontrollably through his grunts of pain. *You were always baking me cookies.* "Ow!"

"What's going on here?" Professor Chao said as he and the other students—some making smooching noises—ran by.

"Nothing, sir!" they both said in unison as Zoe let him go.

"Get back to running, you two."

"Yes, sir!"

They both got up on a knee, Ethan rubbing his shoulder. He looked Zoe in the eye. "Fine. You were confident. More sure of yourself and your Abilities. More certain of who you were and of your role among the Igigi."

"What does that mean, 'my role among the Igigi'?"

Ethan looked away.

"Ethan, I need to know."

He sighed, then turned to her with a pained expression. "It means you were a believer, Zoe. You never had any doubt that our destiny was to destroy the Anunnaki and that it was a righteous cause. You were Master Ragnar's favourite, I think. You and I were his star pupils, but he always favoured you."

Oh no. "Why?" Zoe asked, quietly.

"He loved your killer instinct, I think. The way you would draw on your anger to increase your power, the way you would show no mercy to your opponents. You were more serious back then. More driven."

It was everything she'd feared. Zoe felt like she wanted to vomit. Or cry. Or both. She silently stood and ran away as fast as she could. Ethan called after her. She ran and ran.

■ ■ ■

Zoe told Lin everything. Partly because she needed someone to talk to, but also because she wanted Lin to tell her dad everything should things go wrong.

"What is it that you're most worried about?" Lin asked. They were alone, mucking out the stalls at the sanctuary.

"That I'm a horrible person, like Ethan said. That his suspicion is correct—that I'm a plant, Ragnar's spy, just waiting for his trigger to suddenly activate me and turn me back into my old evil self."

"How could he activate you when he's not even here?"

"Ethan's here," Zoe answered. "Maybe he'll just say a magic word one day and then it's bye-bye me, hello . . . whoever I was."

"You really don't trust him, huh? He clearly loves you. I wasn't sure at first, but I can see it in his eyes whenever he looks at you."

Zoe blushed. She saw it too, though she pretended not to. "I trust that . . . he's my friend. We grew up together and we have a history, even if I don't remember any of it. But that doesn't mean he's telling the truth about defecting. I'm genuinely scared, Lin. You saw what Ethan and I did to all those soldiers. Think of what we could do to the students."

"You would never hurt us, Zoe."

"You don't *know* that."

"Then *do* something about it, Zoe!" Lin cried suddenly, stomping her foot.

Zoe blinked. "What do you mean?"

"I mean you've been obsessing over this forever, saying the same thing over and over, and it's getting you nowhere! You're smart, so use that super brain of yours to figure this out. Get your memories back," she said, poking Zoe in the forehead.

"Ow! Lin . . ."

"See if you're right about that brooch hanging from your neck." This time, she poked Zoe hard in the chest.

"Oof! Lin!"

"Figure out how to get ahead of these Igigi so that if things do go bad, you stay good!"

Lin stormed off, leaving Zoe wondering what had just happened.

"And when you finally have a plan," Lin yelled back without turning around, "tell me how I can help!"

Zoe stared after her friend until she disappeared, then said goodbye to Vincent and the other animals. She walked to her favourite bench down by the frozen lake and sat with her arms wrapped around her knees, thinking.

Fine. A plan.

...

As it turned out, coming up with a plan wasn't that hard. The hard part was actually following through with it. Her plan was scary and dangerous, so she decided to think about it for a few more days, just to be sure that it really was a good idea. A few days became a few weeks and then the next thing she knew, the playoff schedule for Doom had been posted. It looked like the Valkyries would play against the Crushers in the semifinals, if they both got that far. If her plan didn't work out, she didn't want her team to have to face Ethan without her, so she decided to hold off on executing said plan until after the match in May—at least.

If she was being honest with herself, she was deliberately delaying out of fear that her plan would fail—with dire consequences for her, though hopefully not everyone else. However, she *wasn't* being honest with herself and instead, threw herself into her classes with renewed focus, working hard to use her Abilities calmly. She also sparred as much as possible in the dojo during open practice hours, usually against a handful of seniors to see how many she could handle at once. This was the best type of training for an actual battle, she thought, but sometimes she sparred against Ethan one-on-one, which always drew a crowd.

On rare occasions, Professor Chao would spar one-on-one with Zoe or Ethan, which was humbling. She was certain her reflexes were faster than his, but he was just such an experienced fighter that he always seemed to be two steps ahead of her. His movements were so minimal, plus he used his Abilities in such subtle ways, putting her off-balance or making her miss her mark. Each time he defeated her, though, he would explain where she had gone wrong and how he had been able to outmanoeuvre her.

Zoe also kept training hard with the Valkyries, trying to devise new strategies as well as ensuring they had ready-to-use plays for common strategies other teams might employ against them. They won their first match of the playoffs easily and began preparing for their match against the Crushers.

Truthfully, she was nervous about going up against Ethan in Doom. She was pretty sure he was her equal. He might even be her superior. The Valkyries needed a really good strategy. She expressed all this to her team at the start of their final practice before the match. They looked at each other and Makena spoke first.

"We agree," she said. "We've all seen him play and he's like you—at a level above everyone else here. I can't go up against him."

"I can't either, Zoe," Lin said. "It has to be you."

"Luckily," Priya said, "we're better than the rest of those guys. So, if you can keep Ethan busy . . ."

"We can take care of the rest," Paige finished.

Zoe looked at her teammates with pride. "Okay," she said. "Let's brainstorm. How do we do this?"

• • •

When the day of the match arrived, she was a bundle of nerves. But as she donned her uniform in the locker room, a funny thing happened. She could feel herself physically calming down. She'd expected the opposite, but by the time she stepped out onto the court, her heart was steady, and she was as calm as could be. She saw Ethan at the other end, and he looked as focused as she felt. Maybe this was their training kicking in, or maybe it was just their genetics.

She could feel the excitement in the bleachers. The audience knew this was no ordinary match. They were about to watch the two best players in the school—maybe *ever*—face off. Everyone knew it. Even all the professors were in attendance. As the players lined up along their baselines, a hush fell over the crowd. Then, the whistle blew.

Zoe took off, sprinting toward Ethan as fast as she could, the tip of her team's arrow formation. Lin and Makena were on either side of her and slightly behind, followed by Paige in the middle and Priya directly behind her. Their opponents rushed forward with Ethan in the middle and a teammate on each side. Two hung back, though, wary of a repeat of the Valkyries' first game. Both Zoe and Ethan raised their bokkens into striking position. The timing had to be perfect.

At the last possible moment, Zoe dove forward to tackle Ethan's waist. Just before she began her dive, hidden behind her and Paige, Priya—who carried their metal disc—threw it forward as hard as she could, using every ounce of her ferrokinetic strength.

Now! Priya yelled into Paige's mind ahead of her, and Paige dove to the ground as the disc flew over them, adding all of their own telekinetic strength to boost the disc's speed.

Now! Paige yelled into Zoe's mind ahead of them. All of this happened out of Ethan's sight, so as he began his sword swing and saw the metal disc whizzing over Zoe's diving head, aimed directly at his face at incredible speed, he didn't even have time to blink. The disc made a horrible sound as it ricocheted off his forehead. As Lin and Makena took on the other two boys, Priya expertly pulled their disc back in and placed it back on their baseline before sprinting along the sideline toward enemy territory.

Zoe scrambled to her feet and quickly noted that Ethan wasn't moving. She ran toward the two stunned defenders with her bokken held high and screamed at the top of her lungs in their terrified faces. They both raised their bokkens and cringed. Zoe tossed her wooden sword at them as a distraction and sidestepped and ran past. She scooped up their disc telekinetically and threw it to Priya, who pulled it in ferrokinetically and ran back to their baseline as Lin and Makena kept their opponents occupied.

The air horn blasted to signal the end of the match. The crowd erupted. It wasn't what they had expected, but it was still unlike anything they had seen before.

Zoe dropped to her knees beside Ethan. Oh no. He was utterly unconscious. She cradled his head in her lap. "Ethan!" she yelled. "Wake up!" *Ethan! Wake up! Ethan!* She looked around, panicked.

"Professor Yeoh!" she yelled. "Professor Yeoh!" She looked down at Ethan's face. A huge lump had already formed on his forehead. What had she done?

. . .

For the second time in a matter of months, she found herself in the infirmary, sitting on the side of her friend's bed and holding his hand.

"I've healed his injuries," Professor Yeoh said, removing her hands from Ethan's head. "He should wake up soon. The MRI revealed no brain damage—but there easily could have been. He could have died, Zoe. Was winning that important?" She walked away without waiting for an answer.

Zoe was beyond glad that he would be okay, but it didn't make her feel any less guilty. She had known full well their crazy game plan would mean hurting Ethan, yet she went through with it anyway. Was this what he'd meant when he spoke about her killer instinct? Ragnar favoured her because she showed no mercy to her opponents? She was willing to do what others wouldn't? She felt sick to her stomach.

Finally, Ethan stirred and opened his eyes. He looked puzzled, then his eyes darted about before he relaxed.

"Oh, man," he said. "I guess this means we lost."

"Sorry," Zoe said, sheepishly.

"What happened? Why don't I remember anything?"

Zoe filled him in on how the match had unfolded.

"Impressive," he said. "I wish I could've seen it. I hope people weren't too disappointed. I know they were expecting an epic showdown."

"I'm so sorry, Ethan." A tear slid down her cheek. "I was so irresponsible. You could've been killed, just to win a stupid game."

"Killed? Jeez, give me some credit, will you? I'm tougher than I look. Besides, it was brilliant. I mean, I had my own game plan that was also brilliant, but it just didn't work on account of my being unconscious."

He smiled and wiped the tear from her cheek. "Don't worry about it, Zoe. I'm fine. Tell everyone I'll be good to go in this afternoon's bronze medal match, too."

She forced herself to smile back. "I'm glad, Ethan. I'm really glad." She rested her head on his chest. It was time to stop stalling. She simply couldn't live like this anymore, always afraid that she was really a bad person deep down. She needed to be whole again, but in control.

It was time to get her memories back.

17

THE PLAN

"Zoe," Dr. Sharapova said as she opened her office door. "This is a surprise."

"I think I've been going about this all wrong," Zoe said, barging right in. She paced back and forth. "All along, I've been thinking the worst-case scenario would be if my new memories got suppressed when my old memories returned. But that's not it."

"What is?" Dr. Sharapova asked, taking Zoe's abrupt arrival in stride and sitting down.

"The real worst-case scenario would be the literal destruction of my new memories, my new *self*. Is that actually a danger?"

Dr. Sharapova shook her head slowly. "As I said before, blocking your new memories when your old memories return is theoretically possible, if extremely complicated, but I think that destroying them via a trigger would be impossible. Someone would actually have to be in your mind, actively targeting and destroying those memories."

"Excellent," Zoe said. "So, if restoring my old memories results in the blockage of my new memories, then if there's anyone in the world who has the skills to unblock those new memories—so that the new me would exist again—it's you, right?"

The doctor considered this. "I can't guarantee it, Zoe, because if your mind really was split into two personas, then an incredibly skilled person did it. I've been researching this since we stopped our sessions together, but it's difficult to study without human guinea pigs—which would be horribly unethical. So, I don't know for certain that I can either prevent your current persona from being suppressed or that I can restore it . . . but I *can* say that I am the one person in the world who would have the best chance of doing so."

"That's good enough for me." Zoe lay down on the couch. "All right, let's do it."

Dr. Sharapova blinked. "Excuse me? Do what exactly?"

Zoe sighed. "Start poking around in my head, of course. We've waited long enough. I can't live like this anymore. Always afraid that deep down, I'm a bad person. I need to be *whole*. I've been afraid to let you do it in case who I am now disappears, but I've also been worried that some other trigger might *activate* my previous self one day, or a dream might cause a cascade of old memories and I'd vanish in my sleep. But if you can prevent my new memories from being blocked—or at least from being blocked forever—then it's time we try."

"Zoe . . . are you absolutely certain? Don't misunderstand me, I have always been of the opinion that even if your memory loss was intentional, it is highly improbable that your mind has been split in two. If it was, though, and I can somehow restore your old self while preserving your current self, there is no guarantee that having both sets of memories will leave your current persona in charge. Your old personality and beliefs are much more deeply ingrained and may dominate."

"Desperate times," Zoe said. "I have this horrible feeling that I'm running out of time, that if I don't take control of events, events may soon take control of me. We have to try, while I'm still me."

The doctor looked pensive. "Zoe, there is another danger that we haven't talked about. We can certainly do some more poking around and try to regain your memories, but you must understand that the situation is different now. Back when we first started, I had no real reason to believe there was any inherent danger in restoring your memories. Now, though, we know more about our enemy. And we have learned that you were a child soldier—an exceptionally dangerous one."

"I agree," Zoe said. "We have to take precautions. I've come prepared." She reached into her back pocket and pulled out some twine she had taken from the sanctuary. "Do you know how to tie a good knot?"

The doctor nodded.

"Good. Tie my hands and feet so that if the old me wakes up, she can't hurt you. Also, I want you to ask for a password to make sure it's still me and not her."

"All right, the password is . . . something random . . . lilies."

Zoe nodded. "Let's do it."

■ ■ ■

"Last time we started with your first encounter with the Rogues—the Igigi—in the hospital and found a block that prevented you from remembering them from before. This time, let's try another approach. You have recovered some memories since then in the form of dreams. Let's start with one of those."

Zoe lay on the couch with her hands tied behind her and her feet bound. It was uncomfortable, but not nearly as much as the feeling of the doctor sliding into her mind again. "Okay. There was the frog . . ."

"I see it . . . oh, how terrible! This memory is from quite far back, I think. You were only seven, maybe? Incredible, an entire room full of children, all active Telepaths. The teacher's name was . . ."

"Miss Gillespie."

"Right. What did you think of her?"

"I remember wanting to please her, but after she tried to make me kill the frog, I didn't like her much. I think I hurt her by accident . . . to protect the frog."

"Oh . . . yes, I see that. It wasn't your fault, Zoe. No one should be forced to do such a thing, let alone a child. Did she ever try to make you do anything else that was really bad?"

Zoe drew a blank.

"You just tried to access a blocked memory. Hold on."

Zoe felt pressure in her mind.

"Anything?"

"No, I don't think . . . oh."

Ethan sat tied to the chair, maybe twelve years old. Bloodied, bruised, defiant. Zoe stood above him, panting. Her knuckles were sore. Miss Gillespie sat off to the side, very prim and proper, her legs crossed, a clipboard in her hands and a tight smile on her lips.

"You're holding back, Zoe."

"I am not. Look at him!"

"You're not holding back your punches, but that's not what I'm talking about."

"I don't know what you mean."

"Don't play dumb. It's unbecoming. What is the purpose of this interrogation?"

"To determine why he refused to hit me when he had me pinned to the ground, ma'am. But he explained already. He felt he had won and didn't see the point in hurting me further. I don't see why we're continuing with this."

"You know why."

Zoe scowled. "Because I haven't verified his story yet."

"Exactly. What is the fundamental principle of any interrogation?"

"To never rely on what the prisoner says. To instead take the information directly from the prisoner's mind. But his shields are strong, ma'am. I can't get past them to see into his mind."

"And have you tried everything?"

"Well, no, ma'am. But this is Ethan, not an Anunnaki. He's one of us."

"If he were one of us, he would cooperate. We are the Igigi. Our strength lies in our unity, in our unwavering obedience and dedication to the master and the creation of his new world order. Ethan disobeyed a direct order, lied about his reasoning, and continues to resist questioning. He is obviously hiding something, so you will treat him as the enemy."

"But he's my friend, ma'am."

Miss Gillespie grew quiet. "Are you disobeying my direct order, Zoe? Do I need to involve Master Ragnar?"

Zoe swallowed. "No, ma'am."

"Then stop wasting my time and extract the information using whatever means necessary."

Zoe looked down on Ethan and his bloodied face. It was all she could do to keep from crying. "Why are you making me do this, Ethan? Just lower your shields and give her what she wants so we can end this already."

Ethan shook his head. "I can't do that."

"Why not? I understand why you disobeyed. You didn't want to hurt me. Maybe because you'd already won. Maybe because I'm a girl, I don't know! Who cares? It doesn't matter, Ethan."

He locked eyes with her and for a brief moment his defiance disappeared and was replaced with something else, something . . . tender, and then it was gone again behind a mask of strength.

"I've told Master Ragnar and Miss Gillespie why I disobeyed. I accept whatever punishment I get. But my mind is my own."

Zoe took a deep breath. Why wouldn't he listen to reason? What could he possibly have to hide that was worth this? "You know I can get past your shield eventually," she said, probing his shield for any weaknesses.

"I know."

"Then what's the point? Just drop the shield and let's get out of here."

"No."

Zoe felt herself getting angry. This was so stupid! She tried to enter his mind forcefully and bounced back. She hit his shield again, harder. "Drop them, Ethan!"

Ethan shook his head and gripped his chair tightly.

"I don't want to do this!" She began battering his shield with all her telepathic strength. Hitting it over and over, like a giant hammer. "Don't make me do this!" She realized she was crying. What was he trying to prove? She hit him harder, willing herself to double the intensity of her psychic blows. She hit his shield from the right side over and over again, the same type of blunt blow, over and over, and then suddenly switched to a frontal piercing attack, like a drill burrowing in. She'd caught him off guard, made a tiny opening, and she poured all her strength into it, willing herself through.

"No, Zoe! Please!"

And then she forced herself past the last of his resistance and was inside his mind. She could feel him frantically trying to throw her out. She felt sick to her stomach, but began her search.

Stop resisting, Ethan. It's almost over. She needed to find his memories of the incident quickly. *Remember when we were fighting today?* There it was. She zeroed in on the memory that lit up. *You had me on the ground and then you hesitated. Why?*

She felt two strong emotions radiating from him. The first was terror in the here and now. Terror that he was about to be discovered. The second was the emotion he had been feeling so acutely when he'd had her on the ground, his fist raised for the finishing blow. What was this emotion? It wasn't compassion. It wasn't an unwillingness to hurt a classmate. He was looking down on her face with a feeling of absolute . . .

You . . . you love me?

She gently slid out of his mind. He was looking at her, his shields finally down, tears streaming down his cheeks. *Ethan . . . I . . . I didn't know. But why? You know we can never be together. Relationships among us are prohibited. The punishment is severe.*

"What is it?" Miss Gillespie demanded. "What have you learned?"

Zoe up held a hand.

I'm sorry, Zoe. I couldn't help it.

She felt stunned. How long?

Always. Since we were little. Since as long as I can remember.

This was bad. She bit her lower lip. This was so bad. *They could kill you for this, Ethan. They'll say you're weak and can't be trusted anymore.*

Ethan shook his head and stared at the floor. *I don't care. Let them.*

"What. Have. You. Learned?"

Zoe looked at Miss Gillespie. "It's exactly like he said, ma'am. He had already won and didn't think it was necessary to hurt a fellow soldier unnecessarily during training."

Miss Gillespie's eyes narrowed. "And that's why your eyes went wide and your jaw dropped? Because you learned he was telling the truth?"

Zoe stood helplessly, with no clue what she could possibly say.

"Stand aside, child," Miss Gillespie said, standing at last and approaching. "I will see for myself." Zoe could see her reaching out toward Ethan's undefended mind.

"No!" she yelled and threw her teacher against the wall with all the force her mind could muster.

"What are you doing?" Miss Gillespie sputtered.

What *was* she doing? This was the second time she had attacked Miss Gillespie, and she wouldn't be forgiven this time. She quickly applied pressure to the carotid artery and watched as Miss Gillespie's eyes bulged and then glazed over and closed as she slid down to the floor. Zoe untied Ethan from the chair.

"What have you done, Zoe? Now we're both dead."

"Not if you're as good as you say you are."

"What?"

"She needs new memories of what just happened here. I don't have the finesse to do that, but you do."

Zoe opened the door a crack and peeked out into the hall. Nobody had heard anything. She closed the door gently. Ethan was still sitting there, staring at their teacher on the floor. She squatted in front of him and took his head in her hands. "Snap out of it, Ethan. You have to do this. She needs to remember you consenting to a mind probe right from the beginning and me discovering that you simply have an overly acute sense of honour. That's it. You'll be punished, probably put in solitary for a few days, but that's it. Okay? Can you do this?"

Ethan nodded.

"Good. But first we have to clean you up. You can't look like you've been beaten up." She stopped and tenderly touched the bruises on his face. "I'm sorry, Ethan. I am so, so sorry."

Ethan turned away. "It's okay, Zoe. It wasn't your fault. She made you do it. I shouldn't have resisted. I should have just told you that I . . . told you how I felt."

Zoe placed her hands on his face and concentrated. "Be still," she said. She wasn't very good at healing, and they hadn't learned it in any depth, but she knew the basics and did the best she could to heal the cuts and bruises on Ethan's face. When she was done, she wiped off the blood with the bottom of her shirt.

"There. I think that's good enough. Time to get started on Miss Gillespie."

The two of them lifted their teacher back into her seat. While Zoe held her up, Ethan held her head and stared intently.

"She's starting to wake up. This is perfect. She's at that stage between consciousness and unconsciousness where she'll offer no resistance. I can slip in and fix this."

Zoe watched while Ethan went to work on their teacher's brain. She and Ethan had competed with each other their entire lives, but this was one skill she conceded he was better at. Patience and precision were just not her strengths. After several minutes, he gently placed Miss Gillespie's head on the table. "There. That should do it. She'll wake up on my command thinking the interrogation is over, that you did everything she asked of you, and that I cooperated fully." He returned to his chair and handed the ropes to Zoe.

"Wait, Ethan. One more thing. You need to do the same thing to me now."

Ethan's eyes went wide. "What? Why?"

"If my memories of your interrogation are different from hers, I might slip up some day. Or maybe I'll be interrogated myself one day. Also . . ." She paused. "It's not right that I know your secret. Not like this."

Ethan held her gaze. He looked fragile . . . vulnerable. "You don't want to know how I feel about you?"

"I do, Ethan. But it might change how I act toward you. Someone might pick up on it. And besides, it was your secret to tell me if and when you chose to, not for me to forcibly rip from your mind." She shook her head. "I feel sick about it. I don't think I want to remember what I did."

Ethan nodded. He slowly placed his hands on her head.

"And, Ethan, if you ever win against me again in class, don't be stupid. Just finish it. You can't risk this happening again. And I want you to give me a subliminal directive to do the same thing to you, okay? No more interrogations, for either of us."

He nodded again and she hugged him. She was scared. She couldn't believe she was willfully about to lose her memories of this moment. "When you're done, make me tie you up again so everything looks right." She pulled back and took a deep breath.

"Okay. Do it."

■ ■ ■

"Are you all right, Zoe?" Dr. Sharapova laid a gentle hand on her shoulder.

"That was…intense," Zoe managed. "I don't know that this particular memory helps me in any way, but it still feels good to remember anything about my life. And it's good to know that Miss Gillespie was okay after the frog incident."

"What's the password, Zoe?"

"Hmm? Oh, lilies."

"Good. Every recovered memory helps, Zoe. Each one is an opportunity—a jumping-off point to try to find new memories."

"What, one at a time? That's no good. It would take forever, and there would still be no guarantee that I'm not missing key, crucial memories. I need them *all* back. There has to be one particular block that's suppressing everything else, right?"

"Perhaps…but not necessarily. You see—"

Zoe cut her off. "Then let's find it," she said. "Let's start with the fight in the alley. I was on the ground, almost unconscious." She closed her eyes and waited for Dr. Sharapova to slip into her mind again. After a moment, she opened her eyes to see the doctor staring into space, looking concerned. "Doctor?"

"I am not certain we should do this. I have an uncomfortable feeling. I—I think we should wait, Zoe. Make another appointment in the near future. One recovered memory is surely enough for today, yes?" She smiled.

"No," Zoe said, puzzled. "No, it's not. What's going on? We should have done this a long time ago when we first recovered my memories of the alley. You wanted to. I was the one who put on the brakes. But there's no more time to wait. It has to be now."

Still, the professor looked hesitant.

"Please, Natasha. I need your help."

Sighing, Dr. Sharapova placed her hands on Zoe's head again. *All right, go back to the alley.*

Zoe lay on the ground, completely spent, unable to move or even open her eyes. She could hear the fireworks, the people partying in the streets, and someone's footsteps approaching. "It's time," a male voice whispered in her ear. She heard the metallic click of an expanding metal staff, then felt a blow across the back of her head. Then woke up and stumbled out of the alley.

Stop. Go back to when he spoke to you.

"It's time," he whispered. *There. Something happened right there. Right after he said those words and before he hit you. There's a second where I can feel your mind . . . slipping . . . before the blow renders you unconscious.*

Slipping?

It's like . . . this was staged. I think your mind was prepped in advance—all your memories connected within a container so they could be blocked all at once with a trigger. I think the trigger was the phrase, "It's time."

Can you find it? Can you see the block?

Not yet . . . keep running through this memory, Zoe. Over and over, from when you first hear him approaching to when you get hit on the head.

Zoe let the memory replay itself over and over. She concentrated on every detail she could. The pavement pressing up against her face. The taste of blood in her mouth. The feeling of him crouching over her. The familiarity of his whisper. "It's time." Time for what? Time to sleep, presumably. Time to forget her entire life.

Focus on what happens immediately after he says those words, Zoe. Slow it down. Stretch it out into an eternity. Focus on how you feel.

"It's time." She slowed it down. Felt her heart beat in slow motion. What had she been thinking in that last second? She recognized his voice, knew it was. . . . Oh no. It was Ethan. And then . . . confusion? *What's going on? Where am I? Who am I?*

Panic.

I think I found it, Zoe.

Zoe opened her eyes. She was lying on a couch in a small office. A blond woman watched her in concern. It was Natasha Sharapova, the Anunnaki psychologist.

"Zoe? Are you all right? What's the password?"

She tried to move her hands and found they were bound behind her. Incredible. It had worked! She needed to take stock of her situation. First things first.

"It's time to wake up now, Natasha."

The doctor's eyes glazed over.

"Do you remember our time together among the Igigi, Professor?"

"Yes, ma'am," she answered.

"And what's the password you were supposed to reveal to me now?"

"Babylon."

"Good," Zoe said, rising to her feet. "Now, untie my hands."

Natasha did as she was ordered.

Zoe rubbed her wrists, then reached for and found the brooch hanging around her neck beneath her shirt. She pulled it out and examined it closely. Amazing. She could hardly believe the plan had worked. She put the brooch back under her shirt. "What's the date?"

"It's May 4, ma'am."

So long! She'd lost almost a year of her life. "Why did you wait so long to bring me back? You had a subliminal suggestion to start restoring my memories as soon as you arrived and to make sure I was back after no more than four months."

"You were spooked, ma'am. Ethan left a memory bubble in your mind, warning you that if you let me restore your old memories, your new persona would cease to exist."

Zoe's jaw dropped. Ethan had done what? "Give me a full report," she said, striding to the window. It was a bleak, overcast day. There was no snow on the ground, she noted, but there were no leaves on the trees yet, either.

"There were no suspicions regarding my delayed arrival. I said I had come down with typhoid fever during my visit to Thailand, which was true, as it was part of my cover."

"When did I arrive?"

"I was not here, of course, but I was told you arrived on July 3 when the Academy opened. Master Ragnar fought you and Professor Chao in a restaurant in downtown Toronto and all of the Anunnaki were in an uproar and sent their children here ahead of schedule for safety's sake."

"Wait. Professor Chao is dead?"

"No, he survived the encounter."

Zoe raised her eyebrows. "Impressive. I can hardly wait to meet this man." How had Chao survived a fight with Ragnar? And more importantly, what had Ragnar even been doing there? Zoe examined herself. She felt different. Taller. Stronger. She faced Natasha. "The last thing I remember is fighting in the alley. Tell me everything that's happened to me since then. Leave nothing out."

It took Natasha almost an hour to fill her in on everything she knew, from the moment Zoe arrived at the Academy to this moment. It all felt so surreal. Someone had literally taken over her body for months. Made friends with the Anunnaki. Zoe shuddered.

"So, those godlings actually tried to kill me in the hospital and almost ruined the whole plan. Where the hell was Ethan? And then he had the nerve to try to take my brooch and prevent me from waking up? And now we're revealed, not just as rogue Telepaths but as the Igigi, thanks to Ethan, who is here and who blabbed to the Council about pretty much everything regarding the Igigi and Ragnar and Marduk. That was never part of the plan. What the hell is going on? Has he betrayed us? Is that why Ragnar put an arrow through his heart, or was it to make his defection look real so he could become a student here, too?"

"I don't know, ma'am."

"Of course you don't know," Zoe snapped. "I was talking to myself. You served one purpose here and that was to bring me back. You took your time about it, too. Now, you're a liability." She paused to think. There was no way she could pretend to be the new Zoe for long before someone figured it out. But should she act now, or had Ethan's arrival changed everything? Was he here to fix something, or had he actually left the Igigi for her? She had sometimes suspected he had feelings for her, but he knew why she was here, so why would he defect? She shook her head.

"I have to go." She stood up. "I assume the map of the school you drew for us months ago hasn't changed in any way?"

"No, ma'am."

"Good. Then it's time for you to go back to your real self. You will forget everything that's happened since I woke you up." A thought suddenly occurred to her. "Actually, first, I want you to think about every encounter we've had together here at the Academy. I want to see what Zoe 2.0 is like."

She placed her hands on Natasha's head, slipped into her mind, and saw herself through Natasha's eyes. Their first session together. Seeing Zoe in the hallways laughing with Chao's daughter. In the headmaster's office, watching security footage of her and Ethan fighting their own people. It was hard to believe this was real. An entirely different person existed in her mind and was submerged now. All those new memories safely tucked away in a container and blocked off. Did that Zoe still exist? Did she have her own distinct consciousness? Could she be aware of what was going on now and struggling to regain control? No, that wasn't how it worked. She had no memory at all of being conscious these past months.

She also viewed Zoe 2.0's recovered memories that Natasha had seen while in her mind and was startled to find they had recovered one just today—a memory she herself didn't even have! An interrogation in which

Ethan admitted how he felt about her and then erased her memory at her request. So, Ethan was in love with her. That sure explained a lot. It made her wonder even more, though, if he was here for a legitimate reason or if he was just a lovestruck idiot who'd betrayed his own people because he missed hanging out with her.

"Enough," she said, placing her hands behind her back. "Tie me up again, exactly as before." Professor Sharapova complied and Zoe lay down on the couch again. "One more thing. What's the password I need to prove I'm still the other Zoe—the one you asked me for when I woke up?"

"Lilies."

"Good. It's time to go to sleep now, Natasha."

Dr. Sharapova blinked. "Zoe? What's the password?"

"I'm all right, Doctor," she said. "It's lilies. I'm afraid I still don't remember anything from before, though."

"Oh, I am sorry, Zoe," Natasha said, perplexed. "I really thought I had found it. We were close, I know it."

The doctor untied her feet and hands.

"Thank you, Natasha. I really do appreciate you trying. But I think we should try again another day. I feel really tired all of a sudden."

"Of course. Of course."

Zoe left Sharapova's office and strode purposefully down the hallways of the Anunnaki Academy. Her first course of action was to find Ethan and determine his reasons for being here.

Ethan. There was no immediate reply, so she tried again more forcefully. *Ethan!*

Whoa! Zoe? What's wrong? And how are you even doing this?

Doing what?

Initiating our mindlink when we're physically apart from each other. I know you're not here.

Haven't we been doing this since we were little?

Yeah, but you haven't been able to initiate it since I got here.

Oops. *Well, I guess I can now. We have to talk. Where are you?*

Where am I? I'm playing Doom! The bronze medal match, remember? I was hoping you'd be here to watch, actually.

What the hell was Doom? Oh, that game Sharapova had said she played. *Fine. Be right there.*

· · ·

Doom turned out to be awesome. Sure, it wasn't as brutal as the training they'd gone through growing up, but it was still way more violent than she'd expected of these decadent Anunnaki and, more importantly, it was exciting! They weren't training to infiltrate a compound or anything—there seemed to be some objective involving a metal disc that she still hadn't quite grasped—but they were being imaginative and working as a team and a crowd of spectators was going crazy! It was impossible not to get caught up in all of it.

Ethan was clearly the best one out there. He was faster and smarter and . . . taller and more muscled than she remembered. She shook her head.

"Zoe!"

Oh no. A girl waved to her, smiling. Chao's daughter Lin made her way through the bleachers to sit next to her and immediately hugged her.

"I'm so sorry!"

"For what?"

"For letting you do it. I should've stopped you. You must feel so guilty. Poor Ethan! I mean, he's obviously fine now, but we could've seriously hurt him. I saw you in the infirmary, but when I looked for you later, I couldn't find you."

Right. Sharapova had told her that she'd played against Ethan this morning and seriously hurt him. How to respond to this girl? The best lies are those that are closest to the truth. "I went to see Dr. Sharapova to see if she could recover any more memories."

"Whoa. I didn't expect that. What made you do that all of a sudden?"

Zoe shrugged. "I just felt like it was time."

"How did it go?"

Zoe told her about the interrogation and Ethan's confession. There didn't seem to be any harm, and sharing such a personal story would make the girl trust her more.

"Wow. I thought Miss Gillespie was a horrible person before, but the frogs were nothing compared to this! Poor Ethan. And poor you, too! It must have been awful to have to hurt him like that. So, he was in love with you even back then, huh?"

Zoe forced herself not to look shocked. She knew about Miss Gillespie and the frogs? Of course she did; Sharapova had said Zoe 2.0 had recovered that memory as a dream. Wait, "even back then"? That implied Ethan was in love with her now and Lin knew about it. Apparently, Zoe 2.0 had shared everything with Lin, which meant it was probably reciprocal—which meant she probably wouldn't be able to fool Lin for long.

"I guess so. I'm not sure what to think about that."

"I think it's sweet. And we both know you love him, too."

"What?" she blurted.

"Oh, don't act so shocked, Zoe. I see how you look at him. And I saw you holding his hand in the infirmary. You two have known each other forever and been through who knows what. Assuming that he's actually been truthful about everything, I can't imagine a better couple."

Zoe's face felt hot. She didn't know what to say. She was not in love with Ethan.

"I am not in love with Ethan," she said, finally.

"Mm-hmm," Lin said, turning back to the match. "So you keep saying."

Scowling, Zoe stood up and walked away. Who did this girl think she was?

"Where are you going?" Lin asked, grabbing her sleeve.

Zoe grabbed her wrist and applied the Aikido wrist control *nikyo*, making Lin cry out in pain. "Don't touch me. And don't tell me how I feel about Ethan." She let go and stalked off without glancing back. That was a mistake. She'd let her temper get the better of her and most likely acted out of character. Hopefully she wouldn't have to play this part much longer. She met Ethan's gaze briefly as she left the gymnasium.

Leaving so soon? Ethan asked, flashing her an impish grin before elbowing a boy in the gut and leaping out of another's way.

Finish playing your game, Ethan. We'll talk after.

She decided to explore as much as she could. Memorizing a map of the Academy was one thing, but she needed to get as familiar with this place as she could and she only had a short amount of time. Her wanderings eventually took her to the dojo in the deconsecrated church. She peeked in and, finding it empty, slipped quietly inside.

Now *this* was her kind of place. Weapons *everywhere*. She walked along the walls, touching each weapon gently and nodding approvingly. When she reached the large mirror along the front wall, she drew up short. She looked . . . different than she remembered. She touched her face. A little more adult. She fought back tears. What had she missed while she was gone? How much of her childhood had she willingly sacrificed for this mission? What had she been thinking? All those months, all those memories she might never get back. She grasped her brooch.

The door opened and someone switched on the lights. "Zoe, what are you doing here? I would have thought you'd be at the match."

Zoe wiped a tear away and quickly composed herself. Turning, she recognized the man from the dossier she'd studied before the mission. Professor Chao. The man who fought Ragnar and lived. The man she was supposed to kill.

18

THE MISSION

"I'm sorry, Professor. I just needed to get away from that crowd," Zoe said, innocently. "It's so noisy there. I wanted a quiet place to think. And this has always been my favorite room." Smile. Don't give him any reason to be suspicious.

"The dojo has always been my favorite as well," Professor Chao said, as he walked to the centre of the mats. He spread his arms wide. "This is where life is at its simplest and most pure. There are no politics here, no schemes, no dangers from the outside world. Here we meditate and train and find our true selves. We enter this room and always leave a slightly better version of ourselves." He sat in seiza and gestured for her to join him.

"I never thought of it that way, Professor," she said, sitting beside him and placing her hands in her lap. She closed her eyes when he did. "I just enjoy the thrill of combat. Testing myself against others. I find it cathartic, a way to channel and vent my rage."

"I certainly understand the excitement that comes with combat, Zoe, but what have I told you about relying on anger?"

Uh-oh, what *had* he said? Ragnar had taught her that with anger comes strength. It sounded like this man disagreed. "I know," she said.

"But old habits."

"Yes, old habits are indeed the hardest to overcome," the calm voice beside her said. "Even harder when they are formed during childhood. It must have been very difficult for you and Ethan, growing up with the type of training you received."

Zoe suddenly went on high alert. Had she slipped up, talking about old habits like that? Was he fishing? Did he suspect she'd awakened? "You know I don't remember anything, Professor. Except for a few dreams."

"Of course, but we have both learned much of the manner in which you and your peers were raised. You and Ethan are both very skilled, and there is no doubt that anger can make you stronger. But it also clouds your judgment, makes you reckless. Perhaps more importantly, it becomes addictive. You become dependent on it, and when you need to keep yourself angry all the time, you can easily be manipulated by others. It is only with a calm mind that one can properly reflect on events and employ critical thinking."

Zoe opened one eye to stare at her enemy. She was no one's puppet, she wanted to rage at him. She knew how to think for herself. Her hatred of the Anunnaki was utterly justified—they were a scourge on the face of the earth who needed to be wiped out. Instead, she bit her lip and said, "I'm trying, sir."

"Meditation can help," Professor Chao continued. "The trick is not to try to rid yourself of anger, or distance yourself from it, but rather to embrace your anger as a natural and useful part of yourself. If you do not allow yourself to ever feel anger, you will prevent yourself from feeling any other emotion as well. You simply want to control your anger rather than allowing it to control you."

Zoe wondered if she could just kill Chao right now while he sat there pontificating. He would never expect it. She had no weapon in hand, though. Would the element of surprise be enough? She couldn't afford to fail. She had to be certain of success before she made her move. "Tell me more, Professor."

"Start by forgetting about whatever it is that you think has caused your anger. Instead, focus on the *feeling* of your anger. It will express itself as a physical sensation somewhere in your body. It is usually hot, but it can be cold or sometimes just numb. Move your focus throughout your body until you can pinpoint where the anger manifests itself."

They sat quietly together, the professor meditating like a fool while Zoe scanned the walls for the closest weapon. The sword was her best weapon, and it was the most lethal. There was a long katana and a shorter *wakizashi* sitting on a stand just five feet away. She could roll to it, have it in her hand, and strike a blow in under two seconds. He would surely hear her, though, and she wasn't sure if she could best this man even if he was unarmed and sitting. She needed absolute surprise, to kill him before he was aware a blow was even coming. She could will the sword into her hand, but he might sense that.

"You are not trying," Professor Chao said, calmly, still sitting peacefully with his eyes closed.

Zoe furrowed her brow and closed her eyes. How could he possibly know that? "I'm sorry, sir." He might be in her mind, she thought, suddenly panicked. She fought the impulse to raise her shields and instead took a deep breath to calm herself and looked with her third eye. She saw no tendrils emanating from him.

"Better. Start with the breathing. Deep and controlled. Calm yourself enough to allow your thoughts to rise above the anger so that you can see it and recognize it."

This was ridiculous. "Professor, I really have to go."

"Nonsense. You came here to be away from the crowds. This is important, and long overdue. Now, breathe."

Zoe screamed inside her mind. She wanted nothing more than to kill this man where he sat, and instead, she had to play along with his mystical, New Age garbage. She forced herself to calm down. This was part of the mission. Pretending to respect him was not the same as actually respecting him, she told herself. She would play the part of the Zoe he knew and when he least expected it—when he was at his most vulnerable—she would end his life. Until then, she would breathe as he instructed.

"Excellent. Now, tell me when you are able to rise above the turbulence of your anger so that you can see it as something separate from yourself."

Zoe thought about faking it, but maybe he would know she was lying, so she turned her thoughts inward and began to explore her body, looking for her stupid "anger." After several minutes, she was surprised to learn that she *could* actually sense something. It was like a burning, churning cauldron inside of her. "I can sense it," she said. "I can't tell where it is in my body, though."

"Very good. Your anger actually resides, of course, in your mind, but our body is a remarkably holistic system. Everything is interconnected. When we love someone, we literally *feel* it in our heart, even though that love exists in our mind. The same is true for anger. I want you to move your awareness through your body until you feel the spot where your anger seems to reside."

Zoe did as she was told, intrigued. She focused all her awareness within her head and slowly moved down her body. After some minutes, she said, "I don't feel it, sir."

"Try this," he said. "As you breathe in and out, imagine your breath is like a wave breaking over rocks. Locate where your breath breaks and you will locate your anger."

Zoe did as she was told. But just as she was about to give up on finding rocks in her lungs, she realized that she did feel her breath meeting something. His waves on rocks analogy didn't feel right, though. This was more like a cool wind bending around a hot blade fresh from the forge. She described the sensation to the professor.

"Yes, that sounds like you have found it. Now, let each breath meet that hot blade. Feel them touch. Let your awareness meld with your breath and completely envelop the blade. Once your awareness has surrounded the physical manifestation of your anger, do not fight it, but embrace it, for it is a part of you. In this state, you may suddenly become enlightened as to the source of your anger, or you may feel it suddenly dissipate into energy, which you can redirect in a manner of your choosing."

Zoe could hardly believe this mystical nonsense, but there was no denying the sensations. She did as he instructed, trying to "become one" with her breath and surround the hot blade that was her anger manifested. With each breath, she felt more at ease, and more intrigued. She had been angry for as long as she could remember. Her temper had always been a source of pride, especially when she used it to overpower an opponent. Even Ethan could rarely stand against it. But she had never really allowed herself to consider *why* she was so angry all the time. Did she want to know? If she discovered the source, would her anger abandon her? Who would she be without it?

"I'm afraid," she blurted. Why had she said that?

"Of course you are," Professor Chao said. "It is not an easy thing to come face to face with your own inner demon." He was quiet for a moment. "I told you of my youth, when the Mongols attacked my village. I told you how I killed many of them before being left for dead." He took a deep breath. "What I did not tell you was that after I was healed, I hunted them down. I was so angry. They had killed everyone I'd ever loved, save those in the Academy—my parents, my brothers and sisters, and my beloved. I wanted revenge so badly it consumed me for months. When I finally found them, I was ruthless. I was an avenging spirit let loose in their camp and they were terrified. They begged for mercy and I showed them none. I killed each and every one of them as painfully as I could manage. Vengeance was mine."

Zoe arched an eyebrow. Maybe this man wasn't as bad as she'd been told.

"After the killing was done and the morning sun revealed all that I had wrought, I thought I would feel at peace. But that was not the case. My anger remained, stronger than ever, except now with my mission completed and my people avenged, I had nothing to feed it. And so, it began to consume me. For many years, I was lost. A violent man, wandering aimlessly, seeking every possible outlet for my rage." He took another breath. "Eventually, I met someone who guided me in taking control of my anger—and my life—again. It would pain me beyond measure to see you spend even a fraction of the time I did in such misery. If you wish, Zoe, I could be *your* guide."

Zoe realized she was staring. Tears ran down her cheeks again, but this time, she made no move to brush them away. This man, whom she had sworn to kill, had just bared his soul to her, divulged his deepest secret, and offered to help her. This was the single greatest act of kindness anyone had ever shown her. She felt confused and conflicted. She'd been raised to believe that Chao was her enemy, that he was selfish and decadent and arrogant. That he cared only about himself, allowing the world to rot under some lofty pretense of non-interference and free will. But this man sitting beside her seemed nothing like that. He seemed kind. He seemed to actually care about her well-being, as she thought a parent might. Was this what it felt like to have someone care about you? She opened her mouth to speak, but nothing came out. She had no idea what to say.

"Do not say anything," Professor Chao said, smiling, his eyes still closed. "Just know that the offer is always there, should you wish to accept it. A guide can only show you the way when you are ready."

They sat together awhile longer while Zoe, feeling like a lost child, tried to compose herself. She had always known that killing this man would be difficult because of his abilities, but it had never occurred to her that it would be difficult because she genuinely liked him. She had a mission, she told herself. She had known from the beginning that this wouldn't be easy.

. . .

Though the sky was dark with the threat of rain, Zoe suggested that Ethan join her for a walk, so she could familiarize herself with the layout of the grounds while also learning why he was here. She began delicately.

"Ethan, do you think I've changed much from how I used to be, back before my memory loss?"

"Of course," he said. "I've told you so."

"Tell me again, in more detail this time. I really want to know what I was like before."

Ethan put his hands in his pockets and shrugged. "You were . . . intense. Serious. Quick to anger. Always focused on training and being the best. You never had time for friendships. You seemed to have walls around you to keep anyone from getting too close."

"Weren't we friends?"

He grinned. "Yeah, but only because I was persistent. You used to beat me up when we were little."

She remembered. She'd beat him up and he'd cry, yet he kept hanging around her anyway. Always volunteering to be her sparring or studying partner. No matter how mean she was to him, he was always there for her. And then she apparently discovered why, that day Miss Gillespie forced her to interrogate him, only to ask him to make her forget all about it.

"I'm sorry," she said.

"It's okay. We were kids."

Kids. To the rest of the world, they were still just kids. But she hadn't felt like one in a long time. Children run and laugh and play. She couldn't remember anything like that.

"Congratulations on winning the match. You looked like you were enjoying yourself out there. I don't think I've ever seen you so carefree." Oops. She regretted saying that as soon as it left her mouth. The new Zoe only knew him from here, not from childhood. Ethan didn't seem to notice, though.

"It's surprising how fun it is," he said, "to pit yourself against others without it being a simulated battle to the death. It's still violent, of course, so I have to be really careful to curb my instincts. An elbow to the ribs, not the throat. You know what I mean—you've played it longer than I have."

Uh-oh. She hoped this wasn't a test. She had to assume so for now. Still, it would be safest to change the subject. "Do you really think I've changed that much? I'm still short-tempered."

"You are, but Zoe—you *laugh* now. You have a best friend now. You and Lin are inseparable. I see you two goofing around together, eating together, having serious conversations together. I think she's been a great influence on you. I think that forgetting our childhood, getting a clean slate, has actually been *good* for you. It's allowed you to become more like the person you'd have been if we'd grown up normally, with parents and friends and a normal school, or maybe at least *this* school. With a future that's all yours to decide, not determined for you by a self-professed god bent on world domination."

Oh, wow. He was either playing a role and saying what he thought Zoe 2.0 wanted to hear or he had actually flipped sides. She'd need to tread carefully.

"So, you don't believe what you were taught anymore?"

"You mean that Marduk is a god, and that we're the good guys and they're the bad guys?" He snorted. "Zoe, I don't think I was ever the believer you were. But I don't think these people here are as virtuous as they pretend to be either. We know they exist in key positions in every country in the world, but the kids here haven't even thought to ask what they're supposed to do with their Abilities once they've graduated."

"So, who's side are you on?" Zoe asked.

"I told you, I'm on your side."

"Which is?"

"The side of the Anunnaki, at the moment. But if you get your memories back and you feel that you're still Igigi, then I'm on the side of the Igigi."

"So, you don't care whose side you fight on?"

"They can go to war and kill each other until no one is left for all I care. As long as you and I are still standing at the end."

Zoe hardly knew what to say. He had abandoned his people. He had no loyalty—except to *her*. "Why?" she finally blurted. "Why are you here, Ethan?"

Ethan's step faltered and he stiffened for a split-second. "You asked me that exact question in the infirmary after I arrived here. Do you remember?"

Zoe stayed calm but was now on high alert. She might have just given herself away. "Of course."

"And you remember what I said?"

Here we go. "For me," she guessed, readying herself for whatever would happen if she was wrong.

Ethan visibly relaxed. "That's right," he said. "So, why are you asking again?"

"Because you told the Council *everything*. I don't understand how you can betray your own people like this."

"Yes, you do, Zoe." He stopped suddenly and took her hand and turned her toward him. "You understand full well." He looked into her eyes intently. "I told you in the memory bubble I left for you. I've been scared to say the words to you in person, but you *know*." He took her other hand now. "I love you, Zoe. I always have. You're the only person I care about in this world, and I will do *anything* to keep you safe."

Zoe's palms were sweaty. Why did her stomach feel like it was full of butterflies trying to escape? And why was her heart beating so fast? And why couldn't she look away? How had she never noticed how beautiful his eyes were? She swallowed. "I—I don't know what to say, Ethan."

"Don't say anything," he said, and kissed her.

It was a nice kiss. It was her *first* kiss. Raised as a child soldier, the idea of a first kiss had never really been particularly important to her. When the kiss ended, though, she wished it could go on awhile longer, and she surprised herself by pulling him closer and kissing *him*. And then they were walking hand in hand, her head against his shoulder, and she wasn't paying attention to the layout of the grounds anymore.

Oh, Ethan, she thought to herself. What was she going to do with him? When her mission here was done, even if he helped her complete it, the Igigi would never welcome him back if he had actually defected. She hoped he was just playing a part—that he'd really been sent here by Ragnar to see why she hadn't awakened yet. There was no way to know, though, so her safest course of action was to wait until it no longer mattered before revealing herself to him.

■ ■ ■

Where to go from here, she wondered as she wandered the halls. Her other self seemed to have gained the trust and confidence of Professor Chao, which was everything she could have hoped for upon awakening. Lin was his adopted daughter, so she should apologize and patch up their friendship before Lin told her father and aroused any suspicion. Ethan was the only unexpected variable, but no matter his reasons for being here, he should support her mission.

The longer she waited, the more likely she would be discovered. She had to act as soon as possible. She made her way to Sharapova's office and knocked. The door opened.

"Zoe. I wasn't expecting to see you again so—"

"It's time to wake up now, Natasha," she said, wasting no time as she strode inside and locked the door behind her. She removed the painting of the fishing village from the wall and turned it over. "You know," she said, pulling off one side of the frame, "We were originally going to surgically implant this inside you." She pulled out a small flash drive from its hidden compartment. "But when you returned from Thailand with this gift, they decided to just hide it in the frame and give you a subliminal suggestion to hang this in your office." She banged the frame back into place and rehung the painting. "I argued that surgery was safer." She shrugged. "But it worked."

She sat at the desk and plugged the flash drive into the professor's laptop. After installing the malware, she removed the drive and put it in her pocket. The Igigi should now be able to disable the security systems just prior to the assault.

"Give me your phone," she said.

She texted, "Miss you" to the number she'd memorized, then deleted the message and returned the phone. No turning back now. "It's time to go to sleep now, Natasha," she said, closing the door behind her as she left. She went to the girls washroom and flushed the drive down the toilet. Nothing to do now but wait.

. . .

"I'm sorry," she said to Lin at dinner. She put on her best sorry face, which wasn't easy. Even when she'd been forced to apologize to teachers in the past, she always made sure to keep her eyes defiant so they'd know she was really just reciting the words. Being a spy was hard. "I didn't mean to hurt you. I don't know what got into me. I just . . . what you said about Ethan . . . it struck a nerve, I guess." She made brief eye contact, then averted her gaze again in what she hoped was a suitably humble fashion. "I'm really sorry, Lin."

"It's okay," Lin said. "But it wasn't like you, Zoe. I don't understand why you reacted like that."

Zoe took her time responding. The best lies were close to the truth. "Ethan and I went for a walk after the match. He . . . told me he loved me."

"What?" Lin spat out her food. "In person finally? Wow! What did you say?"

"I said that I didn't know what to say. And then he kissed me."

Lin's eyes bulged out of their sockets. "He kissed you??"

Zoe nodded. "And then I kissed him back."

"You kissed him back???"

Zoe covered her eyes and nodded again.

"Zoe, that's great!" Lin beamed, all thought of their fight forgotten. "Oh, Zoe, I'm so happy for you! But why didn't you say that you love him too?"

"What? Because I don't!"

"Well, you kissed him."

"Yeah, but—"

"So, you obviously like him."

"That's different from *loving* him!"

Lin crossed her arms. "Fine. Live in denial."

Zoe scowled and they ate in silence. "Why does the idea scare you so much?" Lin finally asked. "So much that you got so angry about it?"

"Because I don't fall in love," Zoe blurted.

"What, as a rule?"

"Yes, as a rule."

"Since when?"

"Since *always*," she said, starting to get angry again. "Love is a weakness."

Lin opened her mouth to say something, but stopped and stared at Zoe. Her expression spoke volumes. She was the sort of person who should never play poker. She *knew*.

"Zoe . . . what's the password?"

"What password?" she asked, buying time while thinking frantically. They were in the middle of the Great Hall, surrounded by at least a hundred students. She had no doubt she could escape, but how could she complete her mission if she was on the run? The entire plan was predicated on earning Professor Chao's trust. Her only chance of maintaining her cover was to—

And then Lin raised her shields, preventing her from rendering her unconscious without physical force.

"The password you told me to ask you, in a public space with lots of people around, should I ever suspect you weren't you anymore," Lin said, her eyes narrowed.

"Lin—" Zoe began.

"Did you really think my Zoe would be less clever than you? She came up with this plan ages ago. Do you like my shield? You're probing it right now, aren't you? Looking for faults. Don't bother. You taught me how to make mine so well that even you couldn't break it."

Zoe tried to keep her expression bewildered while she thought. Okay, so her choices now were to run or fight, both of which would expose her and almost certainly result in the failure of the mission. She would be disgraced. Almost a year of her life lost, for nothing.

"Whatever you're here for, you've been discovered. You can run or you can fight but both are pretty bad options, so I'm going to offer you a third."

Zoe waited.

"Open the box brooch."

Zoe was shocked. She'd never expected this. How—?

"Open the brooch and then tell me the password. If my Zoe's guess was right, only you can open it, and its purpose is to restore your new memories."

Zoe sat dumbstruck.

Lin continued. "My Zoe figured that *if* she was actually a sleeper agent, that her thought processes and logical reasoning would still be the same as yours. She said that if this was all an Igigi plan to allow her to infiltrate the Academy, they probably wouldn't want to risk her Anunnaki persona poisoning her Igigi persona, so they'd rig her brain so that when Zoe 1.0 awakened, Zoe 2.0 would go to sleep. She said that she wouldn't like the idea of losing months of her life, though, so she'd create a back door to assimilate her new persona with all those memories. She wouldn't want to jeopardize the mission by using it before her mission was complete, but there would always be the chance that she would actually *need* those new memories in order to complete the mission. She would want to have that option available to her, in case of an emergency, and also for after the mission was over, so she'd create a trigger for that back door—maybe a word written on a piece of paper—and she'd hide it someplace that only she could access. Like that box brooch. And then she'd hide that someplace where she knew she would go looking for clues after losing her memory. Like the alley where it all began."

Zoe had to admit that she was impressed her other self had deduced it all. Zoe 2.0 was clearly every bit as smart as she was.

"Is that why Ethan tried to take it from you in the alley? He was in on Marduk's or Ragnar's plan and knew you weren't supposed to have it?"

"It wasn't *their* plan," Zoe said, abandoning all pretense. "It was *my* plan. It was always my plan. Only me, Ragnar, and Ethan knew that my defection and memory loss was staged. I can only assume Ethan tried to take it from me for the same reason Ragnar didn't want me creating a back door in the first place: He didn't want the new me to corrupt the old me. As if it were Ethan's choice to make. And as if it were even possible. I know who I am. I've been Igigi my entire life. She's existed for less than a year."

"But you didn't open it yet or you'd know the password," Lin said. "So, you must be a little worried that the new Zoe could influence you.

Maybe you just wanted to play it safe and only open it in an emergency, to recover the memories needed to prevent discovery, hoping that you'd stay in control. Well, this is an emergency."

"Except I'm still caught, aren't I?" Zoe said. "So, why would I possibly open it? I'll still wind up a prisoner here."

"Because if you can give me the password and prove to me that my Zoe is back—even though you're still here too—I'll lower my shields."

Zoe's eyes widened. "Why would you do that?"

"Yeah, this isn't part of my Zoe's plan. In fact, this is very much *against* my Zoe's plan. She'd kill me if she knew I was doing this."

"Then why?"

"Because she's my *friend*," Lin said, emphasizing the word. "My very best friend. And no matter who she may have been in the past, I don't believe that she would hurt me or this school, and I don't want anything bad to happen to her."

Zoe could hardly believe her good luck. This girl was an idiot. Her decision was an easy one, but she pretended to consider carefully it. "And what then? Assuming you're right and I don't reach into your mind and make you forget this entire conversation, what then? You'll just tell your father and he'll put me in a cell."

"I won't tell anyone. Not unless it looks like I have no other choice."

Zoe pretended to weigh the pros and cons. "All right," she said. She fished her brooch out from under her shirt and held it in her hand. She looked at it. Master Ragnar had never explained why he'd given it to her—only that he was proud of her for stepping up and showing initiative, that she reminded him of someone he once knew, and he wanted her to have it. She remembered how shocked she was. It was the only time he had ever expressed any particular interest in her, as far as she knew, despite Ethan's claims that she was his favourite. He would be very displeased to learn that she'd used it to do something he had expressly forbidden. While he liked her plan, he'd refused to allow her to remember any of her time here at the Academy. The temporary Zoe, he said, would be the enemy. Her entire life, short though it must be, would be formed under the influence of the Anunnaki and thus couldn't be trusted. Better to be captured and killed, he said, than to allow herself to become infected by the teachings of the enemy.

She didn't agree but knew better than to argue. She was confident in who she was, confident in her beliefs and their cause. There was no way that a few months among the Anunnaki would change her. She thought back to how she had formulated her side-plan. Sharapova had finished segmenting her brain into two isolated sections, with a trigger phrase to bring the new Zoe into existence. Ethan, who was himself quite good at neural manipulation, watched the entire process to learn how Sharapova did it. Zoe then convinced Ethan—with quite a bit of persuasion—to create another phrase that would unlock the new Zoe's memories. He wrote the phrase on a piece of paper and folded it and gave it to her, making her promise not to use it until after the mission when she was in a safe, controlled environment. Zoe promised because she had to, but then hid it in the box brooch. Ethan must have figured it out when he saw her retrieve it from the alley. He wouldn't have been happy that she'd lied to him.

Now she sat across from the enemy, staring at the brooch. She had never considered that she might be forced to open it. She took a deep breath and closed her eyes and began to open the box brooch from the inside, moving the tumblers in the precise combination that only she knew. If she slipped up even slightly, the microexplosive she had stolen from the lab would incinerate the paper within. When the lock clicked, she opened her eyes.

She inspected Lin's shields one last time—yes, this really was her only choice.

She pushed open the circular door on the back of the brooch and fished out the little piece of crumpled paper inside. Taking a deep breath, she unfolded it and read the phrase scrawled in Ethan's handwriting:

We know what we are, but know not what we may be.

The memories flooded her, and she gasped, grabbing the edge of the table to steady herself. Waking up in the alley. Fighting her way out. Encountering Ethan and finding the brooch. Meeting Professor Chao in the library. Fighting alongside him in the restaurant. Meeting the Anunnaki in the safe house. Attending the Academy. Everything she had learned here from the professors. The kindness shown her by Professors Chao and Yeoh. And Lin. She looked up and met her gaze. Her first real friend. Ethan had been her friend, but she had never really been his. She had never lowered her guard enough, become vulnerable enough, for anyone to really know her. Not until she'd met Lin.

And now she'd have to kill her.

Wait—no. Whose thoughts were those? She couldn't kill Lin. Lin was her best friend … but also her sworn enemy. This was really confusing. It wasn't just two sets of memories colliding, it was two personalities, two different sets of morals. She was both Igigi and Anunnaki. Whose side was she on?

"Zoe?" Lin asked, expectantly.

"Yes?"

"The password."

Oh. Right. "Asnasiki," she said. "Quechua for 'wrinkled butt face' or something like that. Pacha told it to us once and we thought it was hilarious."

Lin smiled. "You're back." She lowered her shields.

Zoe didn't hesitate. She jumped into Lin's head and paralyzed her before she could do anything more than widen her eyes in surprise. No one looking their way would have any idea that anything was amiss, but Lin was completely at her mercy. *I'm sorry, Lin. I'm so sorry, but I have to do this. I won't hurt you, I swear, but I can't allow you to remember any of this.*

Why? Zoe tried not to notice the look of betrayal in Lin's eyes.

I need time to figure this out. I have all my memories back, but I've never been more unsure of who I am. The person who I used to be is very different, Lin. I came here with a mission and things have already been set in motion. I don't know what to do now, but I know that I can't do anything if I'm in a cell—and if you tell your dad or your mom or anyone that my memories have returned, that's exactly where I'll be. I'm sorry, but it has to be this way.

She couldn't bring herself to tell Lin what her mission really was, not even if she would wipe her memory. She couldn't cause her such pain even for a second.

Forget all about this conversation. Forget you had any suspicions that my memories returned. The last thing you remember is that Ethan told me he loves me and that he and I just kissed.

She returned the paper to her brooch and tucked it back under her shirt. She exited Lin's mind, removed the paralysis, and watched as Lin's brain reset itself.

"That's amazing!" Lin beamed. "Oh, Zoe, I'm so happy for you! Did you say it back?"

"No," Zoe said. "It's too soon, I don't know how I feel. Feelings like this are new to me. I did hold his hand, though, as we walked."

"Well, I still think you two would make a great couple, but I get wanting to take it slow. You have to follow your heart and do what you think is right."

Zoe forced a smile. "Thanks, Lin. I'll try."

19

SCHISM

Sorting out her feelings for Ethan was the furthest thing from her mind just then, but Lin's advice was still solid—she needed to follow her heart and do what she thought was right. And she had to figure that out within hours, because after the message she'd sent with Dr. Sharapova's phone, it could all go down tonight. She wished she could take that message back. If only she had apologized to Lin before going to see Sharapova. She briefly considered sending another message to abort but knew it would be useless. Once she was awake, there was absolutely no reason for the Igigi to wait—she was either ready and in position or she had been captured and was being interrogated. Either way, the attack would come soon.

When sending that message, she'd thought the easiest way to kill Professor Chao would be during the attack, fighting alongside him until suddenly she thrust her sword through his back. Now, she grimaced. How she could have been so cold-blooded, planning to betray him like that? Then she got angry at her newfound conscience. Her old and new selves were literally disgusted with each other, two warring personalities struggling for dominance.

She wandered the halls, completely at a loss, when a course of action struck her. If she couldn't decide right from wrong, couldn't decide who was good and who was bad, then she needed more information. She soon found herself in the lower levels of the school, where students weren't allowed, and where the former Minister Lafleur was imprisoned. At the end of a long hallway stood two guards, watching in annoyance as she approached. She started working out just how to incapacitate them and wipe their memories when suddenly one spoke into a walkie talkie.

"Sir, we have a student approaching in Sector 3. It's the girl Zoe. Over."

Oh. Well . . . crap, now everyone knew she was here. She approached the guards but before she could speak, she heard someone reply through the walkie talkie: "Minister Chao says to let her through."

Zoe raised an eyebrow, and the guard opened a door and motioned her through into a small room. The guard shut the door behind her. The room held a single chair and a camera mounted in the corner of the ceiling. On the room's far side stood a jail cell. But instead of bars, it was made of some sort of thick glass or transparent plastic. Inside, former Minister Gabrielle Lafleur lay on her bunk, ignoring Zoe's approach.

"Hello," Zoe said, awkwardly, and got no reply. "I was hoping we could talk. I . . . need to know some things. Things that I suspect only you might know."

Again, no response. "Gabrielle?"

"We're on a first name basis now, are we?"

"I'm sorry," Zoe stammered. "I don't know what to call you now that . . ."

"Now that I am no longer minister."

"Yes . . . Madame Lafleur," Zoe tried, hoping she sounded respectful.

"Thanks, in no small part, to you."

Zoe's brow furrowed. "I'm not the reason you're in here."

Lafleur sat upright and furrowed her own brow right back. "No? I was leader of my people for generations, and then mere months after you appeared, I am in a cell, accused of being a criminal."

"We are who we choose to be," Zoe said.

Lafleur paused, then snorted, and let her body relax. "My own words come back to haunt me. To think, I taught that man everything he knows." She sighed. "What do you want, girl?"

Zoe sat in the chair. "You said the Igigi are known to you. You called them beasts. Who are they? How do you know about them when nobody else does? Why do you hate them so much?"

The former minister was quiet for a while, then said slowly and deliberately, "The Igigi—your people—are a scourge on this planet. I know things others do not because I am older than others. I was alive during the height of the Roman Empire and I witnessed its fall. The Igigi played no small part in that. I lived through the Dark Ages that followed, during which time the Igigi hunted us. They claimed to be "liberating" people from our manipulations, but they cared nothing for the welfare of the world. They only wished to impose their will upon it and establish themselves as its rightful rulers."

Lafleur stared into space as she remembered. "They killed everyone I knew. All my friends. Never in open battle, but in the shadows. One by one, whenever we were alone or in small numbers. Our numbers dwindled and we lived in constant fear."

"Was Marduk their leader back then?" Zoe asked.

"Possibly, but I do not know. They certainly worshipped him as their leader, their god, but he always seemed like a fairy tale, not an actual being. I interrogated many of the captured Igigi myself, but none ever claimed to have seen him."

"How did you defeat them?"

"Slowly," Lafleur said. "Methodically. Over many centuries. Until they were too few in number to be called anything other than rogues, people who just weren't happy with the way we do things. I had thought they were all gone."

"You said they claimed to liberate people from the manipulations of the Anunnaki. Is there any truth to their way of thinking? Are the Anunnaki really above criticism? You said the Igigi helped bring about the fall of the Roman Empire. Wasn't that a good thing? Weren't the Romans horribly oppressive, conquering people and ruling through force?"

"The Romans built their empire through force, it is true, but they also brought order and stability and an age of prosperity and enlightenment."

That sounded much like what she was criticizing the Igigi for, but Zoe decided to leave it alone. She was more interested in the here and now than the Roman Empire. "So, what is the way we do things? Since I first got here, I've been trying to figure out what we do out in the world after graduation. We get vague hints about how Telepaths subtly guide the world along the correct course, but the world is hardly peaceful. There are countless wars and atrocities happening right now—just as there have always been. Fascist governments are always rising to power, and in just this past century, leaders have ruthlessly killed millions of their own people. Where were we? What good *are* we?"

Lafleur scowled. "The world is a complicated place, child, and so is what we do—"

"Spare me," Zoe interrupted. "And stop calling me a child to avoid explaining yourself. What exactly do we do out in the world? Why are we the good guys?"

"Because we don't interfere!" Lafleur snapped. "We don't claim moral superiority over Typicals. We don't go into their minds and compel them toward the world order that we prefer."

"We have no qualms about compelling them to keep our existence secret."

"Yes, exactly! We compel them only for the purpose of self-preservation, not to impose our will upon them."

"So, even though we could have prevented genocides, we purposefully did nothing, in the name of some ideology of non-interference? You were minister during World War II. How could you have let the Holocaust happen?"

"Do you think I wanted to? Do you think it's easy to watch a monster come to power, to watch millions of innocents die, knowing that I *could* stop it? You don't understand my burden."

"Then make me understand! Convince me the Igigi are wrong. We aren't aliens here—we're a *part* of this world! We could make it better—and yes, we'd risk being exposed—but instead we cower in fear and do *nothing*!"

Lafleur shook her head. "There was a time when we played a larger role in the affairs of Typicals, in secret, behind the scenes, but when you start to play god, Zoe, where does it end?"

"Why can't it end with the death of one brutal dictator? Or with simply compelling him to step down? How could the end not justify the means when millions would live at the expense of a single, awful man's free will?"

"It would seem like the right thing to do at first, guiding humanity in a way we see fit. And in the past, we have done so. But once we go down that path, it is inevitable that we begin to interfere more and more."

"I still don't see why that's bad."

"Because our morality is not any better than theirs. Indeed, the temptation to use our Abilities for our own benefit makes us much more susceptible to being *immoral*."

"So, what *do* we do, if we don't make the world a better place?"

"We stop each other from making it worse, mainly. And we stop each other from exposing the rest of us."

Zoe was speechless.

"When students graduate from the Academy, Zoe, they go home, back to whichever country they came from. Everyone has nationalistic tendencies, the desire to help their own people, which often comes at the expense of other nations' people. We cannot allow that. We try, during a student's formative years, to instill a sense of identity, a sense of belonging to a group outside of our respective countries, of being a part of something greater. We are Telepaths first, citizens second. Our loyalty must be to each other first, to our country second."

"And does that work?" Zoe asked.

Lafleur shrugged. "Yes and no. There will always be those who cannot resist the temptation to effect change on a grand scale, whether it be for good or bad. It can be very difficult to spot, so we have spies everywhere, watching to ensure this doesn't happen."

"So, we're not allowed to use our Abilities at all? That must be pretty hard to enforce."

"We're only human, Zoe. With the same needs and desires and failings as any Typical. If we were to try to force Telepaths to never use their Abilities, we would fail spectacularly. So, we turn a blind eye to Telepaths using their Abilities to amass wealth and power on a small scale. But we will not tolerate anyone trying to influence world events."

Zoe sat quietly for a while, letting it all sink in.

"I'm not sure," she said, slowly, "that I have any better sense now of who is right and who is wrong than I did when I came in here. I understand what you're saying about how power can easily go to our heads and how we should adopt a policy of non-interference. But it seems to me that what you are most concerned about is hiding our existence, and that this fear stops us from using our Abilities for the greater good. We have great power, yet we are abdicating our responsibility because we are afraid to put ourselves at risk."

"No," Lafleur said, shaking her head once more. "You have it wrong. It is our responsibility to prevent those among us who covet power from obtaining it. We must not give in to our desires to rule this planet."

"But this is our planet every bit as much as it is theirs! And this planet is in danger. The human race could go extinct from nuclear war, or from the climate crisis. What good are your principles of non-interference and non-exposure when everyone—Telepaths and Typicals—are dead?"

"So, you agree with the Igigi then," Lafleur spat. "You think we should take over the world, reveal ourselves, and rule the Typicals with an iron fist."

"I don't know what I think! I only know that doing nothing, out of fear of maybe doing evil, when we could do so much good, can't be the way! There is so much we could do to help people and all you do is use your Abilities for your own gain! And do you even think you can prevent the Typicals from learning of our existence for much longer? In the age of the Internet? When anyone can post a video from their phone and have it go viral within minutes? I can't believe it hasn't happened already. And the Igigi could just decide to expose us all at any time. Telepaths will soon be known to the world and there's nothing any of us can do to stop it. Do you have a plan for that?"

Lafleur was silent.

"That's what I thought," Zoe said, standing. "You're a dinosaur, leading your people and the entire world toward extinction."

She turned back at the door. "I wanted so badly for you to convince me who was in the right and who was in the wrong. Would that have been so hard?"

Slamming the door behind her, she strode past the guards, down the hallway, and up the stairs. She soon found herself in the Main Hall where she had stood wide-eyed nearly a year ago upon first arriving at the Academy. Groups of students walked this way and that, laughing and giggling. They didn't know what was coming. She pictured what this room might look like soon, perhaps in a matter of hours. Would this hall be filled with their blood?

She felt lost. Her whole life had led to this mission and now she faltered. She was a soldier. It wasn't her job to decide who was right and wrong—it was her job to follow orders and complete her mission. Except, of course, it was more complicated than that. Had anyone ever been in her position before? Led two completely different lives, indoctrinated into two different and opposing worldviews? Lived among the enemy and become their friend?

She was furious with Lafleur, who had basically validated everything that she had been taught growing up—that the Anunnaki cared nothing for the welfare of others, using their gifts solely for their own benefit. But just because Lafleur was wrong didn't necessarily make the Igigi right. Could change only be effected through murdering the Anunnaki? They hadn't even tried talking to them. She'd been told that talking had proved useless in the past and this time they would take no chances—but it sounded like "the past" was well over a thousand years ago! As far as she could tell, only Lafleur had even been alive back then. Was attacking first truly justified?

She felt sick to her stomach. The fact of the matter was she was going to have to betray someone—either those who had raised her or those who had befriended her. Unless . . .

Unless she betrayed both sides.

What if she didn't choose any side? What if she just left? She could walk out those doors and never look back. She wouldn't have to kill Professor Chao. She wouldn't have to fight her people. She could absolve herself of everything by simply refusing to play the game. She would spend her life on the run, true, but better that than a life spent wracked with guilt.

She took a step toward the door and stopped. How would she feel if she ran and Lin died in the attack?

"You'd feel horrible," Zoe said aloud. "She's your best friend. You'd spend your life thinking maybe Lin would still be alive if you'd stayed and helped."

"She's not my responsibility!" Zoe said, angrily. "It's not my fault she chose to befriend someone she knew full well might be a spy. Why would she do that? And why would her parents allow it? They're all idiots!"

"They did it because they're good people, and you know it. They did it because they believe that everyone deserves a chance to prove who they really are—a chance to choose who they really are."

"Oh, enough already with Chao's pseudo-philosophical babble. How are we supposed to choose? We're perfectly balanced, you and I. You want me to choose team Anunnaki, but what if I don't? What if I stay true to my people and shove a sword straight through your precious professor's—"

She stopped at the sight of a crowd of students staring at her. She opened her mouth to speak but was cut off by the sudden blare of sirens. A voice came over the loudspeaker.

"To arms! To arms! We are under attack! This is not a drill! To arms! To arms! We are under attack! This is not a drill!"

20

ENDGAME

Students ran in every direction. Over the last few months, they had all been instructed where to go and what to do in the event of an attack. The youngest would go deepest within the school, into the great hall, and only fight as a last resort if the enemy managed to penetrate that far. The older children would position themselves further out from the centre and protect the youngest only if necessary. The oldest students, though, would fight alongside their teachers and the security forces on the front lines. If they had to fall back, they would all make their last stand together, young and old, in the Great Hall. Zoe wondered where Lin would be—in the Great Hall like her parents insisted or fighting outside like she wanted.

Zoe! Where are you? Ethan said in her mind.

Zoe ran outside into the rain. Floodlights lit up the lawns. Security guards yelled about how there had been no warning. She was the reason for this—she had sabotaged their security systems with her virus.

Men jumped over the west wall and ran toward the school. Bullets flew and explosions riddled the lawn. She looked up to see people on the rooftop firing rocket-propelled grenades at the dozen or more helicopters in the air. They really had beefed up the school's defences following the last attack. Then, she saw something else—dark things dropping from the sky. They were people! No parachutes—just soldiers dropping fast and slowing down at the very last second with telekinesis. Some landed on the roof and the rockets suddenly stopped.

Zoe! Ethan yelled again. *Tell me where you are!*

She spun slowly in place, taking stock of the situation, then leapt to the side as a sword shot down from above like a bullet. The wielder literally stood in the crater he'd just made. Zoe stepped in, yanked up his mask, and delivered a lethal blow to his exposed throat. In the back of her mind, she noted that despite the guilt she had felt before, she was still fully capable of killing when necessary. There was no time to reflect on this as she took the fallen man's sword. What now? That was instinct, self-preservation. She still hadn't actually chosen a side.

I'm outside the main entrance, she said to Ethan, walking away from the action so she could think.

A swarm of security guards tried to assemble themselves into a row to meet the oncoming soldiers, but the dark, armoured ninjas dropping behind the front line were causing chaos. Teachers and seniors streamed from the school and engaged the enemy. And she just stood and watched, paralyzed with indecision. Then, she saw Professor Chao striding confidently through the main doors, barking orders as he pointed this way and that. On his left was Professor Yeoh, holding a long metal staff. On his right was—Zoe blinked—Lafleur! She wielded a katana, her face a mask of terrible hatred. She sprinted toward the front line and entered the fray, screaming like a berserker.

An attacker suddenly dropped in front of Chao, but before he could react, Professor Yeoh stepped between them, her staff a blur as she hit the assailant more times than Zoe could count. Leaving him a crumpled heap on the ground, she turned to her husband, clearly daring him to object to how she'd put herself between him and harm's way. He nodded and she did the same before rushing to assist a group of students who were clearly in trouble.

Chao hadn't noticed Zoe yet. Sword in hand, he walked purposefully toward the front line, with five security personnel marching in front of him—clearly determined to protect him as long as they could. Zoe followed. This was it. Nobody was paying her any attention. If she was going to kill him, this was her chance. She closed the distance.

Ten feet. She twirled her sword to get a feel for its weight. Was she actually going to do this? She could only keep telling herself that she was keeping her options open for a few seconds more.

Nine feet. She remembered her first encounter with Chao in the Toronto Reference Library and his incredulous reaction to her pathetic attempt to use compulsion on him.

Eight feet. Eating the meal he had bought for her at the restaurant, as he spoke about Telepaths and their place in the world.

Seven feet. *You are who you choose to be*, he had said to her. *There is always a choice.*

Six feet. Sitting in seiza, side by side in the dojo. *If you wish, Zoe, I could be your guide.*

Five feet. Striking distance. The world slowed, the time between her heartbeats stretching to an eternity. She had delayed as long as she could and still felt balanced on a knife's edge. Two radically divergent paths lay before her and she literally had one second left to decide. She took a deep breath and adjusted her grip on the sword.

Suddenly, Professor Chao pivoted, sweeping his left leg behind him in classic tenkan and stood facing her in the rain. His sword still sheathed, his hands at his sides. He looked into her eyes, not with puzzlement or betrayal, but with kindness. He *knew*. He knew what she was thinking of doing and didn't even try to prevent it. He would simply force her to look him in the eyes as she did it. In what felt like slow motion, she took a step forward and yelled at the top of her lungs as she threw Chao to the side with her left hand—and a considerable amount of telekinetic force—and thrust her sword into the belly of the man lunging at Chao from behind. She kept yelling as she grabbed the dying man's sword arm and threw him violently to the ground. She screamed into his face as his surprised eyes began to dim. She didn't know why she was screaming. Maybe it was a scream of pure anger and frustration at having been forced to make such an impossible decision, or maybe it was a scream of catharsis, of relief at having finally made the impossible choice.

She screamed until tears ran down her face and a dead man's eyes gazed blankly up at her and she had no more breath left in her lungs, and then she rose to one knee and yanked out her sword and took stock of her surroundings. It seemed like a lifetime had just passed. Professor Chao's guards stood slack-jawed and sheepish, knowing they had failed to protect him. Professor Chao himself stood just feet away, looking concerned. He extended his hand to her and she took it, rising to her feet.

"You chose," he said, putting his hand on her shoulder. "I can only imagine how difficult that must have been for you."

"But I almost chose differently, Professor," she confessed. "I honestly don't even know what would have happened if this man hadn't tried to attack you. You were wrong to put your faith in me."

He shook his head. "What matters is that when the moment presented itself, you decided what sort of person you wanted to be. So, don't think any more on what might have been." He drew his sword. "There's a battle to be fought. Come!" he yelled, launching himself into the fray. Zoe ran after him.

. . .

The battle raged. So many Anunnaki had arrived over the past few months to protect the Academy. Many wore security uniforms, but many more appeared to be civilians, some of whom she even recognized from that first emergency meeting at the safe house. The earlier rockets and bullets had given way to a pure melee between two hordes of warriors, viciously battling in hand-to-hand combat. Zoe doubted the world had seen a battle like this in centuries.

Twenty meters away, Professor Martinov displayed what a master of telekinesis could do. His hands empty, his cloak swirling like an angry storm, he stood within a whirlwind of knives that darted in and out among his wary assailants, finding their vulnerabilities with pinpoint accuracy.

Ethan had fought his way to her side, and together, they did their best to protect the students who were fighting bravely, especially considering this was their first real battle. Most of the Doom teams stuck together, she saw, taking advantage of their ability to work as a team. Nevertheless, most students were outmatched and overwhelmed by the trained soldiers.

Is it you? Ethan asked as they fought.

Of course it's me, she replied, as she gutted a soldier who was about to kill Takeshi Yamamoto, captain of the Flying Dragons. *Who else do you think called in the attack?*

Ethan dispatched the man who had launched himself at her exposed back. *Then why didn't you tell me you woke up? And why didn't you take out Chao? Why are we fighting against our own people?*

She rounded on him and stuck her finger in his chest. "I don't even know why you're here, Ethan. I don't know whose side you're on or what games you're playing, but *I* have made my choice, and *I* am fighting with my friends."

Suddenly, she heard someone yelling her name. She looked around and heard it again, this time realizing it was Lin's voice in her head.

Zoe, help! Help me!

She searched for Lin's face in the chaos. *Where are you?*

In the Great Hall! Hurry!

The Great Hall? How could she be communicating via mindlink from there? Adrenaline, she guessed, and maybe Lin was stronger than they knew. But how could she be in trouble? Of course! How could she have been so stupid? The majority of the Igigi had come over the wall, but some came from the sky—landing on the rooftops! She had to get there as quickly as possible, but she couldn't abandon these students.

Ethan, stay here and—

In the distance, she saw him.

Ragnar.

Across the battlefield, she locked eyes with her former master. He was shirtless and covered in tattoos and blood, a huge sword in his right hand and a shield in his left—an unstoppable Viking warrior come straight out of legend to kill them all.

Traitor, he said in her mind, so powerfully that she dropped to her knees. He knew. Had he been watching when she spared Professor Chao's life? Had he seen her fighting his soldiers? She shook her head and rose to her feet. There was no time for this.

Ethan, stay here and help. Lin's in trouble.

Without waiting for an answer, she disengaged from the fight and dashed back into the school. She raced through the empty hallways and burst through the already broken doors of the Great Hall. A group of first-years huddled together at the far end, clutching each other's hands. Lin stood in front of them, holding a bloodied katana. Pacha stood to her left, his arms outstretched and his brow furrowed. Slightly in front stood Head Housemaid Amelia Zehringer, looking fierce in her apron, a broken mop-turned-makeshift-staff in her hands. At least six men lay unconscious or dead on the floor, and another six eyed them warily, dodging the dinner plates and chairs that Amelia and Pacha were telekinetically hurling at them. They used their own telekinesis to deflect as much as possible while also trying to close the distance without Lin skewering them. As godlings, they weren't as strong as regular Telepaths, but they were still stronger in their Abilities than typical first-years. Pacha, of course, was not typical.

Ethan stopped short at her side.

I told you to stay and help the others! she cried.

Sorry, but I'm not leaving your side, Zoe.

Scowling, she advanced on the godlings, who turned and—

She gasped. There stood Tsuji, Ivan, and Anders. Their eyes narrowed.

"You," said Tsuji.

"You," Zoe answered.

Tsuji ordered the other three godlings to attack. Zoe sidestepped one and skewered him as Ethan chopped down the second. The third man stopped, looked back at Tsuji, looked at Zoe and Ethan again, then dropped his sword and ran.

Zoe approached the remaining godlings slowly, her bloodied sword held low. "I'm not the same person you fought last time," she said. "Surrender and we'll let you live."

Tsuji spat. "We are not expendable grunts. You'll not kill us so easily." The godlings spread themselves out and readied their swords as Zoe neared. Then Tsuji crumpled to the floor, Amelia looming over her, staff held high. Ivan and Anders whirled around only to suffer blows to their heads, too—Anders by the blunt side of Lin's sword and Ivan by a heavy and swiftly plummeting table. Both collapsed.

"Humph," Amelia grunted. "Teach *you* to attack children."

"Don't kill them!" Pacha said, as Zoe knelt to examine the unconscious godlings. She nodded. Killing someone in order to defend yourself or others was one thing, but killing someone who was unconscious and no longer a threat was quite another. She searched the fallen godlings and found zip ties on their belts. She tied their hands behinds their backs, then looked up at Lin.

"Are you all right?" Zoe asked.

Lin nodded. "Are my parents okay?"

"Last I saw."

"Good. We can't stay here. It's not safe."

"Agreed. But where is?"

Lin floundered helplessly. "I don't know. It's not like there's a secret safe room. At least, I don't think there is."

Zoe thought a moment. "There's no choice. The only reason to be here was because it was supposed to be behind the safety of our forces, but with Igigi dropping from the sky, the safest place is actually close to the front, where our forces can offer some measure of protection."

They shared a glance, both knowing how dangerous this suggestion was. Most of these first-years were useless in a fight, and Amelia, for all her ferocity, was hardly a warrior.

"Or we could hide . . ." said a meek voice. It was Liam Murphy. "I mean, think about it. We're first-years. We've barely started our studies. We can't go up against trained soldiers—we'll all get killed. We're not like you. We haven't been training to kill since we were born."

Helen Hawkesbury nodded her agreement. Liam and Helen were two of the strongest first-years, and yet they'd done nothing to help as Lin and Pacha defended them.

Zoe shook her head. "There's no time for this," she said. "Anyone who wants to hide, go hide. Maybe Liam's right and it's your best chance to survive this. But Lin and Ethan and I can't go with you. They need us out there, so anyone who wants to fight alongside us, come with us. Amelia, can you take care of those who wish to stay behind?"

Amelia held her chin high. "They will be safe with me," she said.

Zoe left the Great Hall, with Ethan, Lin, and Pacha close behind. Seconds later, half of the first-years hurried to catch up.

"I hope you're right about this, Zoe," Lin said, glancing back at her frightened peers.

"Me too," she said, "but I don't know what else to do. We can't hide in a closet with them, hoping our side wins. We're way outnumbered—we all have to fight." She broke into a run and soon burst out the doors and into hell.

"Oh my god," Lin and Zoe said in unison, as they took in the scene. The dead and the dying littered the ground, outnumbering the living. A helicopter lay in burning ruins. The attacking forces had flanked the defenders on both sides, and the teachers, students, and security personnel now fought in a semicircle formation.

"We're losing," Lin said, stunned.

"I'm sorry." Zoe took her hand.

"This isn't your fault, Zoe. They're not your people anymore."

Zoe took a deep breath. "You need to know something, Lin. In case . . . just in case. No secrets between us." She turned and placed her hands on Lin's head.

"Zoe, wha—" Lin started to say.

Remember.

Lin's eyes widened, and she knocked Zoe's hands aside as she backed away. "What have you done?"

"I'm sorry, Lin. I had already taken down the security systems and called in the assault before you made me open the brooch. And then I was confused, and I needed time to think. To assimilate my two personas. But I chose, Lin. I was here to gain your dad's trust and, once I regained my memories, to betray him—to kill him—either before or during this assault . . . to reduce the Igigi casualties."

Lin shook her head, looking at Zoe like she didn't know her anymore.

"But I didn't," Zoe said, quickly. "You brought back my memories of the last year, so that I could have the chance to decide what sort of person I wanted to be. I had the opportunity to kill him, Lin, but I didn't. I saved his life instead. I chose my side. I chose who I wanted to be, just like he said."

Zoe looked toward the battle and saw Professor Chao and Ragnar each carving a path toward the other. "And now I have to help him."

She turned back to Lin. "Goodbye, Lin. Thank you for being my friend."

She raced toward the battle. "Professor Yeoh!" she yelled to where Lin's mother was fighting alongside Makena, Priya, and Paige. She wished she could help them. "Professor Yeoh, Lin needs you!" She pointed back to the first-years as she tore past.

Her former master looked invincible, covered in the blood of his enemies. Professor Chao would reach him in seconds. She ran as fast as she could, keeping herself directly behind the professor so that Ragnar might not see her coming, then jumped up and over the professor with as much of a telekinetic boost as she could muster, leaving a crater behind in the ground.

No! Ethan yelled shouted in her mind.

Clearing Chao by almost six feet, she began her silent downward arc, her sword pointed at her former master. Her spontaneous gamble that he might be too busy to notice her attack from above was dashed as he looked up, locked eyes with her, and smiled coldly. Time slowed again. She was helpless in the air, with no way to change her trajectory quickly enough. She watched Ragnar's shield arm rise as his sword arm pulled back. The most reckless act of her life would turn out to be her last.

Ethan charged Ragnar, screaming at the top of his lungs in an obvious attempt at a distraction. But Ethan was too far away, and the Viking didn't take the bait. Her sword's point struck his shield as his heavy broadsword began its swing, when she suddenly felt herself being picked up by invisible hands and hurled past him, Ragnar's sword just nicking her shoulder. Someone had just saved her life. Professor Chao? She landed behind Ragnar and spun to see Ethan diving feet first through the Viking's legs and slashing at his ankles. The large man jumped gracefully and rolled out of the way.

"So," he spat, contemptuously, "it seems both my pupils now serve a new master." His eyes narrowed. "Not for much longer."

Zoe and Ethan readied themselves to attack.

"*Enough!*" Professor Chao yelled with a voice so full of authority that a hush fell upon the battlefield and all eyes turned toward the two leaders facing each other.

"This is our fight," Chao said, looking more steeled and dangerous than Zoe had ever seen him. Ragnar nodded and the two warriors began to slowly circle each other as a ring of combatants from both sides formed around them.

It was like watching two panthers square off—each man so lithe, each movement so deliberate and controlled. Ragnar—a full head taller than Chao and with a huge weight advantage—attacked first. He charged, surprisingly quick for such a large man, attempting to overpower his opponent with his heavier blade and end the fight quickly. Chao evaded his attacks, though, and Zoe could see now why he had so often stressed the importance of proper footwork. Rather than trying to meet force with force, blocking and countering, which could only end in disaster against this giant of a man, Chao was constantly trying to blend with Ragnar's attacks and get in close enough to slide in his blade. But Ragnar was no brute—he was a battle-tested warrior who'd spent centuries pitting himself against fighters of all styles, learning their weaknesses and incorporating their strengths. When Zoe watched him make the same attack pattern twice, she knew that Chao must have noticed it too, and that he would look to take advantage should it happen a third time.

It's a ruse, she said in Professor Chao's mind.

When the same attack sequence happened a third time, Chao moved in to strike but didn't commit to the attack, instead feinting, springing the trap and leaping out of its way. Ragnar grinned. He was enjoying himself. When was the last time he'd had a worthy opponent?

Now Chao began to test Ragnar, darting in and out quickly, attacking so as to provoke a desired response and then changing the attack at the last moment, trying to get inside and end the fight quickly. But Zoe doubted Chao had spent much time fighting against anyone with a shield, because it was his undoing each time. Ragnar used his shield not only to block, or to keep Chao at bay, but as a weapon in and of itself to thrust or even strike.

Suddenly, Chao slipped in the mud and was caught by the shield and knocked backwards. Ragnar didn't give him time to regain his footing, instead rushing him shield-first while hacking at him with his heavy sword, forcing him to retreat. Finally, Chao was forced to leap backwards, performing a back roll and immediately leaping and rolling to the side to avoid a certain death blow. Zoe expected him to increase the distance between them and regain his composure, but instead, Chao made the unexpected decision to go full-in on the attack. As Ragnar lifted his blade from the ground where Chao had been moments earlier, Chao leapt in, attempting to close the distance and thrust his sword into Ragnar's side.

It was a gamble that might have paid off against an orthodox, disciplined fighter. But Ragnar had learned to fight on the battlefield, not in a classroom. When he saw Chao's unexpected attack, he didn't hesitate. He left his sword in the ground and leapt toward Chao with his shield arm outstretched, letting Chao's sword graze harmlessly off his shield until he was close enough to grab Chao's wrist and pin it down to the ground as they both landed gracelessly. Chao tried to scramble to his feet and kick Ragnar but was forced to let go of his own sword and dive away to avoid being tackled and pinned by the much heavier man. Ragnar picked up Professor Chao's katana, dropped his shield, and showed everyone how he too knew how to use the two-handed weapon of the samurai.

With this lighter blade, Ragnar was a whirlwind, and Chao did everything he could to avoid it. Chao attempted to close the distance several times, but each time he aborted, perhaps sensing a ruse. Finally, an opening presented itself—he stepped into Ragnar's attack, slightly to the left to avoid the sword, spinning and sweeping his right foot backwards in an arc so that he stood side-to-side on the man's right, his left hand on Ragnar's right wrist. As Ragnar swung around to face him, Chao performed a classic kotegaeshi, flipping the big man over onto his back.

It was a picture-perfect technique and should have worked. But as he tried to roll the Viking onto his stomach to perform a submissive wristlock to allow him to seize the weapon, Ragnar refused to let go of the sword and roll over. Instead, through sheer strength, he scrambled awkwardly toward Chao, who once again was forced to retreat, but did not let go of Ragnar's wrist. Ragnar grabbed Chao's right hand and bit down. Chao yelled and kicked Ragnar in the face with both feet, knocking him away and landing on his back. Both men rose slowly, Chao's hand bleeding profusely and Ragnar spitting out his enemy's blood.

Ragnar still held Chao's sword. He stood patiently now, watching Chao's blood drip. Zoe knew her professor didn't have much time left to finish this fight. He was weaponless, bleeding, and Ragnar stood between him and the other sword.

Chao darted in and out, trying to get his opponent to commit to an attack so he could manoeuvre past him to the broadsword buried in the ground. But Ragnar refused to take the bait, content to let Chao's life drip from his wound. A chill went up Zoe's spine. Professor Chao wouldn't win this fight.

Chao stopped and stood quietly, staring defiantly as his enemy grinned. Then, Chao closed his eyes, dropped to his knees, and spread his arms wide. The crowd gasped and Zoe heard herself scream. Ragnar approached cautiously, clearly expecting a trap, before finally shrugging and raising his sword for a killing blow.

It all happened so quickly. Ragnar's shield suddenly leapt from the ground behind him and flew toward him. Somehow sensing the attack, he spun around and knocked it out of the air with the katana—only to be impaled by the broadsword that had also been hurtling through the air, hidden behind the shield. Stunned, he dropped the katana and stared down at the sword buried in his gut. Zoe could hardly believe her eyes. He'd done it. Somehow her professor had beat Ragnar.

Chao leapt up and put the man in a chokehold from behind, trying to drag him down to his knees. Ragnar resisted, his neck straining and eyes bulging. He grasped the sword buried in his abdomen by its sharp blade with both hands. Hands bleeding, he wrenched it from his body and thrust it backwards into Professor Chao's midsection.

No.

Stunned, the professor released his chokehold. Ragnar turned and grabbed the hilt of the sword and thrust it in deeper, twisting it as Chao grunted. He pulled out the blade, and Professor Chao dropped to his knees.

Everything was in slow motion. Someone screamed. Zoe looked for the source and saw that it was Lin, held back by her mother. Zoe looked to her teacher. This couldn't be happening. Ragnar held a bloodied hand to his abdomen, looking down on his fallen enemy. Professor Chao looked serene. He scanned the crowd and smiled to his family, then turned to meet Zoe's gaze.

Protect them in the days ahead.

And then Ragnar's sword came sweeping down, and the most noble man Zoe had ever known was gone.

Cheers erupted from the enemy, while the defenders stood shell-shocked. Zoe saw them drop their weapons in surrender, but her grip on her own katana tightened. She could not take her eyes off of the man who had just killed her mentor. She felt hatred, true hatred, and blinding rage bubble up. Ragnar met her stare and laughed.

He had to die.

She launched herself at him with a scream, intending to drive her sword straight through him, when suddenly someone tackled her to the ground. Ethan.

"No!" she screamed before her voice quit. She was paralyzed. Just like that time in the alley. *Get off of me! I have to kill him! Let me go!*

But Ethan held her firm, both physically and psychically. Zoe reached down deep, readying for the most explosive burst of telekinetic force she could muster, when suddenly she saw Ragnar's face appear above hers, his hand on Ethan's shoulder. Ragnar held her gaze.

"You are such a disappointment, daughter," he said, and Zoe felt all her power dissipate instantly. Daughter? Ragnar turned his attention to Ethan. "You could not convince her to stay true?"

"I'm sorry, sir," Ethan stammered. "I don't know why she did it. I didn't even know she'd regained her memories until the assault began."

"And you could not put your sword in his back when she refused to?" he said, nodding toward the body of Professor Chao.

"I'm sorry, sir. There was no opportunity during the battle, and then you were fighting him yourself."

"Hmm. But not before you raised your sword against me yourself," Ragnar said, coldly.

Ethan stared helplessly. "I . . . I'm sorry, sir. . . . I had to protect her."

Ragnar stared at Ethan a moment longer, perhaps deciding whether to kill him or not, before he sighed. "I suppose you could not help it. At least you were useful in the end. I am glad you survived my arrow. I am not sure that I could have defended myself from her in my present condition." He winced as he stood. "He fought well, did he not? I have not had such a challenging fight in centuries." He raised his voice to speak to the crowd.

"I am Ragnar Lodbrok of the Igigi! You should all be proud of how your leader fought today. The man had both courage and skill—but he was deluded, just like the rest of you, in thinking that he was on the side of righteousness. This world could be a paradise were it not for the Anunnaki deliberately letting it fall into ruin and chaos while they profit!" He spread his arms wide. "But most of you here are blissfully unaware of how the world truly works and are not to blame. You will be welcomed into the service of Emperor Marduk, once you have been . . . reeducated."

Ragnar continued his speech, but Zoe heard little of it. She stared into Ethan's eyes, all her rage gone. She felt utterly defeated and empty. *Why?*

Why what? I came here to make sure you were okay when we never got your signal, and to be your backup in case the mission failed. But you didn't even tell me you got your memories back and called in the attack, and then, when I saw you about to make your move against Chao, you chose to join him instead!

You lied to me.

Lied? Ethan shook his head. *What are you talking about? I had to lie to you about defecting before your memories had returned because that wasn't really you, but even then I said I was here for you and I was on your side and I am. I actually fought against my own people today just to keep you safe. But that doesn't mean that I'm suddenly an Anunnaki or that I'm going to let you get yourself killed attacking Ragnar.*

You betrayed me, Ethan. You betrayed everyone.

Ethan looked both confused and hurt. *This was YOUR plan, remember? You called in the assault. I only hope you'll be forgiven for turning against him. And that I'll be forgiven, too. What the hell, Zoe? If you regained your memories, then you shouldn't even remember anything about the past few months, so why did you—* His eyes suddenly widened. *Oh. You used it, didn't you? When I first saw that pendant in the alley, I just thought you had stolen it from Ragnar. But it was worse. You went against his orders—and against your promise to me—and hid the trigger in it, and you used it. And now my Zoe is gone.*

Zoe turned her head away and closed her eyes. *Ragnar would be dead right now if not for you. I'll never forgive you for this, Ethan.*

Ethan winced, then stood resolutely and motioned for two men to assist. They rolled her onto her stomach and tied her wrists behind her back before roughly lifting her upright and leading her away through the nightmare scene. Ragnar had finished speaking and now crouched on one knee while two healers placed their hands on his wounds. The helicopters had all landed and were loading prisoners. Lafleur lay facedown in the mud with a knee in her back, still cursing defiantly as six men tried to subdue her. Professor Martinov lay either unconscious or dead. The headmaster was on his knees with his hands tied behind his back. Most of the students were also on their knees, their hands behind their heads, staring at the ground. Some lay on their backs, staring lifelessly up at the sky. Everyone was covered in mud and blood. Lin sobbed inconsolably as she and her mother were led away in handcuffs.

Zoe landed roughly on the floor of one of the helicopters. As it rose and flew away, she looked down at the carnage below. The once beautiful Academy grounds were pocked with craters and littered with bodies and blood. Some of the trees burned.

This was all her fault. Professor Chao and so many others were dead, and it was all her fault. She closed her eyes tightly.

I'm sorry, Professor. I'm so sorry. I'll protect them. I swear.

ACKNOWLEDGMENTS

A huge thank you to my wife, Jennifer, not only for her love, support, and encouragement, but also for being my sounding board and providing valuable feedback and numerous rounds of editing after the initial draft was complete.

Special thanks to my editor, Constance Renfrow. She dove into my finished draft with passion, pinpointing areas that needed work, and offering excellent suggestions. She was instrumental in taking my manuscript to the next level.

Thank you to my cover designer, Stefanie Shaw, for providing the final touch in turning a manuscript into a beautiful book that people can spy on a shelf and hold in their hands.

Finally, thank you to my daughters, Breana and Belinda, for whom I first started writing this novel. Their enthusiasm for the many iterations they read over the years convinced me that this was a story worth finishing and worth sharing.

Thank you all.

9 780099 360576 5